THE INCREDIBLE ROCKHEAD

THE COMPLETE COMICS COLLECTION

SCOTT NICKEL
WRITER

C.S. JENNINGS
ARTIST

STONE ARCH BOOKS
a capstone imprint

THE INCREDIBLE ROCKHEAD

WRITTEN BY **SCOTT NICHEL**

ILLUSTRATED BY **C.S. JENNINGS**

DESIGNER: **HILARY WACHOLZ**

EDITOR: **CHRISTOPHER HARBO**

Stone Arch Graphic Novels are published
by Stone Arch Books, an imprint of Capstone.
1710 Roe Crest Drive, North Mankato, Minnesota 56003
www.capstonepub.com

Library of Congress Cataloging-in-Publication Data is available
on the Library of Congress website.
ISBN: 978-1-4965-8732-9 (library binding)
ISBN: 978-1-4965-9321-4 (paperback)
ISBN: 978-1-4965-8736-7 (eBook PDF)

Summary: When Chip Stone is injected with a mysterious formula,
he instantly transforms into a hulking hero with a giant rock noggin!
With his new power, Chip quickly learns he can smash through his
fears—until a stone-cold evil plot by The General rocks his world. Now
Chip and his trusty sidekick, Scissorlegz, must get to the bottom of
the mutant mystery. Can they save their friends at Banner Elementary
before it's too late?

Printed and bound in China.
2493

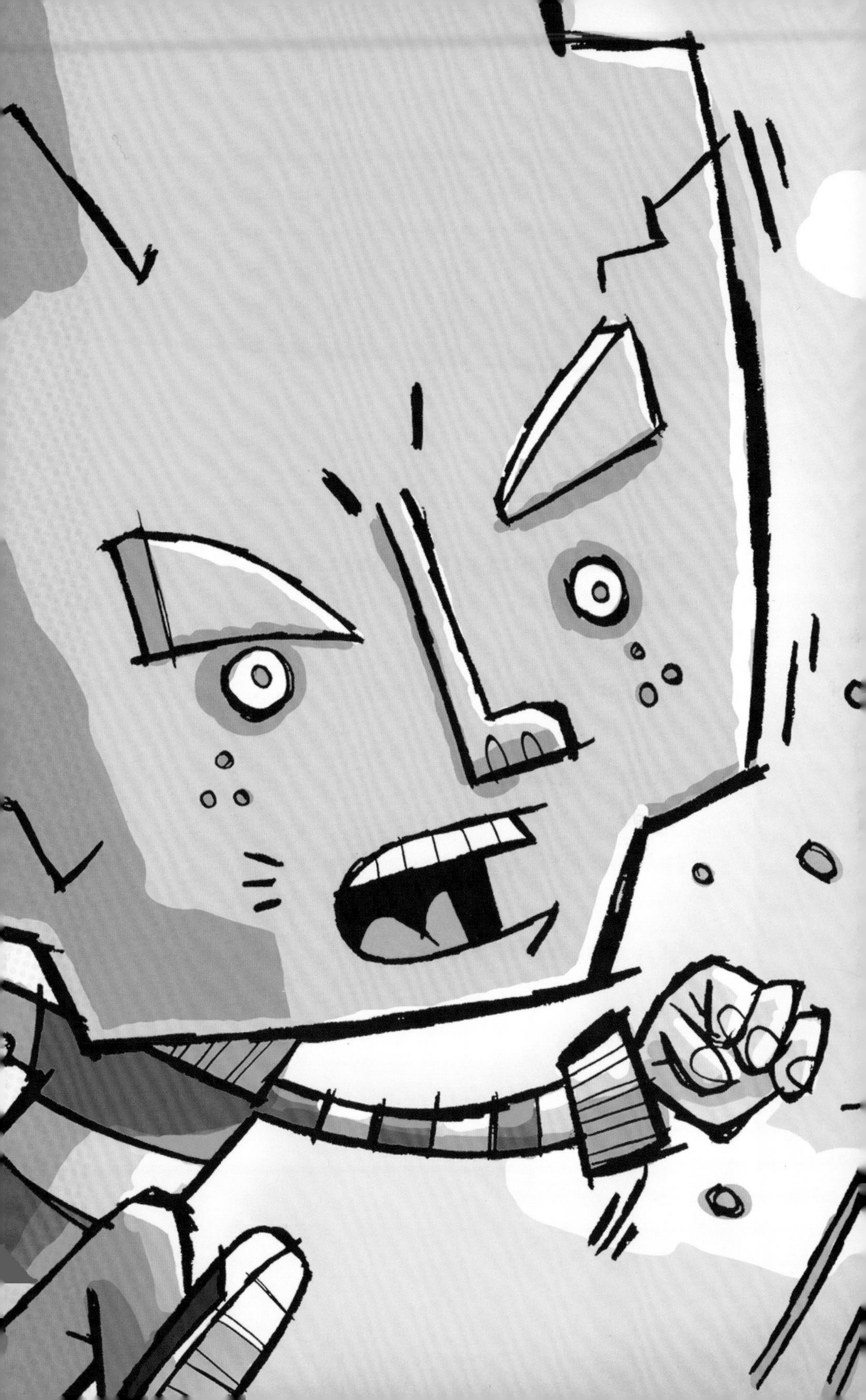

TABLE OF CONTENTS

WHO IS HE?!

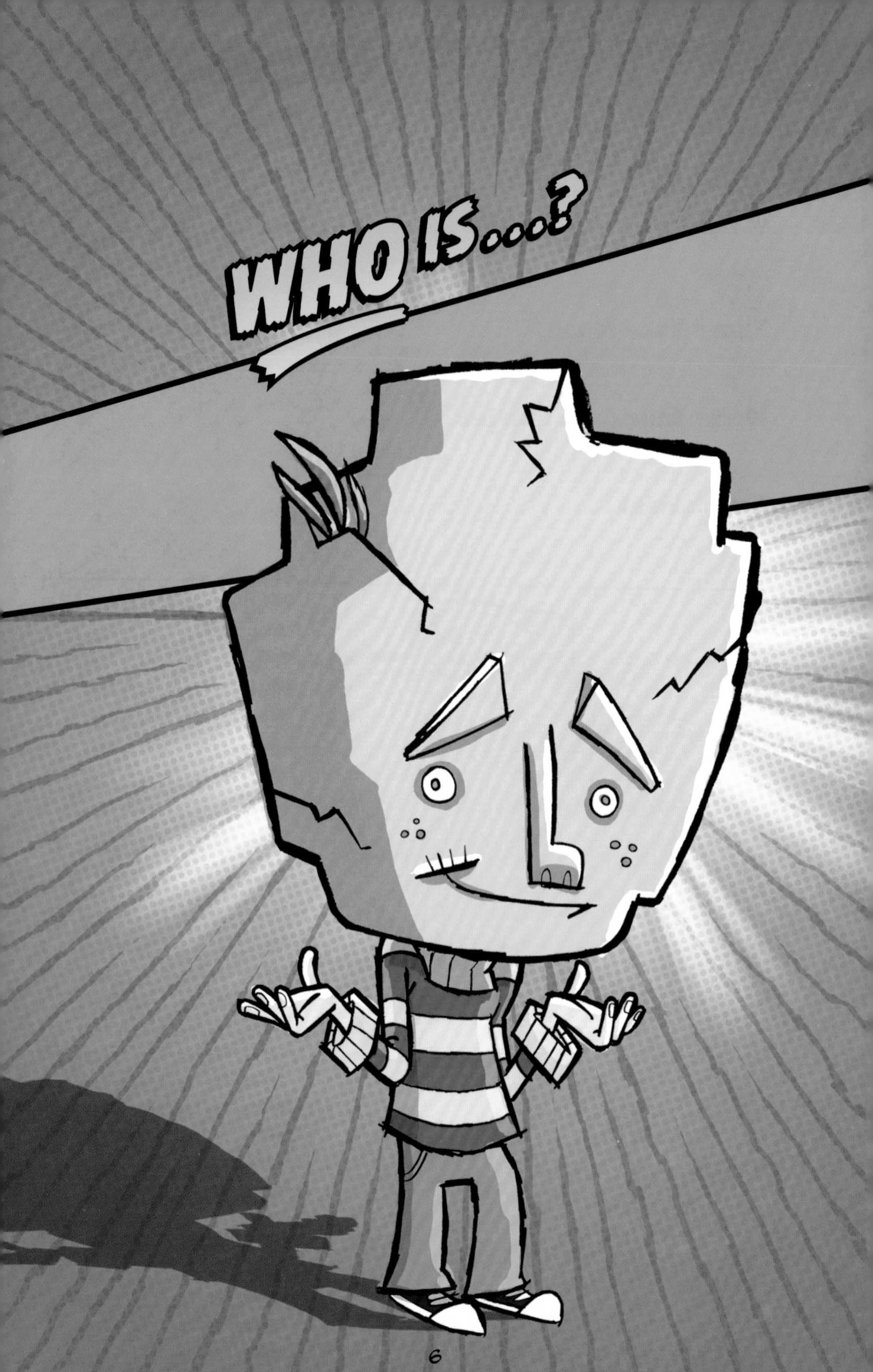
WHO IS....?

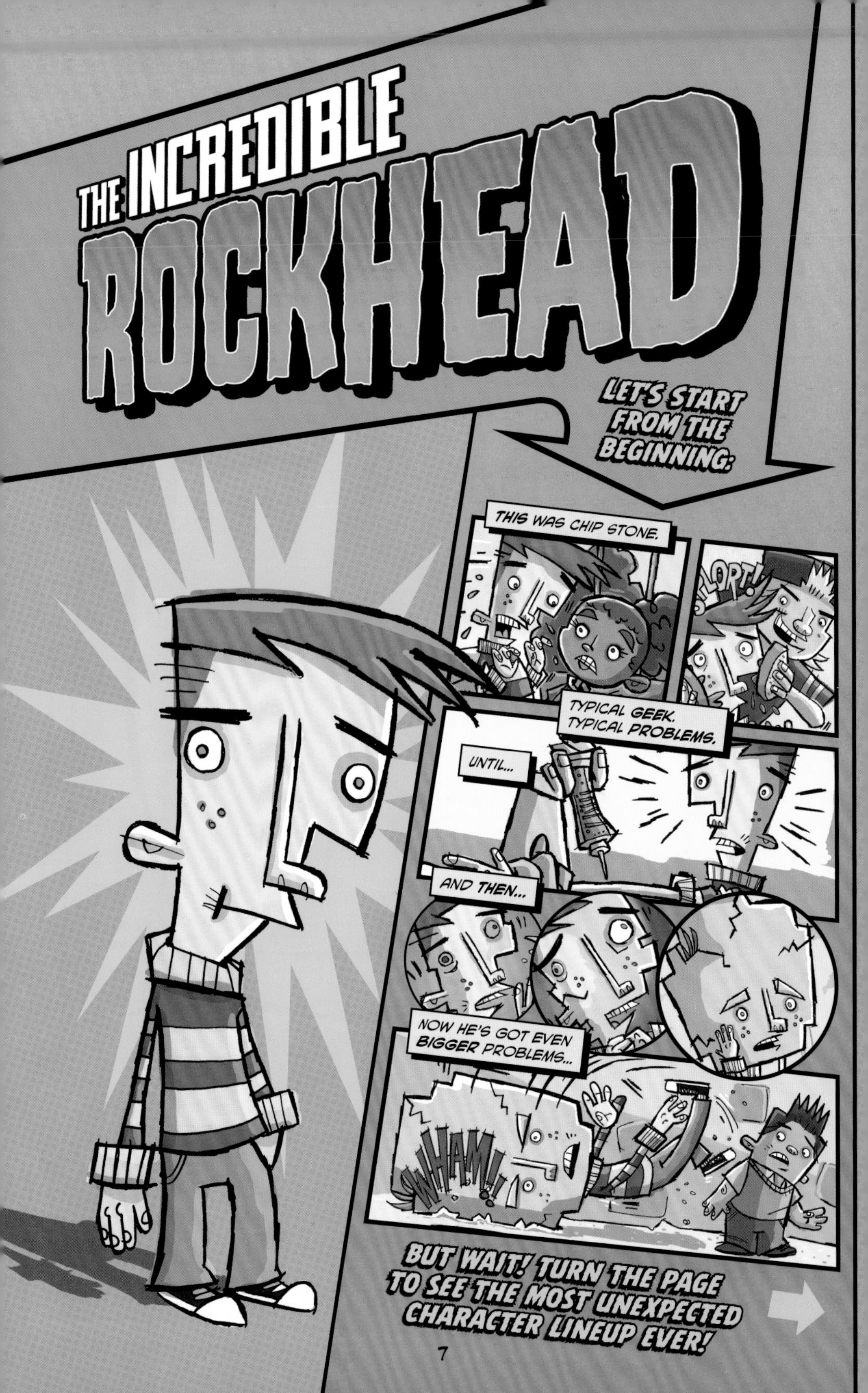
THE INCREDIBLE ROCKHEAD
LET'S START FROM THE BEGINNING:
THIS WAS CHIP STONE.
SPLORT!
TYPICAL GEEK. TYPICAL PROBLEMS.
UNTIL...
AND THEN...
NOW HE'S GOT EVEN BIGGER PROBLEMS...
WHAM!!
BUT WAIT! TURN THE PAGE TO SEE THE MOST UNEXPECTED CHARACTER LINEUP EVER!

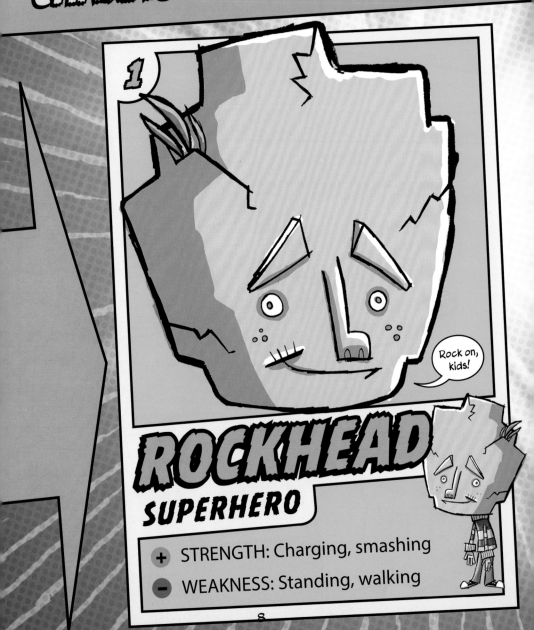

COLLECT THEM ALL!

THE MOST UNEXPECTED CHARACTER LINEUP EVER!

1

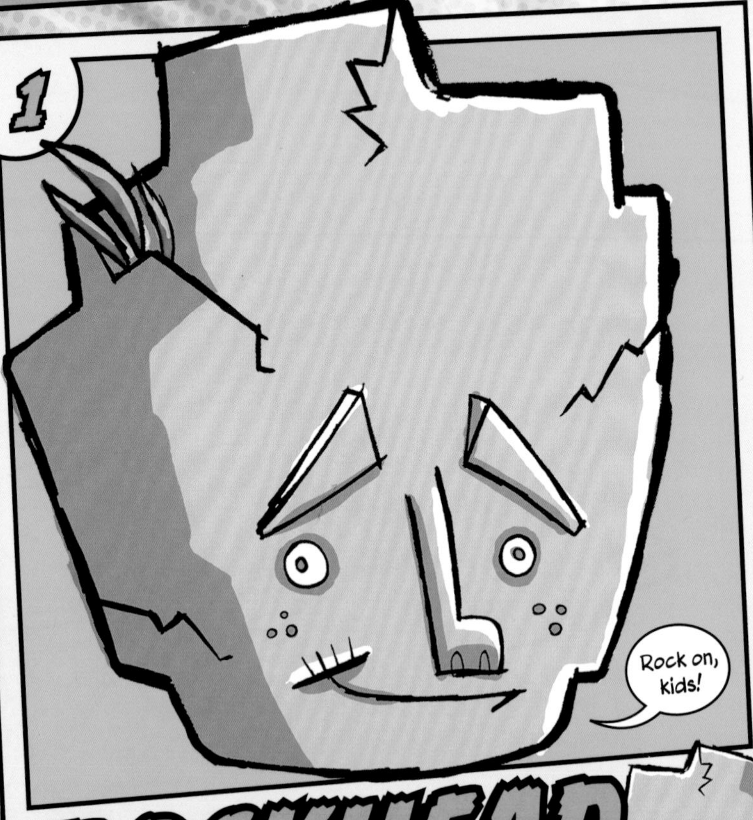
Rock on, kids!

ROCKHEAD

SUPERHERO

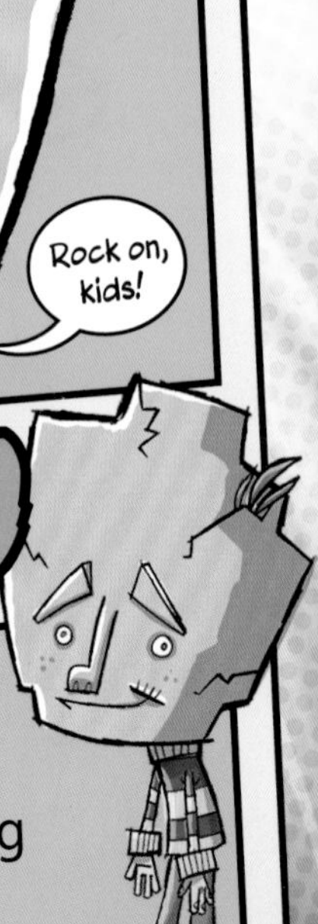

- STRENGTH: Charging, smashing
- WEAKNESS: Standing, walking

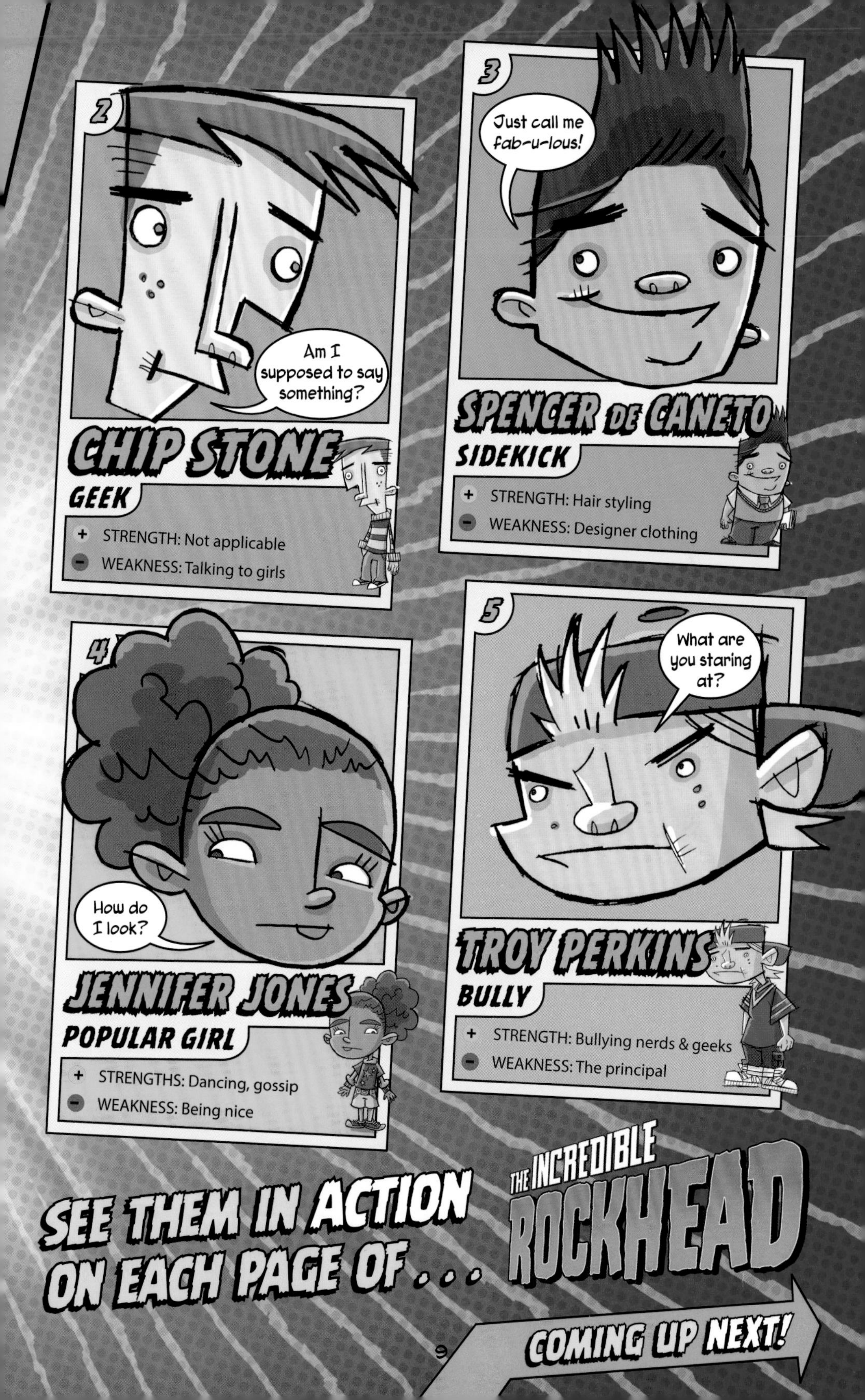
2
Am I supposed to say something?
CHIP STONE
GEEK
+ STRENGTH: Not applicable
– WEAKNESS: Talking to girls
3
Just call me fab-u-lous!
SPENCER DE CANETO
SIDEKICK
+ STRENGTH: Hair styling
– WEAKNESS: Designer clothing
4
How do I look?
JENNIFER JONES
POPULAR GIRL
+ STRENGTHS: Dancing, gossip
– WEAKNESS: Being nice
5
What are you staring at?
TROY PERKINS
BULLY
+ STRENGTH: Bullying nerds & geeks
– WEAKNESS: The principal
SEE THEM IN ACTION ON EACH PAGE OF . . .
THE INCREDIBLE ROCKHEAD
COMING UP NEXT!

IS HE A CREATURE FROM THE STARS, OR A VICTIM OF A CRUEL EXPERIMENT? UNCOVER THE ANSWERS TO THESE QUESTIONS AND MORE AS THE STORY UNFOLDS!

CAPSTONE *PROUDLY PRESENTS:*

THE INCREDIBLE ROCKHEAD!

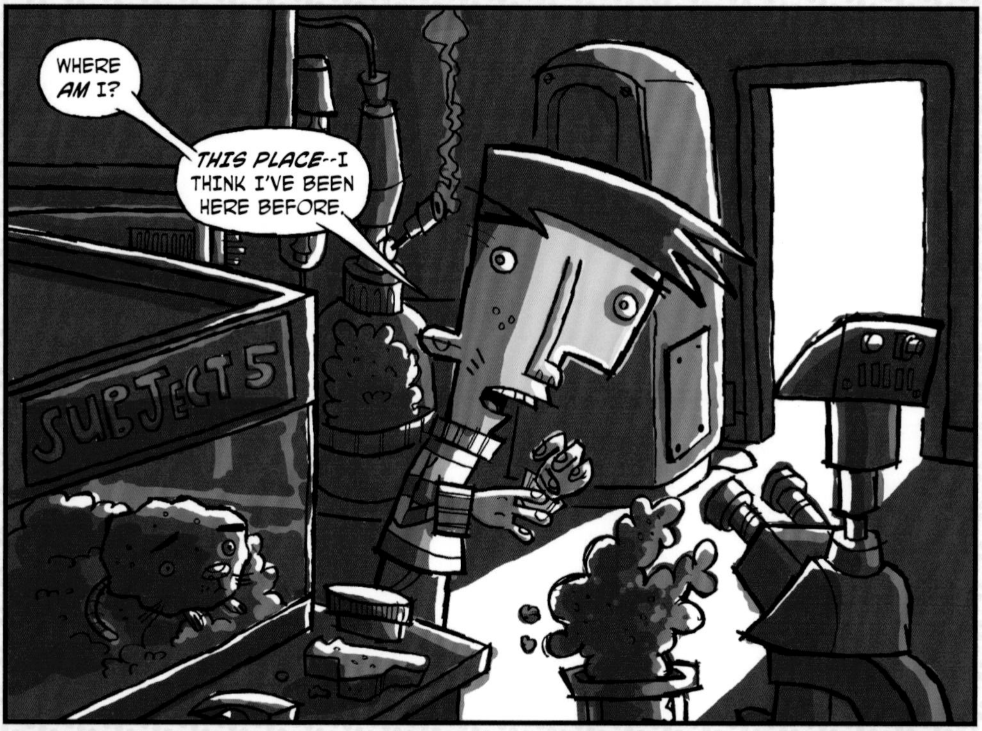

WHERE *AM* I?
THIS PLACE--I THINK I'VE BEEN HERE BEFORE.
SUBJECT 5

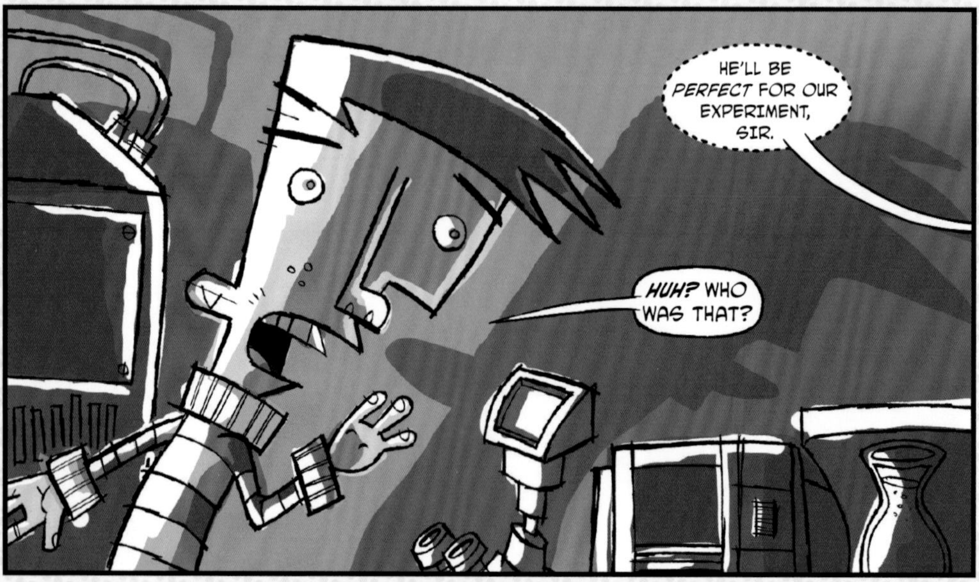

HE'LL BE *PERFECT* FOR OUR EXPERIMENT, SIR.
HUH? WHO WAS THAT?

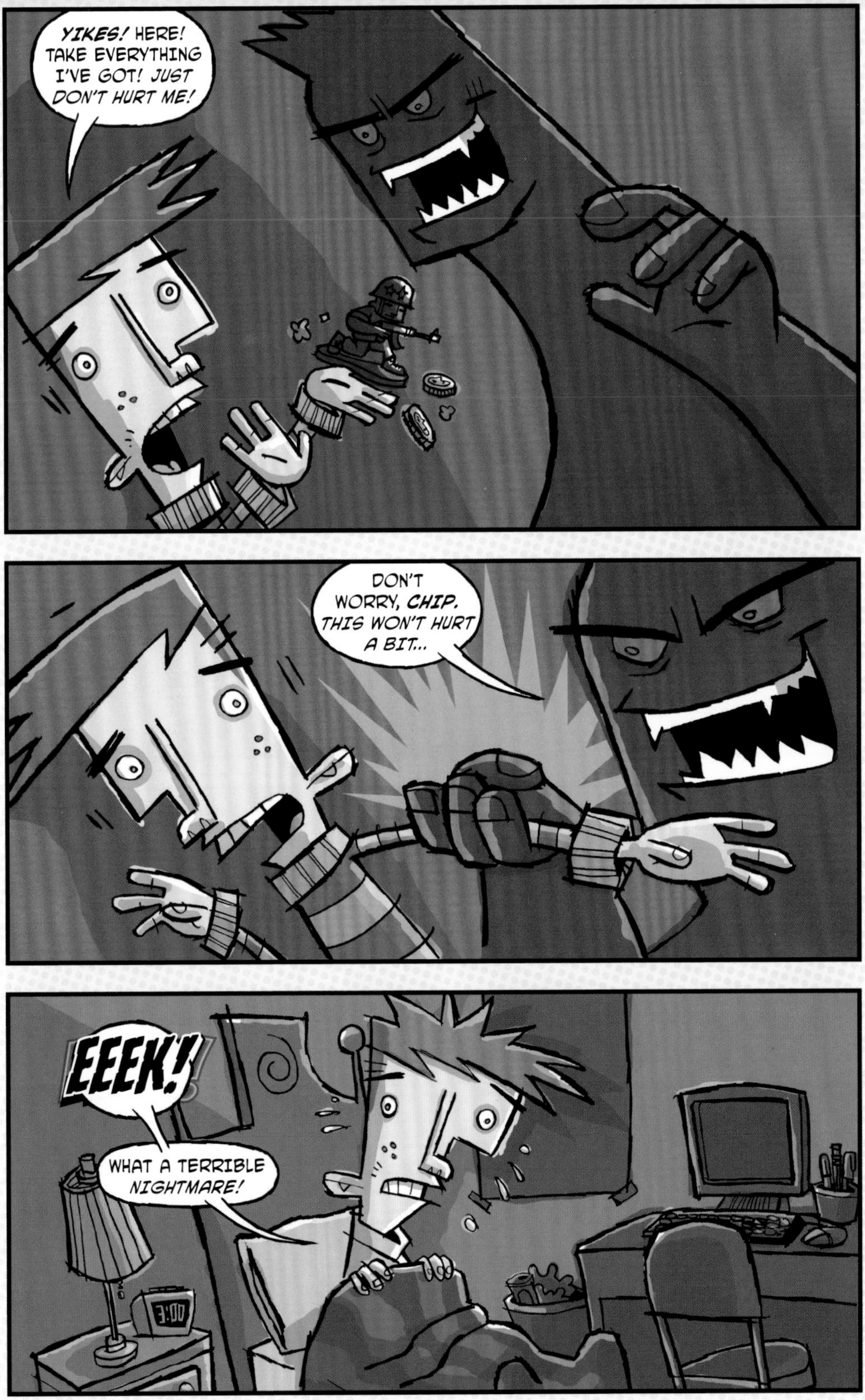
YIKES! HERE! TAKE EVERYTHING I'VE GOT! JUST DON'T HURT ME!
DON'T WORRY, CHIP. THIS WON'T HURT A BIT...
EEEK!
WHAT A TERRIBLE NIGHTMARE!
3:00

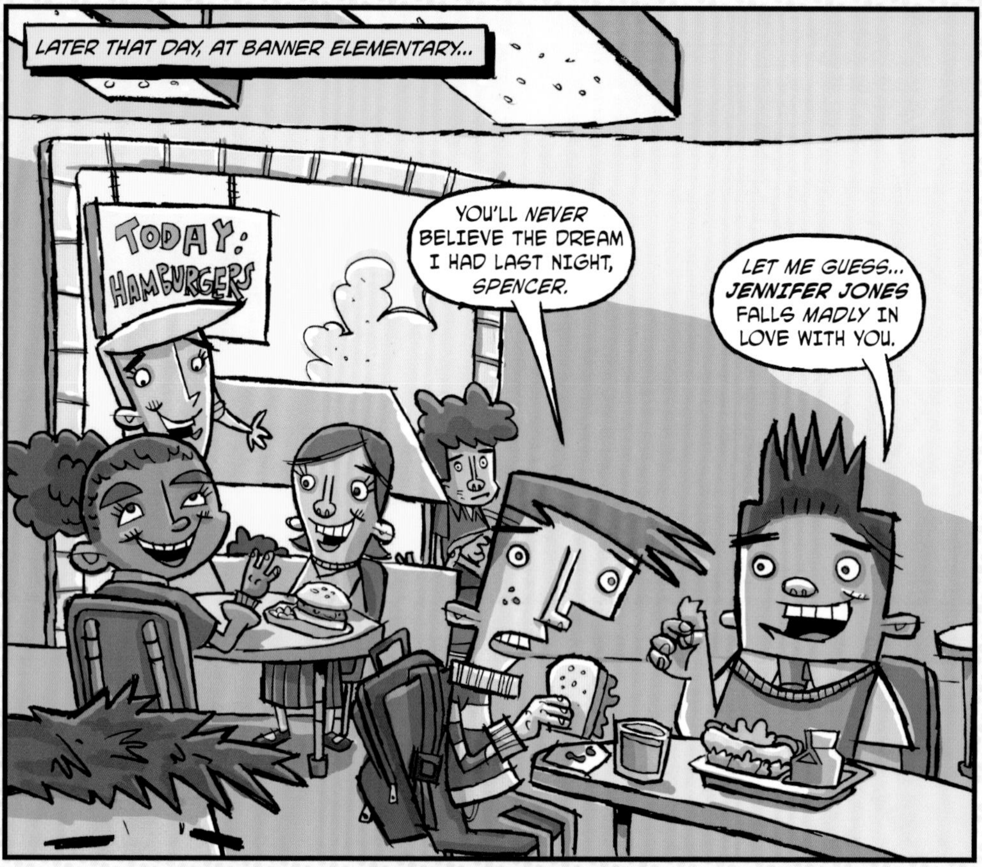
LATER THAT DAY, AT BANNER ELEMENTARY...
TODAY: HAMBURGERS
YOU'LL NEVER BELIEVE THE DREAM I HAD LAST NIGHT, SPENCER.
LET ME GUESS... JENNIFER JONES FALLS MADLY IN LOVE WITH YOU.

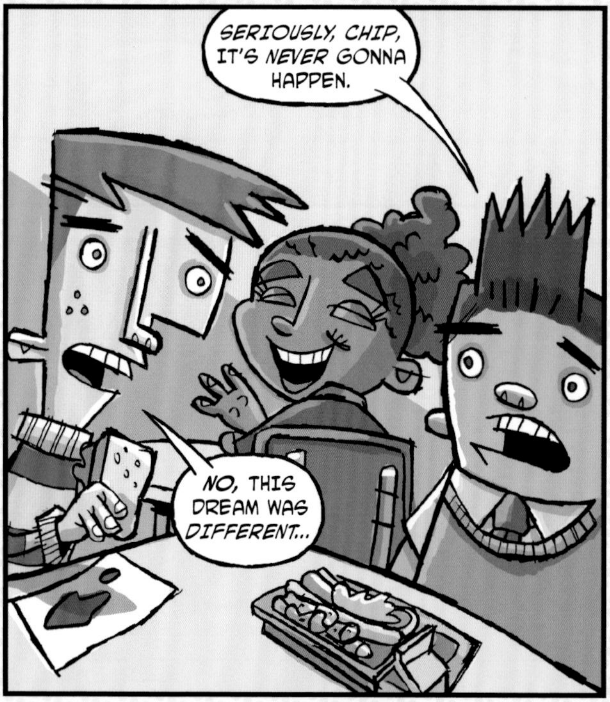
SERIOUSLY, CHIP, IT'S NEVER GONNA HAPPEN.
NO, THIS DREAM WAS DIFFERENT...

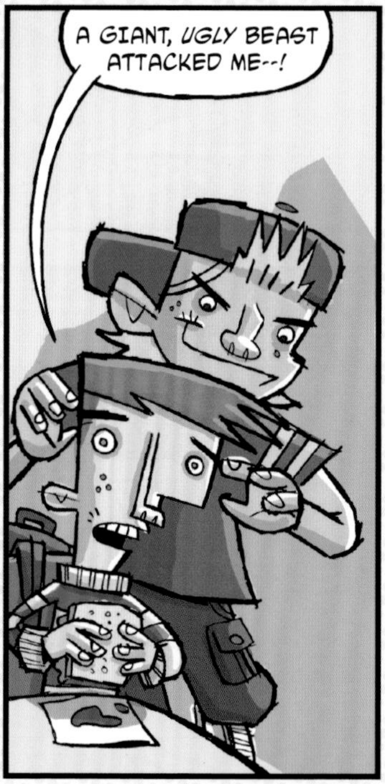
A GIANT, UGLY BEAST ATTACKED ME--!

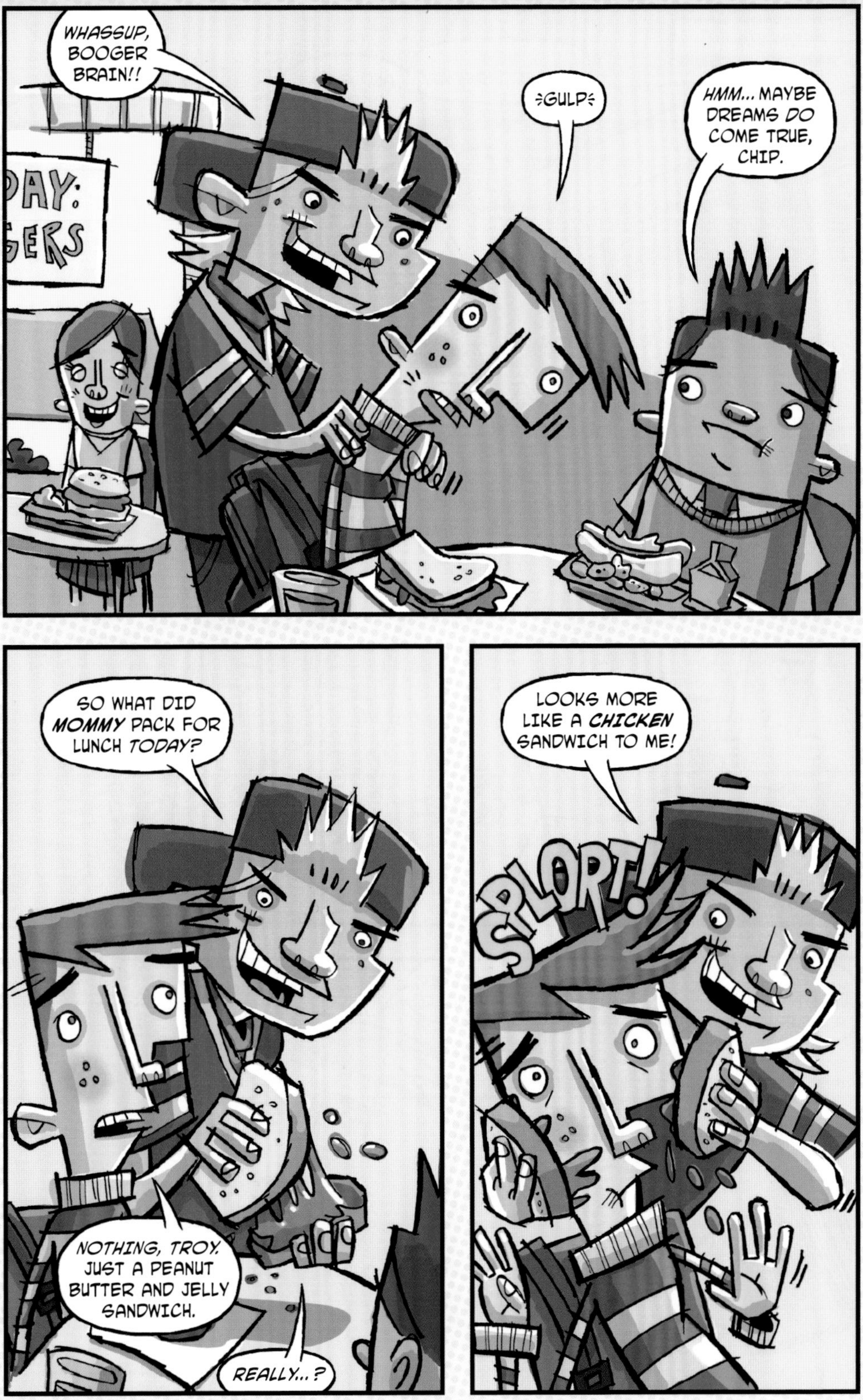
WHASSUP, BOOGER BRAIN!!
GULP
HMM... MAYBE DREAMS *DO* COME TRUE, CHIP.
SO WHAT DID ***MOMMY*** PACK FOR LUNCH *TODAY?*
NOTHING, TROY. JUST A PEANUT BUTTER AND JELLY SANDWICH.
REALLY...?
LOOKS MORE LIKE A ***CHICKEN*** SANDWICH TO ME!
SPLORT!

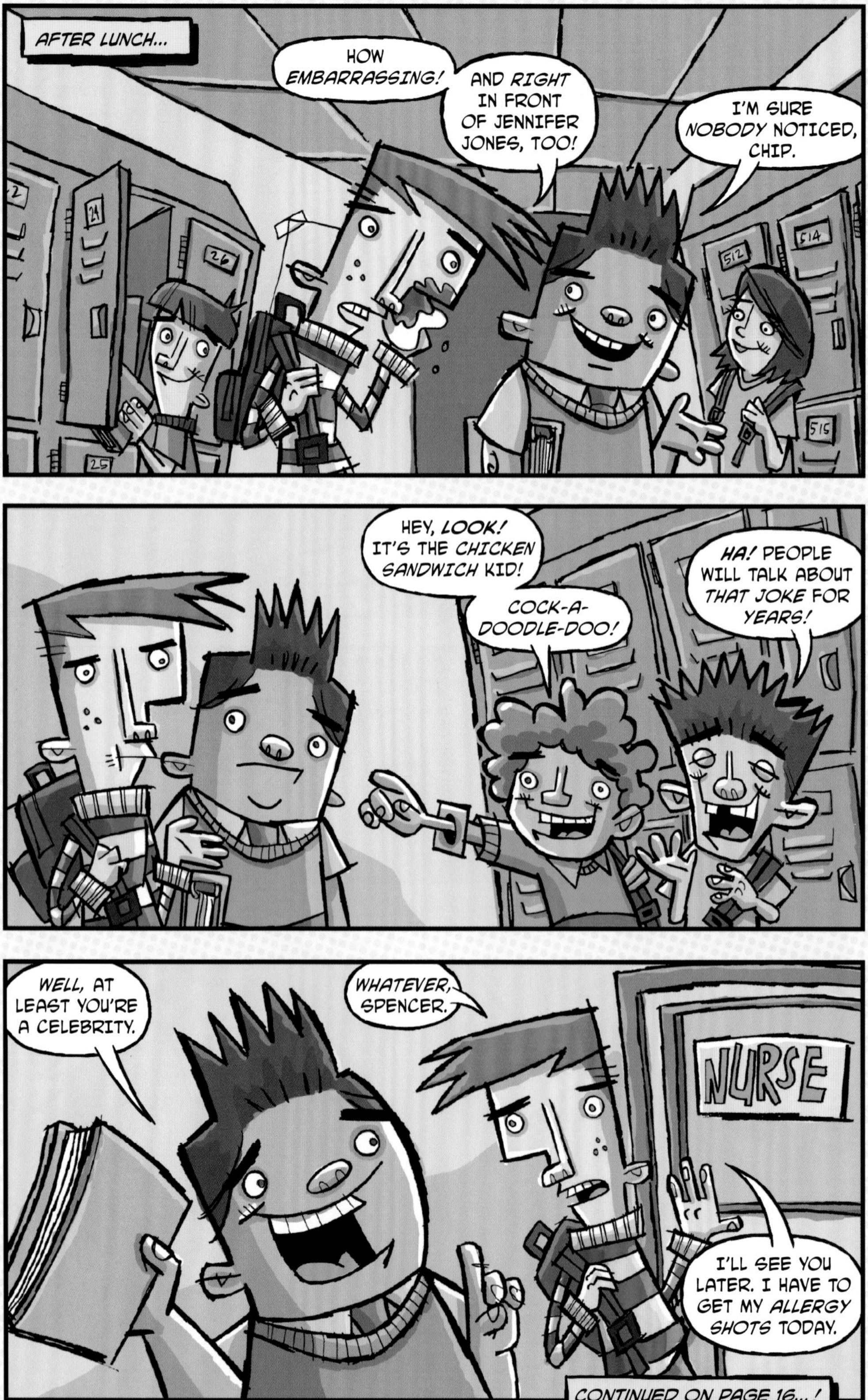
AFTER LUNCH...
HOW EMBARRASSING!
AND RIGHT IN FRONT OF JENNIFER JONES, TOO!
I'M SURE NOBODY NOTICED, CHIP.
HEY, LOOK! IT'S THE CHICKEN SANDWICH KID!
COCK-A-DOODLE-DOO!
HA! PEOPLE WILL TALK ABOUT THAT JOKE FOR YEARS!
WELL, AT LEAST YOU'RE A CELEBRITY.
WHATEVER, SPENCER.
NURSE
I'LL SEE YOU LATER. I HAVE TO GET MY ALLERGY SHOTS TODAY.
CONTINUED ON PAGE 16...!

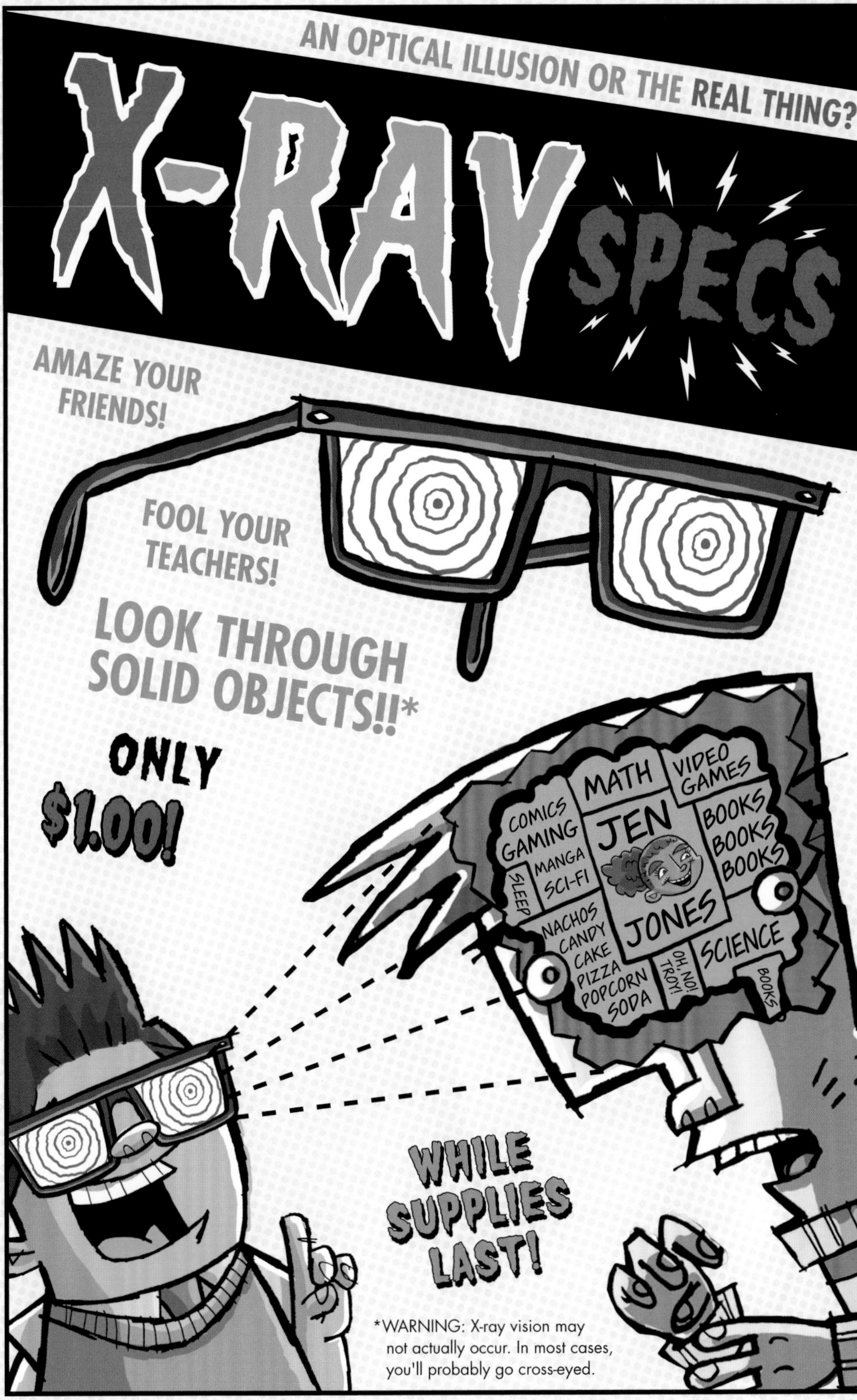

AN OPTICAL ILLUSION OR THE REAL THING?
X-RAY SPECS
AMAZE YOUR FRIENDS!
FOOL YOUR TEACHERS!
LOOK THROUGH SOLID OBJECTS!!*
ONLY $1.00!
MATH
VIDEO GAMES
COMICS GAMING
JEN
BOOKS BOOKS BOOKS
MANGA SCI-FI
SLEEP
JONES
NACHOS CANDY CAKE PIZZA POPCORN SODA
OH, NO! TROY!
SCIENCE
BOOKS
WHILE SUPPLIES LAST!
*WARNING: X-ray vision may not actually occur. In most cases, you'll probably go cross-eyed.

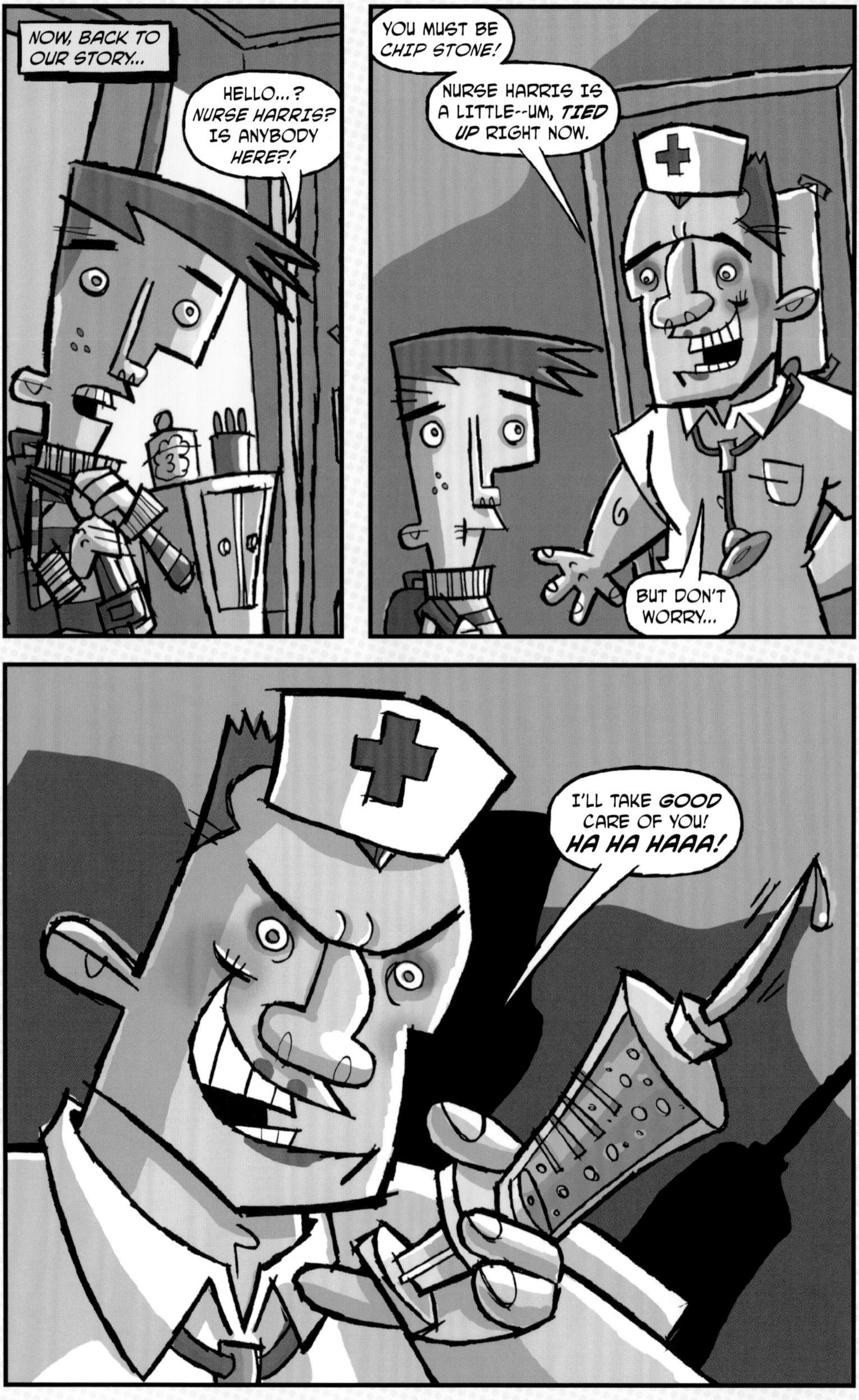
NOW, BACK TO OUR STORY...
HELLO...? NURSE HARRIS? IS ANYBODY HERE?!
YOU MUST BE CHIP STONE!
NURSE HARRIS IS A LITTLE--UM, TIED UP RIGHT NOW.
BUT DON'T WORRY...
I'LL TAKE GOOD CARE OF YOU! HA HA HAAA!

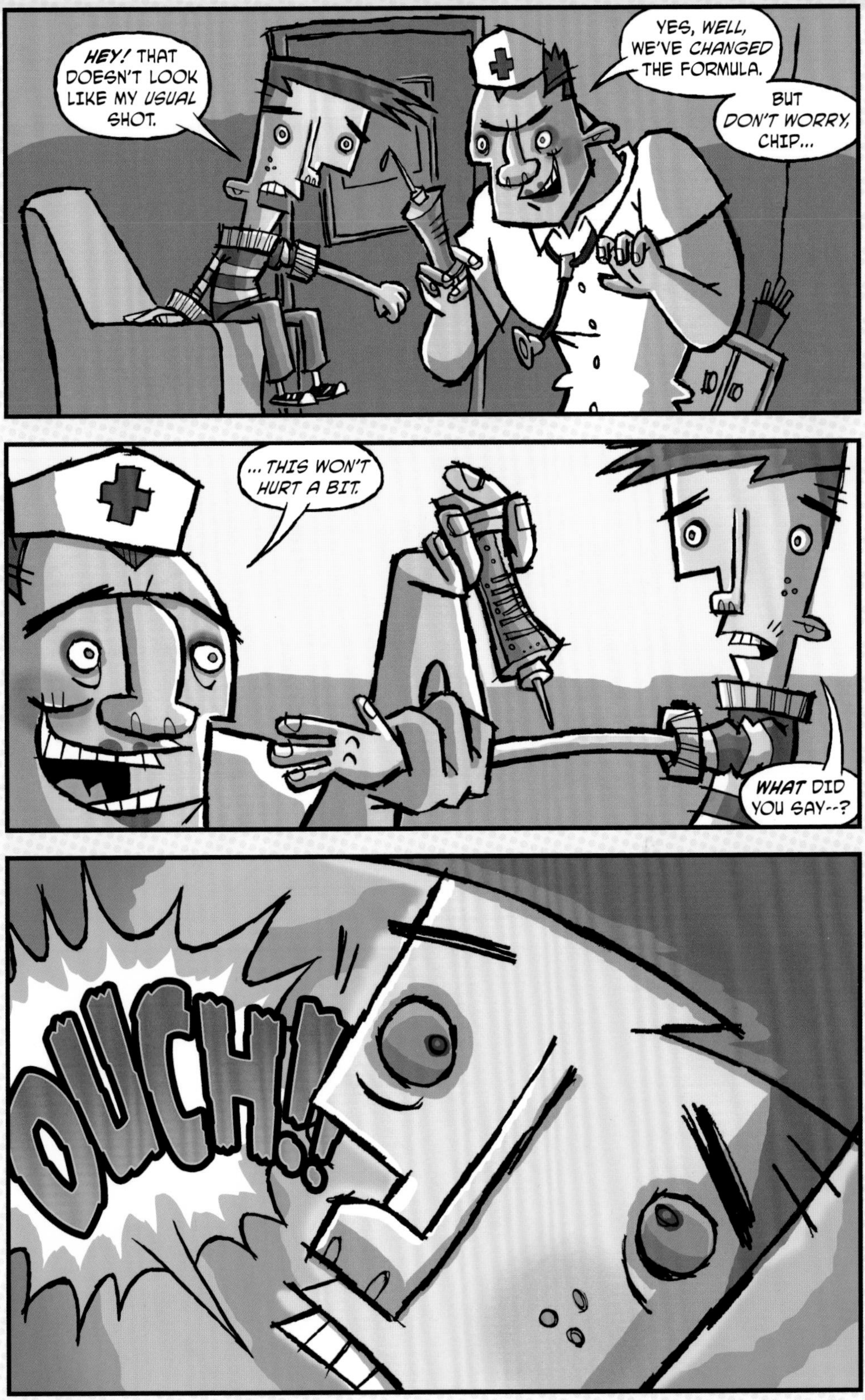
HEY! THAT DOESN'T LOOK LIKE MY USUAL SHOT.
YES, WELL, WE'VE CHANGED THE FORMULA.
BUT DON'T WORRY, CHIP...
...THIS WON'T HURT A BIT.
WHAT DID YOU SAY--?
OUCH!!

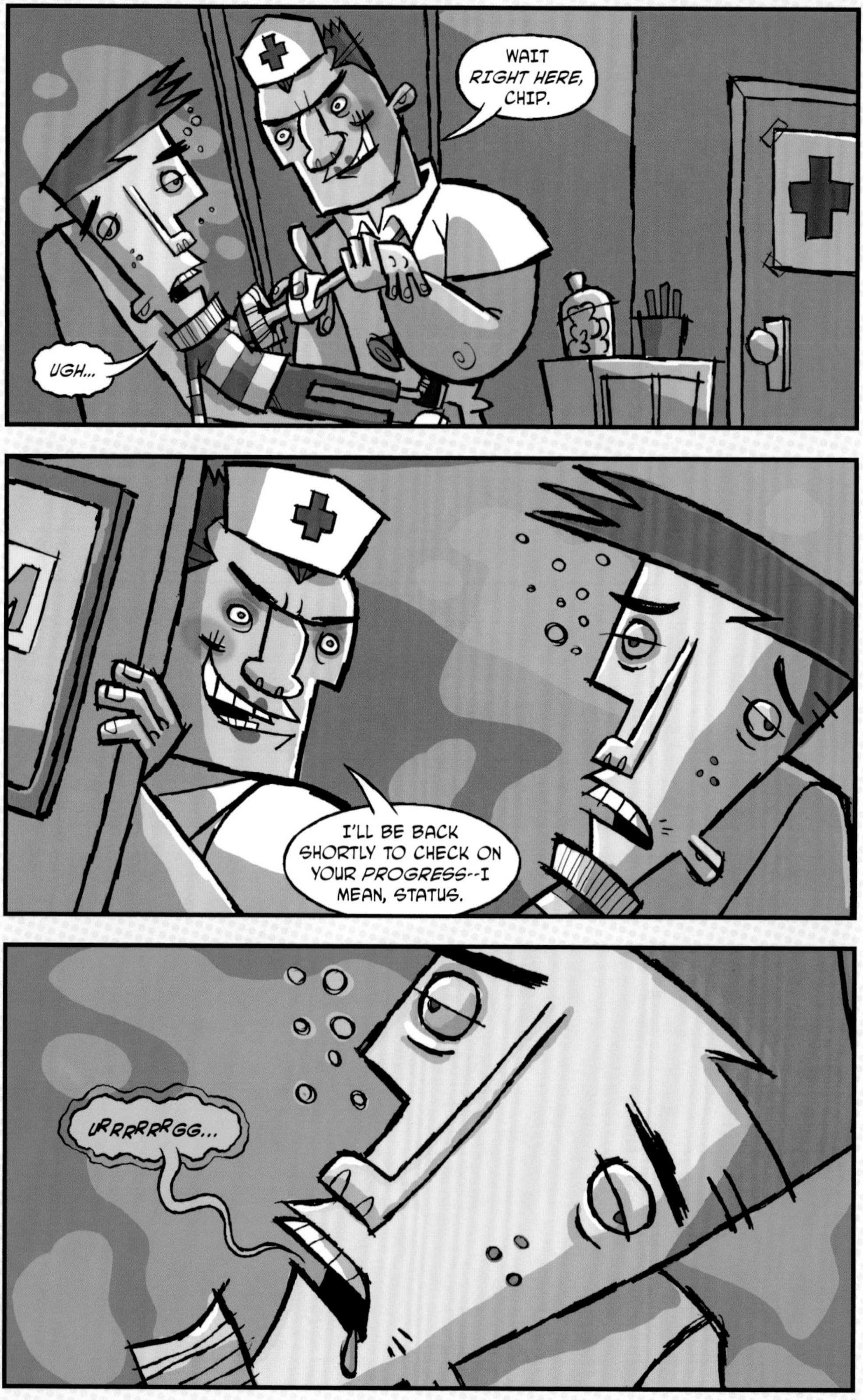
WAIT *RIGHT HERE,* CHIP.
UGH...
I'LL BE BACK SHORTLY TO CHECK ON YOUR *PROGRESS*--I MEAN, STATUS.
URRRRRRGG...

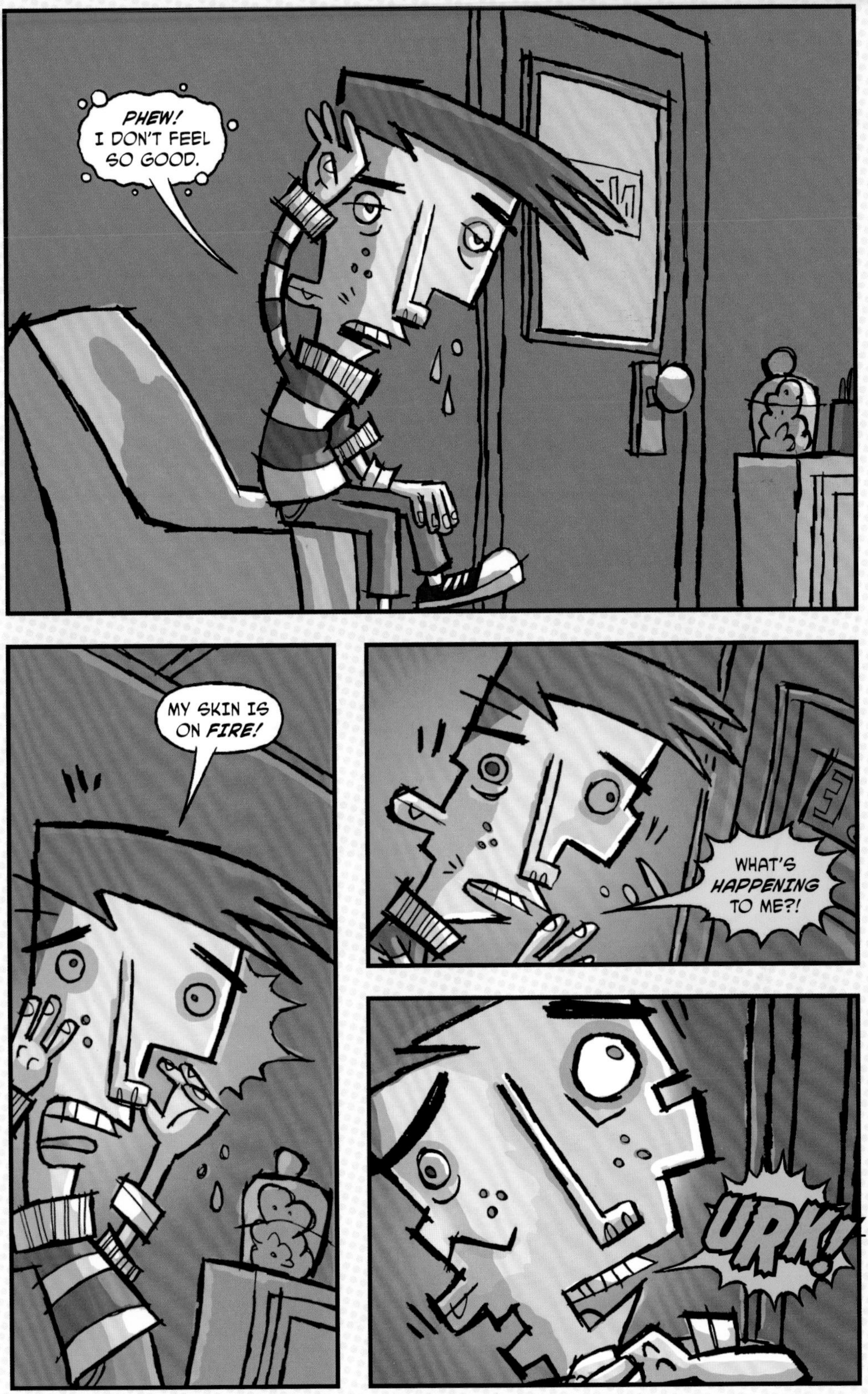
PHEW! I DON'T FEEL SO GOOD.
MY SKIN IS ON FIRE!
WHAT'S HAPPENING TO ME?!
URK!

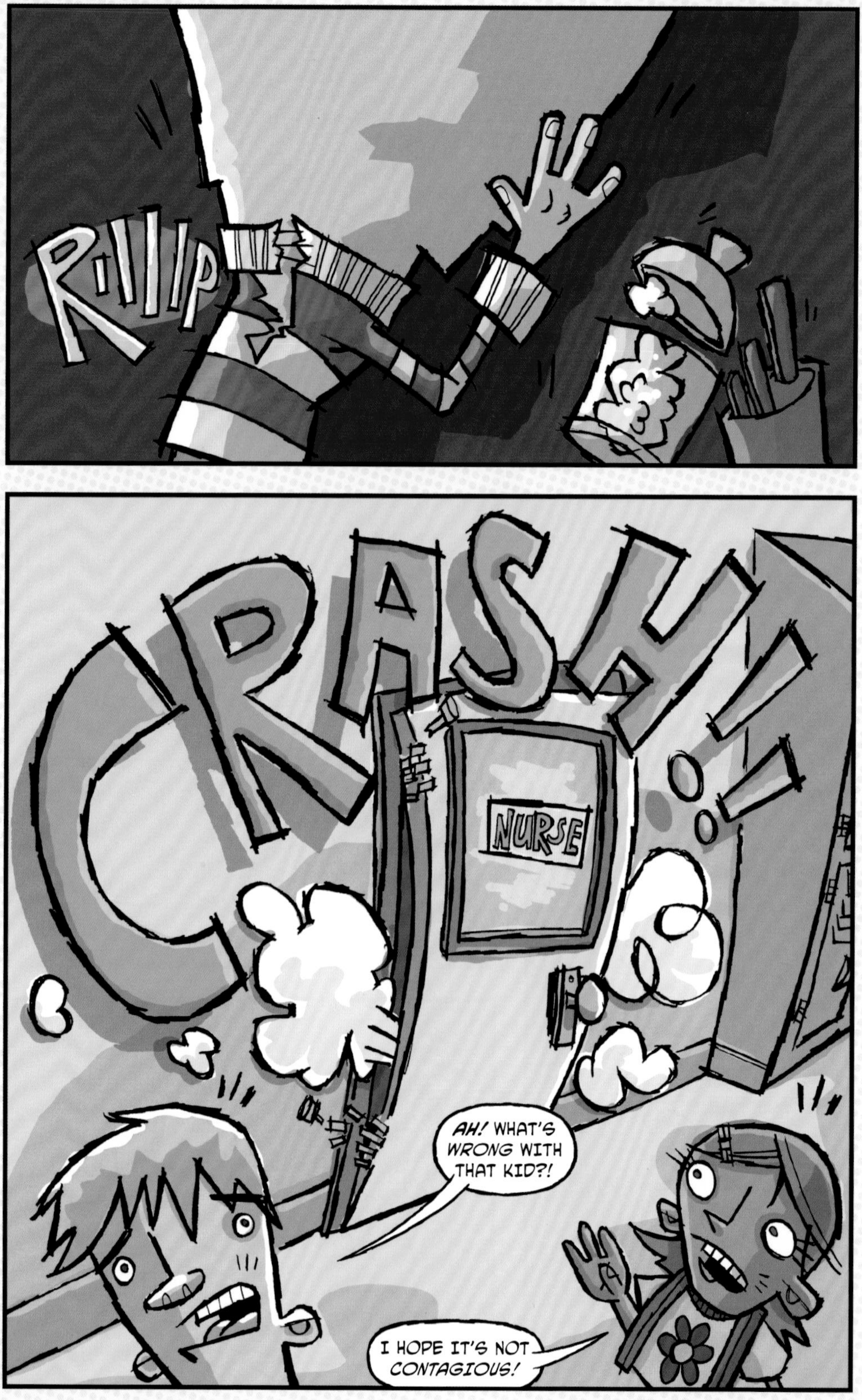
RIIIP
CRASH!!
NURSE
AH! WHAT'S WRONG WITH THAT KID?!
I HOPE IT'S NOT CONTAGIOUS!

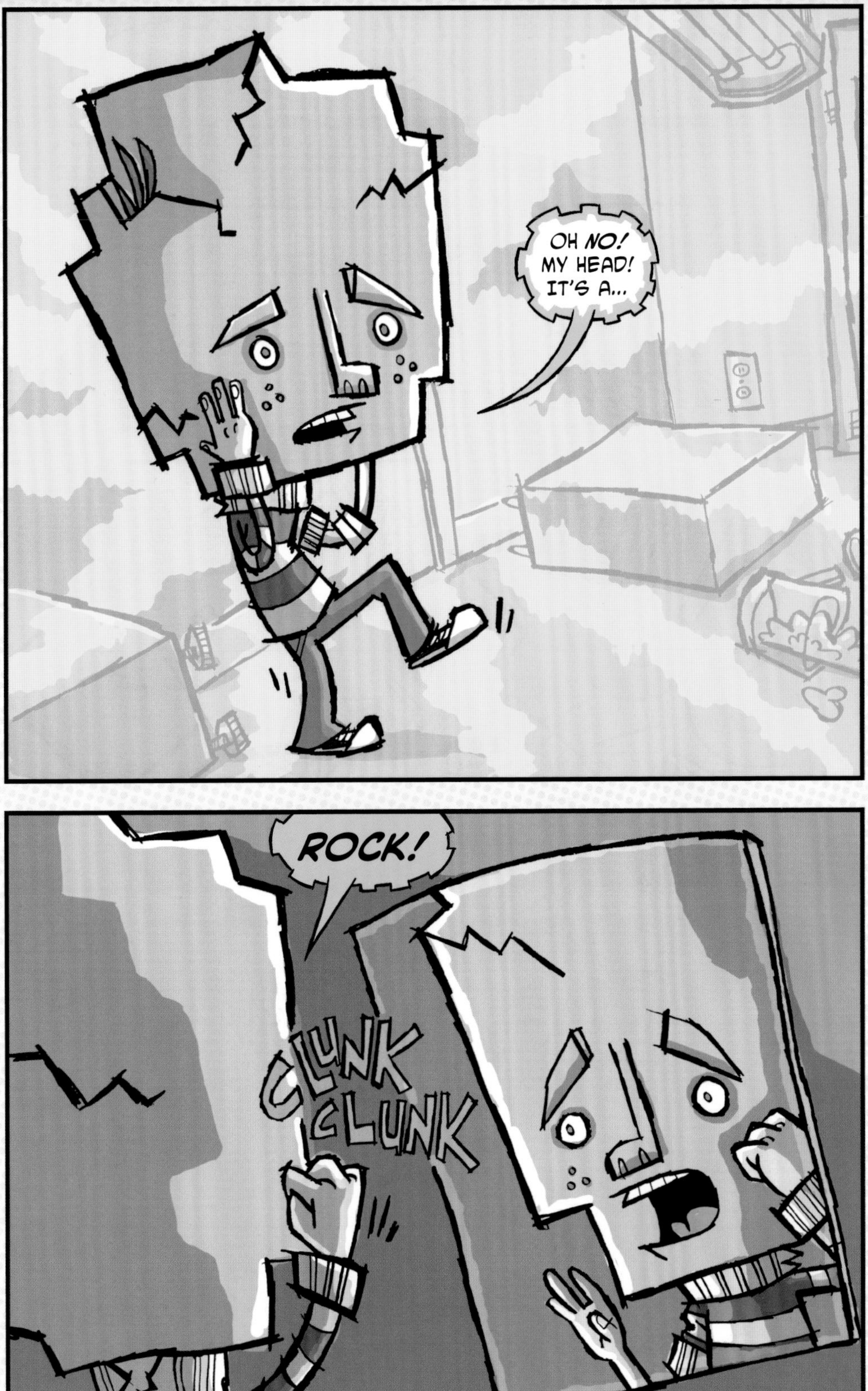
OH NO! MY HEAD! IT'S A...
ROCK!
CLUNK CLUNK

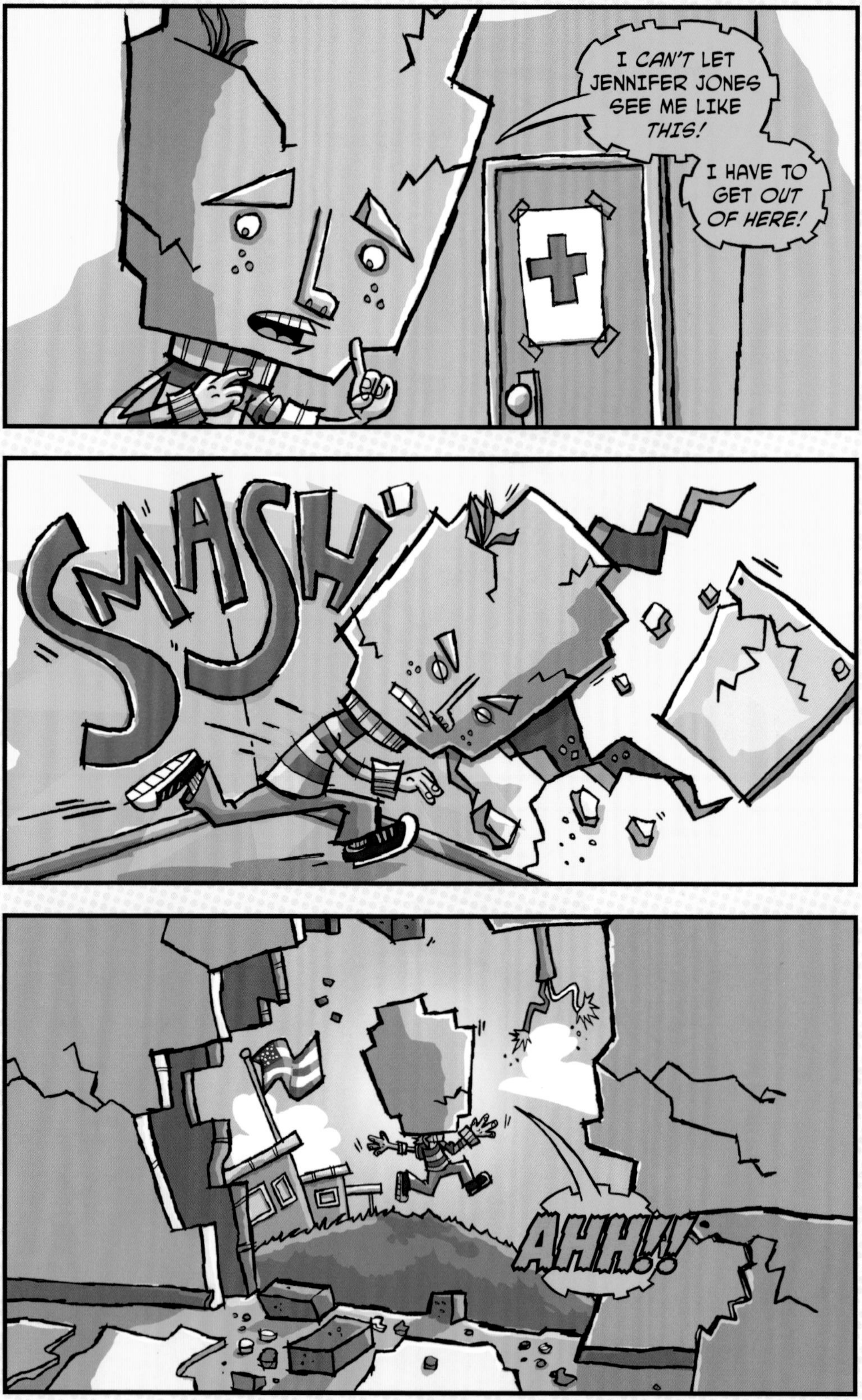
I CAN'T LET JENNIFER JONES SEE ME LIKE THIS!
I HAVE TO GET OUT OF HERE!
SMASH
AHH!!!

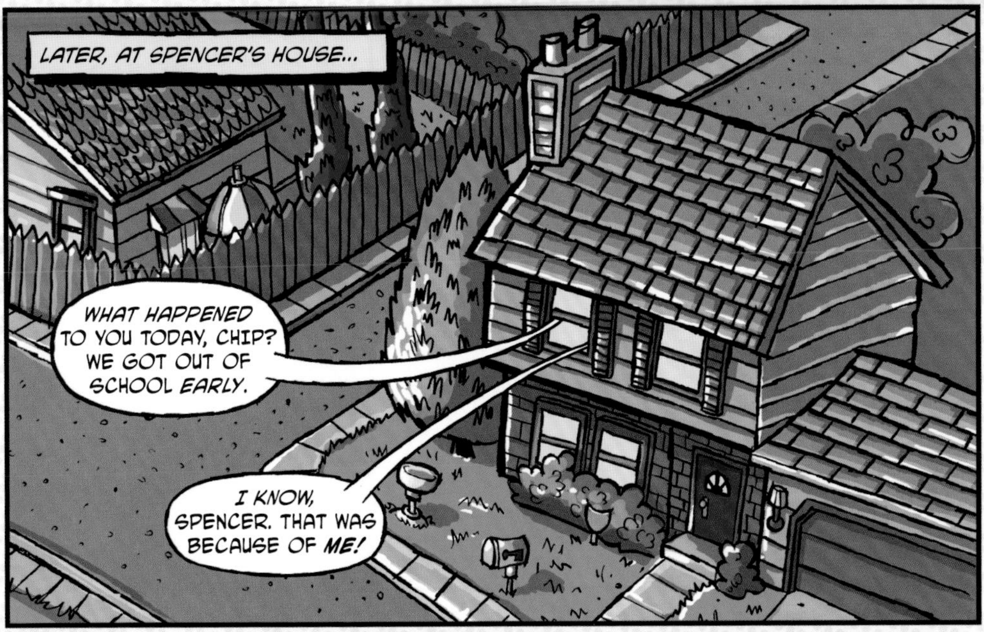
LATER, AT SPENCER'S HOUSE...
WHAT HAPPENED TO YOU TODAY, CHIP? WE GOT OUT OF SCHOOL EARLY.
I KNOW, SPENCER. THAT WAS BECAUSE OF ME!

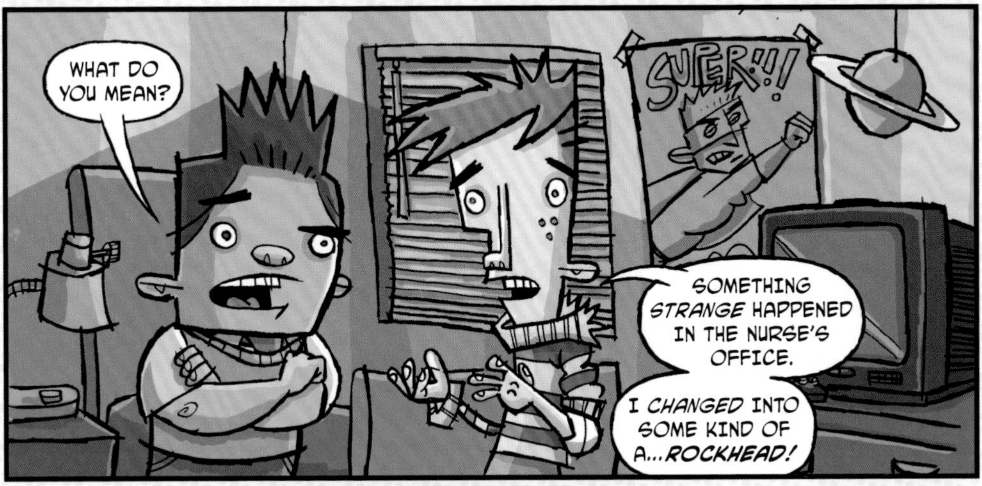
WHAT DO YOU MEAN?
SOMETHING STRANGE HAPPENED IN THE NURSE'S OFFICE.
I CHANGED INTO SOME KIND OF A...ROCKHEAD!
SUPER!!!

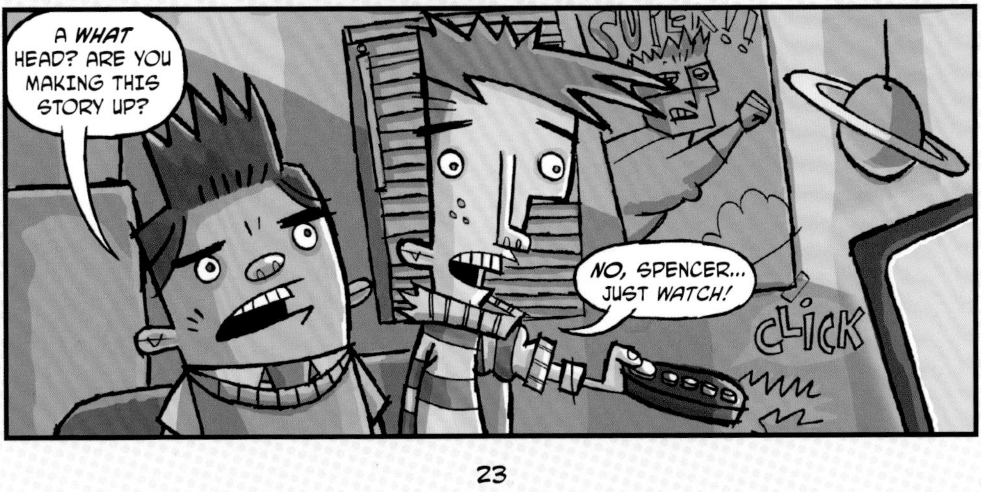
A WHAT HEAD? ARE YOU MAKING THIS STORY UP?
NO, SPENCER... JUST WATCH!
CLICK

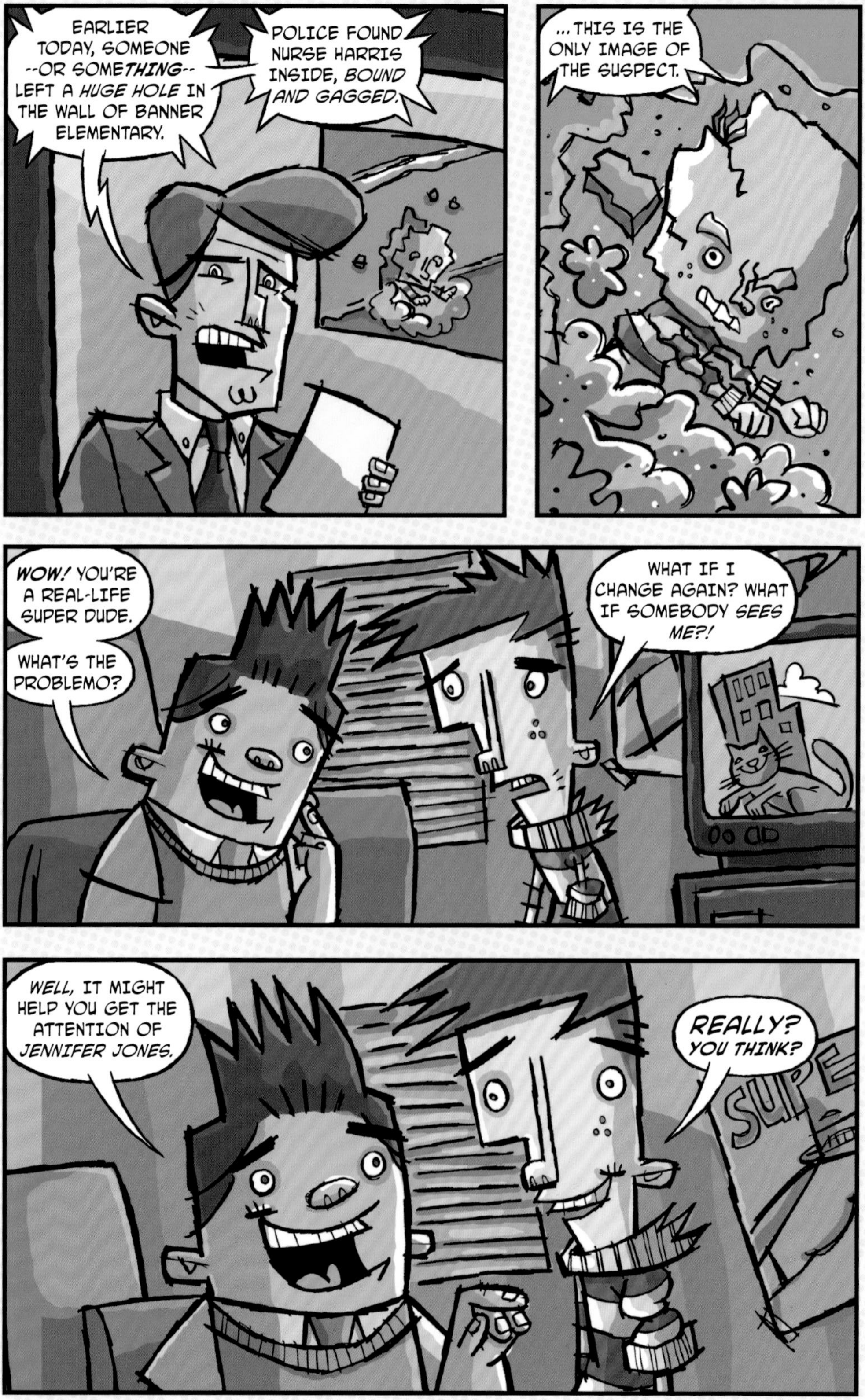
EARLIER TODAY, SOMEONE --OR SOMETHING-- LEFT A HUGE HOLE IN THE WALL OF BANNER ELEMENTARY.
POLICE FOUND NURSE HARRIS INSIDE, BOUND AND GAGGED.
...THIS IS THE ONLY IMAGE OF THE SUSPECT.
WOW! YOU'RE A REAL-LIFE SUPER DUDE.
WHAT'S THE PROBLEMO?
WHAT IF I CHANGE AGAIN? WHAT IF SOMEBODY SEES ME?!
WELL, IT MIGHT HELP YOU GET THE ATTENTION OF JENNIFER JONES.
REALLY? YOU THINK?

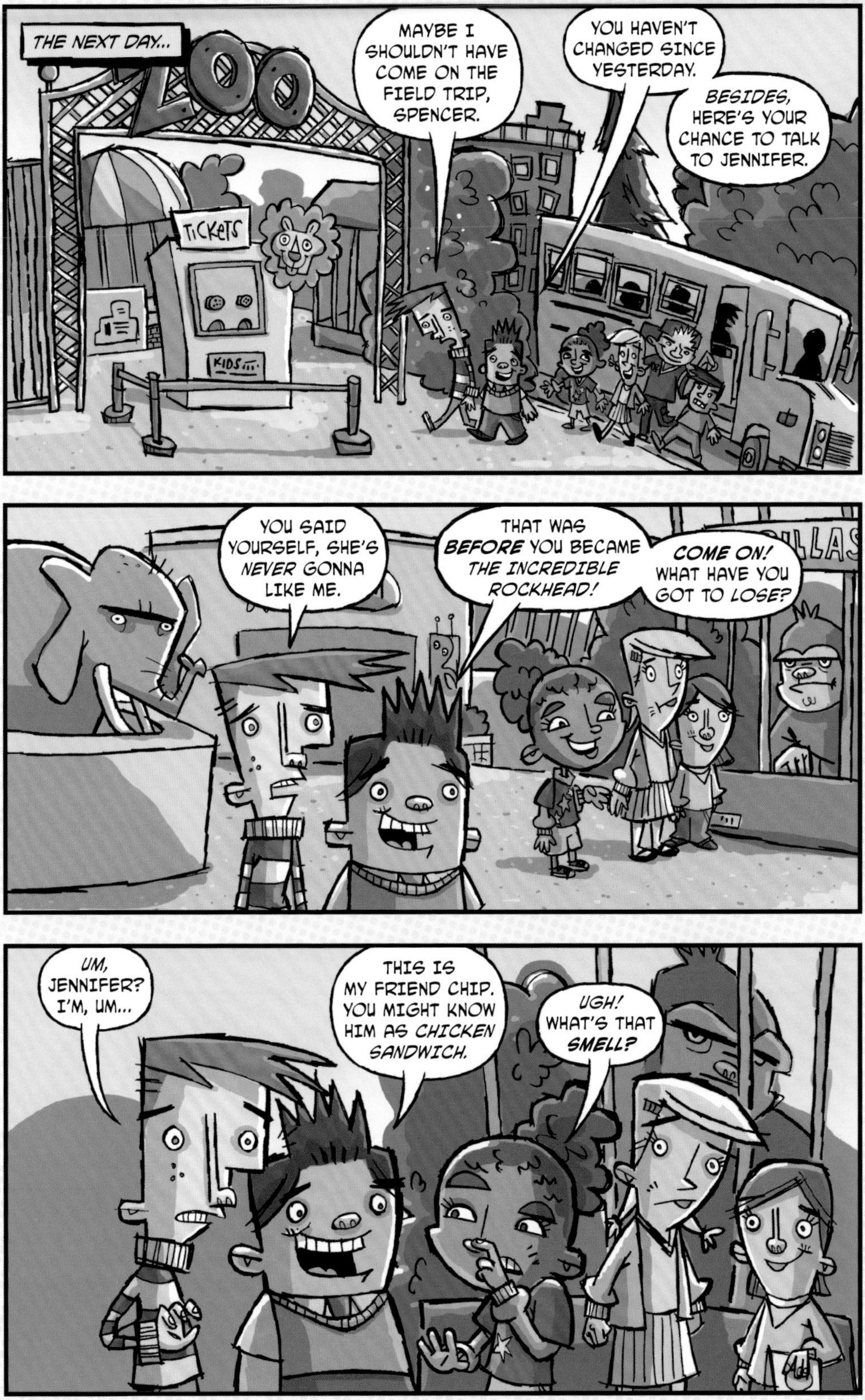
THE NEXT DAY...
ZOO
TICKETS
KIDS
MAYBE I SHOULDN'T HAVE COME ON THE FIELD TRIP, SPENCER.
YOU HAVEN'T CHANGED SINCE YESTERDAY.
BESIDES, HERE'S YOUR CHANCE TO TALK TO JENNIFER.
YOU SAID YOURSELF, SHE'S NEVER GONNA LIKE ME.
THAT WAS BEFORE YOU BECAME THE INCREDIBLE ROCKHEAD!
COME ON! WHAT HAVE YOU GOT TO LOSE?
UM, JENNIFER? I'M, UM...
THIS IS MY FRIEND CHIP. YOU MIGHT KNOW HIM AS CHICKEN SANDWICH.
UGH! WHAT'S THAT SMELL?

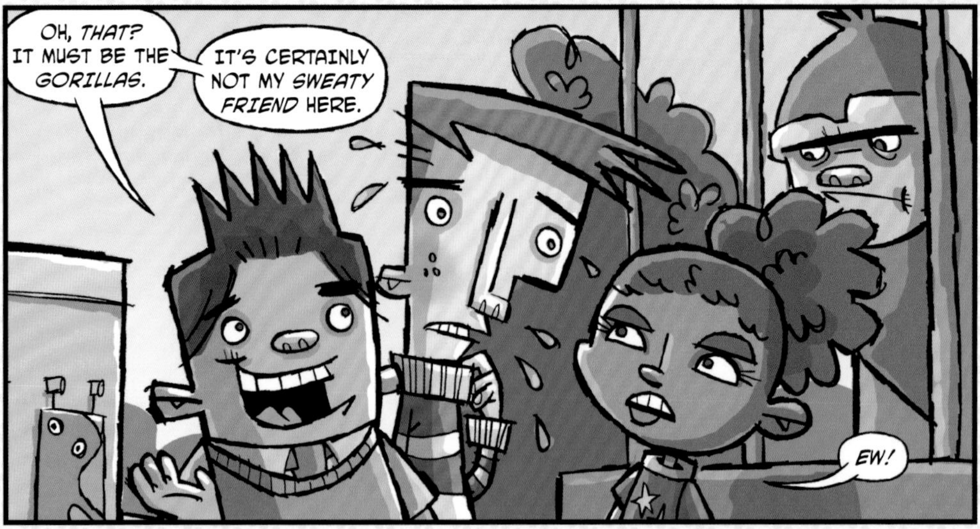
OH, THAT? IT MUST BE THE GORILLAS.
IT'S CERTAINLY NOT MY SWEATY FRIEND HERE.
EW!

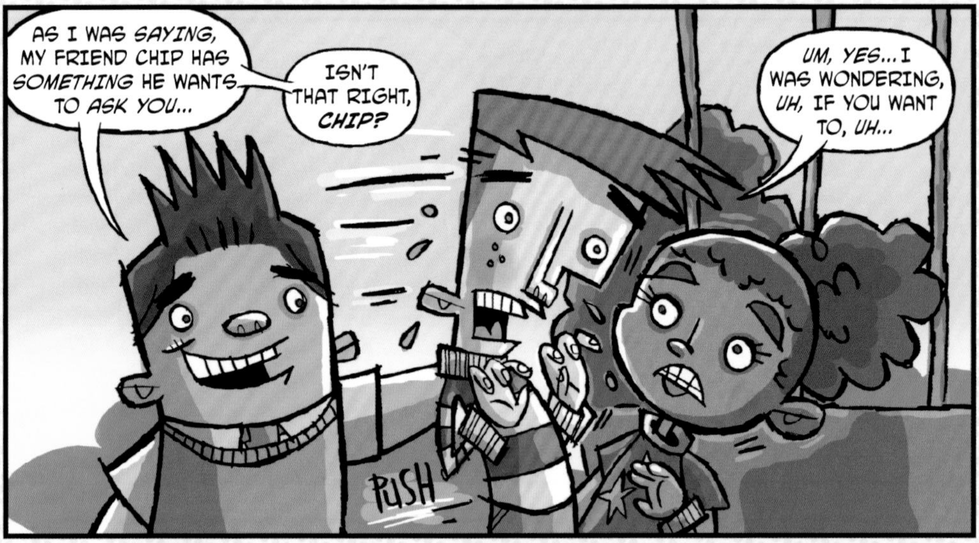
AS I WAS SAYING, MY FRIEND CHIP HAS SOMETHING HE WANTS TO ASK YOU...
ISN'T THAT RIGHT, CHIP?
UM, YES... I WAS WONDERING, UH, IF YOU WANT TO, UH...
PUSH

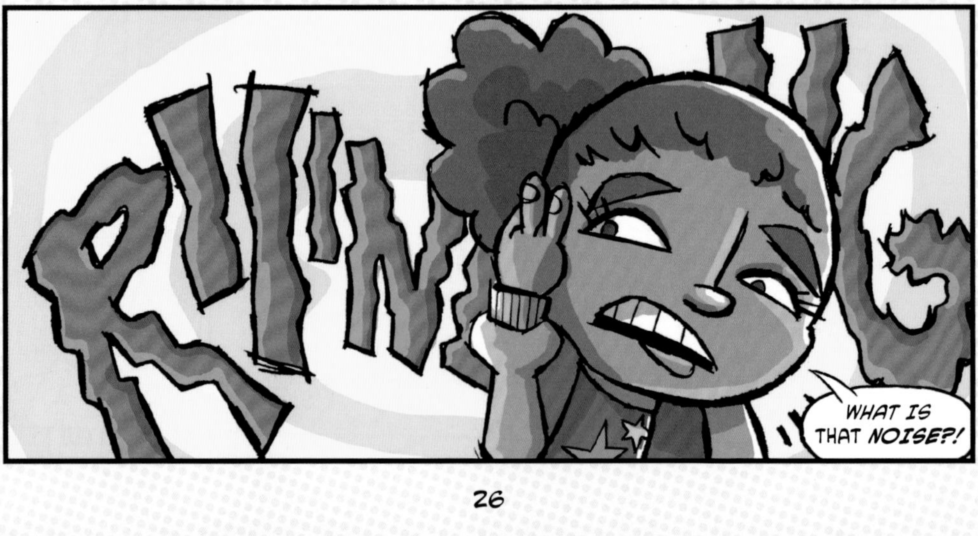
WHAT IS THAT NOISE?!

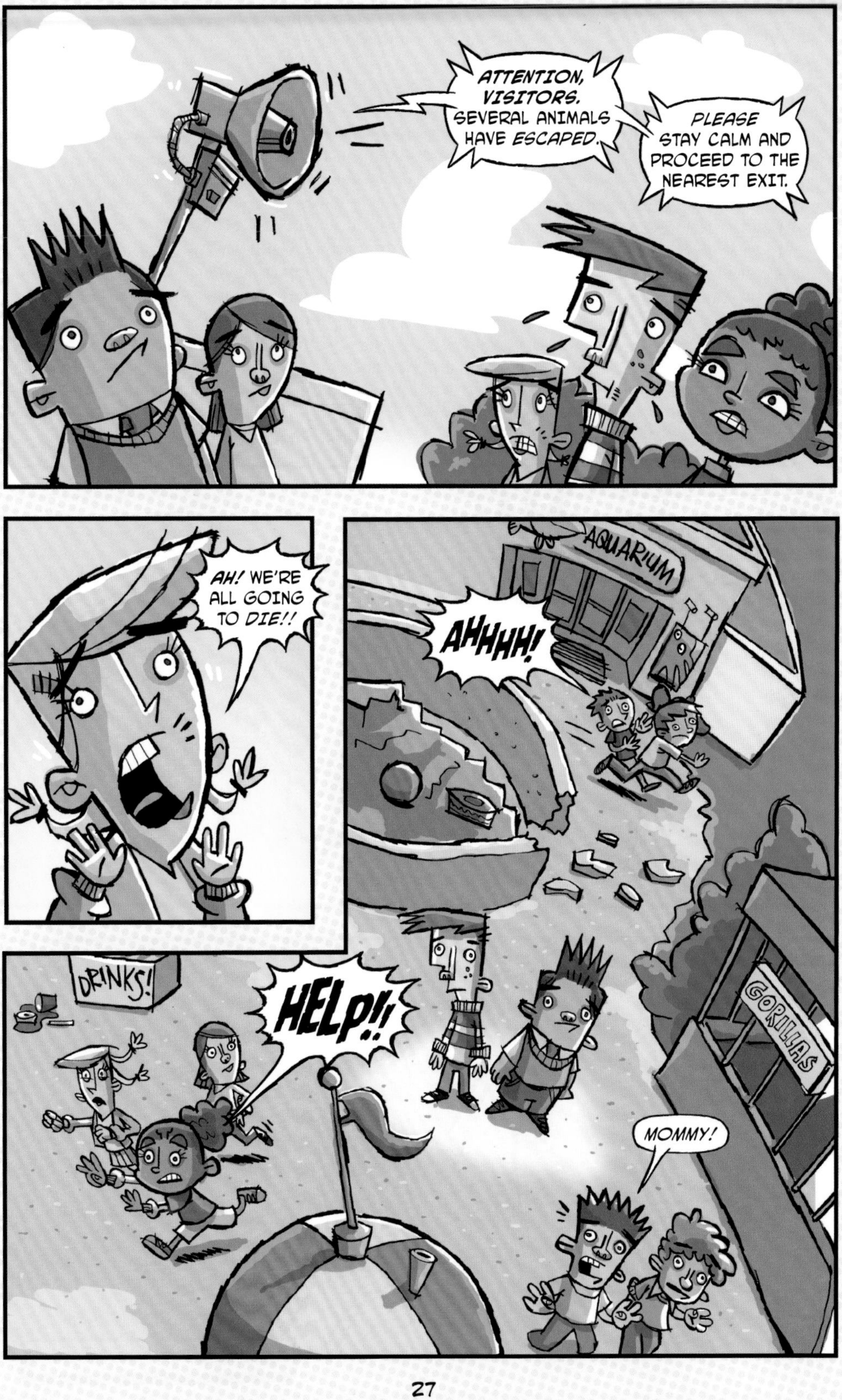
ATTENTION, VISITORS. SEVERAL ANIMALS HAVE ESCAPED.
PLEASE STAY CALM AND PROCEED TO THE NEAREST EXIT.
AH! WE'RE ALL GOING TO DIE!!
AQUARIUM
AHHHH!
DRINKS!
HELP!!
GORILLAS
MOMMY!

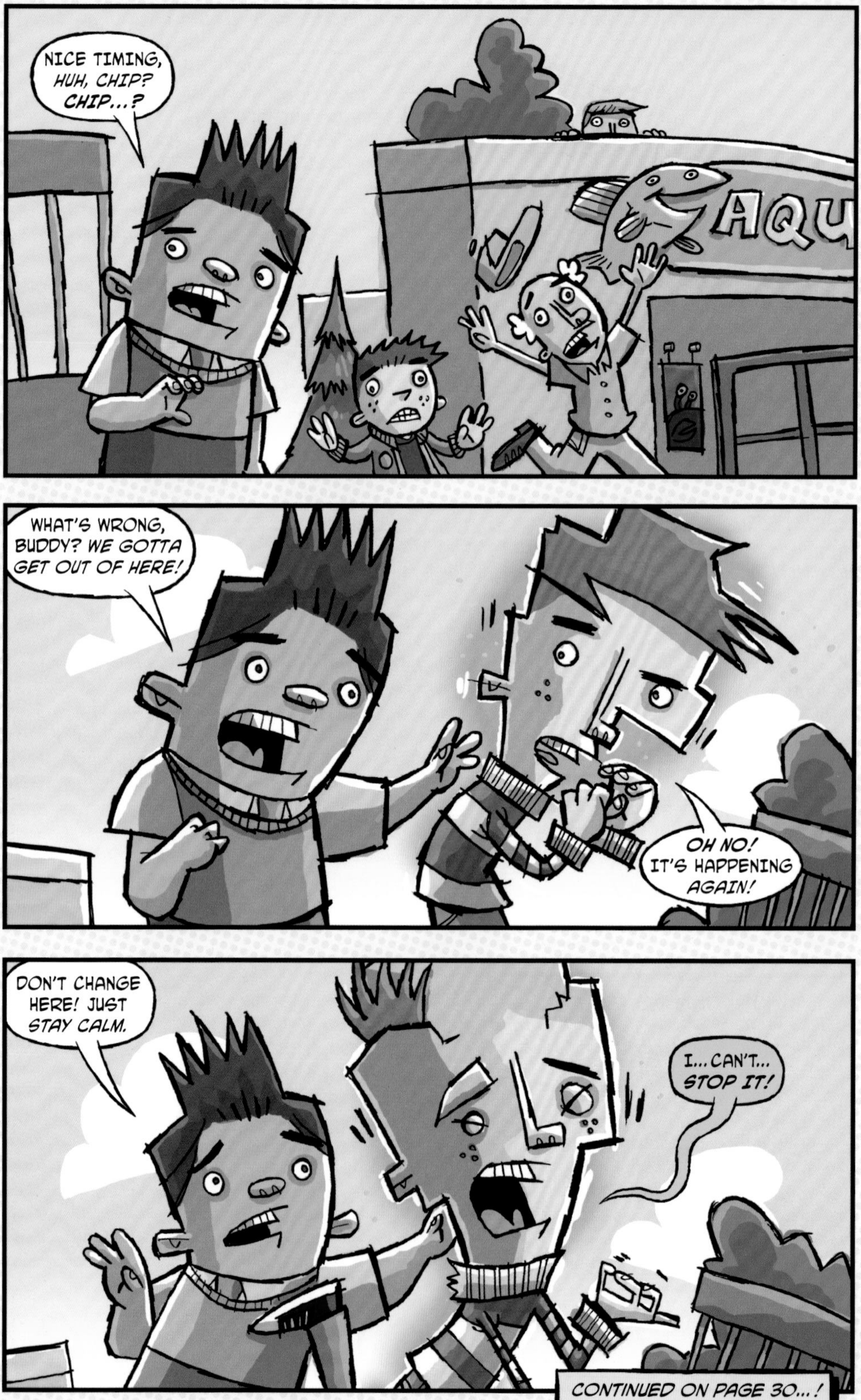
NICE TIMING, HUH, CHIP? CHIP...?
AQU
WHAT'S WRONG, BUDDY? WE GOTTA GET OUT OF HERE!
OH NO! IT'S HAPPENING AGAIN!
DON'T CHANGE HERE! JUST STAY CALM.
I... CAN'T... STOP IT!

CONTINUED ON PAGE 30...!

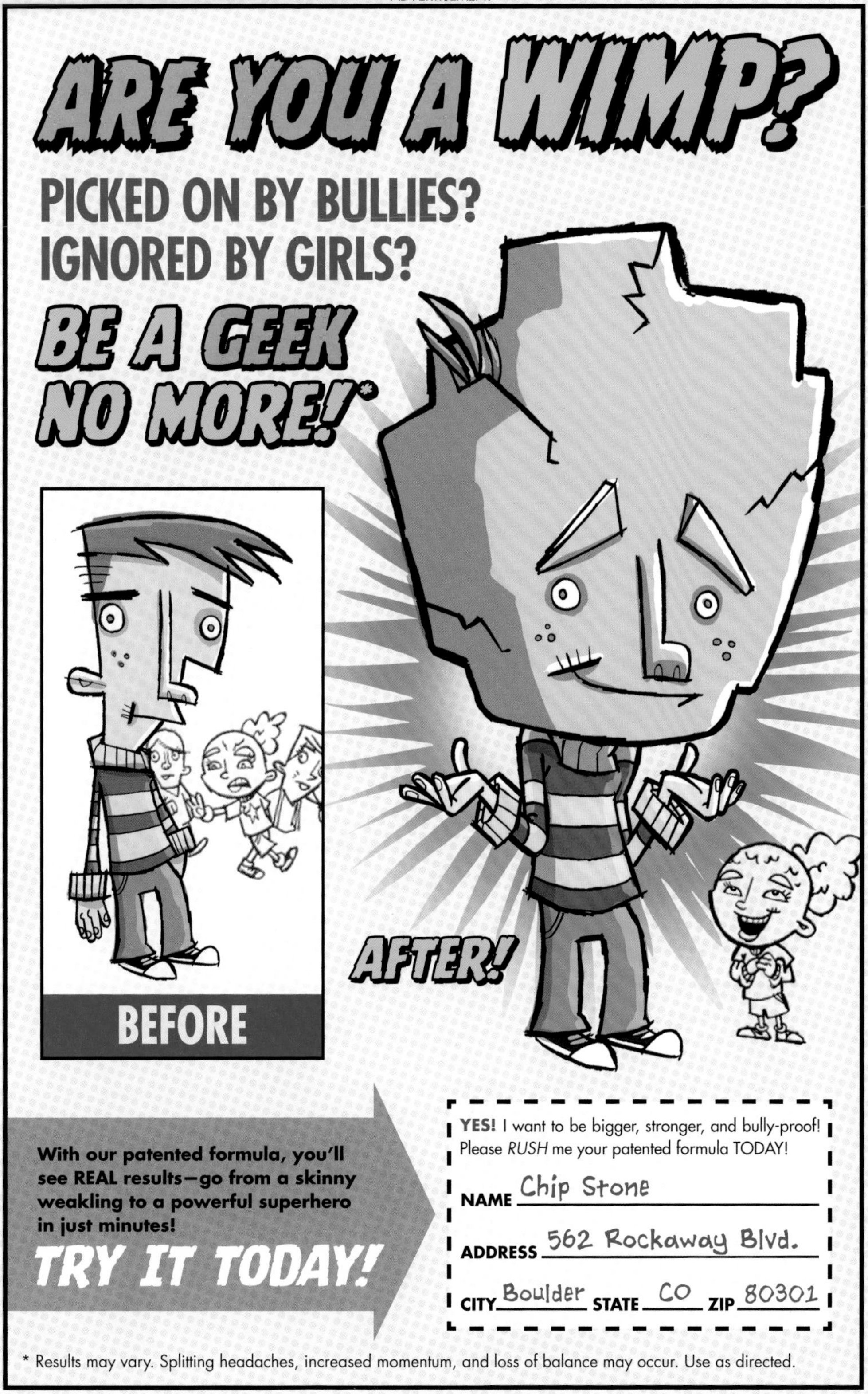
ARE YOU A WIMP?
PICKED ON BY BULLIES?
IGNORED BY GIRLS?
BE A GEEK NO MORE!*
BEFORE
AFTER!
With our patented formula, you'll see REAL results—go from a skinny weakling to a powerful superhero in just minutes!
TRY IT TODAY!
YES! I want to be bigger, stronger, and bully-proof! Please RUSH me your patented formula TODAY!
NAME Chip Stone
ADDRESS 562 Rockaway Blvd.
CITY Boulder STATE CO ZIP 80301
* Results may vary. Splitting headaches, increased momentum, and loss of balance may occur. Use as directed.

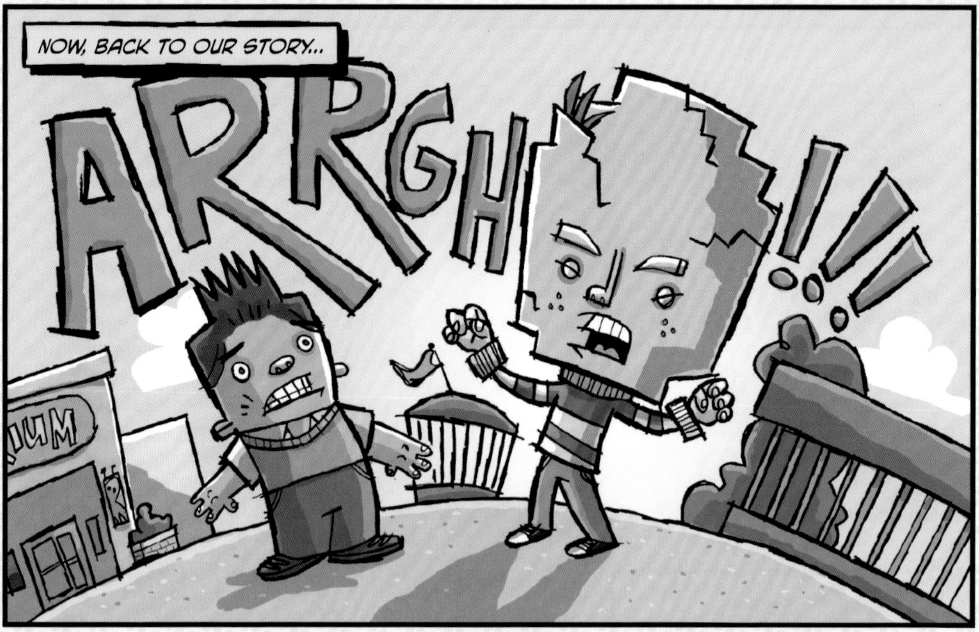
NOW, BACK TO OUR STORY...
ARRGH!!!!

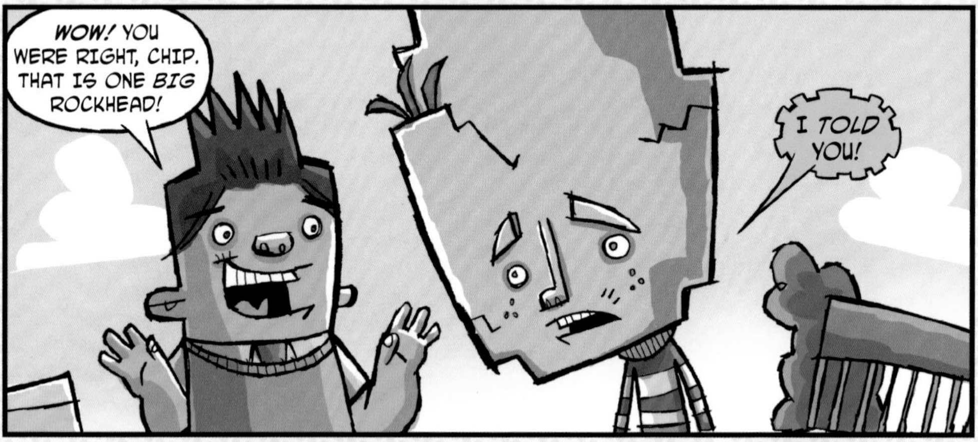
WOW! YOU WERE RIGHT, CHIP. THAT IS ONE BIG ROCKHEAD!
I TOLD YOU!

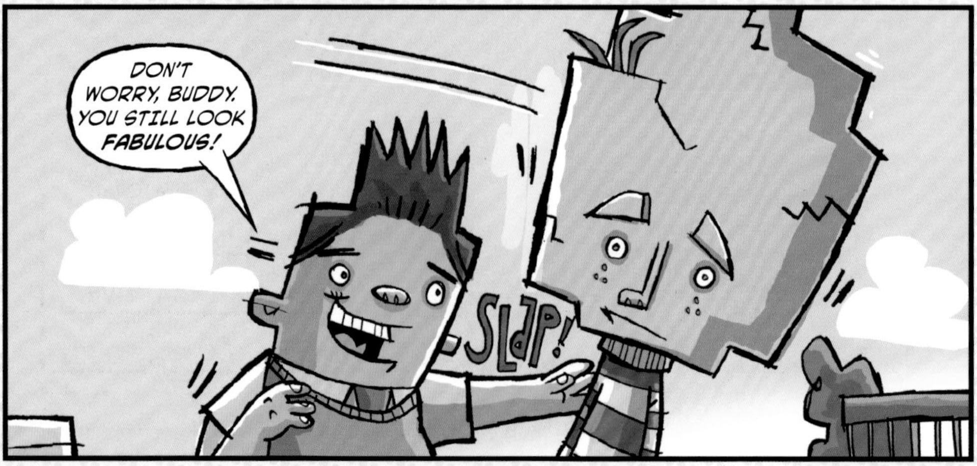
DON'T WORRY, BUDDY. YOU STILL LOOK FABULOUS!
SLAP!

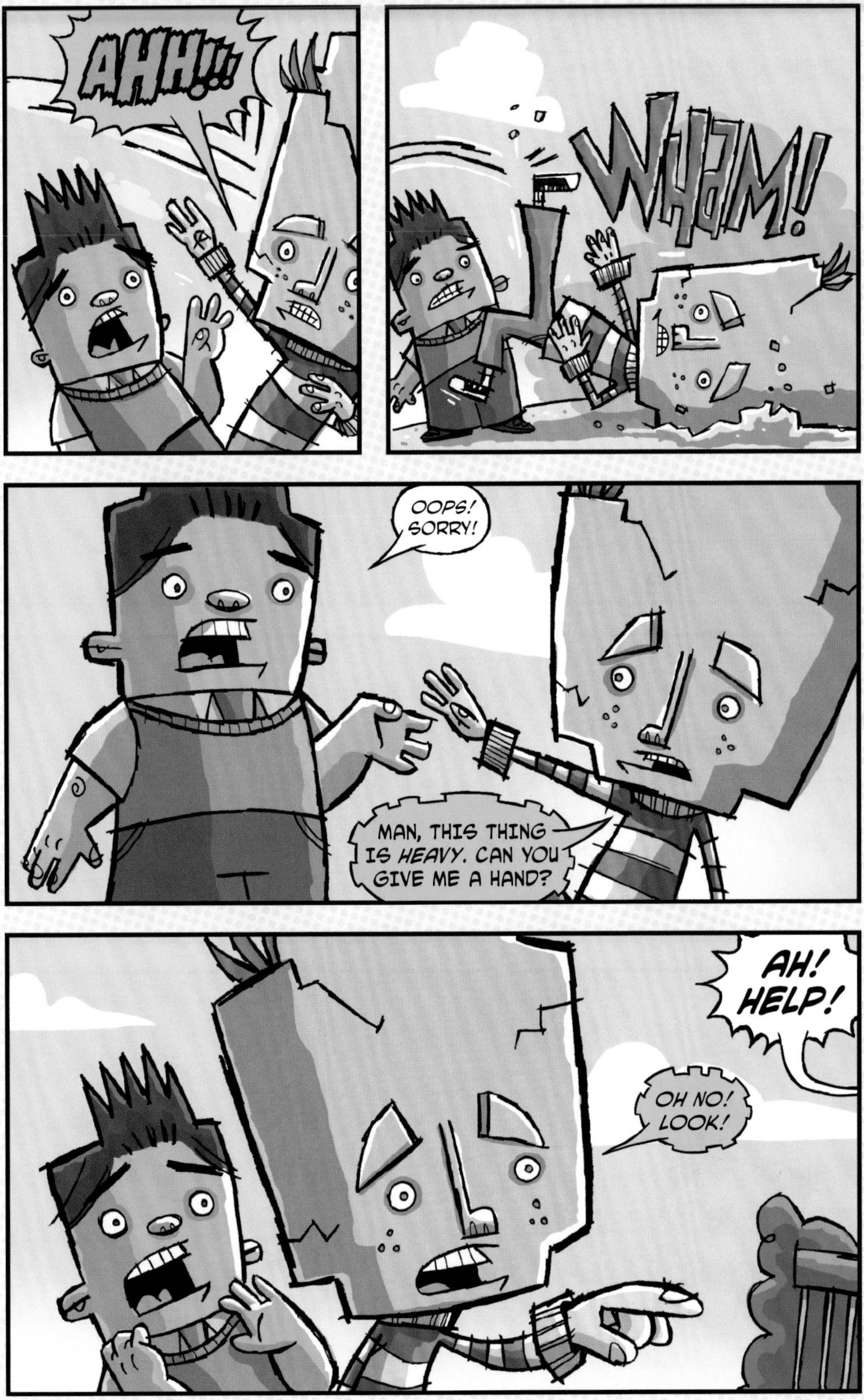
AHH!!!
WHAM!
OOPS! SORRY!
MAN, THIS THING IS HEAVY. CAN YOU GIVE ME A HAND?
AH! HELP!
OH NO! LOOK!

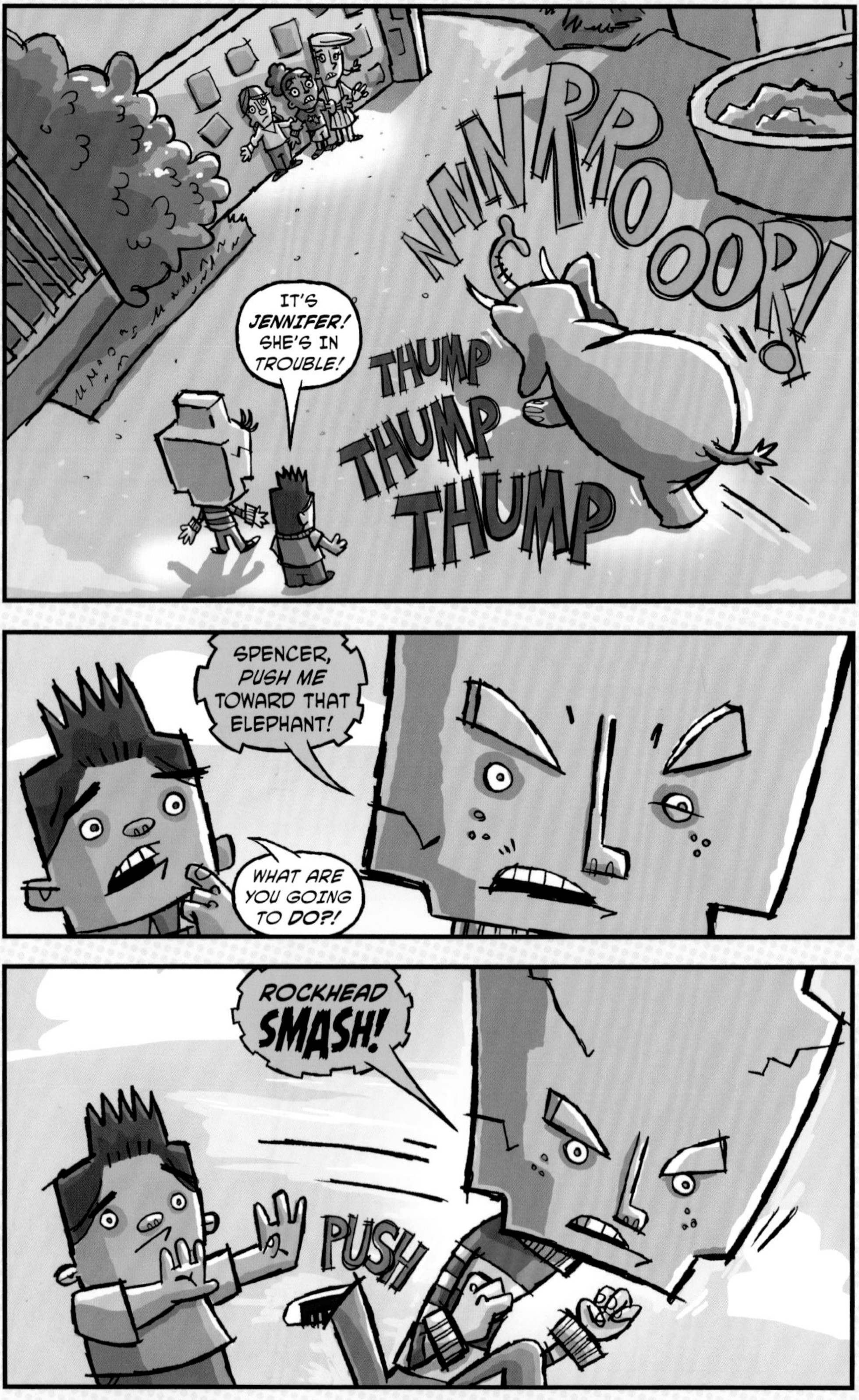
NNNNRROOOOR!
IT'S JENNIFER! SHE'S IN TROUBLE!
THUMP
THUMP
THUMP
SPENCER, PUSH ME TOWARD THAT ELEPHANT!
WHAT ARE YOU GOING TO DO?!
ROCKHEAD SMASH!
PUSH

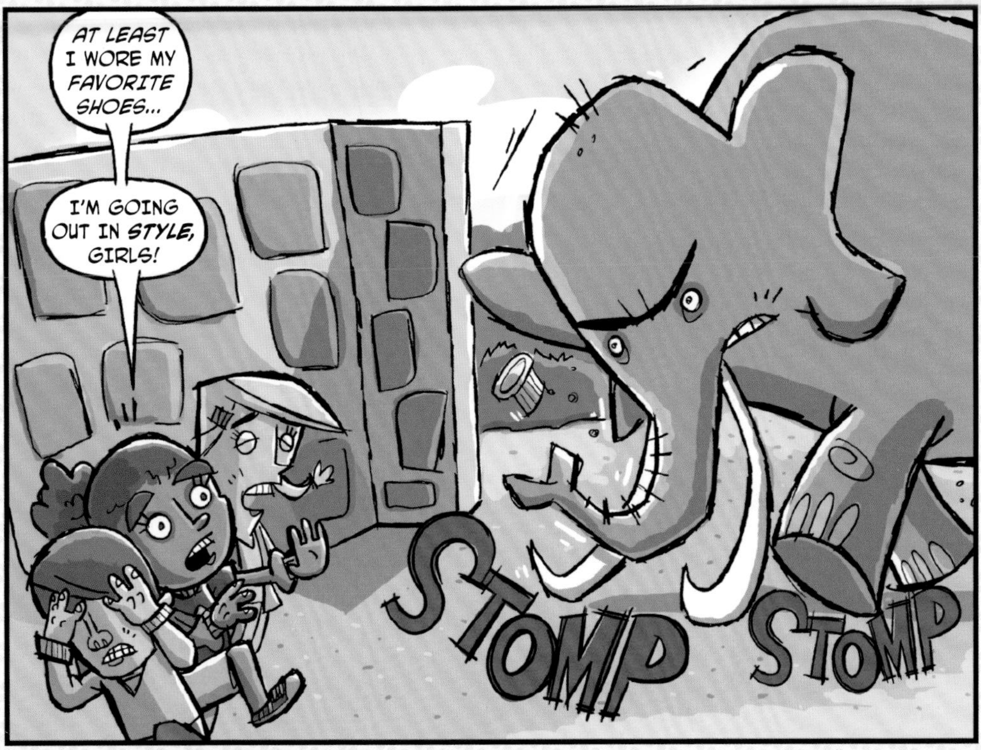
AT LEAST I WORE MY FAVORITE SHOES...
I'M GOING OUT IN STYLE, GIRLS!
STOMP STOMP

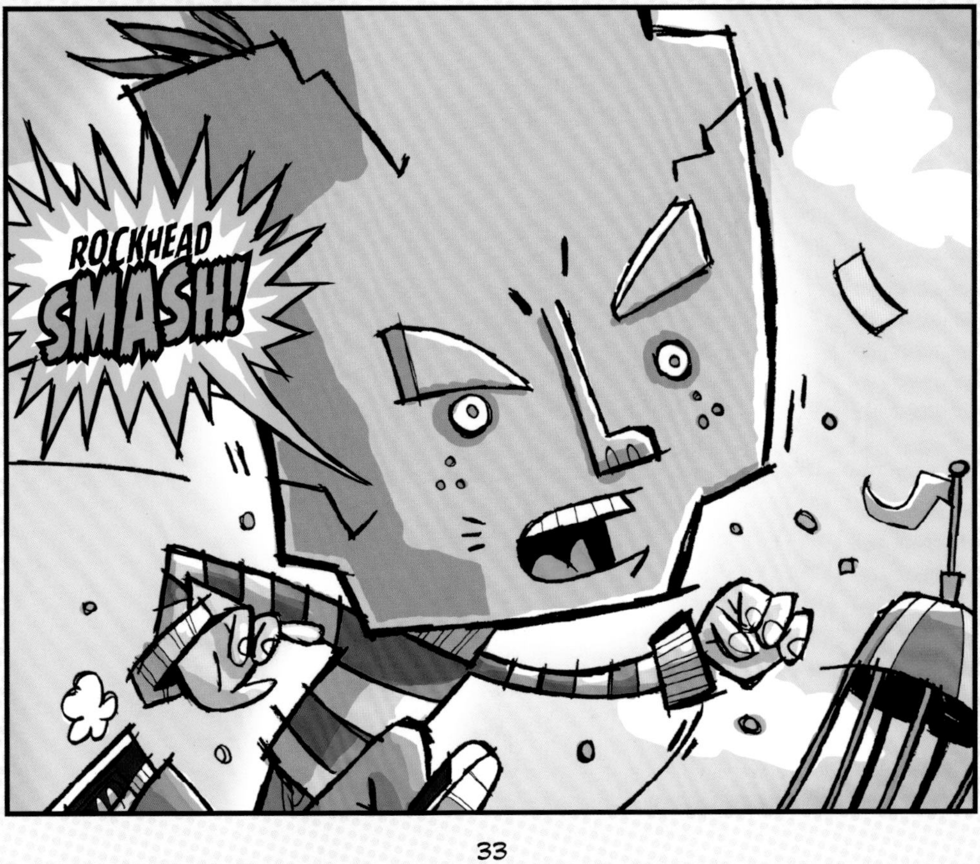
ROCKHEAD SMASH!

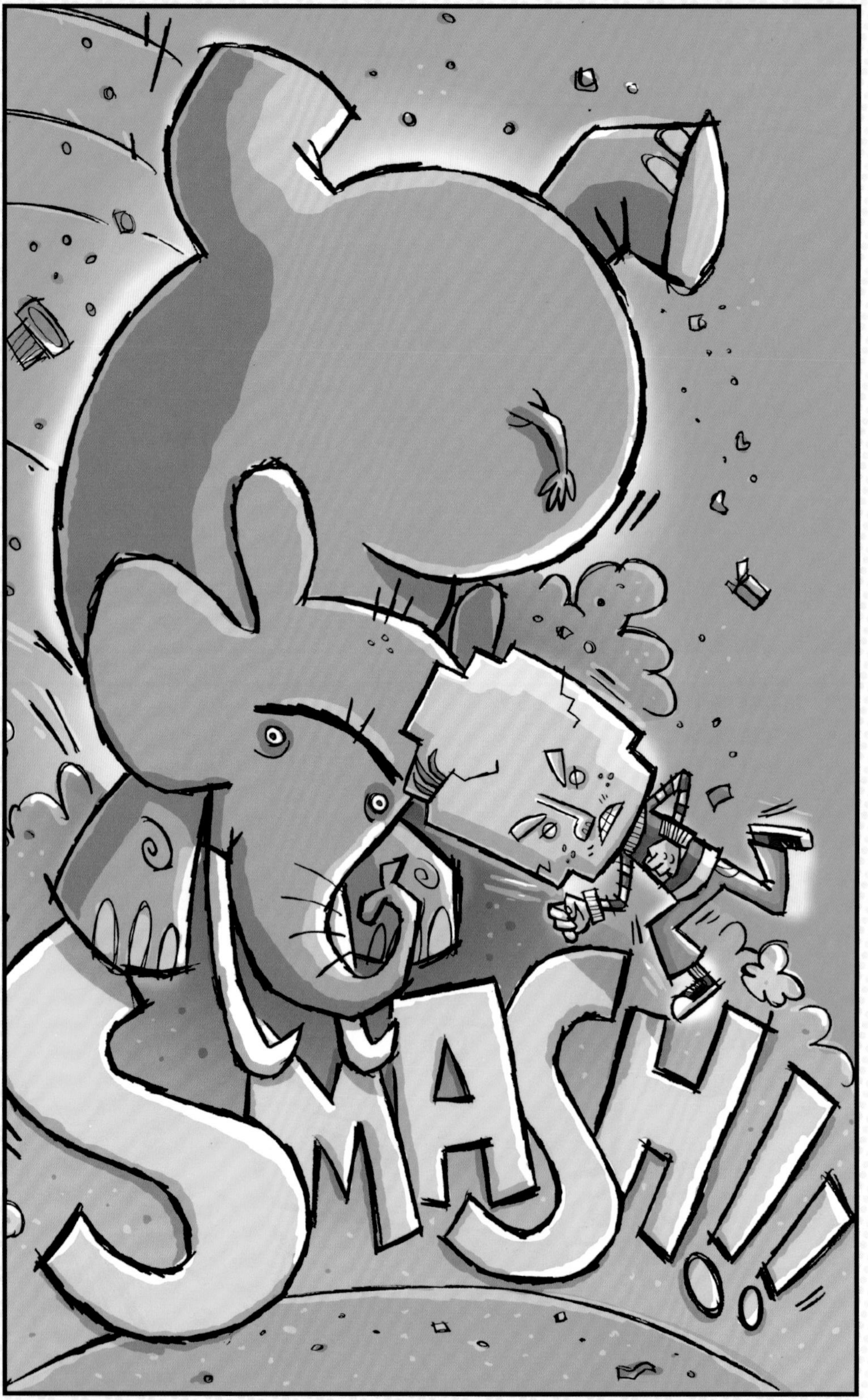
SMASH!!!

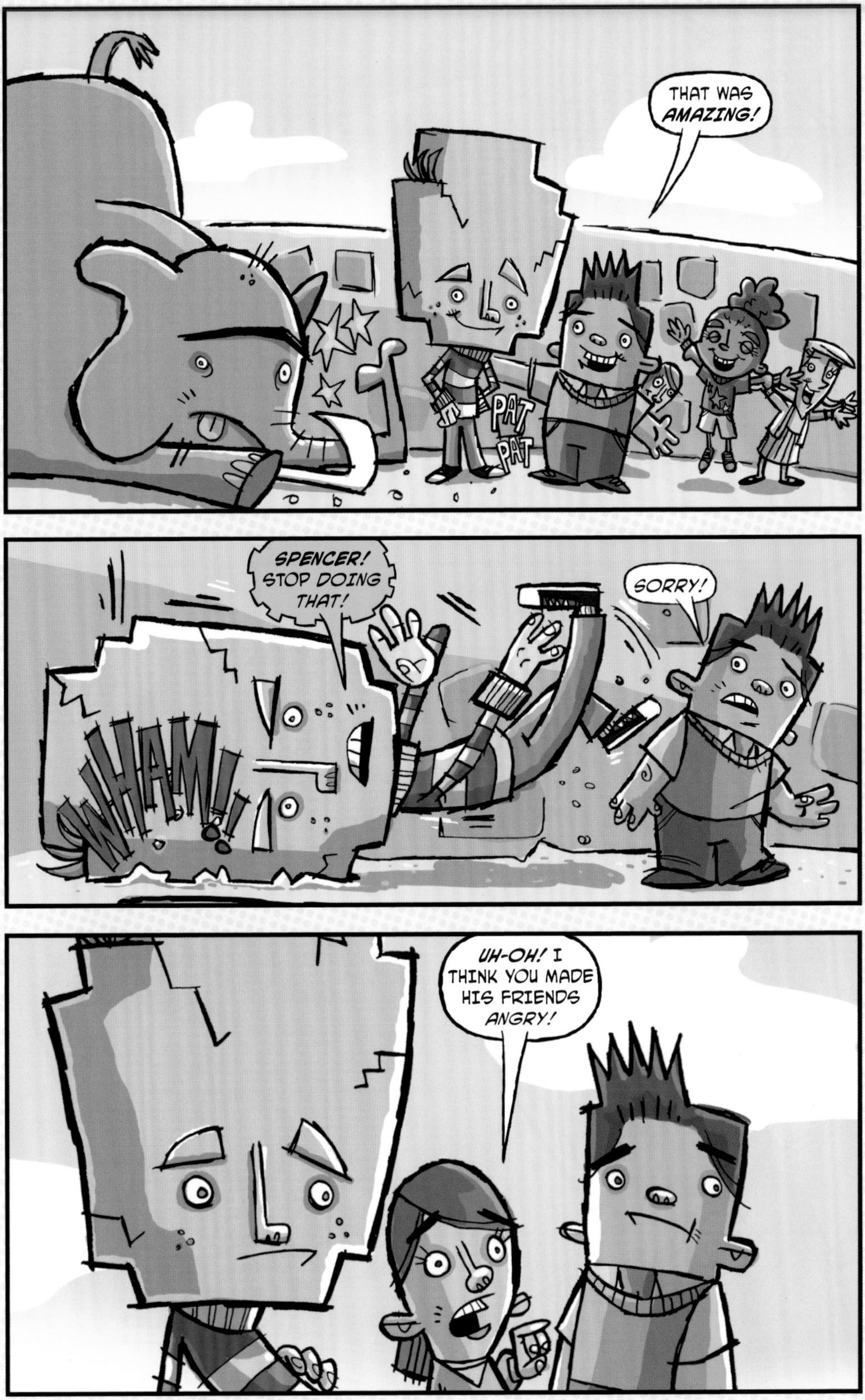
THAT WAS AMAZING!
PAT PAT
SPENCER! STOP DOING THAT!
SORRY!
WHAM!!
UH-OH! I THINK YOU MADE HIS FRIENDS ANGRY!

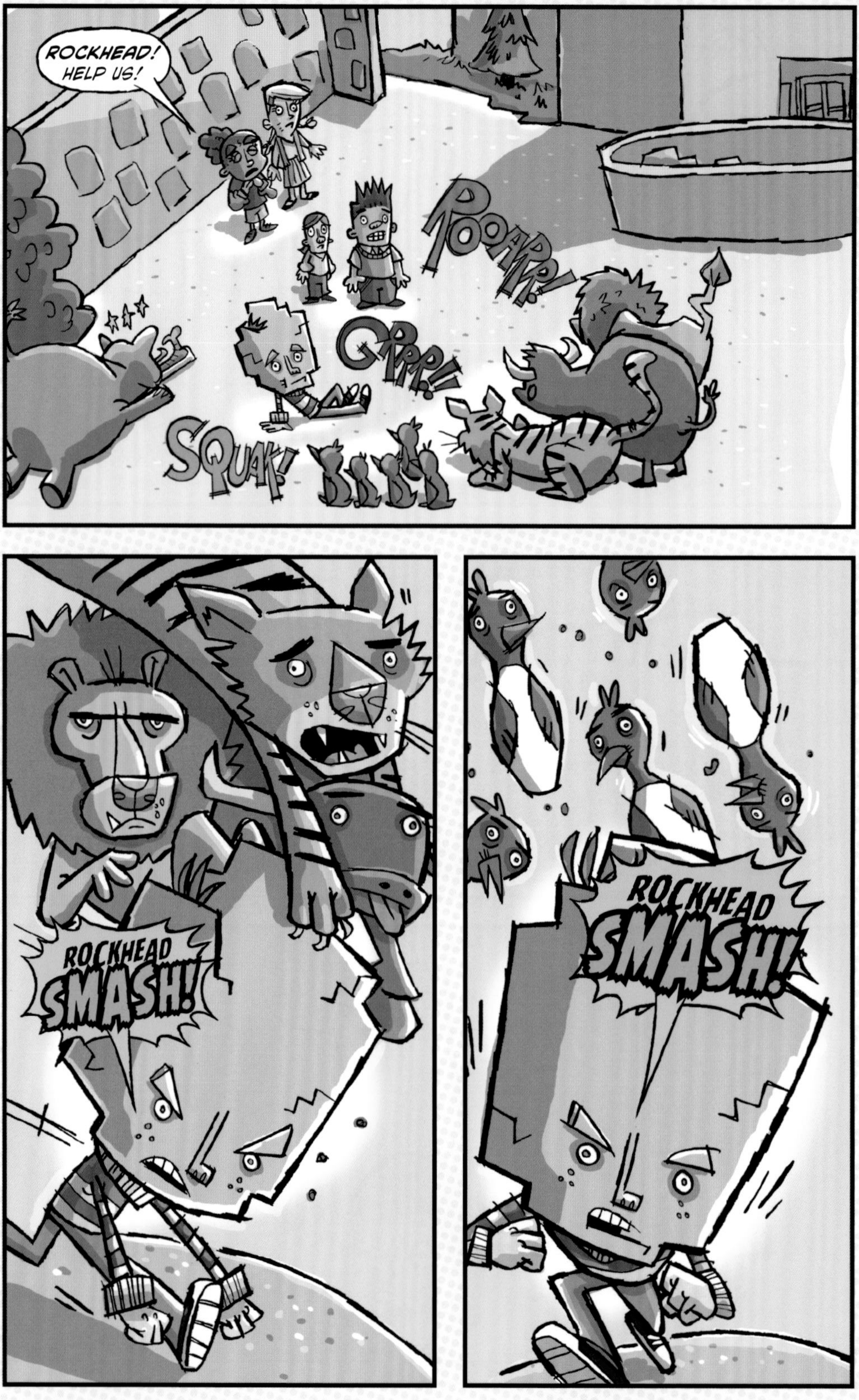
ROCKHEAD! HELP US!
POOARRR!
GRRR!!
SQUAK!
ROCKHEAD SMASH!
ROCKHEAD SMASH!

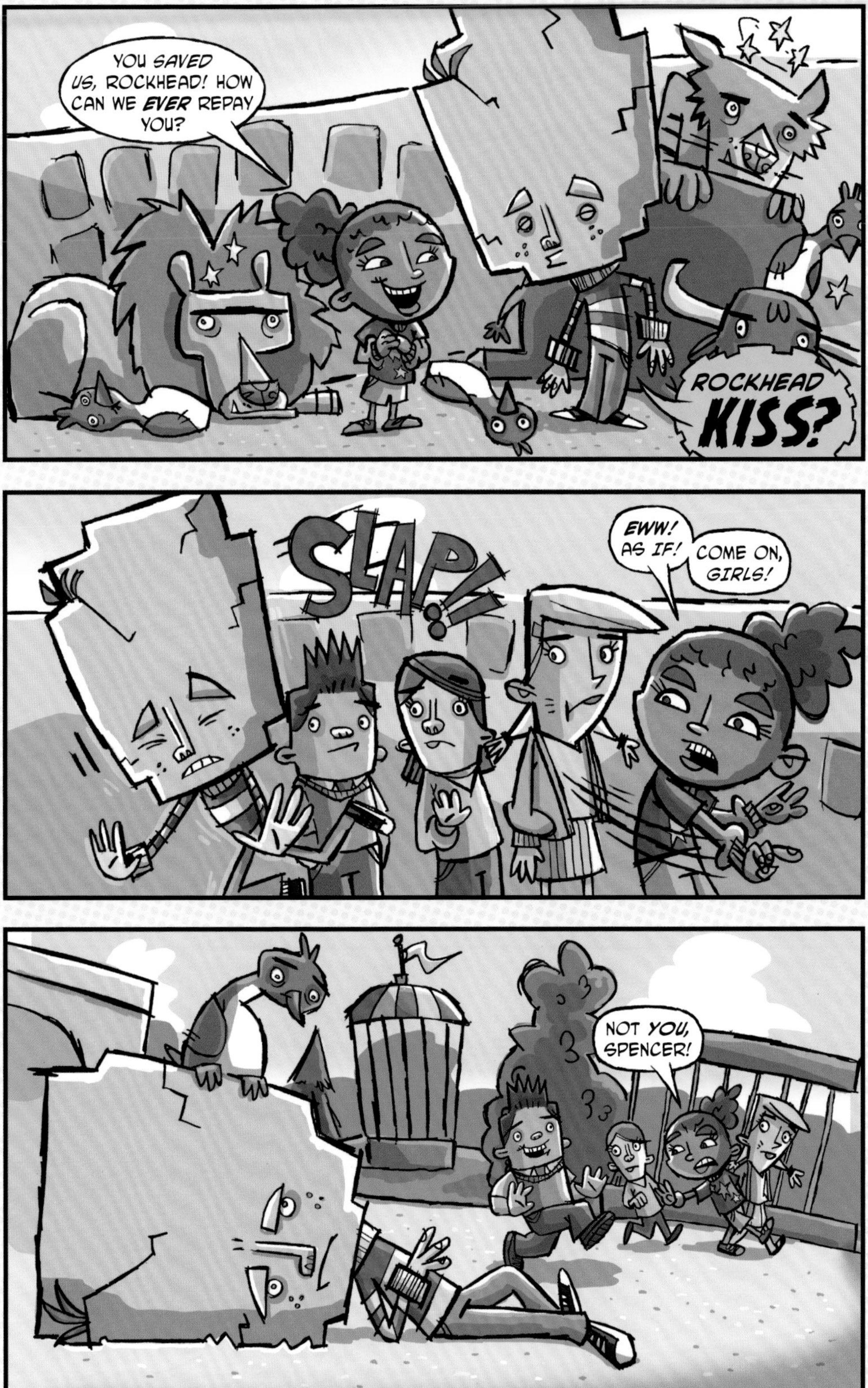
YOU SAVED US, ROCKHEAD! HOW CAN WE EVER REPAY YOU?
ROCKHEAD KISS?
SLAP!!
EWW! AS IF!
COME ON, GIRLS!
NOT YOU, SPENCER!

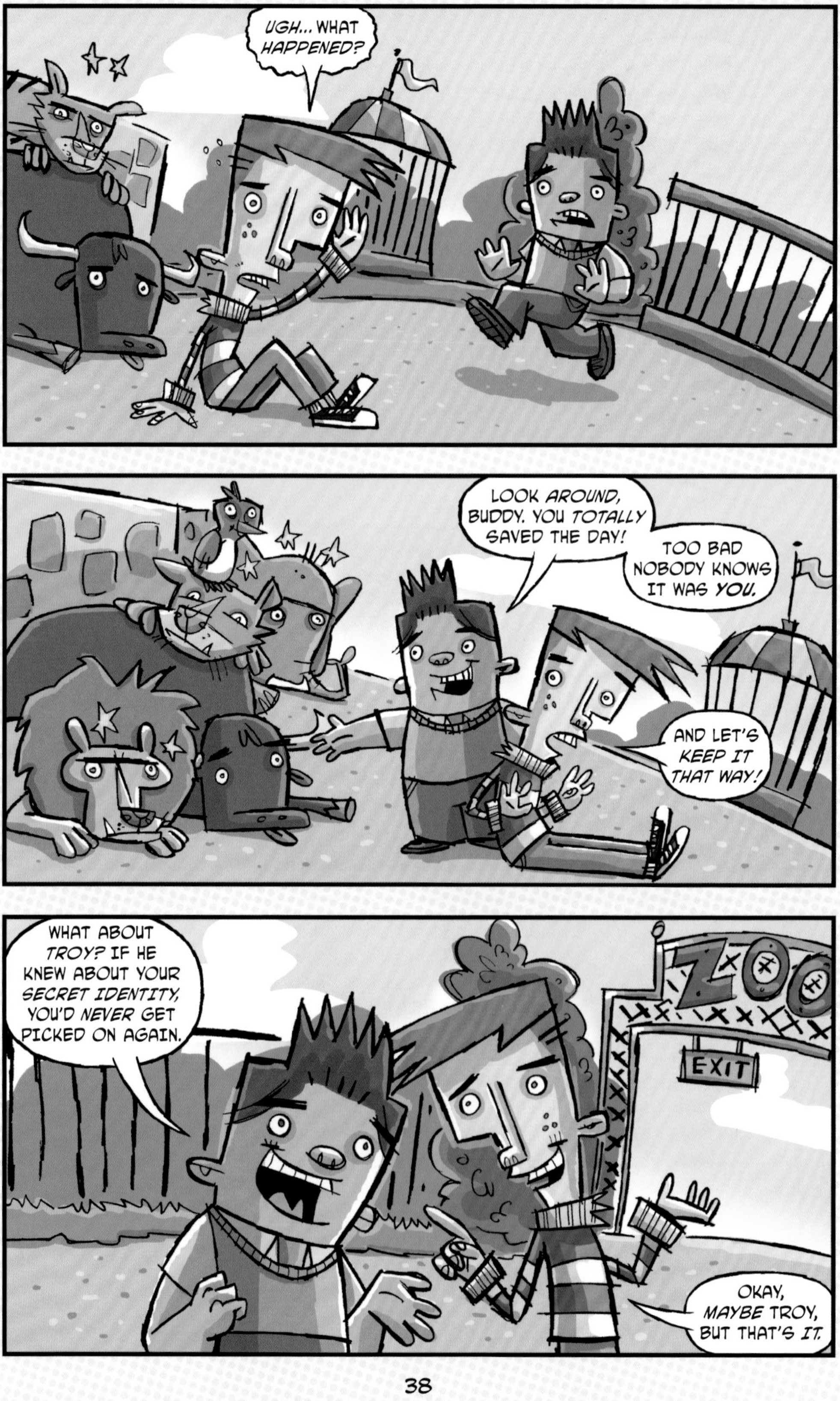
UGH... WHAT HAPPENED?
LOOK AROUND, BUDDY. YOU TOTALLY SAVED THE DAY!
TOO BAD NOBODY KNOWS IT WAS YOU.
AND LET'S KEEP IT THAT WAY!
ZOO
EXIT
WHAT ABOUT TROY? IF HE KNEW ABOUT YOUR SECRET IDENTITY, YOU'D NEVER GET PICKED ON AGAIN.
OKAY, MAYBE TROY, BUT THAT'S IT.

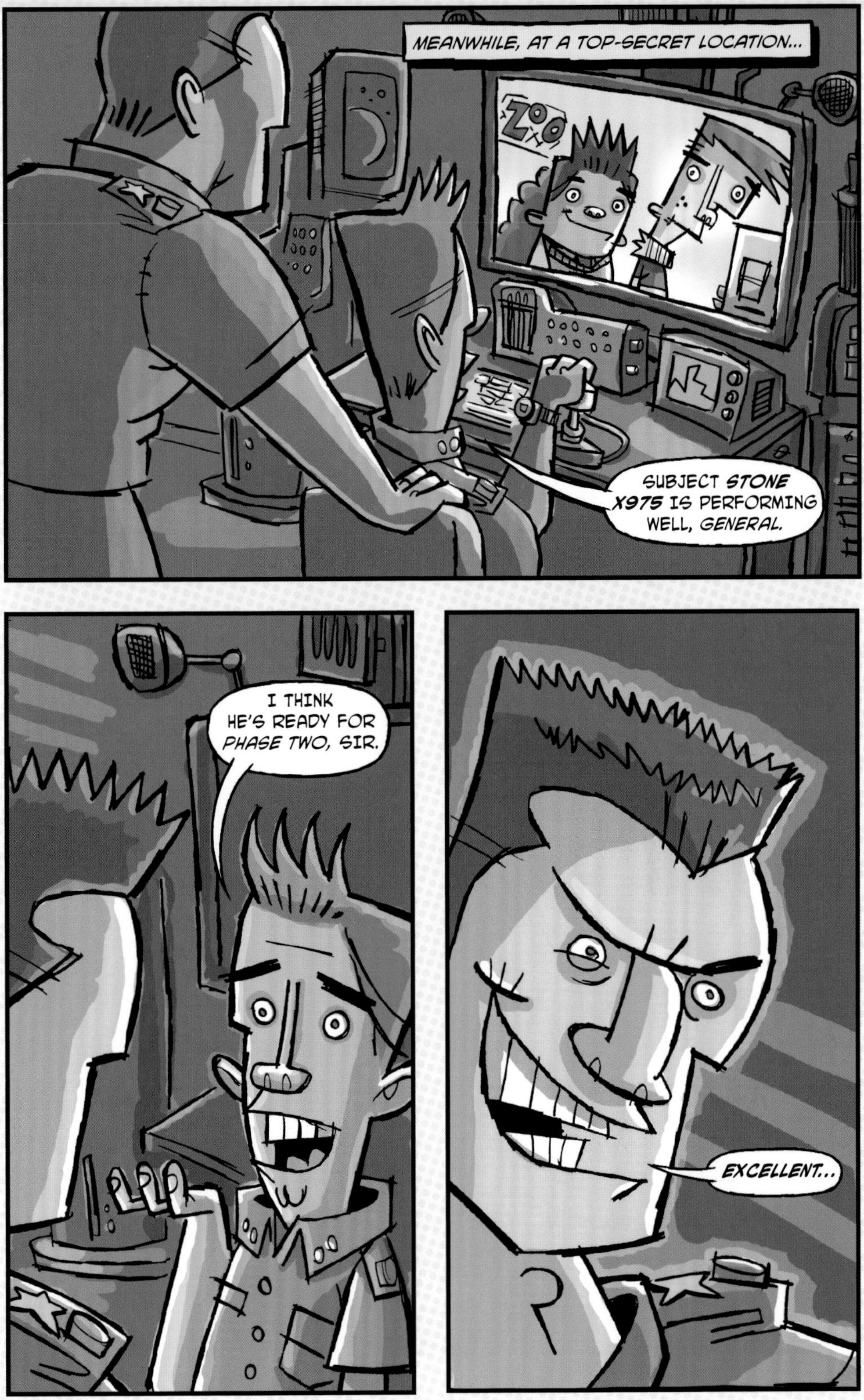
MEANWHILE, AT A TOP-SECRET LOCATION...
ZOO
SUBJECT STONE X975 IS PERFORMING WELL, GENERAL.
I THINK HE'S READY FOR PHASE TWO, SIR.
EXCELLENT...

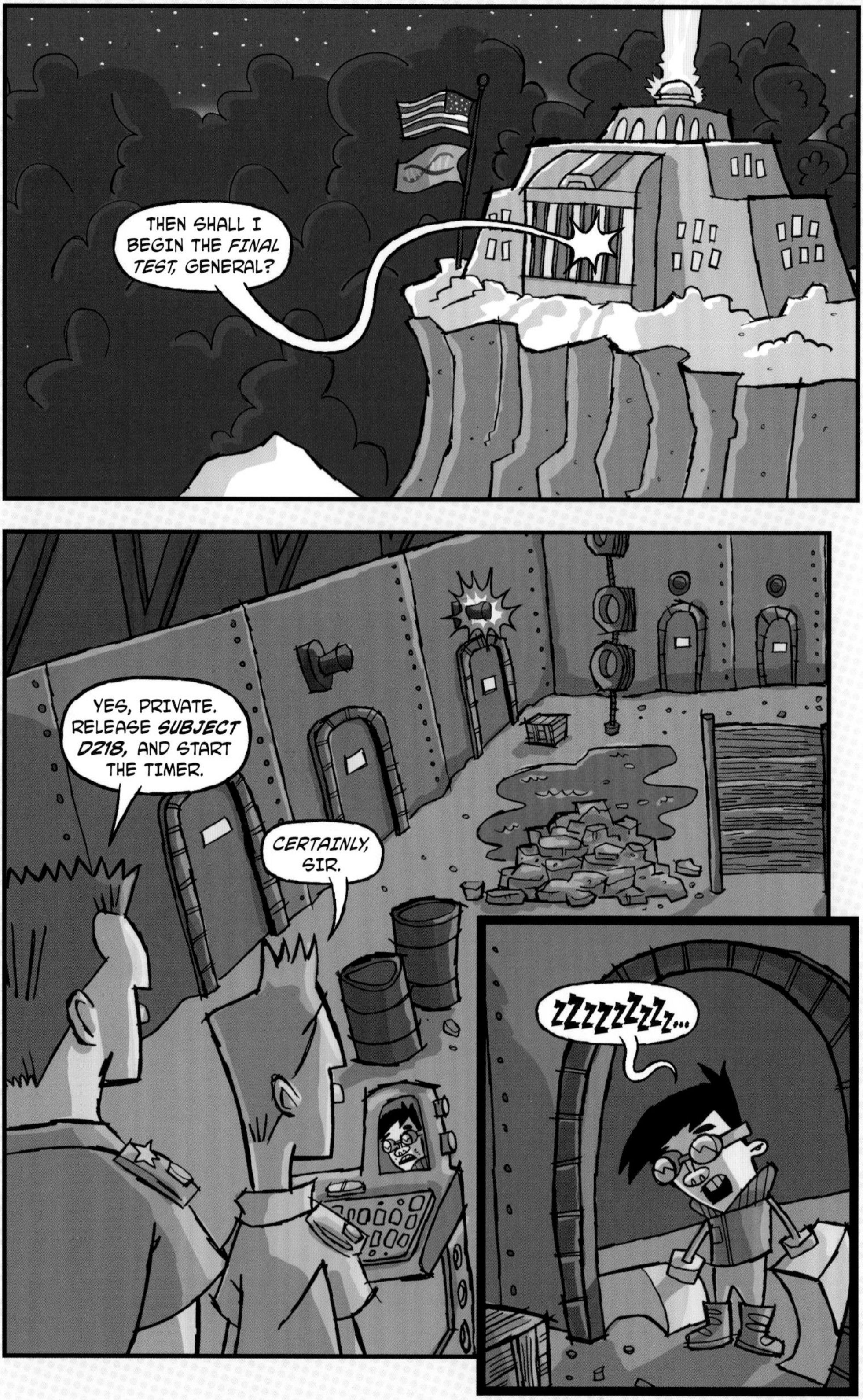
THEN SHALL I BEGIN THE *FINAL TEST,* GENERAL?
YES, PRIVATE. RELEASE *SUBJECT D218,* AND START THE TIMER.
CERTAINLY, SIR.
ZZZZZZZZZ...

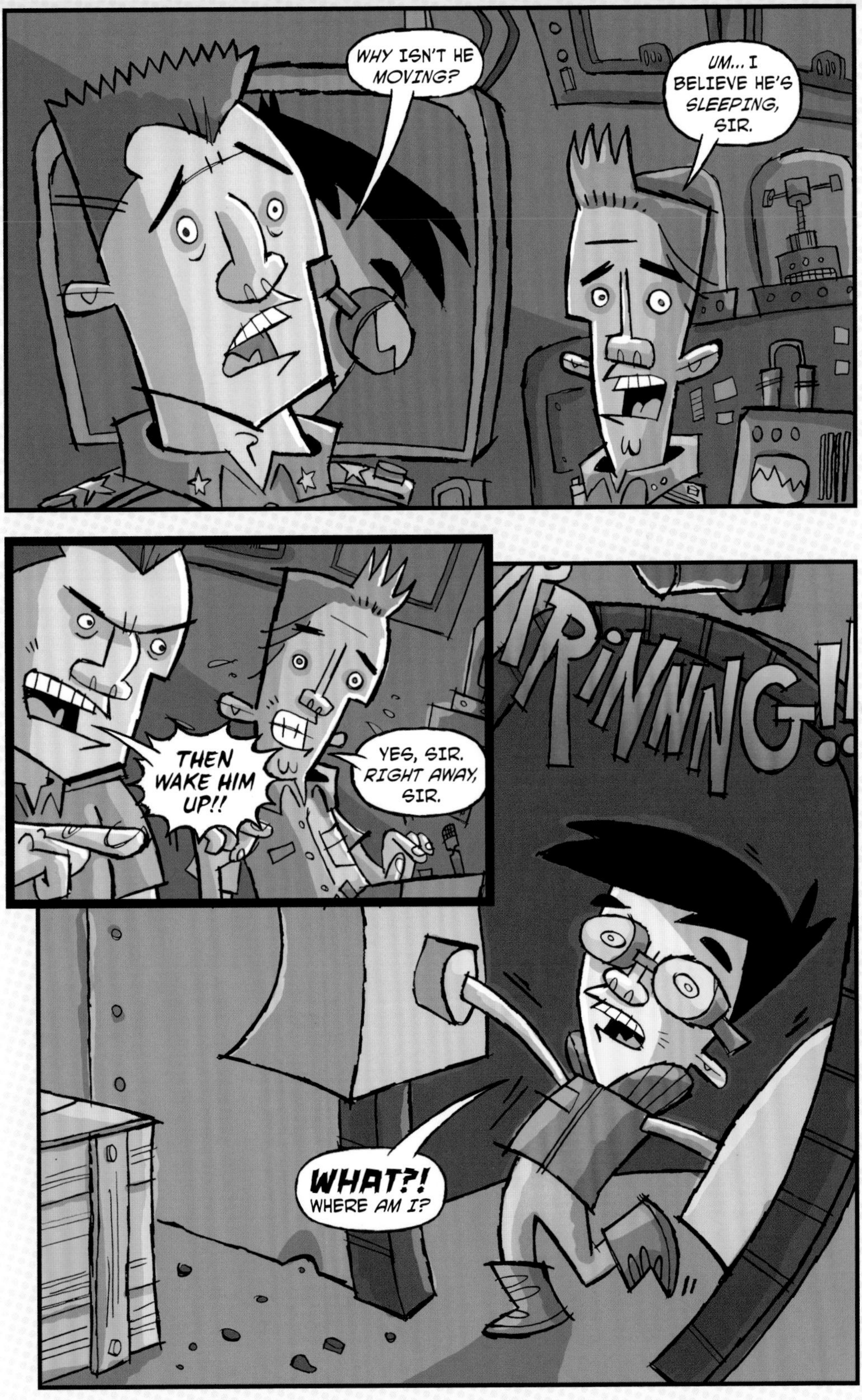
WHY ISN'T HE MOVING?
UM... I BELIEVE HE'S SLEEPING, SIR.
THEN WAKE HIM UP!!
YES, SIR. RIGHT AWAY, SIR.
TRINNNG!!
WHAT?! WHERE AM I?

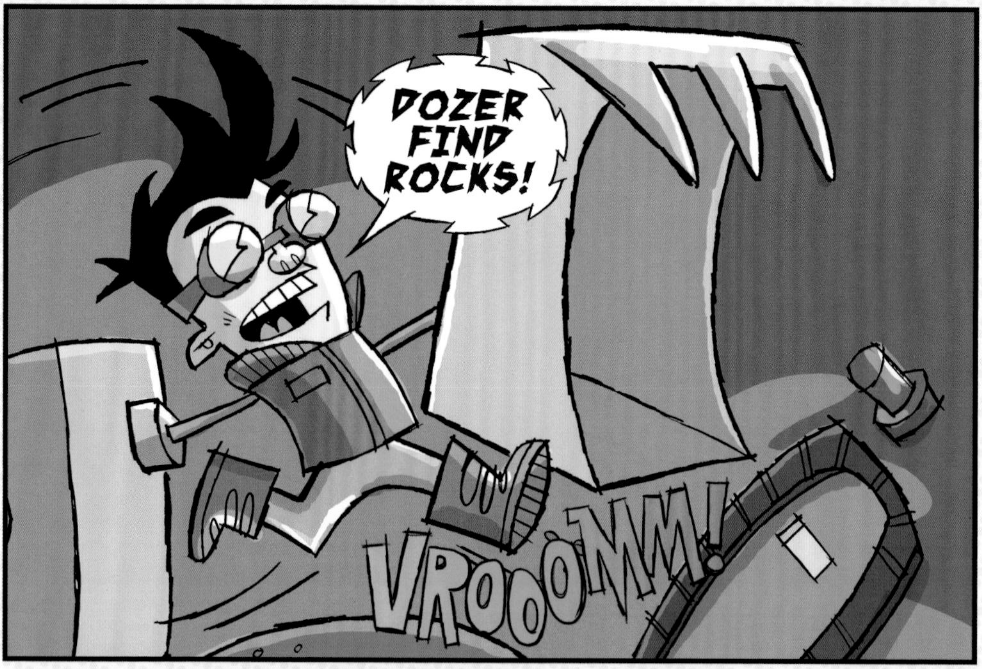
DOZER FIND ROCKS!
VROOOMM!

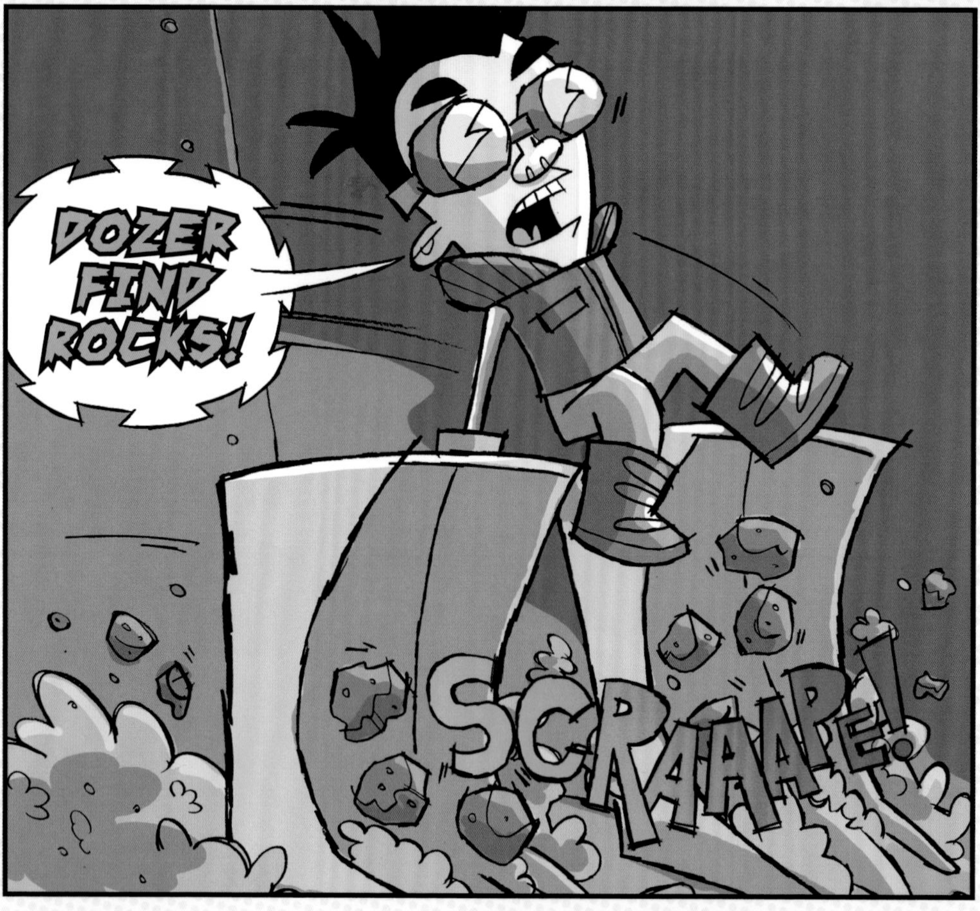
DOZER FIND ROCKS!
SCRAAAPE!

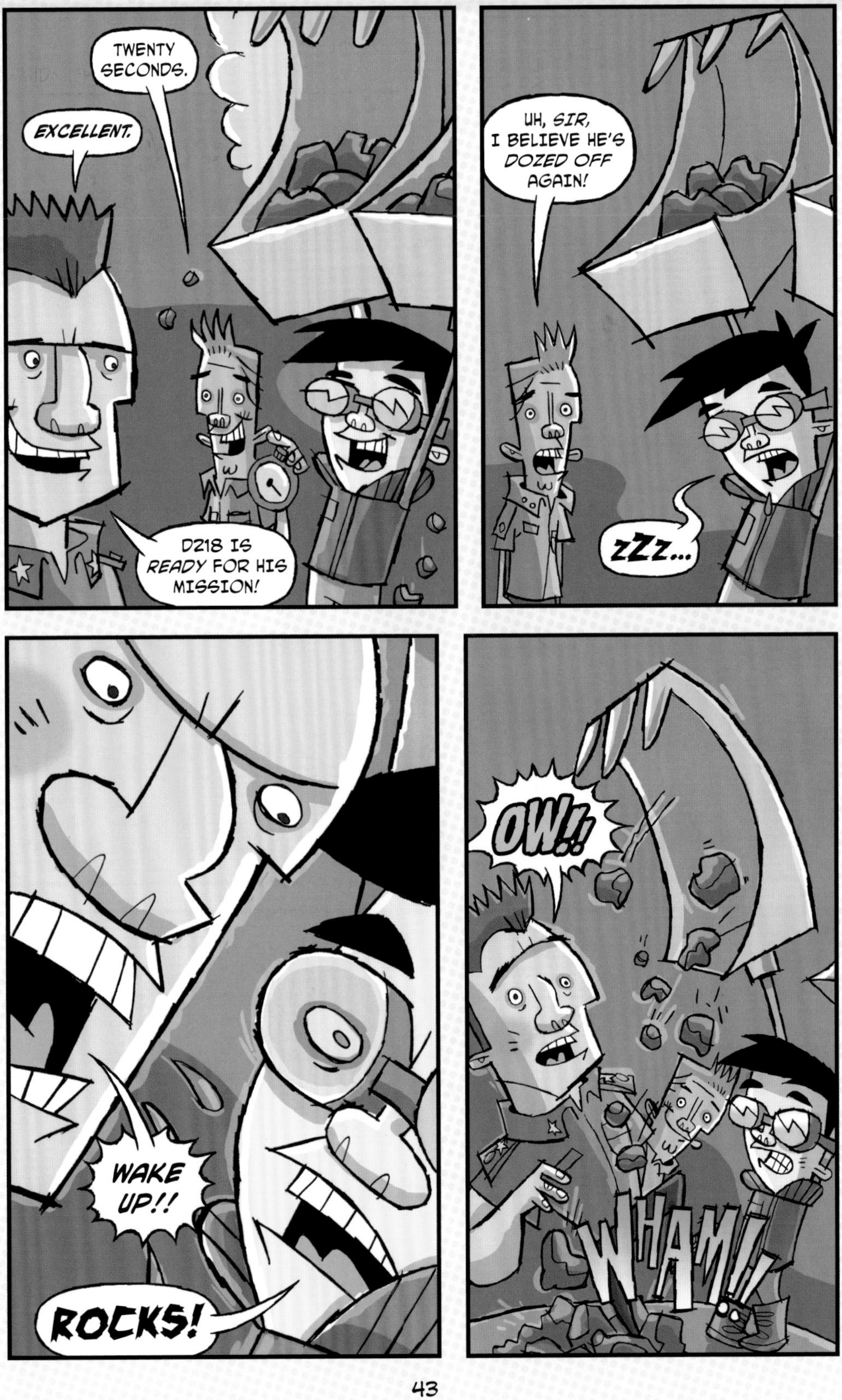
TWENTY SECONDS.
EXCELLENT.
D218 IS READY FOR HIS MISSION!
UH, SIR, I BELIEVE HE'S DOZED OFF AGAIN!
ZZZ...
WAKE UP!!
ROCKS!
OW!!
WHAM!!

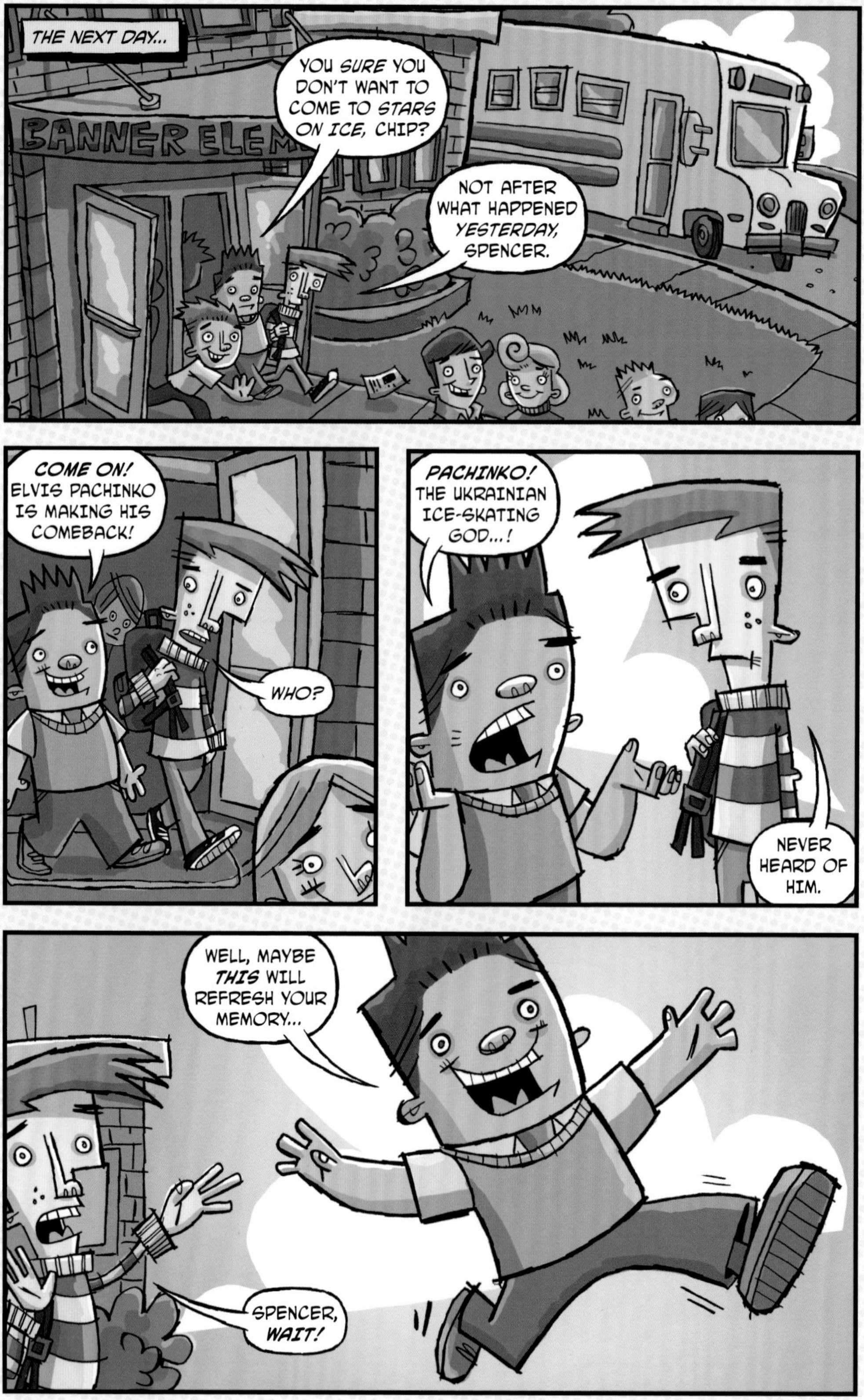
THE NEXT DAY...
BANNER ELEM
YOU SURE YOU DON'T WANT TO COME TO STARS ON ICE, CHIP?
NOT AFTER WHAT HAPPENED YESTERDAY, SPENCER.
COME ON! ELVIS PACHINKO IS MAKING HIS COMEBACK!
WHO?
PACHINKO! THE UKRAINIAN ICE-SKATING GOD...!
NEVER HEARD OF HIM.
WELL, MAYBE THIS WILL REFRESH YOUR MEMORY...
SPENCER, WAIT!

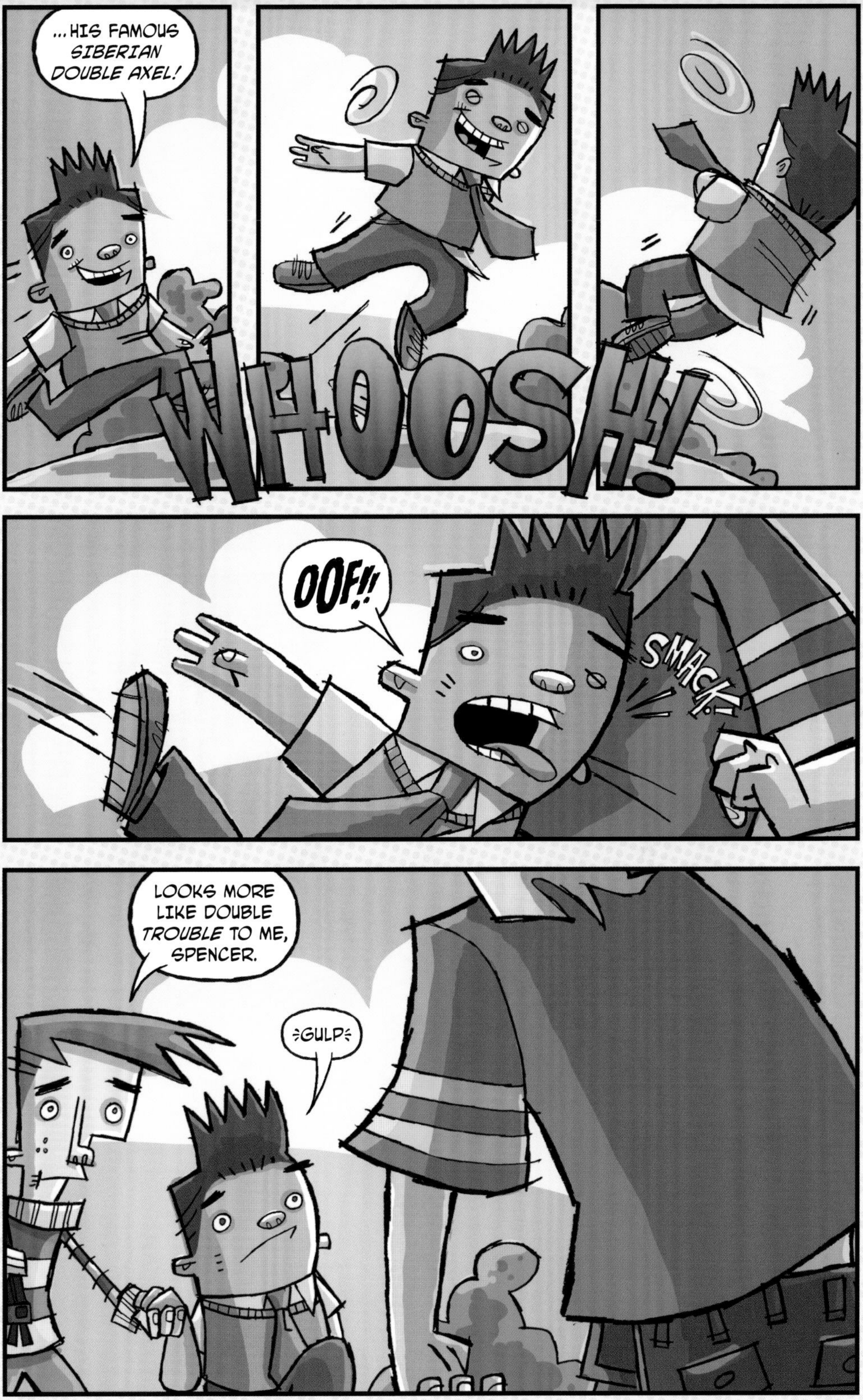
...HIS FAMOUS SIBERIAN DOUBLE AXEL!
WHOOSH!
OOF!!
SMACK!
LOOKS MORE LIKE DOUBLE *TROUBLE* TO ME, SPENCER.
GULP

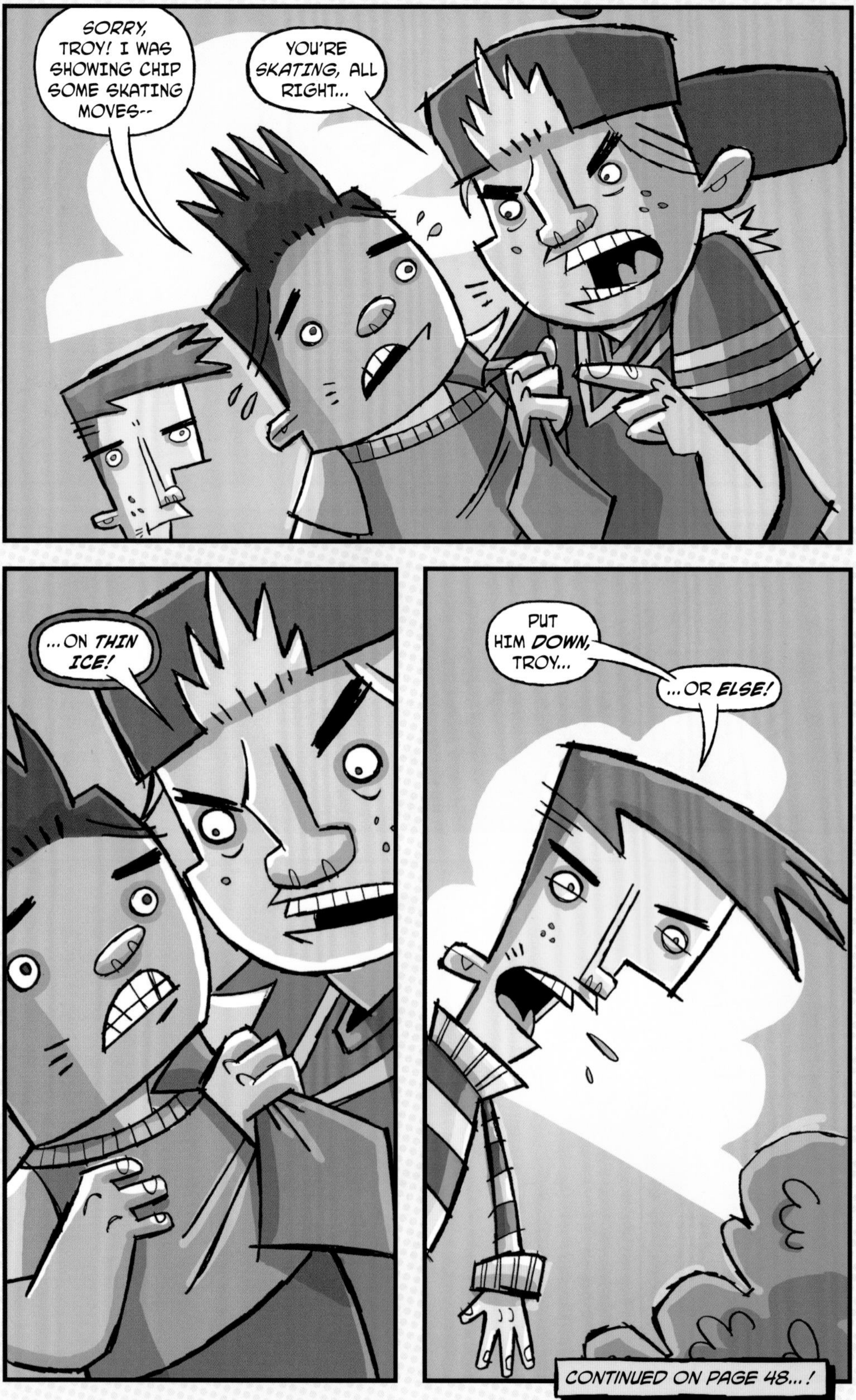
SORRY, TROY! I WAS SHOWING CHIP SOME SKATING MOVES--
YOU'RE SKATING, ALL RIGHT...
...ON THIN ICE!
PUT HIM DOWN, TROY...
...OR ELSE!
CONTINUED ON PAGE 48...!

MISSING!
HAVE YOU SEEN ME?

CRYSTAL FROST

The eleven year-old was last seen at Afton Alps Ski Resort near Boulder, Colorado.

SKIP LODER

The eleven year-old was last seen sleeping at a rock concert near Boulder, Colorado.

POSSIBLE KIDNAPPING SUSPECT?

IF YOU HAVE ANY INFORMATION REGARDING THESE MISSING CHILDREN, PLEASE CONTACT
THE GENERAL

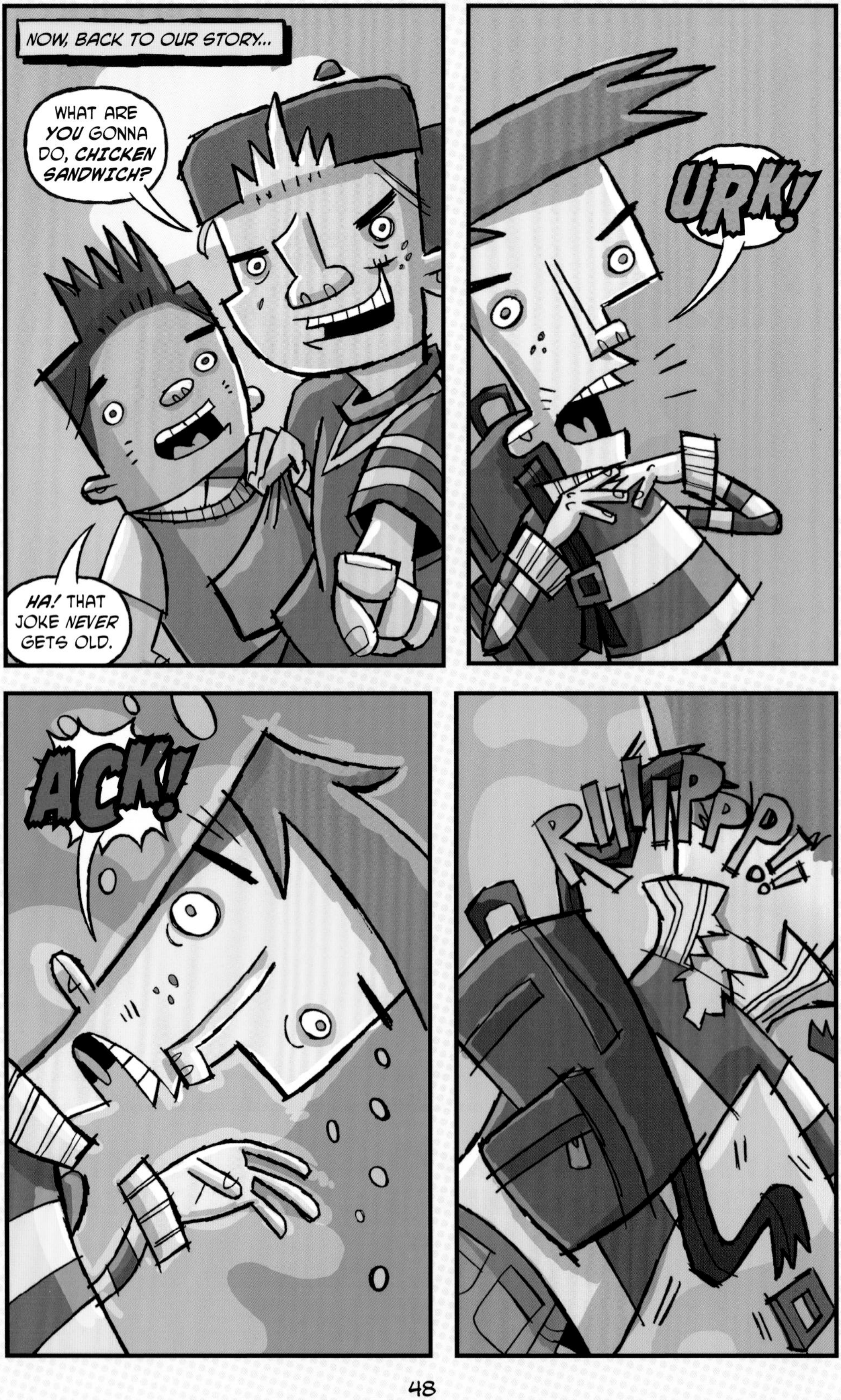
NOW, BACK TO OUR STORY...
WHAT ARE *YOU* GONNA DO, *CHICKEN SANDWICH?*
HA! THAT JOKE *NEVER* GETS OLD.
URK!
ACK!
RIIIPPP!!

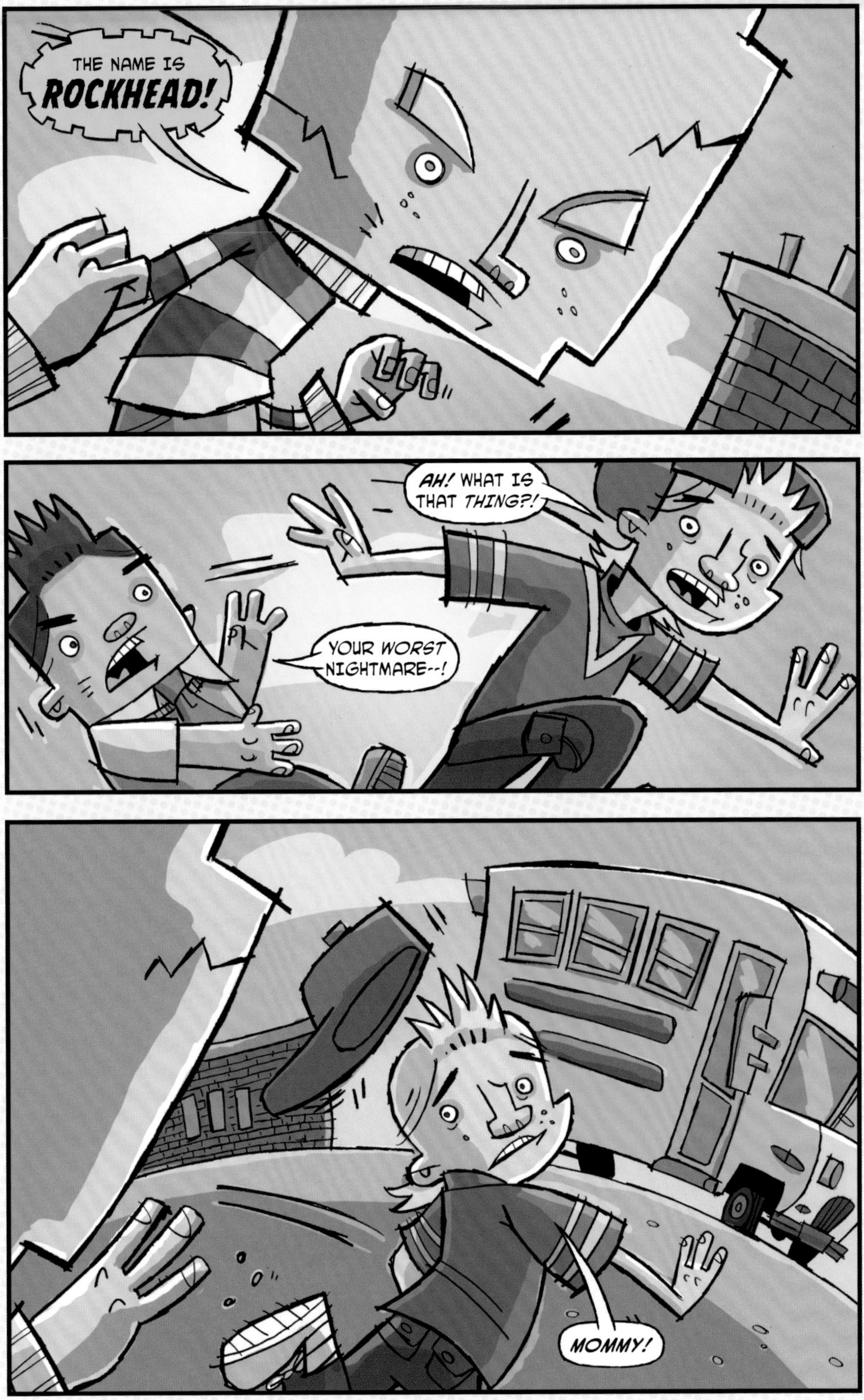
THE NAME IS ROCKHEAD!
AH! WHAT IS THAT THING?!
YOUR WORST NIGHTMARE--!
MOMMY!

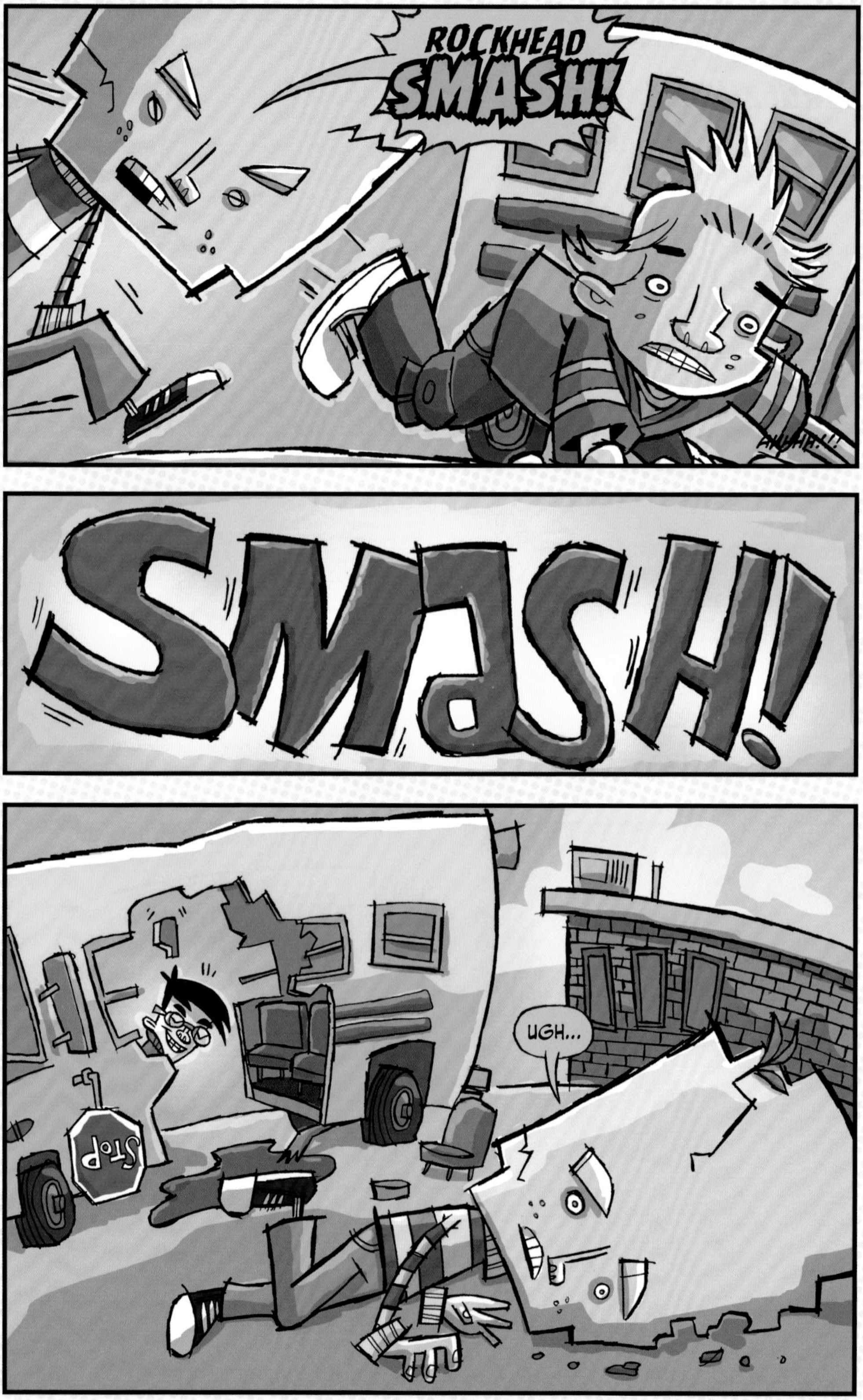
ROCKHEAD SMASH!
SMASH!
UGH...
STOP

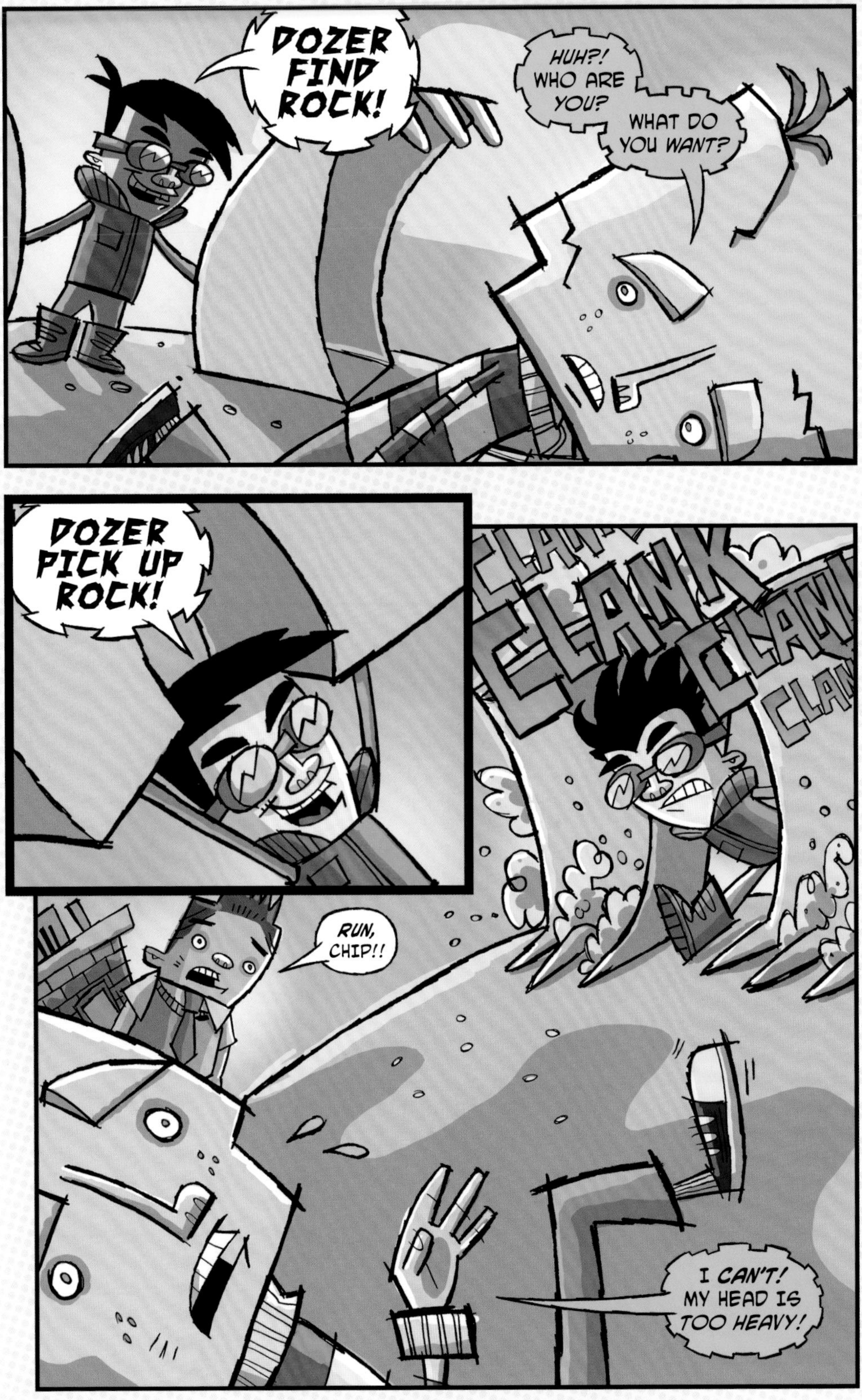
DOZER FIND ROCK!
HUH?! WHO ARE YOU?
WHAT DO YOU WANT?
DOZER PICK UP ROCK!
CLANK
CLANK
RUN, CHIP!!
I CAN'T! MY HEAD IS TOO HEAVY!

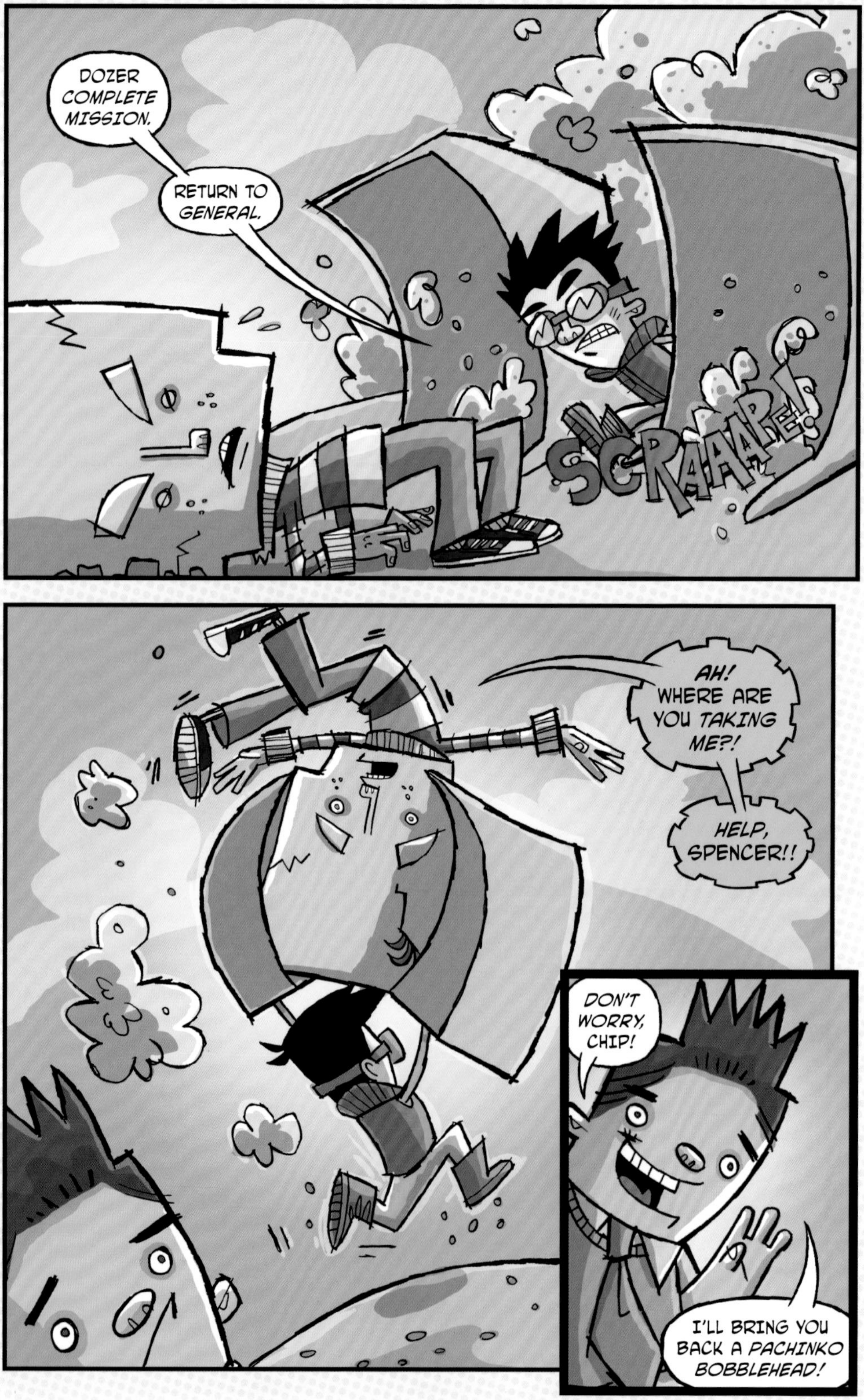
DOZER COMPLETE MISSION.
RETURN TO GENERAL.
SCRAAAPE!
AH! WHERE ARE YOU TAKING ME?!
HELP, SPENCER!!
DON'T WORRY, CHIP!
I'LL BRING YOU BACK A PACHINKO BOBBLEHEAD!

A SHORT TIME LATER...

LET ME GO!

GENERAL WANT ROCKHEAD.

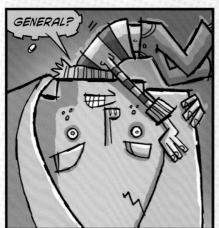

GENERAL?

AM I BEING DRAFTED?

DOZER RETURN TO LAB.

ROCKHEAD MEET OTHERS.

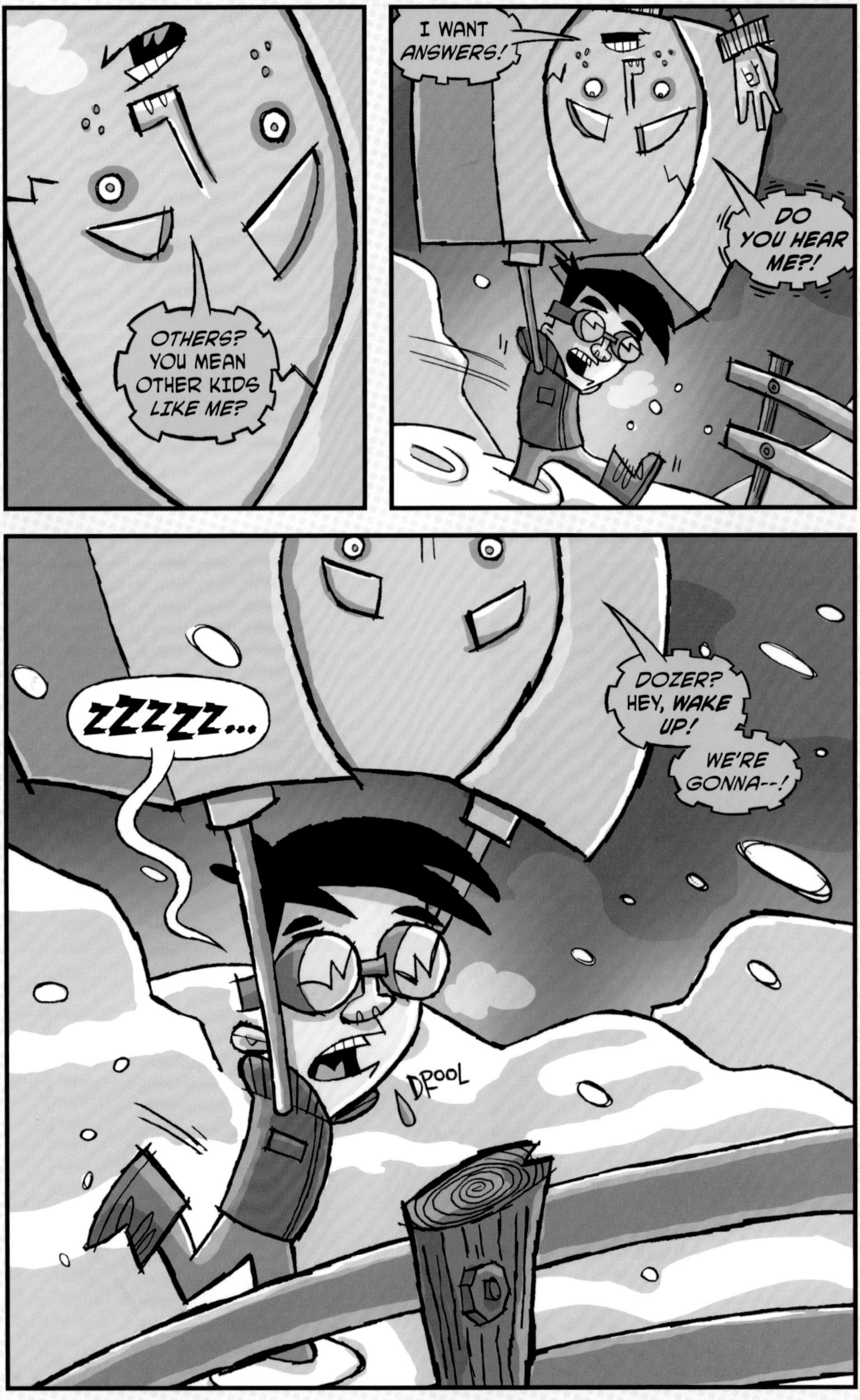
OTHERS? YOU MEAN OTHER KIDS LIKE ME?
I WANT ANSWERS!
DO YOU HEAR ME?!
ZZZZZ...
DOZER? HEY, WAKE UP!
WE'RE GONNA--!
DROOL

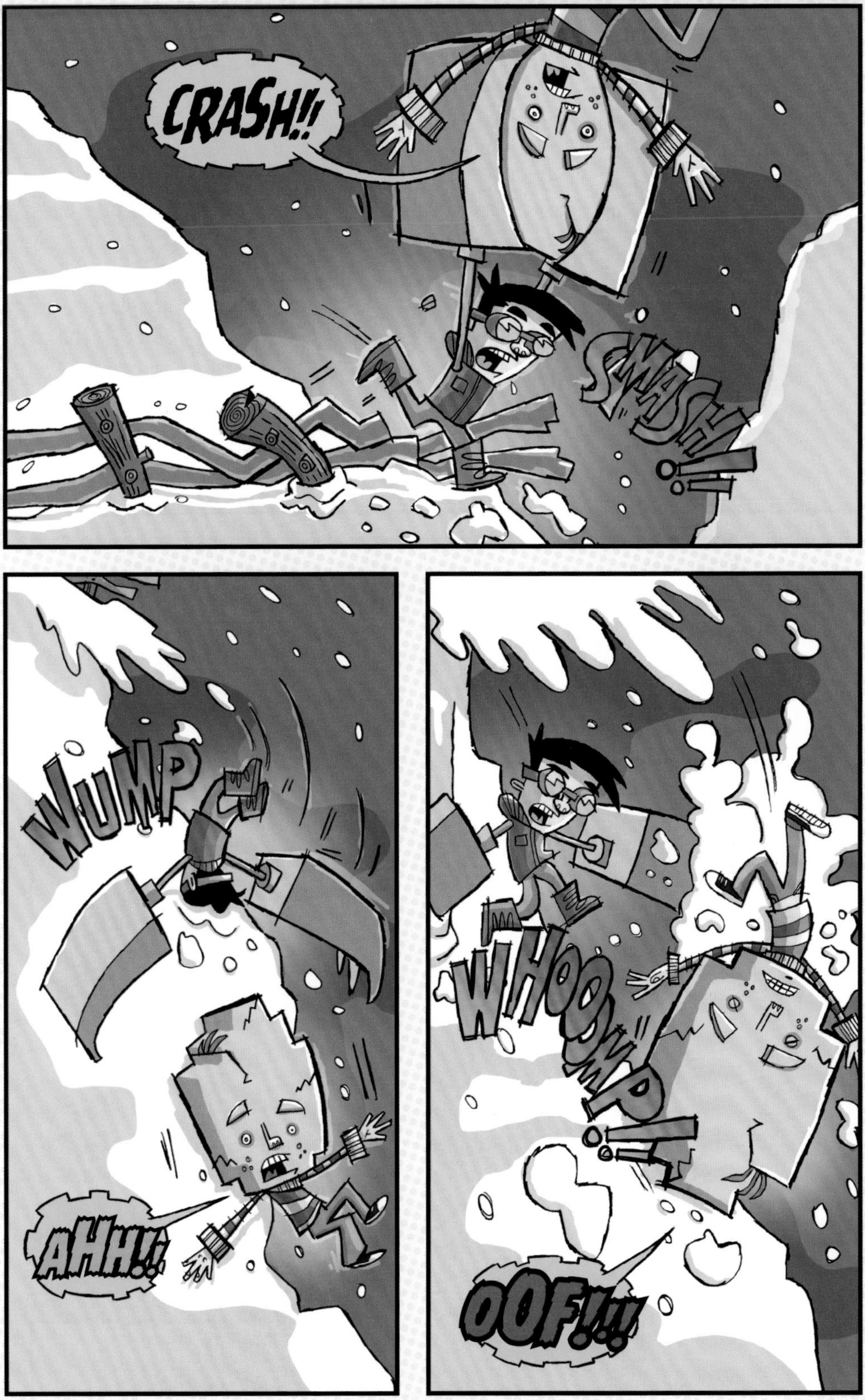
CRASH!!
SMASH!!
WUMP
AHH!!
WHOOOMP!!
OOF!!!

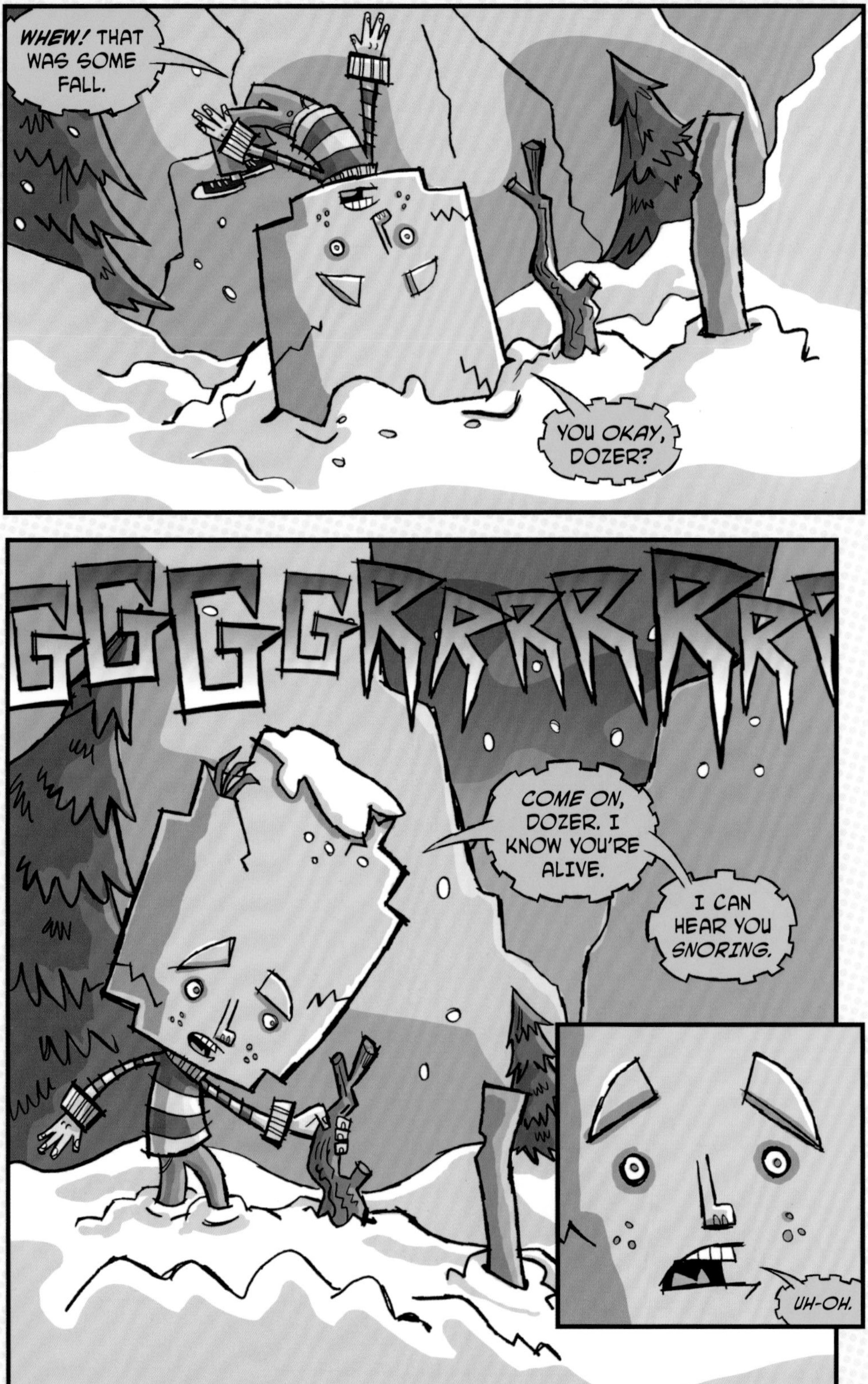
WHEW! THAT WAS SOME FALL.
YOU OKAY, DOZER?
GGGGRRRRRR
COME ON, DOZER. I KNOW YOU'RE ALIVE.
I CAN HEAR YOU SNORING.
UH-OH.

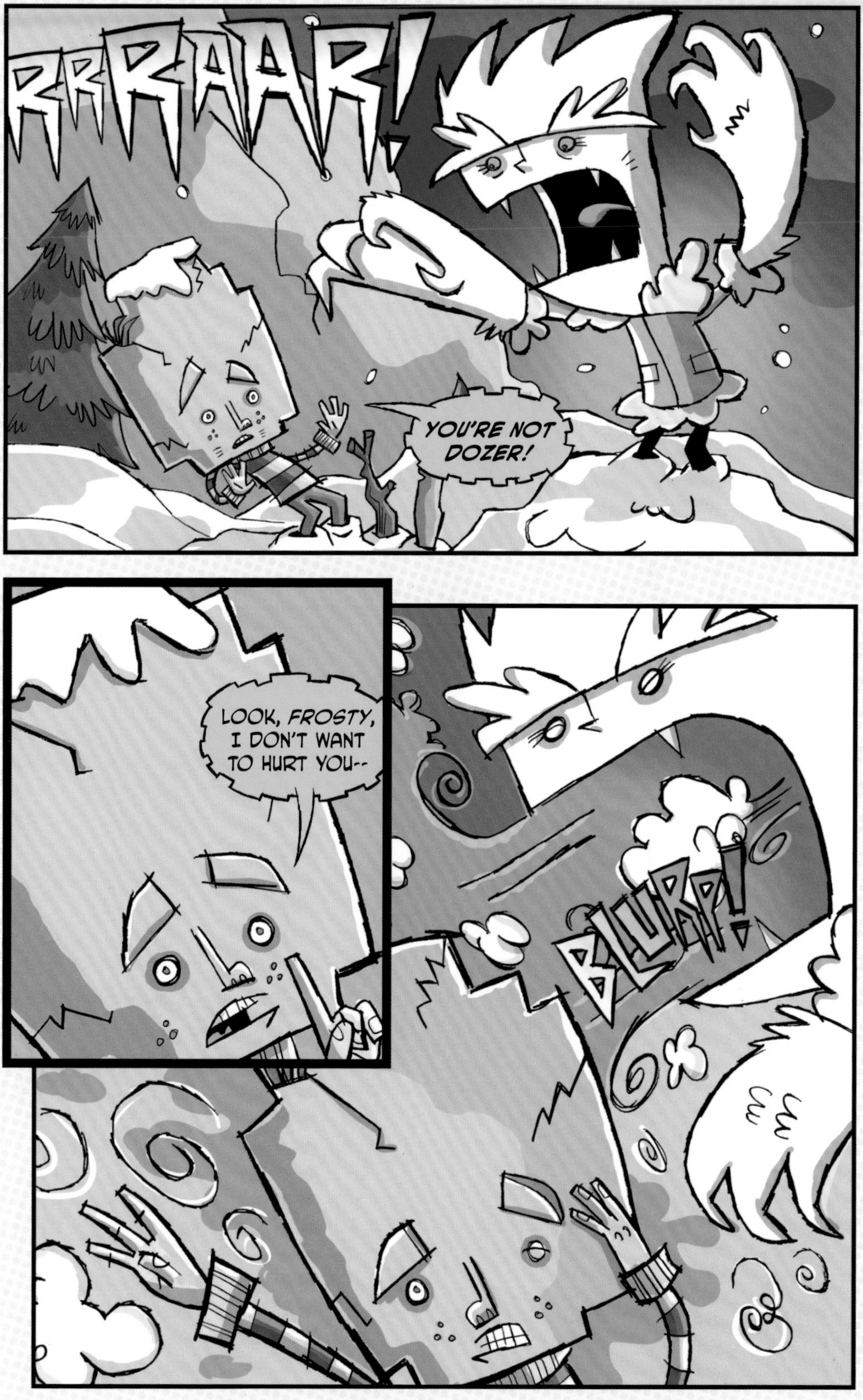
RRRAAAR!
YOU'RE NOT DOZER!
LOOK, FROSTY, I DON'T WANT TO HURT YOU--
BLURP!

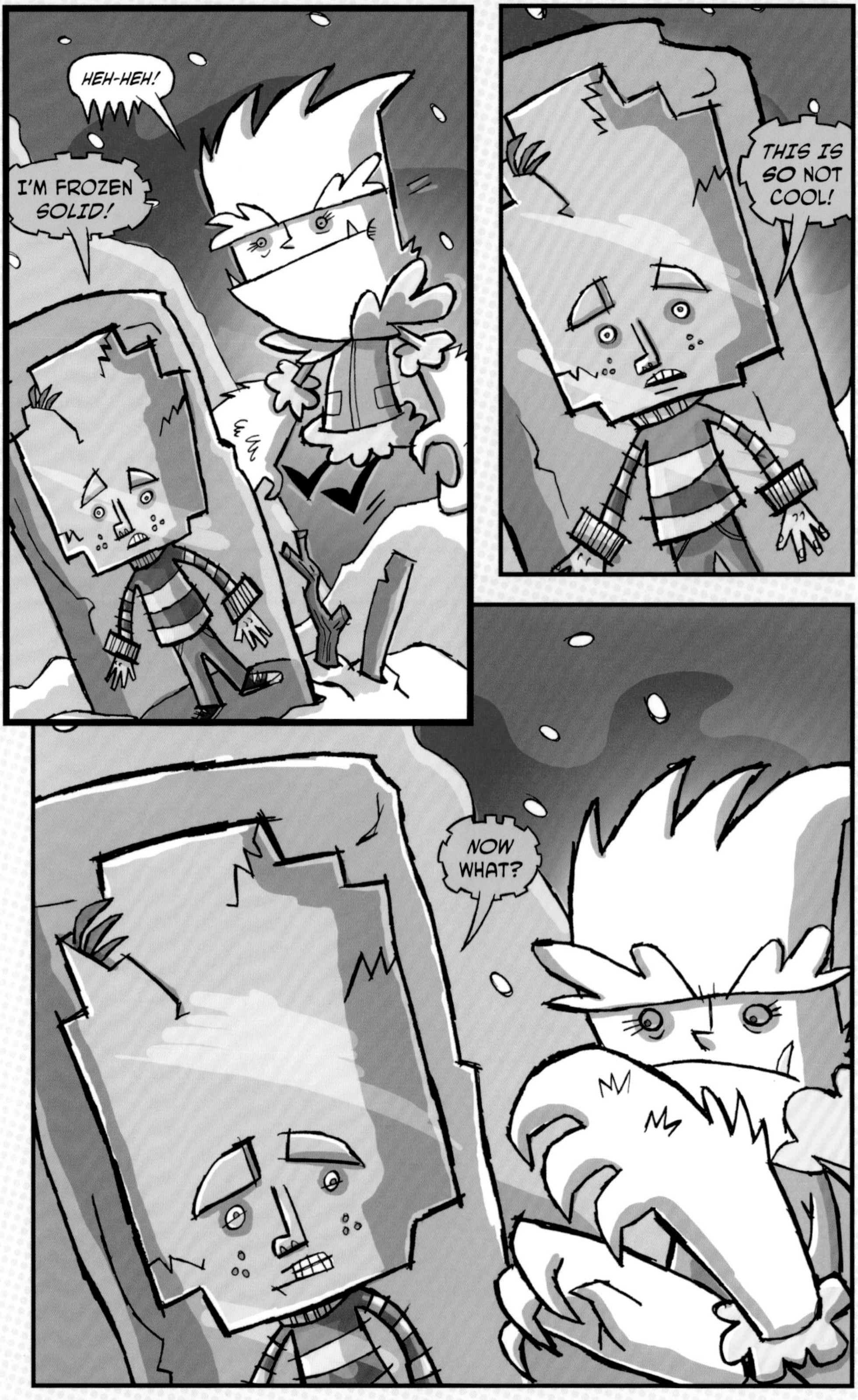
HEH-HEH!
I'M FROZEN SOLID!
THIS IS SO NOT COOL!
NOW WHAT?

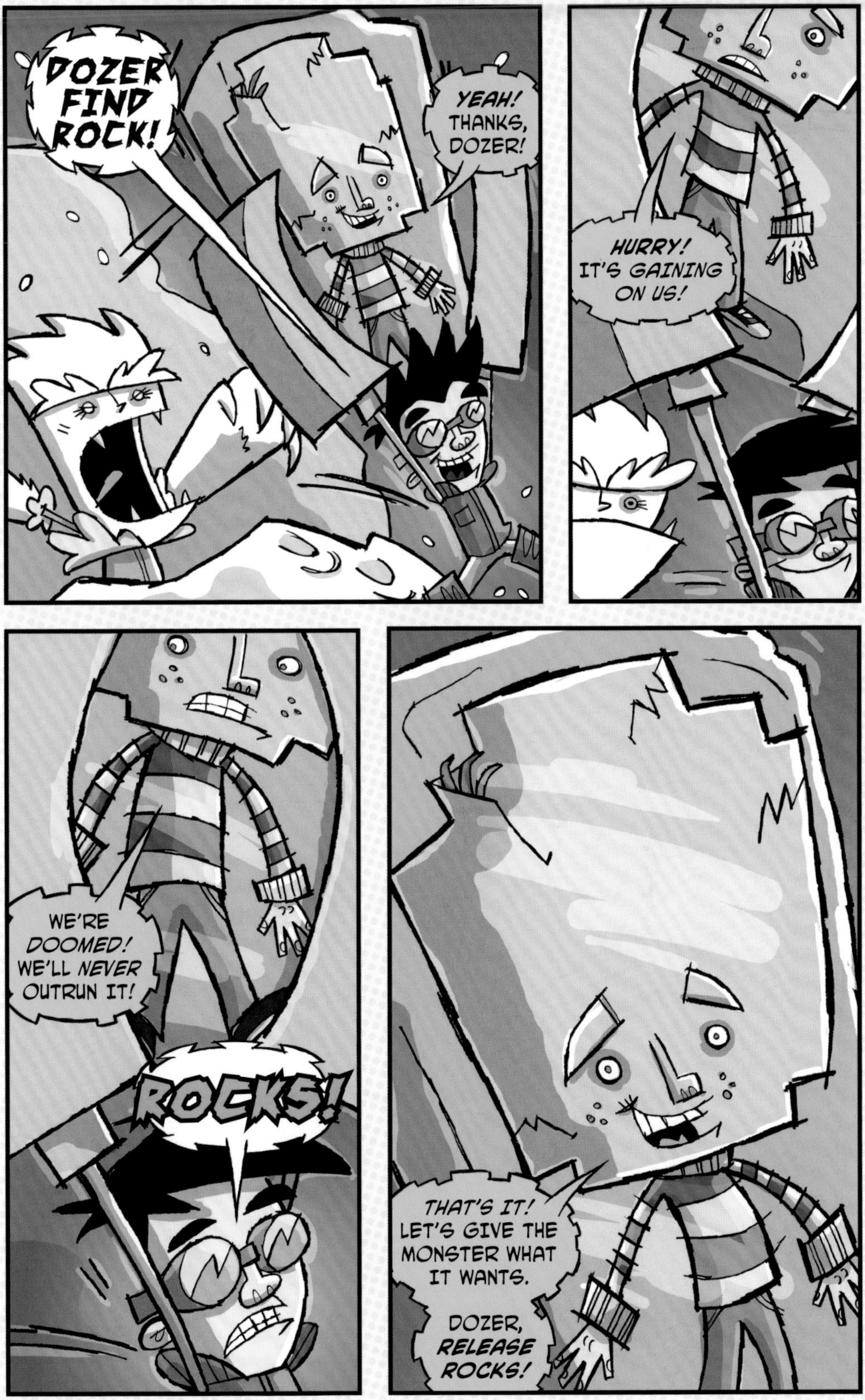
DOZER FIND ROCK!
YEAH! THANKS, DOZER!
HURRY! IT'S GAINING ON US!
WE'RE DOOMED! WE'LL NEVER OUTRUN IT!
ROCKS!
THAT'S IT! LET'S GIVE THE MONSTER WHAT IT WANTS.
DOZER, RELEASE ROCKS!

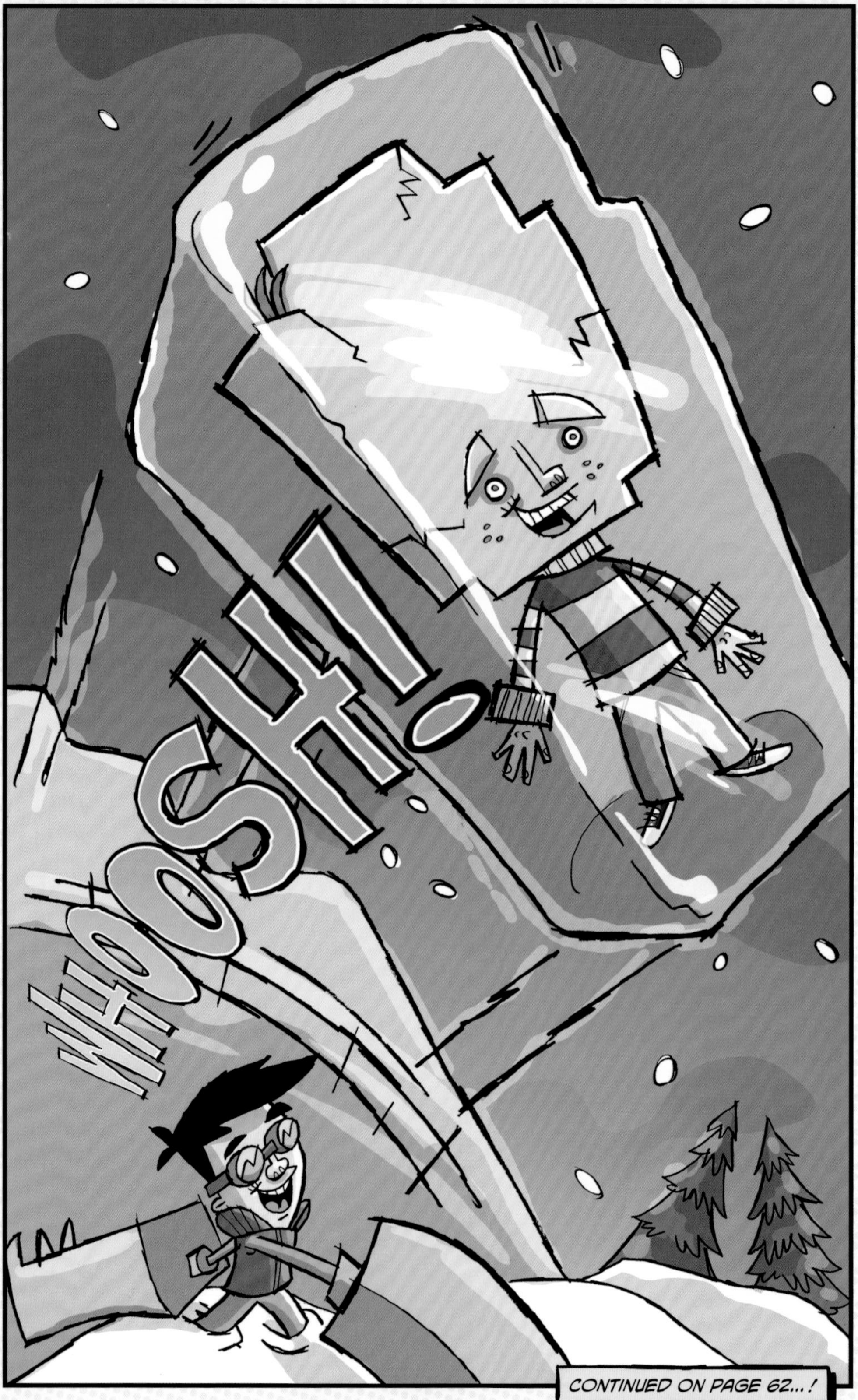
WHOOSH!

CONTINUED ON PAGE 62...!

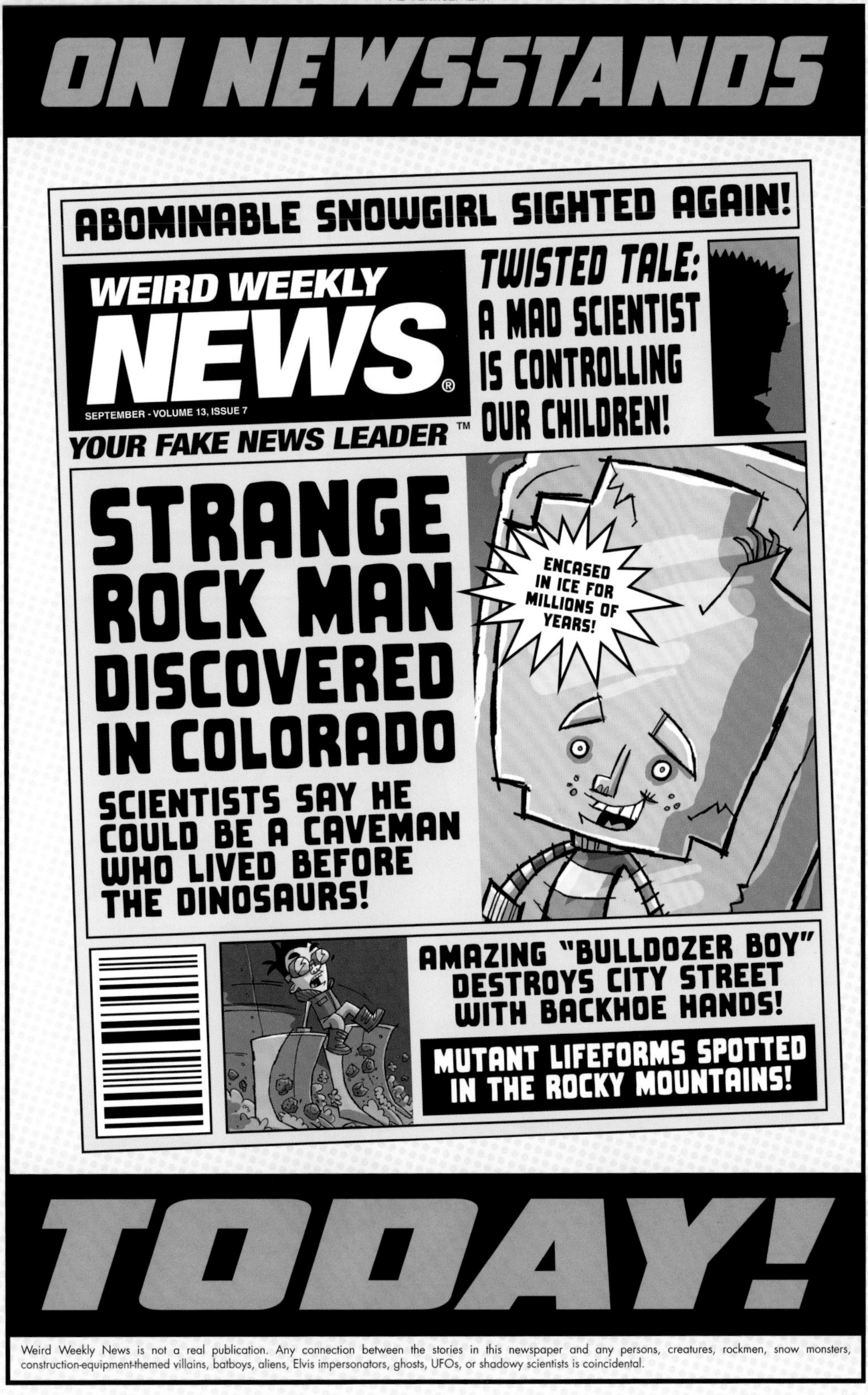
ON NEWSSTANDS
ABOMINABLE SNOWGIRL SIGHTED AGAIN!
WEIRD WEEKLY NEWS®
SEPTEMBER - VOLUME 13, ISSUE 7
YOUR FAKE NEWS LEADER ™
TWISTED TALE: A MAD SCIENTIST IS CONTROLLING OUR CHILDREN!
STRANGE ROCK MAN DISCOVERED IN COLORADO
SCIENTISTS SAY HE COULD BE A CAVEMAN WHO LIVED BEFORE THE DINOSAURS!
ENCASED IN ICE FOR MILLIONS OF YEARS!
AMAZING "BULLDOZER BOY" DESTROYS CITY STREET WITH BACKHOE HANDS!
MUTANT LIFEFORMS SPOTTED IN THE ROCKY MOUNTAINS!
TODAY!

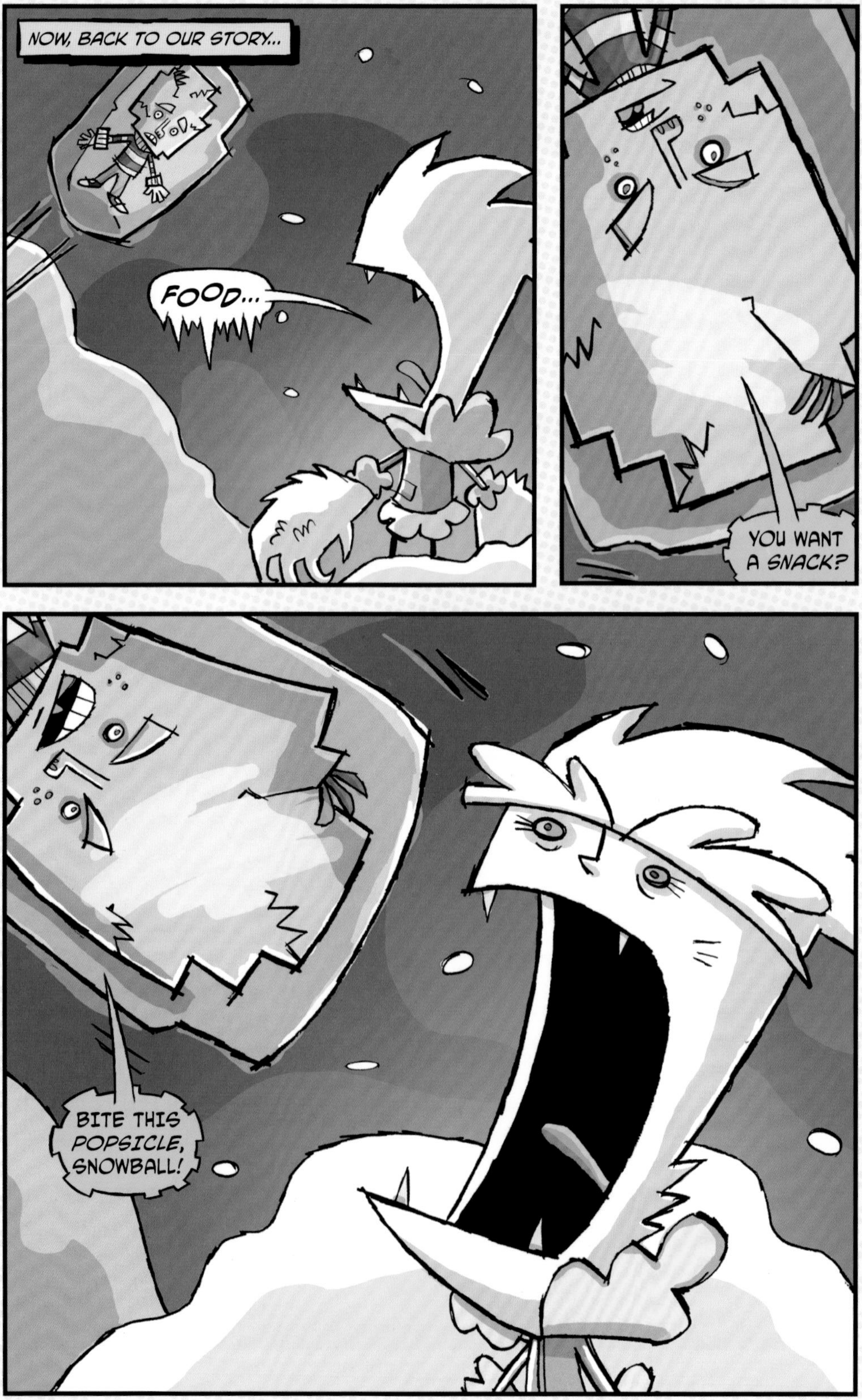
NOW, BACK TO OUR STORY...
FOOD...
YOU WANT A SNACK?
BITE THIS POPSICLE, SNOWBALL!

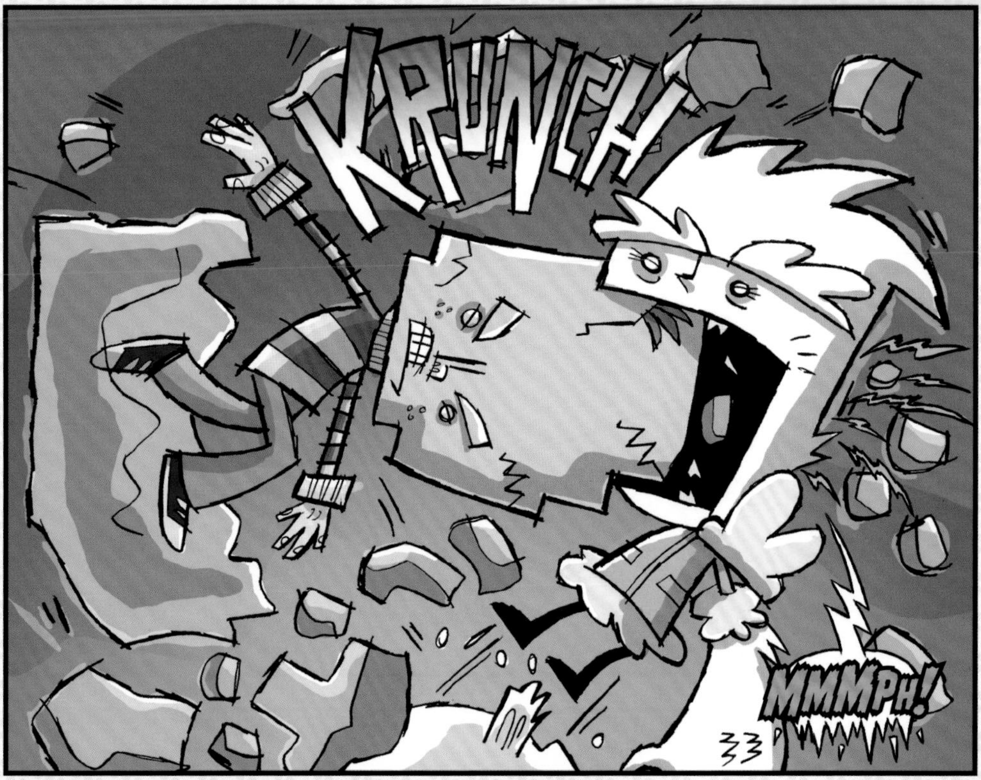
KRUNCH
MMMPH!

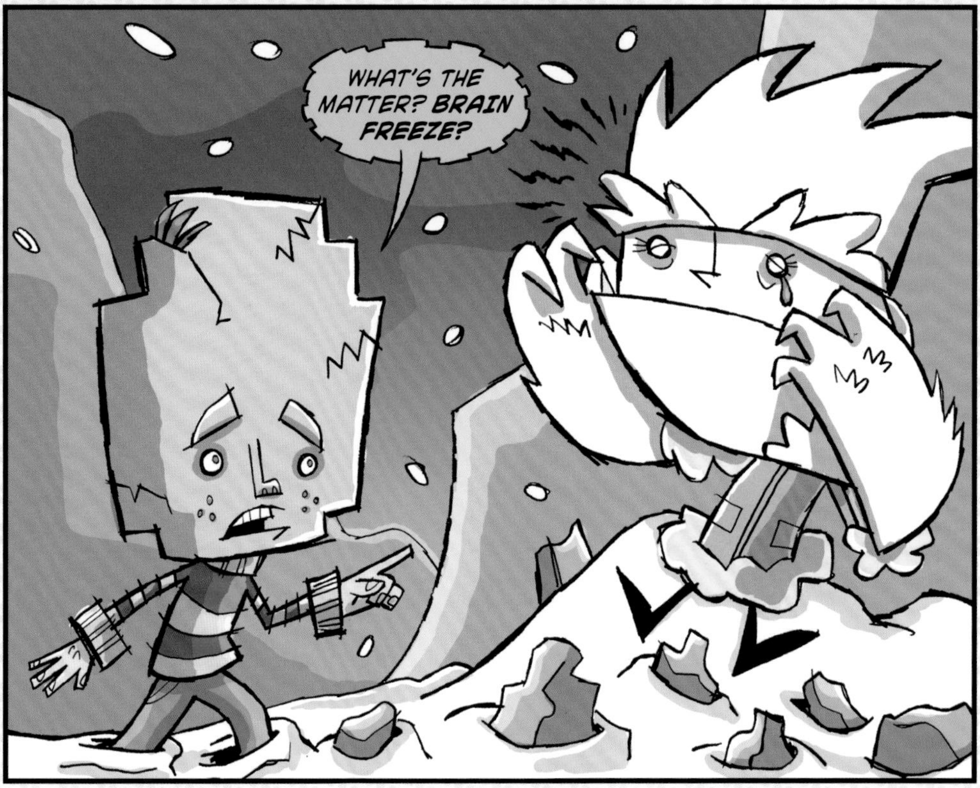
WHAT'S THE MATTER? BRAIN FREEZE?

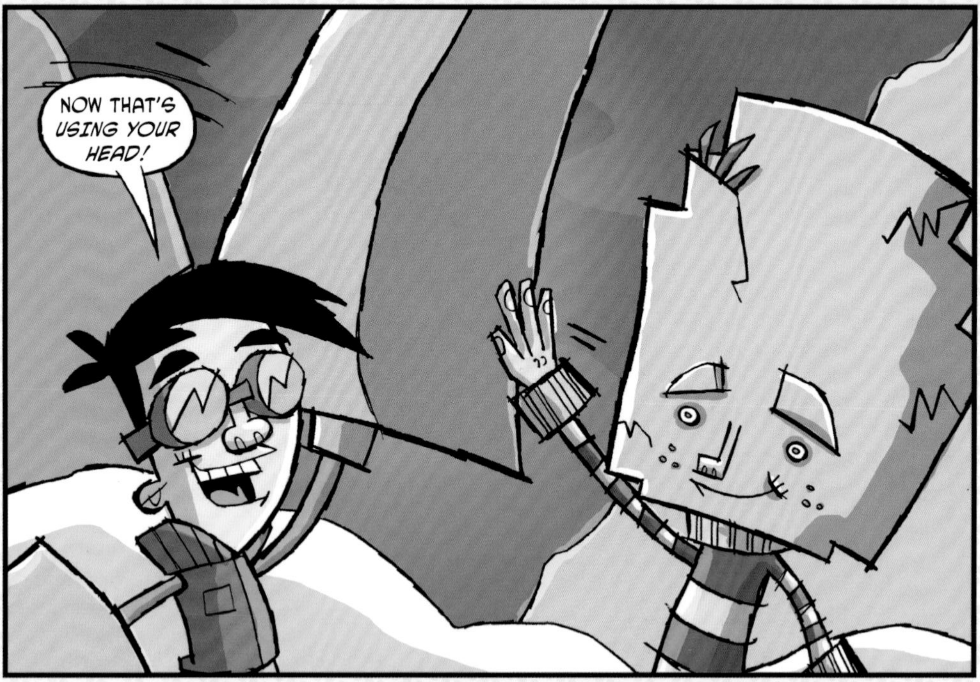
NOW THAT'S *USING YOUR* HEAD!

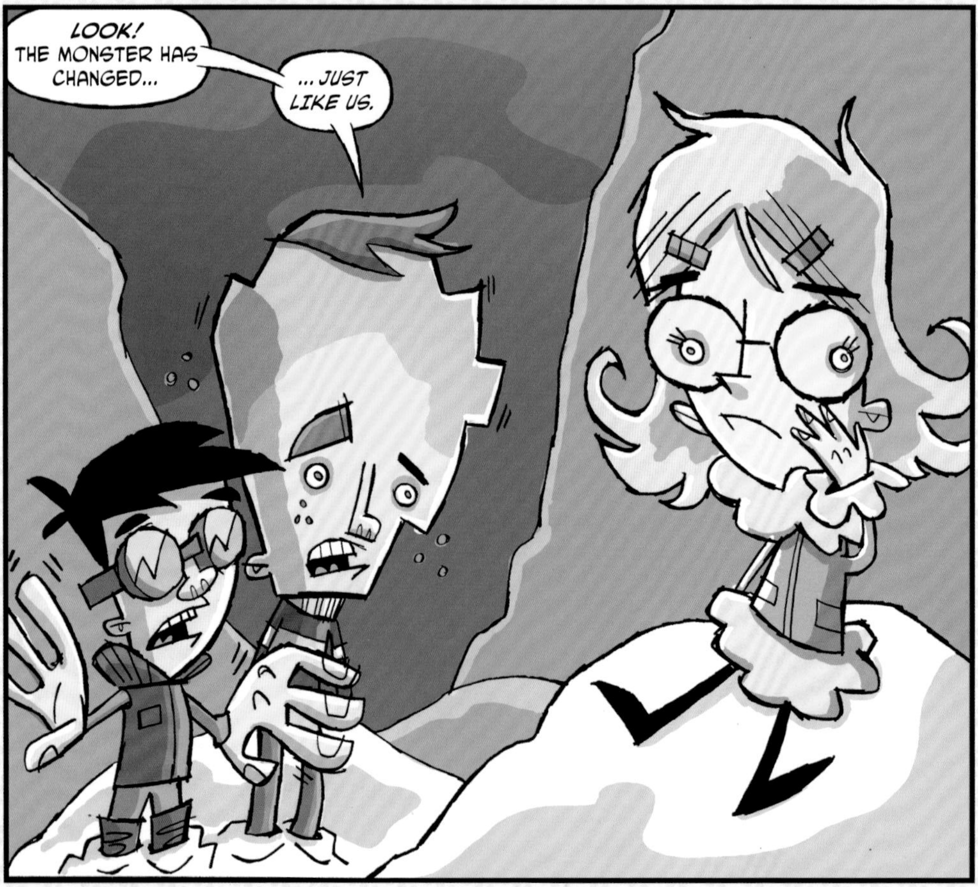
LOOK! THE MONSTER HAS CHANGED...
... JUST LIKE US.

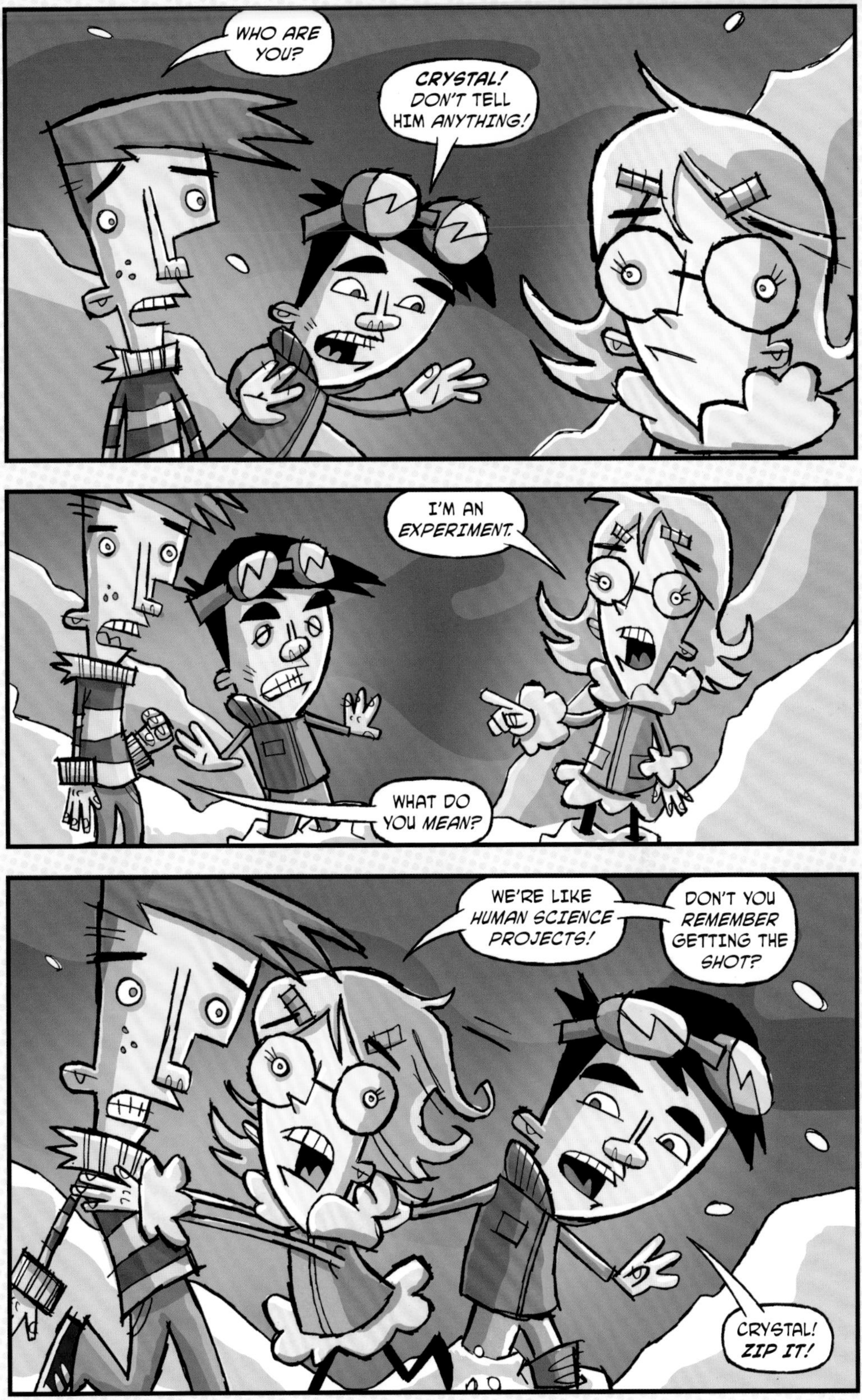
WHO ARE YOU?
CRYSTAL! DON'T TELL HIM ANYTHING!
I'M AN EXPERIMENT.
WHAT DO YOU MEAN?
WE'RE LIKE HUMAN SCIENCE PROJECTS!
DON'T YOU REMEMBER GETTING THE SHOT?
CRYSTAL! ZIP IT!

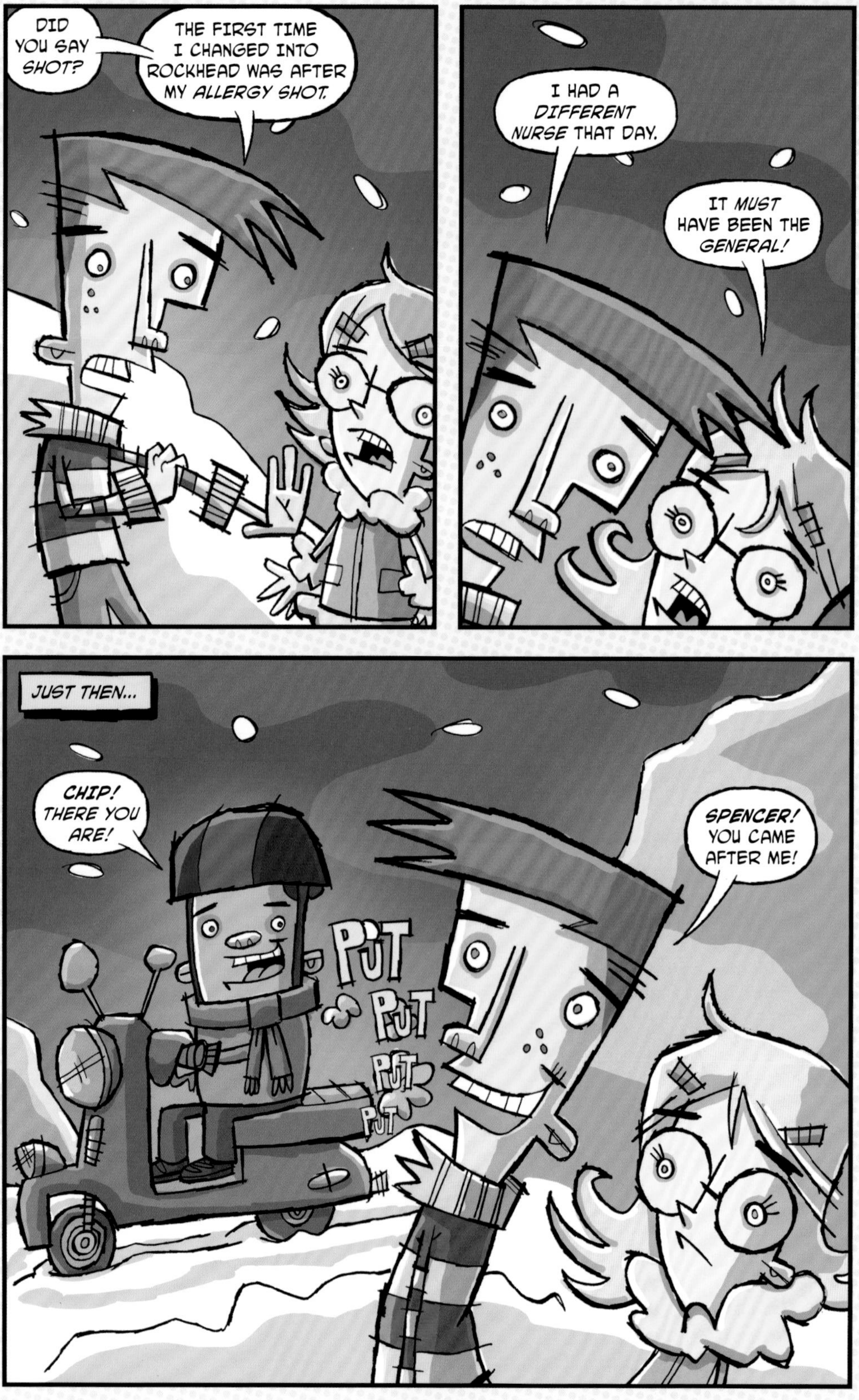

DID YOU SAY SHOT?
THE FIRST TIME I CHANGED INTO ROCKHEAD WAS AFTER MY ALLERGY SHOT.
I HAD A DIFFERENT NURSE THAT DAY.
IT MUST HAVE BEEN THE GENERAL!
JUST THEN...
CHIP! THERE YOU ARE!
PUT
PUT
PUT
PUT
SPENCER! YOU CAME AFTER ME!

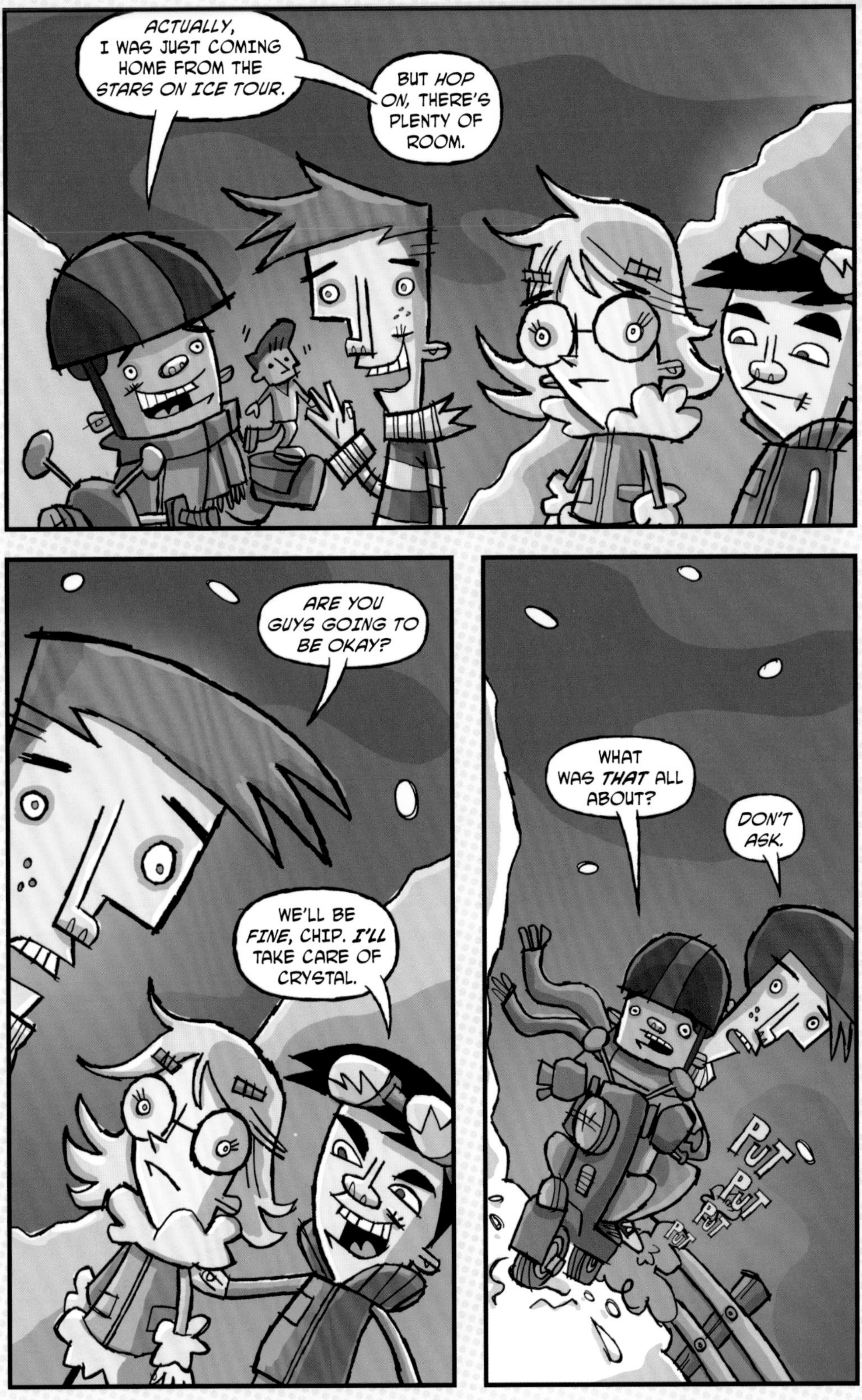
ACTUALLY, I WAS JUST COMING HOME FROM THE STARS ON ICE TOUR.
BUT HOP ON, THERE'S PLENTY OF ROOM.
ARE YOU GUYS GOING TO BE OKAY?
WE'LL BE FINE, CHIP. I'LL TAKE CARE OF CRYSTAL.
WHAT WAS THAT ALL ABOUT?
DON'T ASK.
PUT PUT PUT PUT

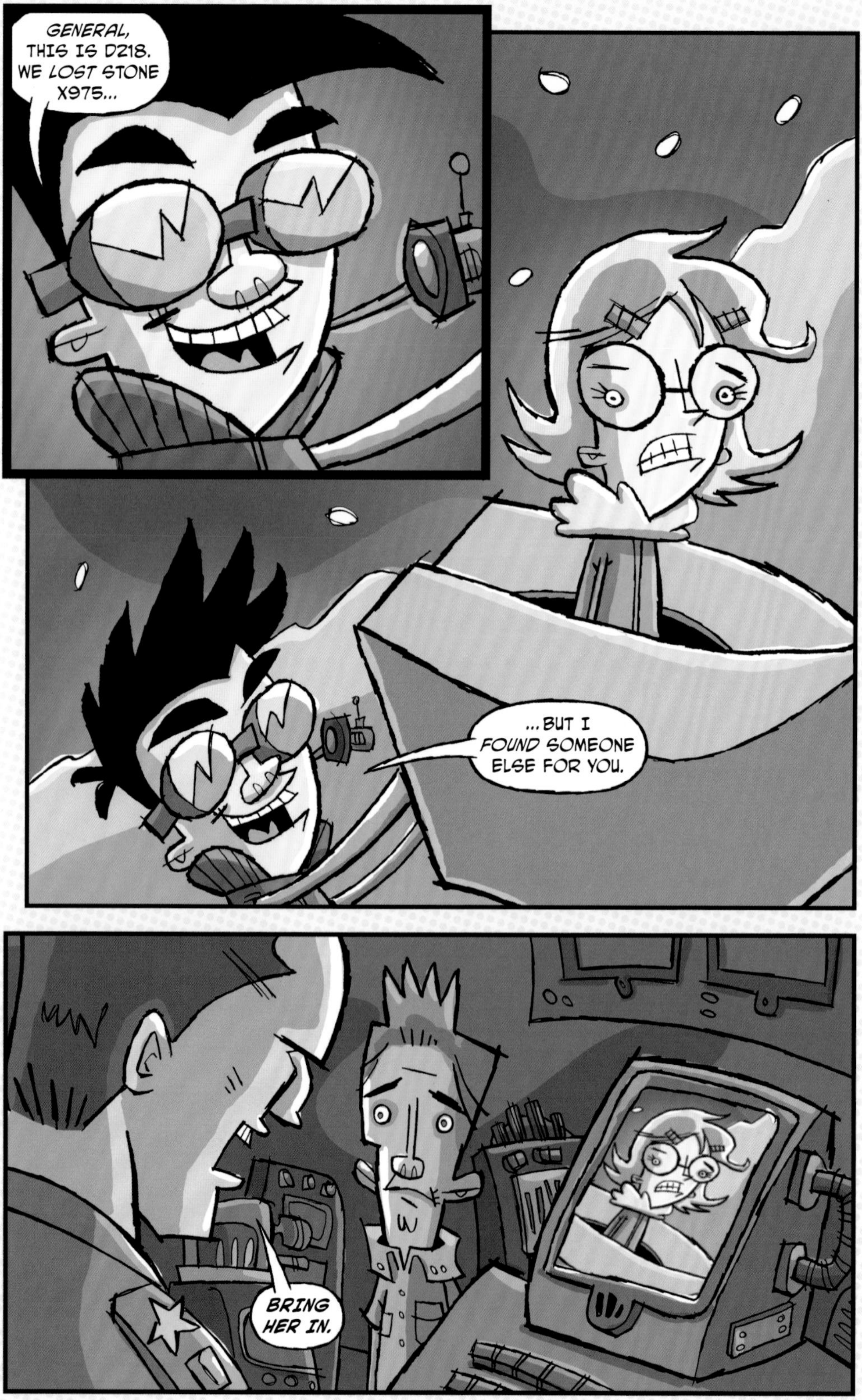
GENERAL, THIS IS D218. WE LOST STONE X975...
...BUT I FOUND SOMEONE ELSE FOR YOU.
BRING HER IN.

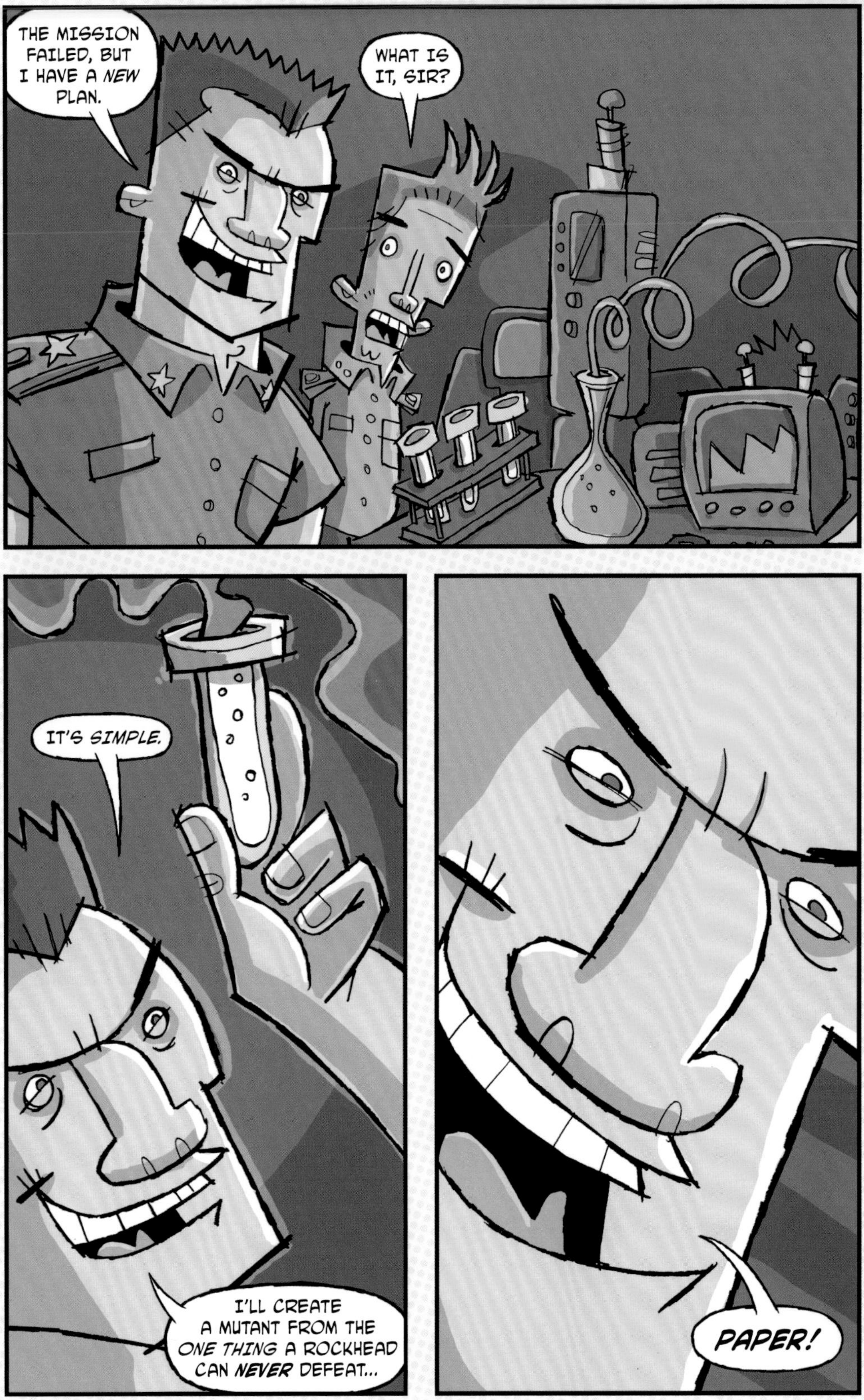
THE MISSION FAILED, BUT I HAVE A *NEW* PLAN.
WHAT IS IT, SIR?
IT'S *SIMPLE.*
I'LL CREATE A MUTANT FROM THE *ONE THING* A ROCKHEAD CAN ***NEVER*** DEFEAT...
PAPER!

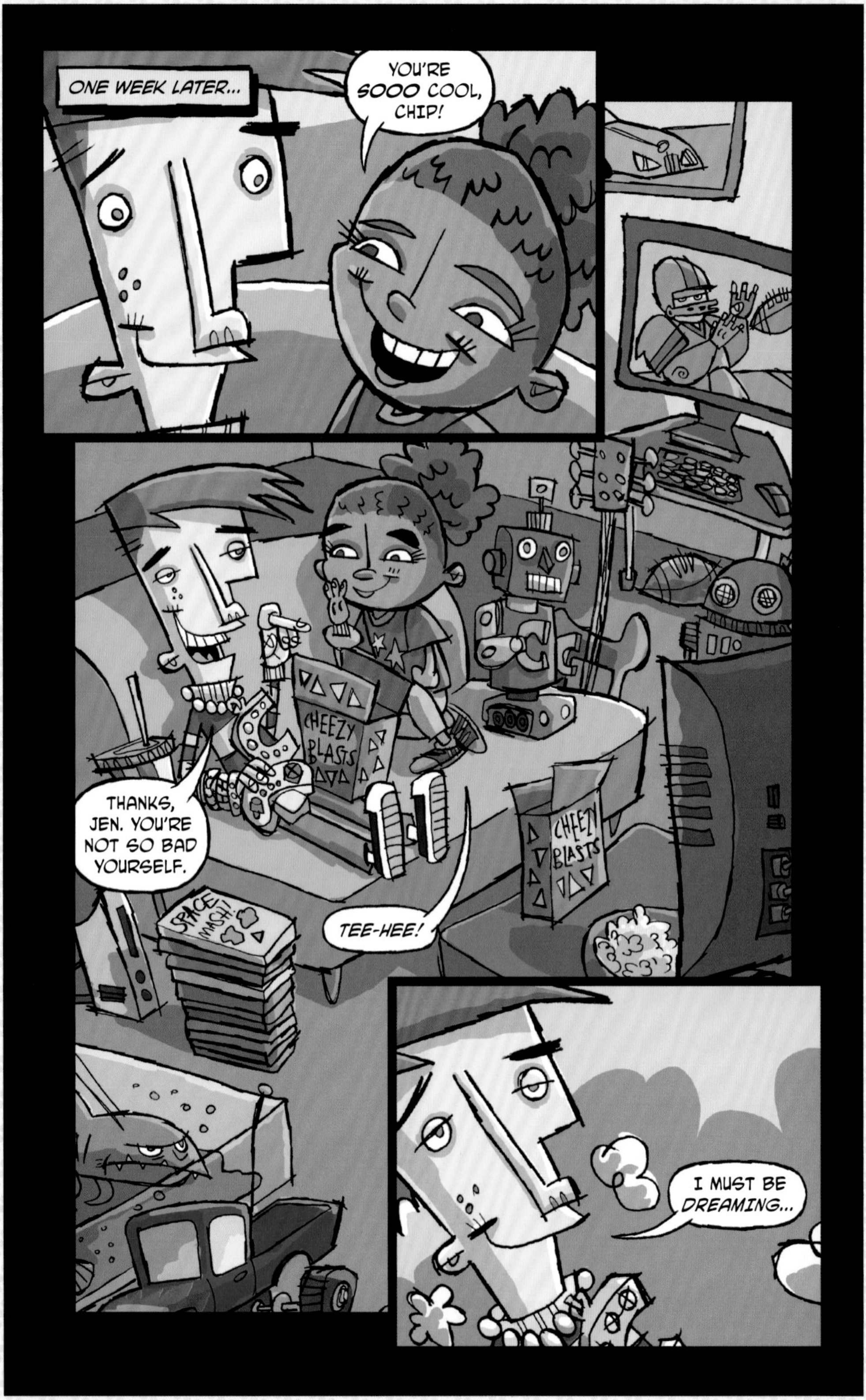
ONE WEEK LATER...
YOU'RE SOOO COOL, CHIP!
THANKS, JEN. YOU'RE NOT SO BAD YOURSELF.
TEE-HEE!
I MUST BE DREAMING...
CHEEZY BLASTS
CHEEZY BLASTS
SPACE MASH!

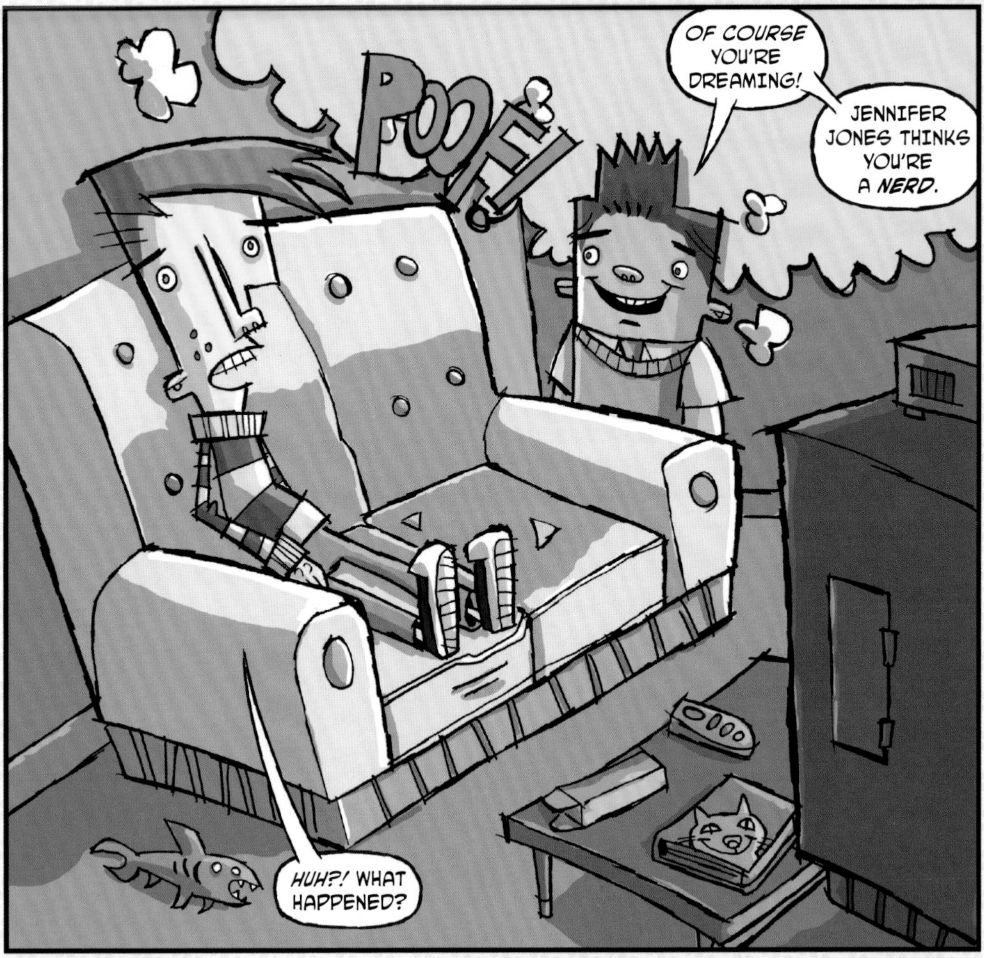
POOF!
OF COURSE YOU'RE DREAMING!
JENNIFER JONES THINKS YOU'RE A *NERD*.
HUH?! WHAT HAPPENED?

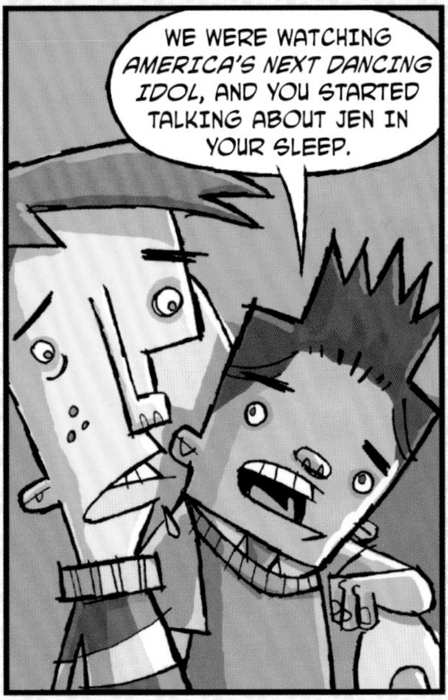
WE WERE WATCHING *AMERICA'S NEXT DANCING IDOL*, AND YOU STARTED TALKING ABOUT JEN IN YOUR SLEEP.

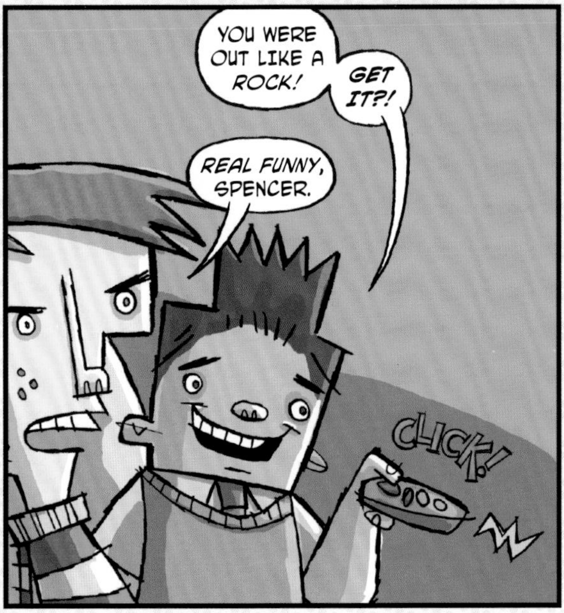
YOU WERE OUT LIKE A *ROCK!*
GET IT?!
REAL FUNNY, SPENCER.
CLICK!

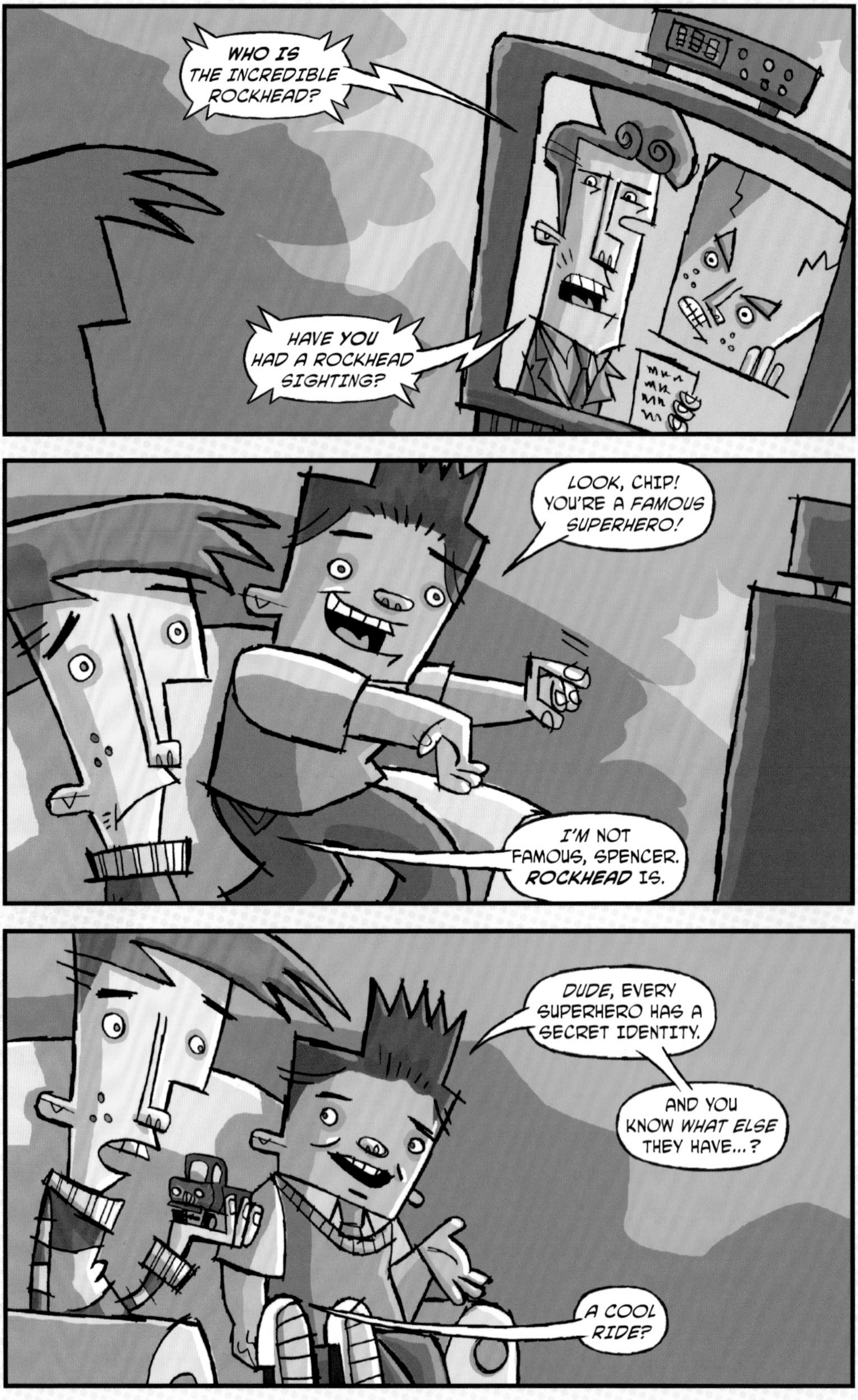
WHO IS THE INCREDIBLE ROCKHEAD?
HAVE YOU HAD A ROCKHEAD SIGHTING?
LOOK, CHIP! YOU'RE A *FAMOUS* SUPERHERO!
I'M NOT FAMOUS, SPENCER. ***ROCKHEAD*** IS.
DUDE, EVERY SUPERHERO HAS A SECRET IDENTITY.
AND YOU KNOW *WHAT ELSE* THEY HAVE...?
A COOL RIDE?

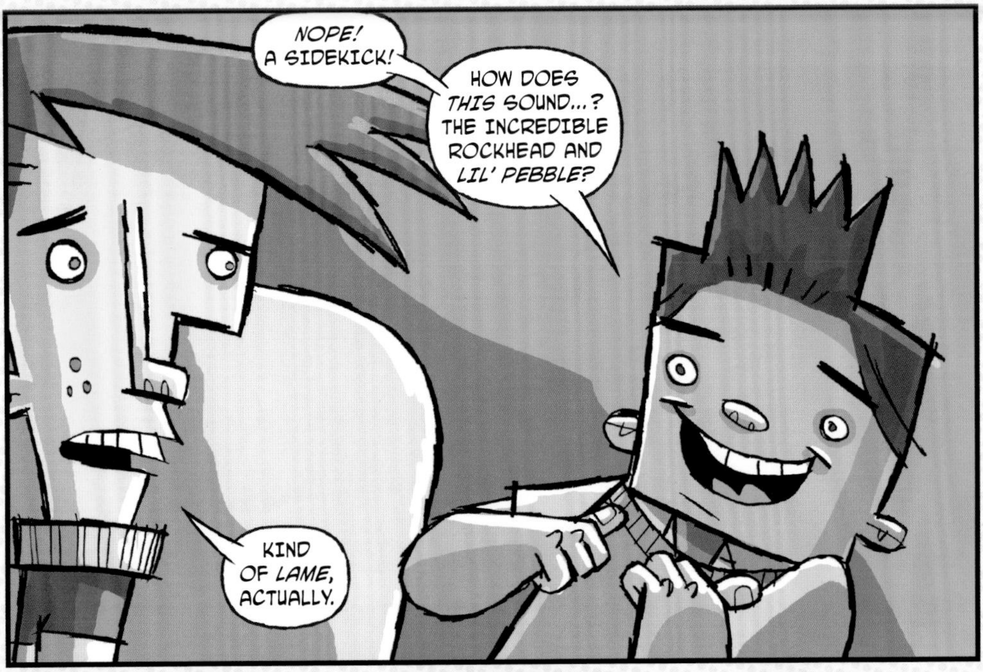
NOPE! A SIDEKICK!
HOW DOES THIS SOUND...? THE INCREDIBLE ROCKHEAD AND LIL' PEBBLE?
KIND OF LAME, ACTUALLY.

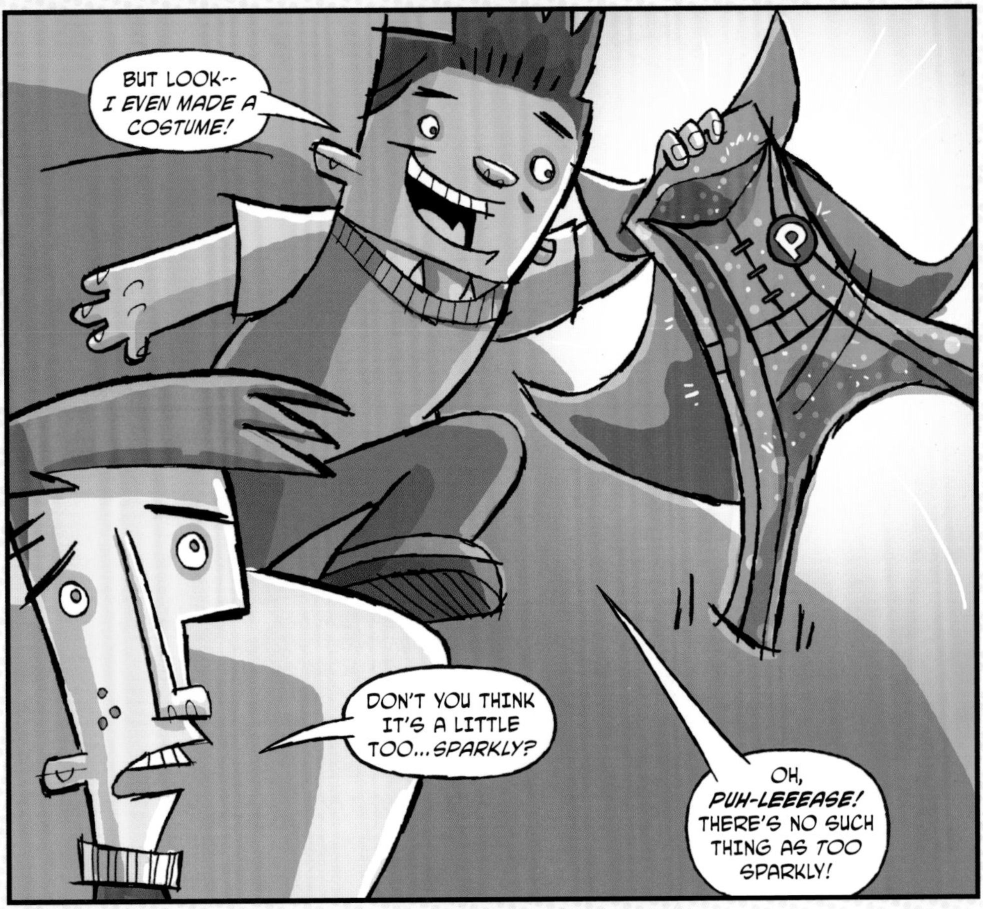
BUT LOOK-- I EVEN MADE A COSTUME!
DON'T YOU THINK IT'S A LITTLE TOO...SPARKLY?
OH, PUH-LEEEASE! THERE'S NO SUCH THING AS TOO SPARKLY!

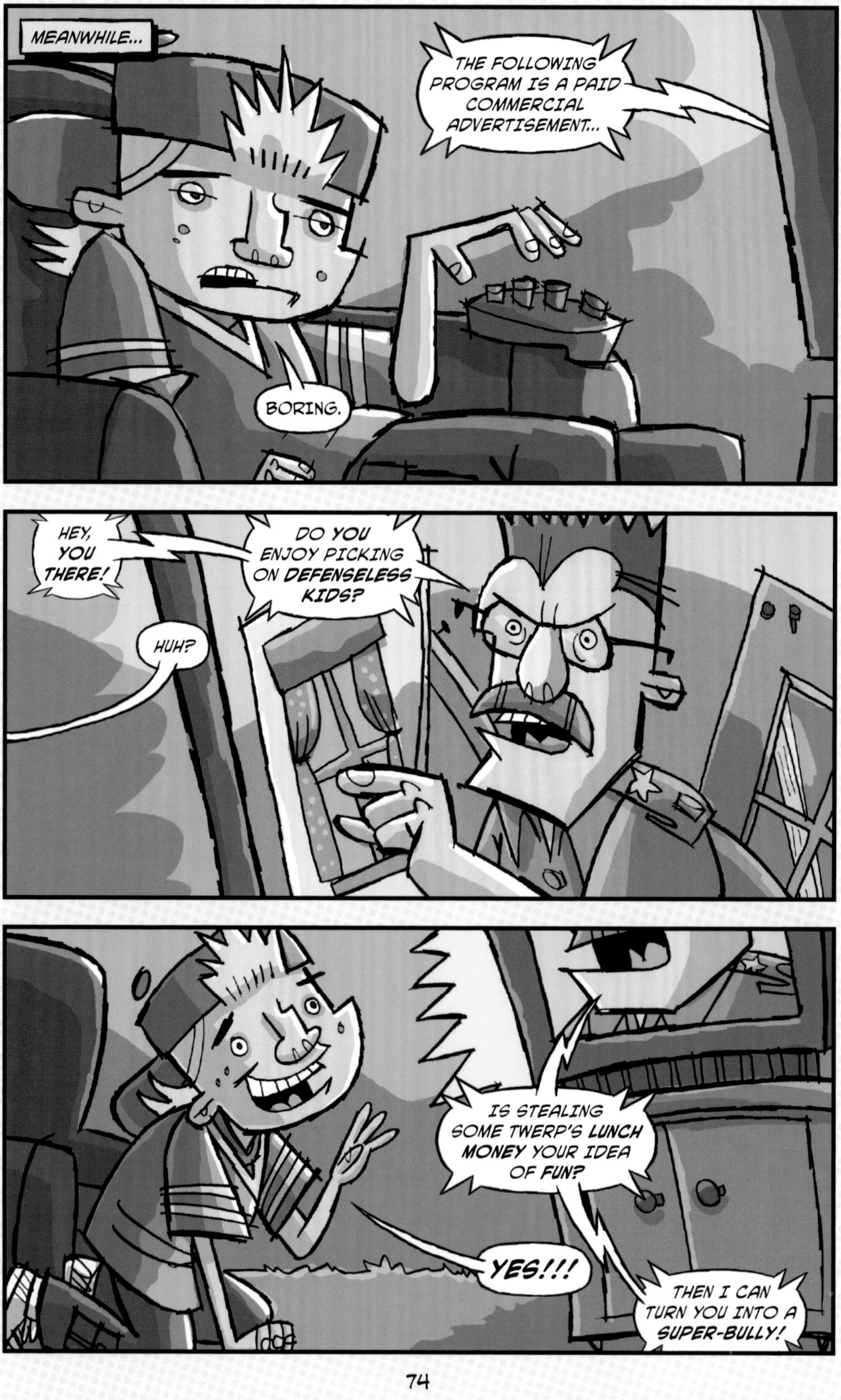
MEANWHILE...
THE FOLLOWING PROGRAM IS A PAID COMMERCIAL ADVERTISEMENT...
BORING.
HEY, YOU THERE!
DO YOU ENJOY PICKING ON DEFENSELESS KIDS?
HUH?
IS STEALING SOME TWERP'S LUNCH MONEY YOUR IDEA OF FUN?
YES!!!
THEN I CAN TURN YOU INTO A SUPER-BULLY!

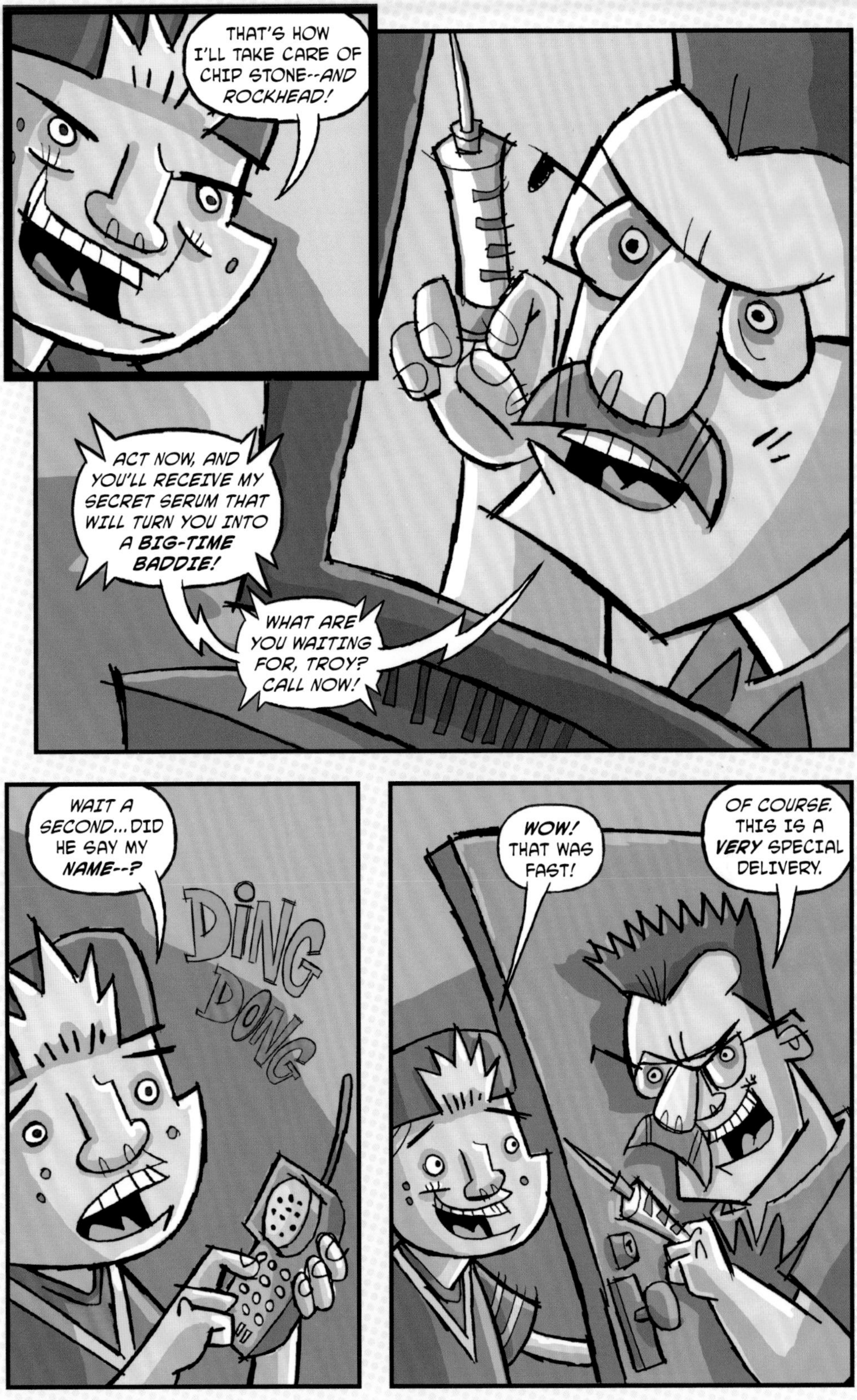
THAT'S HOW I'LL TAKE CARE OF CHIP STONE--AND ROCKHEAD!
ACT NOW, AND YOU'LL RECEIVE MY SECRET SERUM THAT WILL TURN YOU INTO A BIG-TIME BADDIE!
WHAT ARE YOU WAITING FOR, TROY? CALL NOW!
WAIT A SECOND... DID HE SAY MY NAME--?
DING DONG
WOW! THAT WAS FAST!
OF COURSE. THIS IS A VERY SPECIAL DELIVERY.

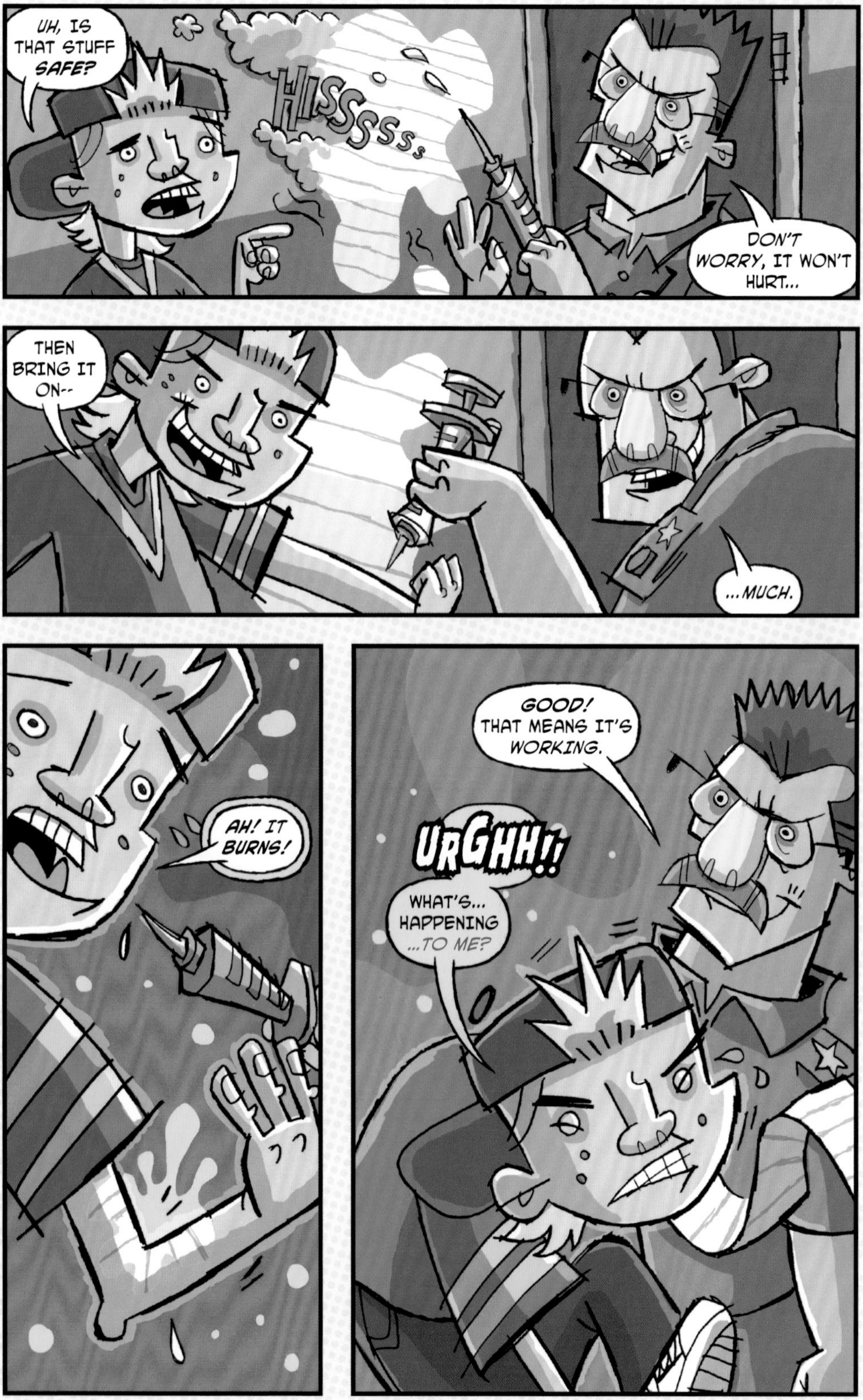
UH, IS THAT STUFF SAFE?
HISSSSSs
DON'T WORRY, IT WON'T HURT...
THEN BRING IT ON--
...MUCH.
AH! IT BURNS!
GOOD! THAT MEANS IT'S WORKING.
URGHH!!
WHAT'S... HAPPENING ...TO ME?

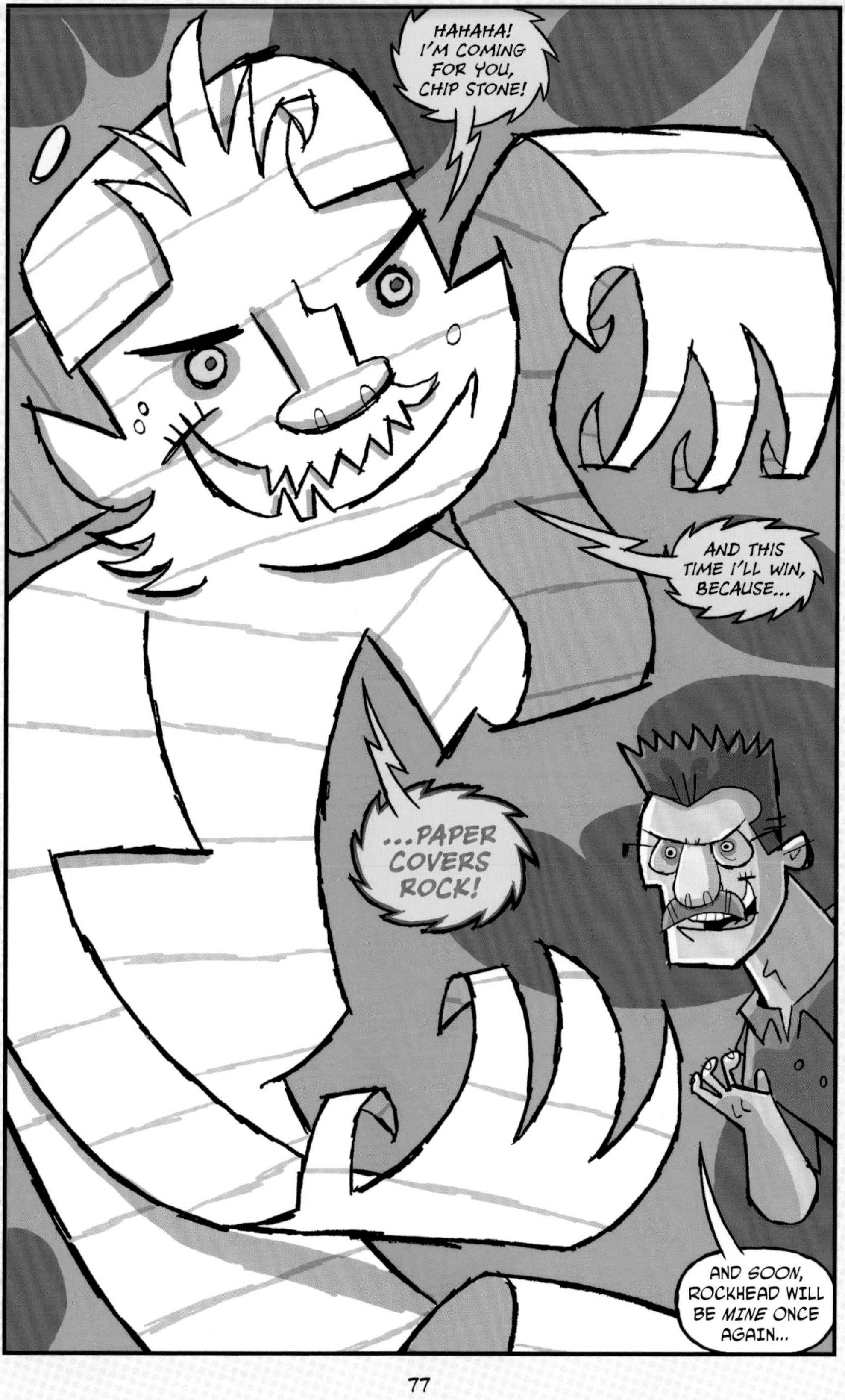
HAHAHA! I'M COMING FOR YOU, CHIP STONE!
AND THIS TIME I'LL WIN, BECAUSE...
...PAPER COVERS ROCK!
AND SOON, ROCKHEAD WILL BE *MINE* ONCE AGAIN...

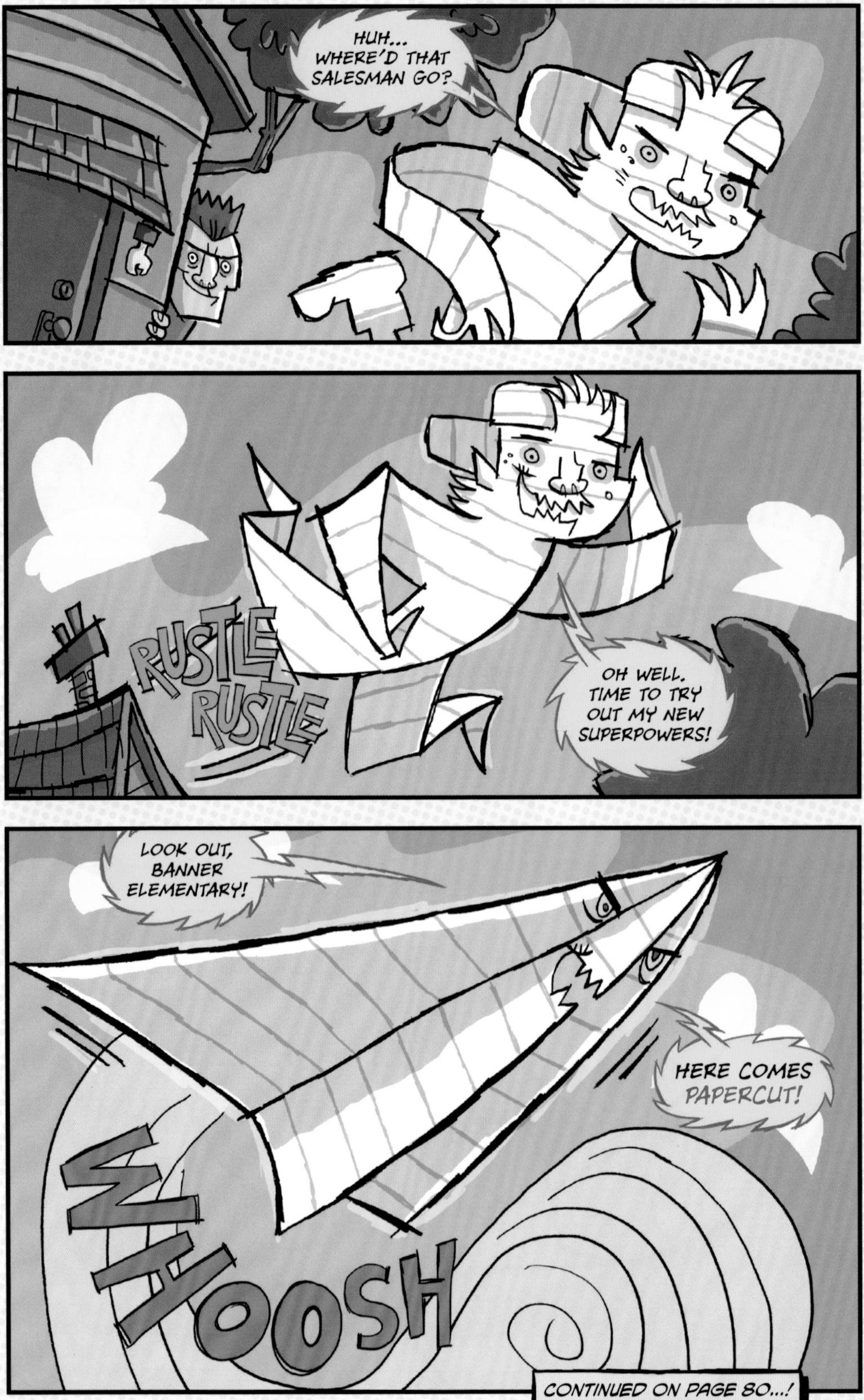
HUH... WHERE'D THAT SALESMAN GO?
RUSTLE RUSTLE
OH WELL. TIME TO TRY OUT MY NEW SUPERPOWERS!
LOOK OUT, BANNER ELEMENTARY!
HERE COMES PAPERCUT!
WHOOSH

CONTINUED ON PAGE 80...!

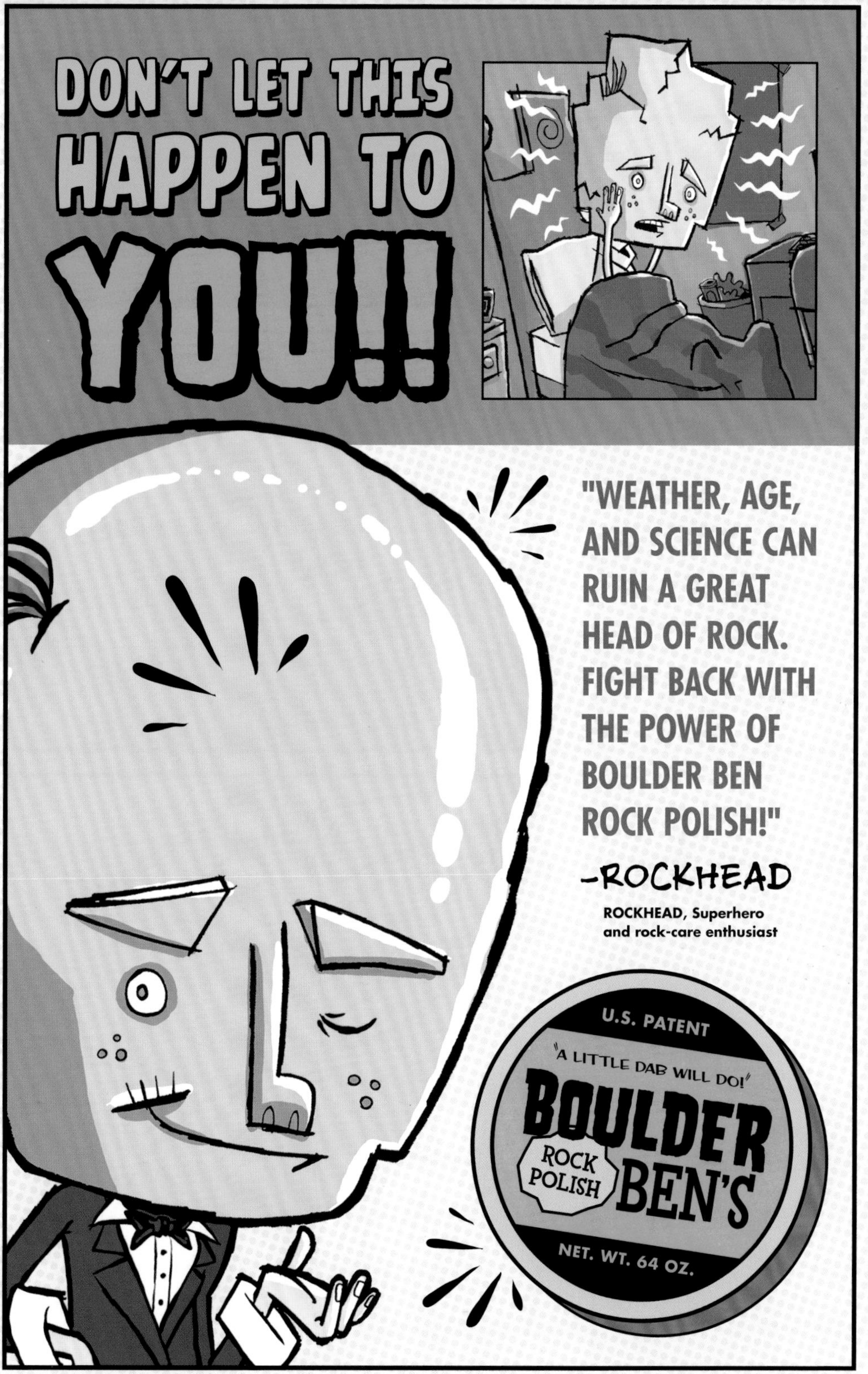
DON'T LET THIS HAPPEN TO YOU!!
"WEATHER, AGE, AND SCIENCE CAN RUIN A GREAT HEAD OF ROCK. FIGHT BACK WITH THE POWER OF BOULDER BEN ROCK POLISH!"
-ROCKHEAD
ROCKHEAD, Superhero and rock-care enthusiast
U.S. PATENT
"A LITTLE DAB WILL DO!"
BOULDER BEN'S
ROCK POLISH
NET. WT. 64 OZ.

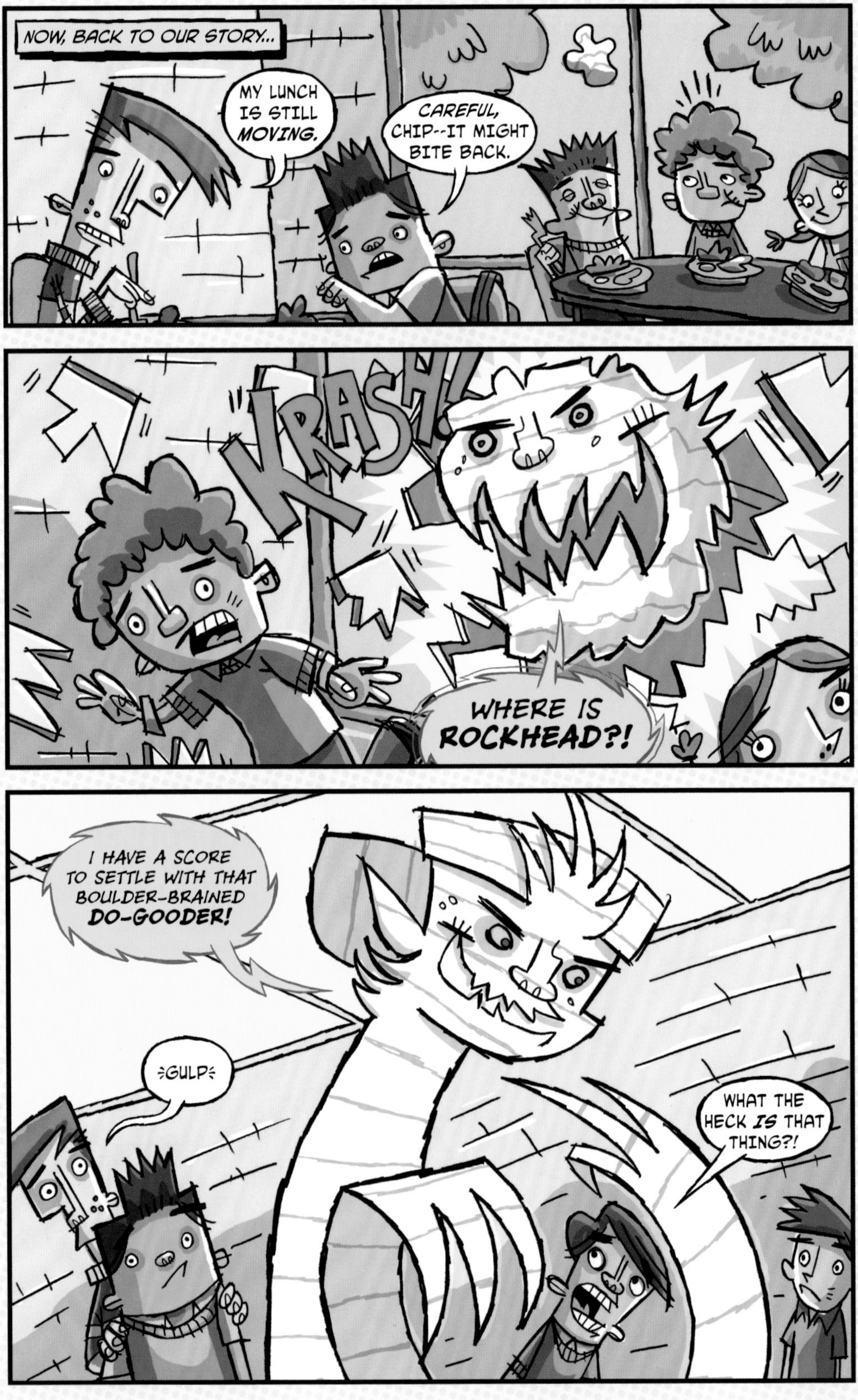
NOW, BACK TO OUR STORY...
MY LUNCH IS STILL MOVING.
CAREFUL, CHIP--IT MIGHT BITE BACK.
KRASH!
WHERE IS ROCKHEAD?!
I HAVE A SCORE TO SETTLE WITH THAT BOULDER-BRAINED DO-GOODER!
GULP
WHAT THE HECK IS THAT THING?!

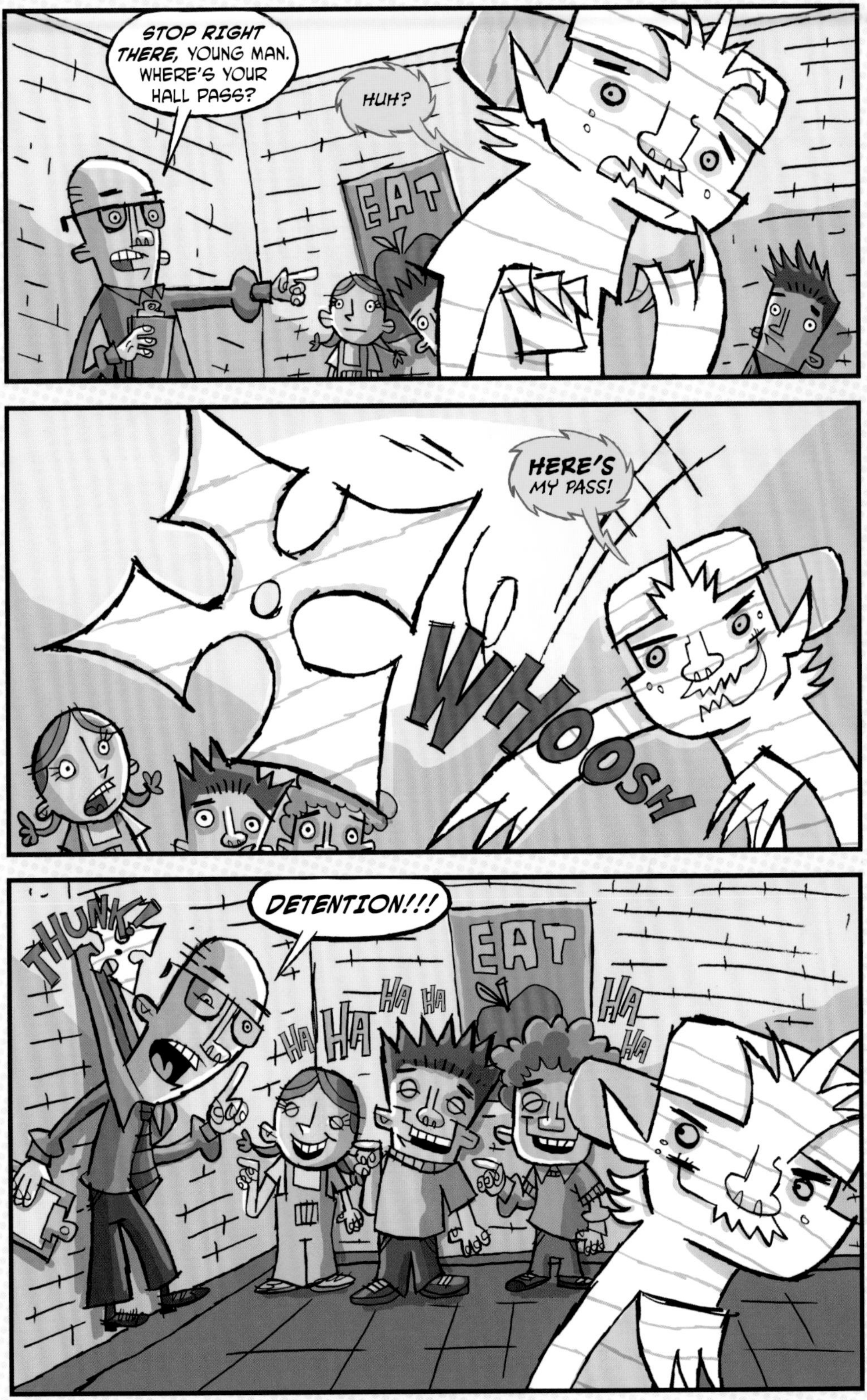
STOP RIGHT THERE, YOUNG MAN. WHERE'S YOUR HALL PASS?
HUH?
EAT
HERE'S MY PASS!
WHOOSH
THUNK!!
DETENTION!!!
EAT
HA HA HA HA HA HA HA

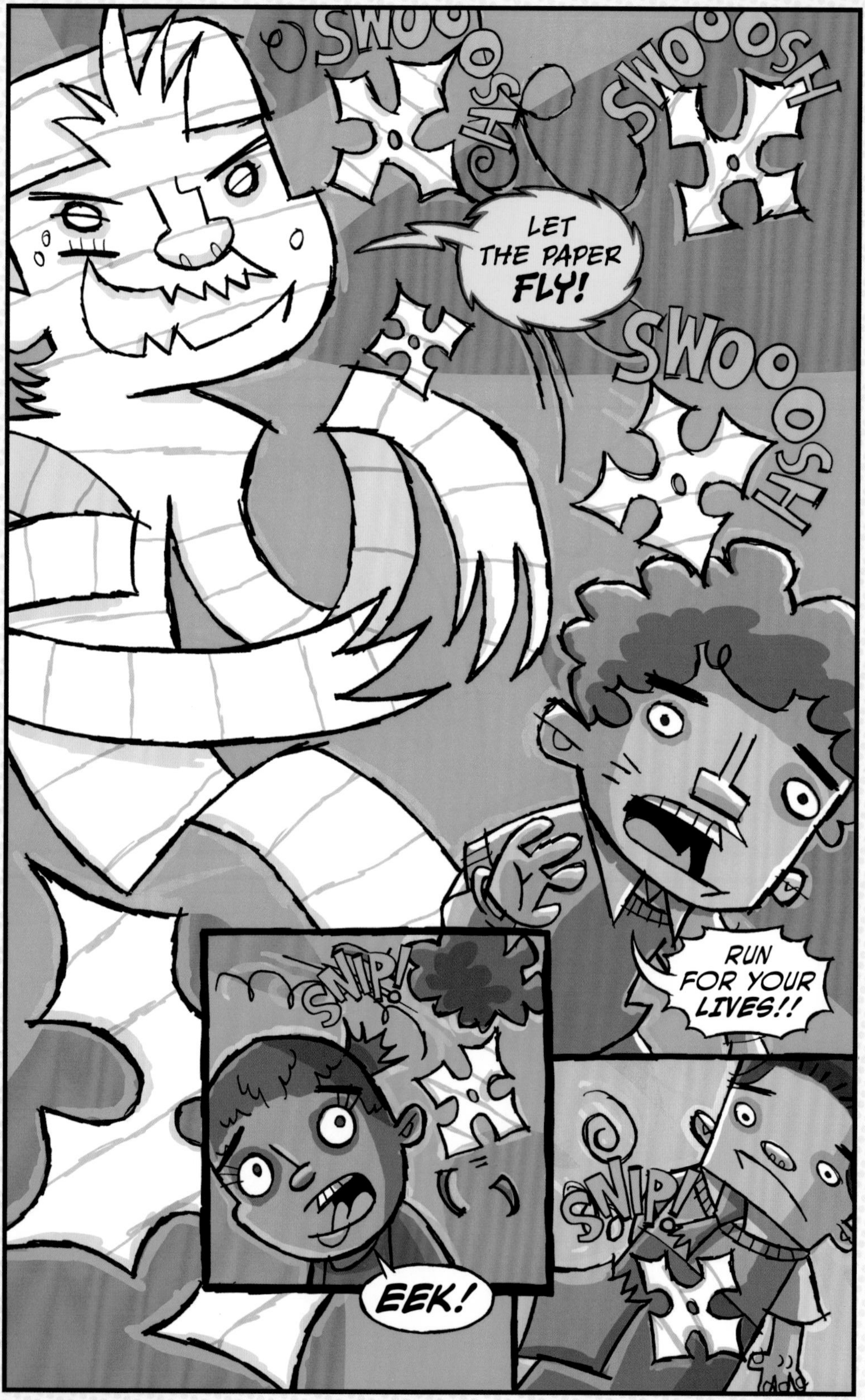
SWOOOSH
SWOOOSH
LET THE PAPER FLY!
SWOOOOSH
RUN FOR YOUR LIVES!!
SNIP!
EEK!
SNIP!

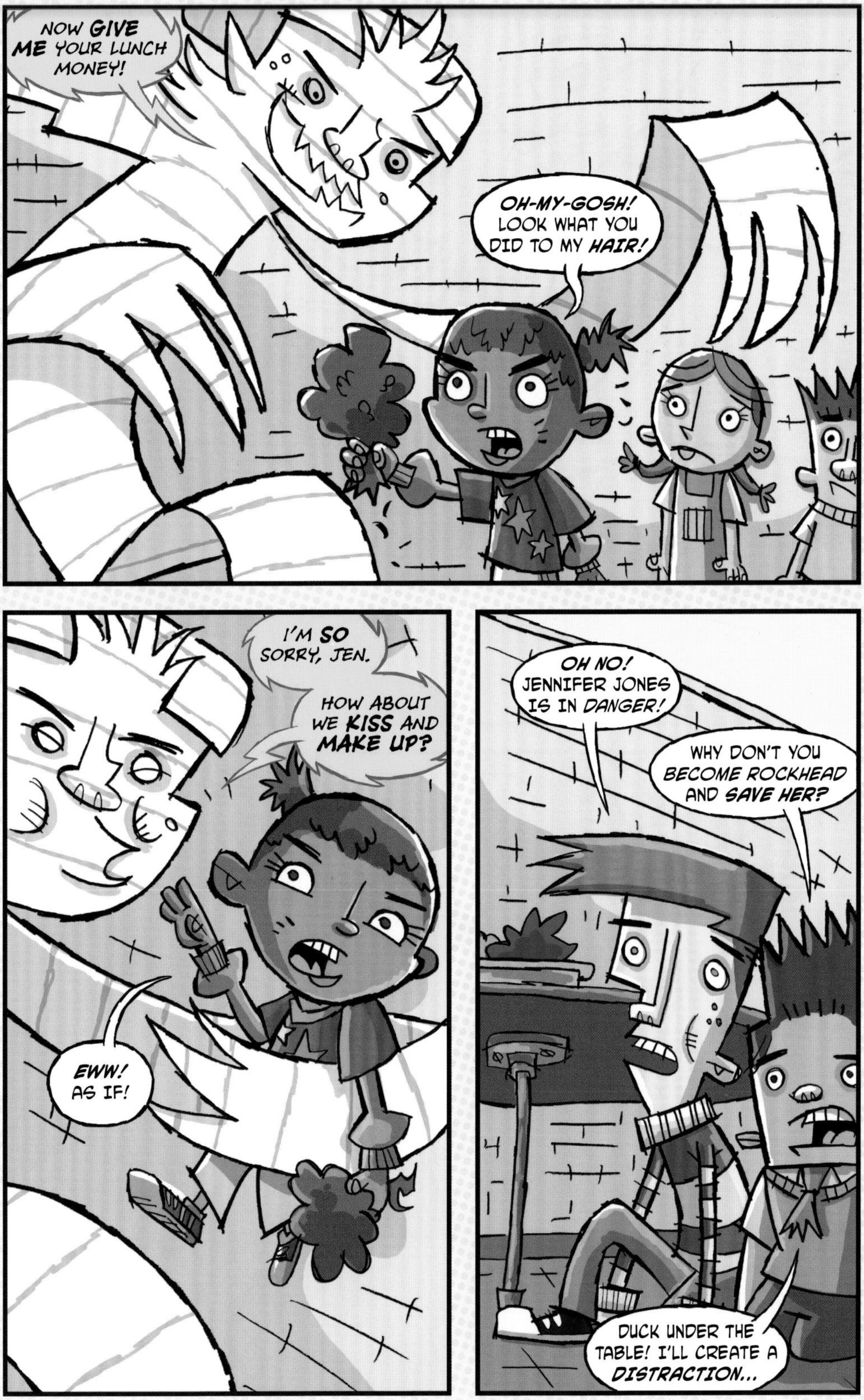
NOW GIVE ME YOUR LUNCH MONEY!
OH-MY-GOSH! LOOK WHAT YOU DID TO MY HAIR!
I'M SO SORRY, JEN.
HOW ABOUT WE KISS AND MAKE UP?
EWW! AS IF!
OH NO! JENNIFER JONES IS IN DANGER!
WHY DON'T YOU BECOME ROCKHEAD AND SAVE HER?
DUCK UNDER THE TABLE! I'LL CREATE A DISTRACTION...

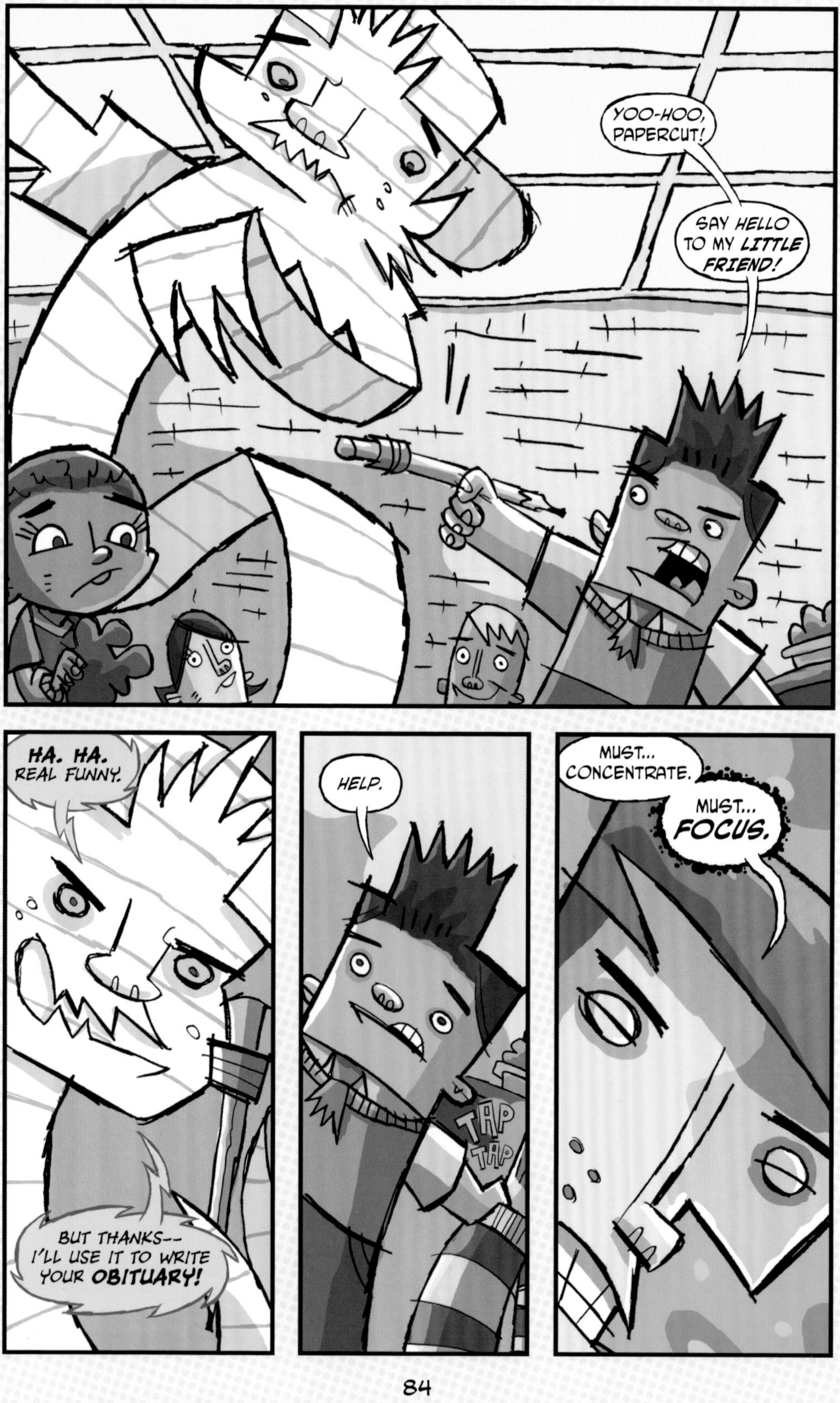
YOO-HOO, PAPERCUT!
SAY HELLO TO MY LITTLE FRIEND!
HA. HA. REAL FUNNY.
BUT THANKS-- I'LL USE IT TO WRITE YOUR OBITUARY!
HELP.
TAP TAP
MUST... CONCENTRATE.
MUST... FOCUS.

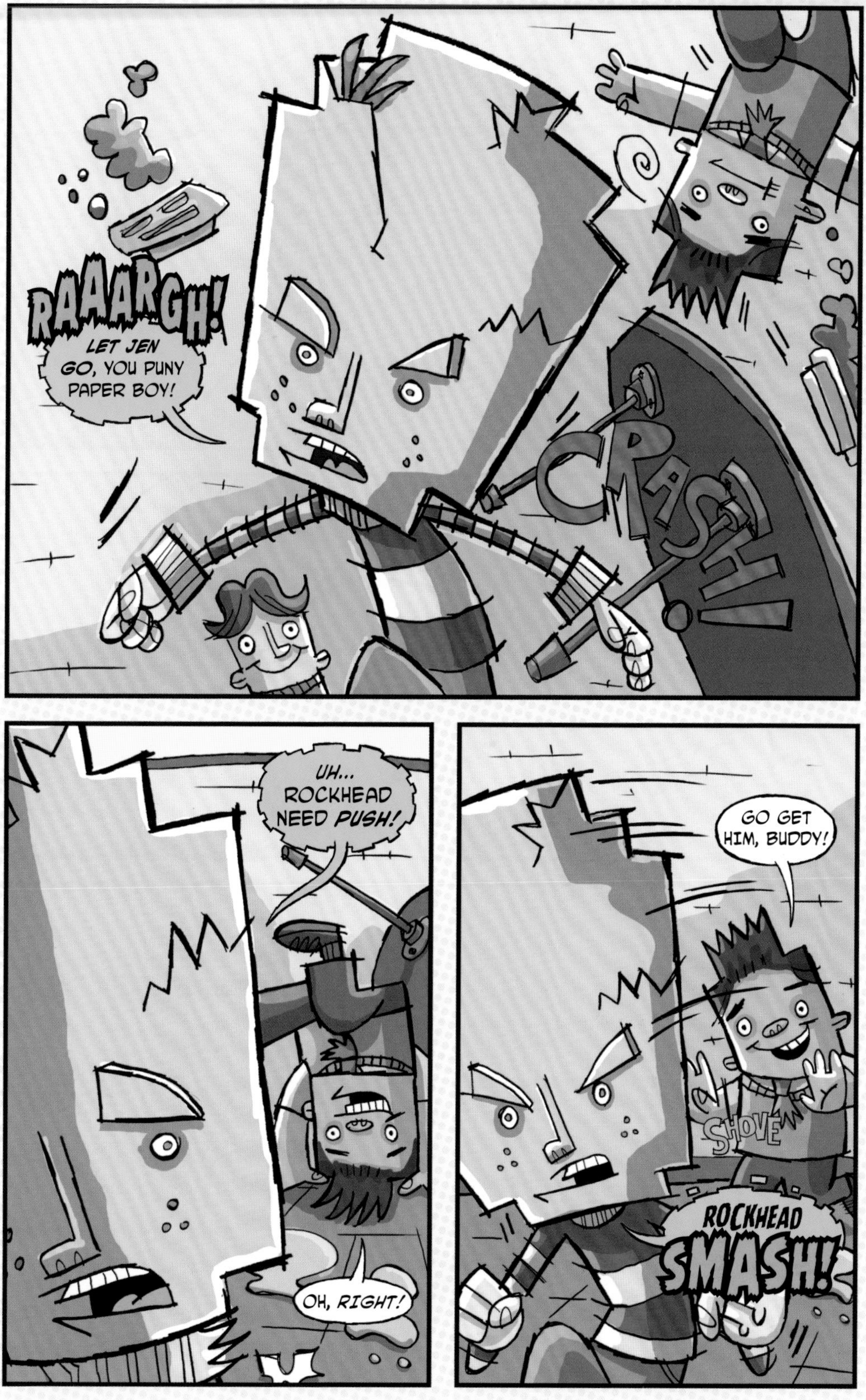
RAAARGH!
LET JEN GO, YOU PUNY PAPER BOY!
CRASH!
UH... ROCKHEAD NEED PUSH!
OH, RIGHT!
GO GET HIM, BUDDY!
SHOVE
ROCKHEAD SMASH!

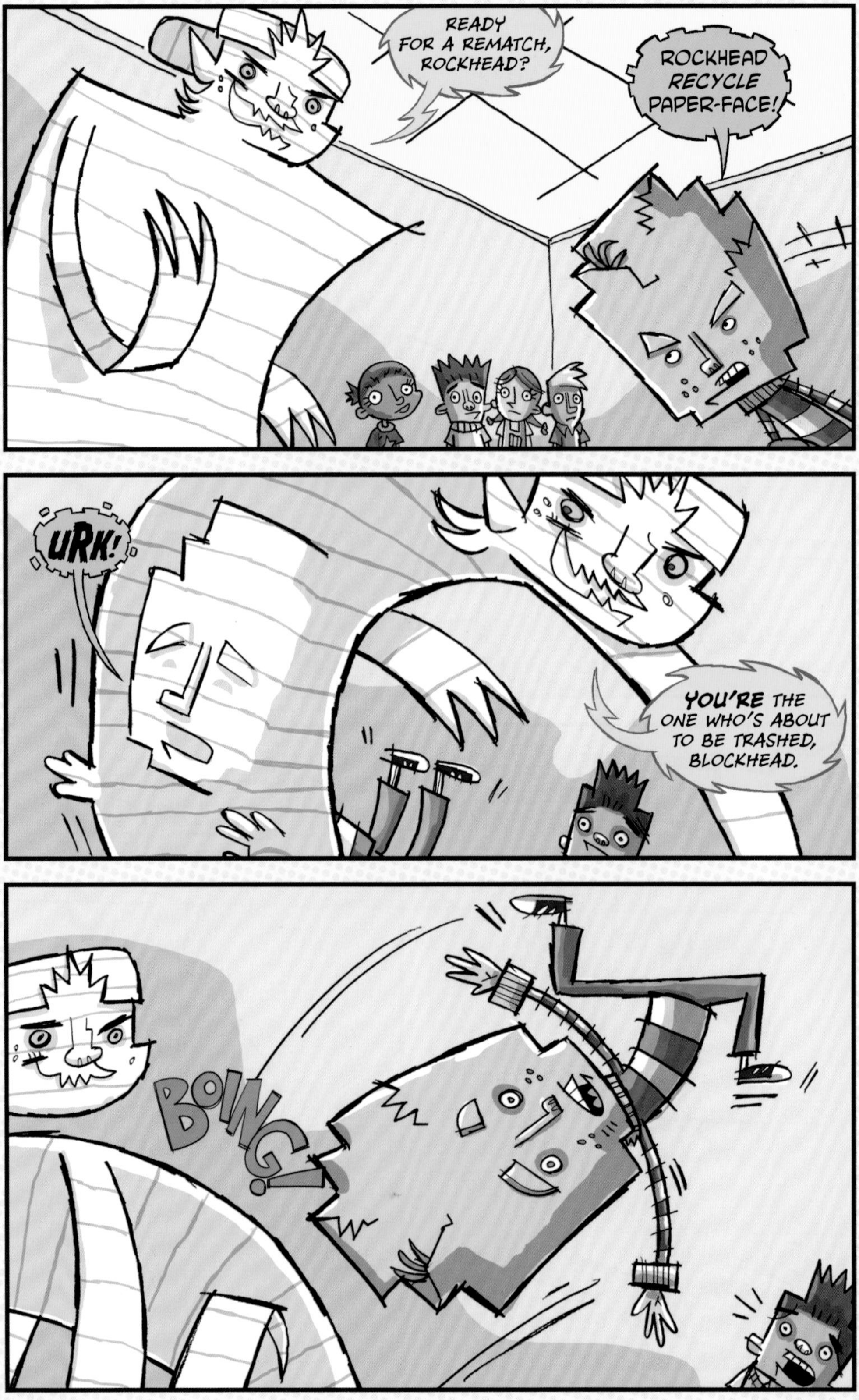
READY FOR A REMATCH, ROCKHEAD?
ROCKHEAD RECYCLE PAPER-FACE!
URK!
YOU'RE THE ONE WHO'S ABOUT TO BE TRASHED, BLOCKHEAD.
BOING!

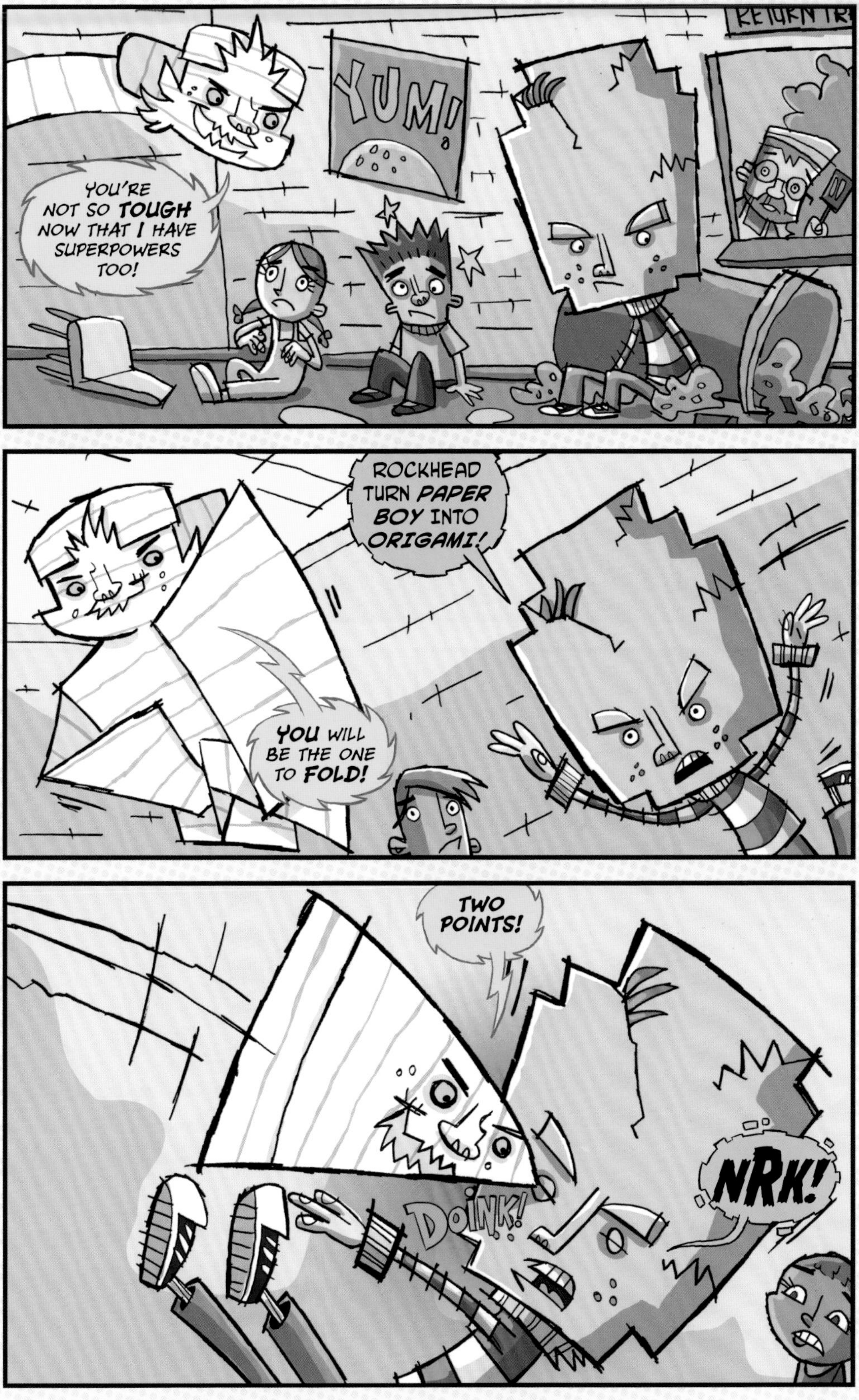
RETURN TR
YUM!
YOU'RE NOT SO TOUGH NOW THAT I HAVE SUPERPOWERS TOO!
ROCKHEAD TURN PAPER BOY INTO ORIGAMI!
YOU WILL BE THE ONE TO FOLD!
TWO POINTS!
DOINK!
NRK!

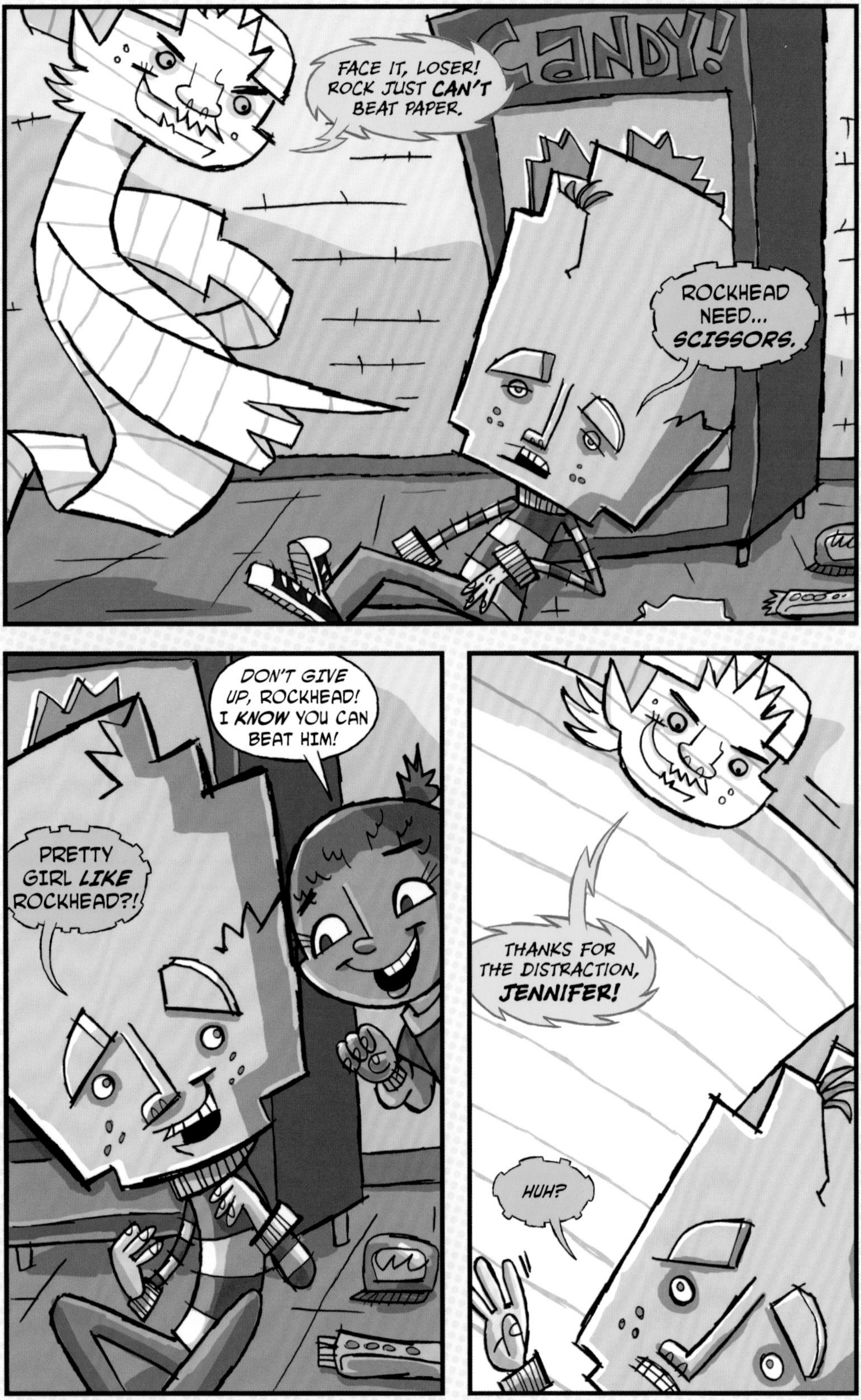
FACE IT, LOSER! ROCK JUST CAN'T BEAT PAPER.
ROCKHEAD NEED... SCISSORS.
CANDY!
DON'T GIVE UP, ROCKHEAD! I KNOW YOU CAN BEAT HIM!
PRETTY GIRL LIKE ROCKHEAD?!
THANKS FOR THE DISTRACTION, JENNIFER!
HUH?

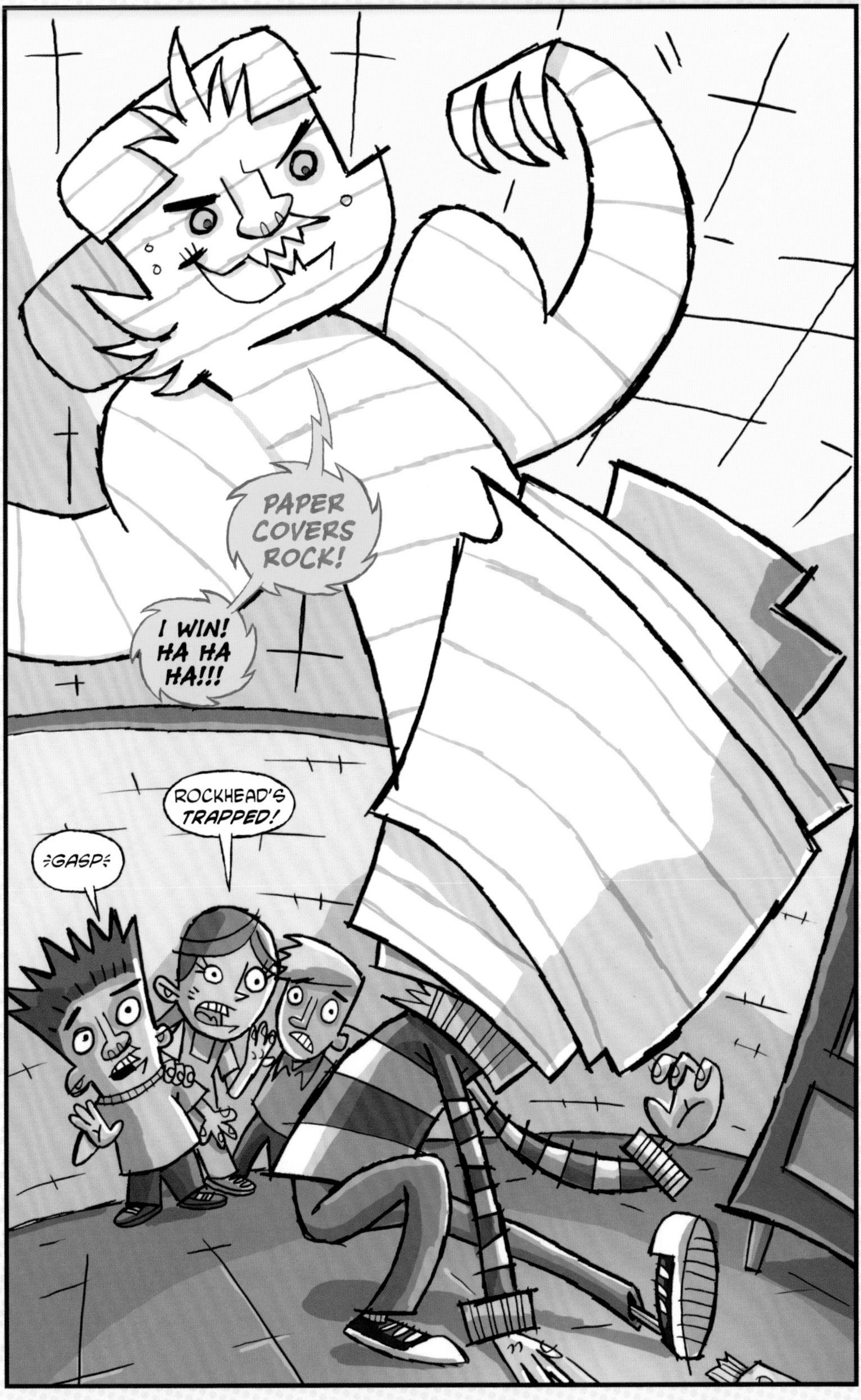
PAPER COVERS ROCK!
I WIN! HA HA HA!!!
ROCKHEAD'S *TRAPPED!*
GASP

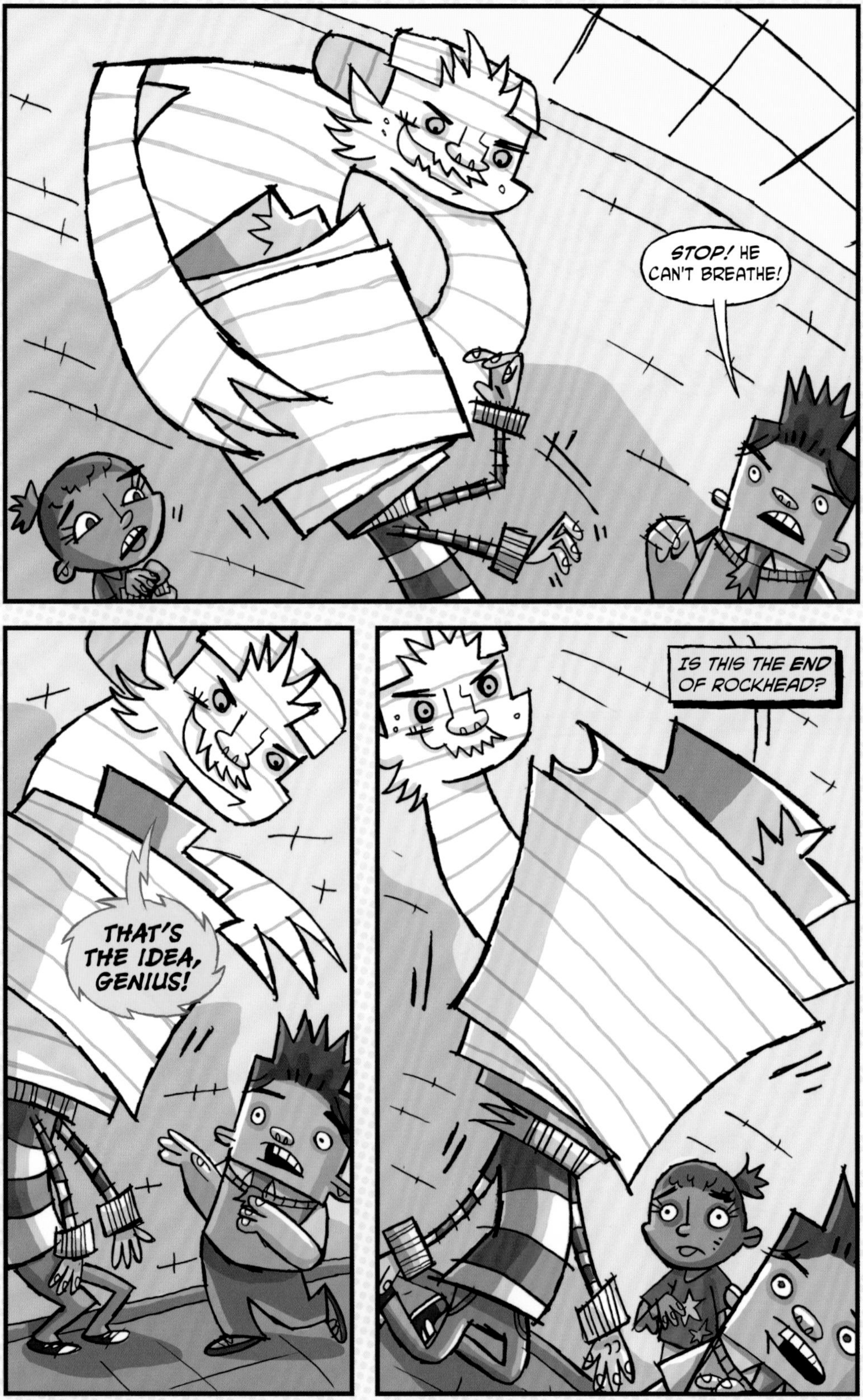
STOP! HE CAN'T BREATHE!
THAT'S THE IDEA, GENIUS!
IS THIS THE END OF ROCKHEAD?

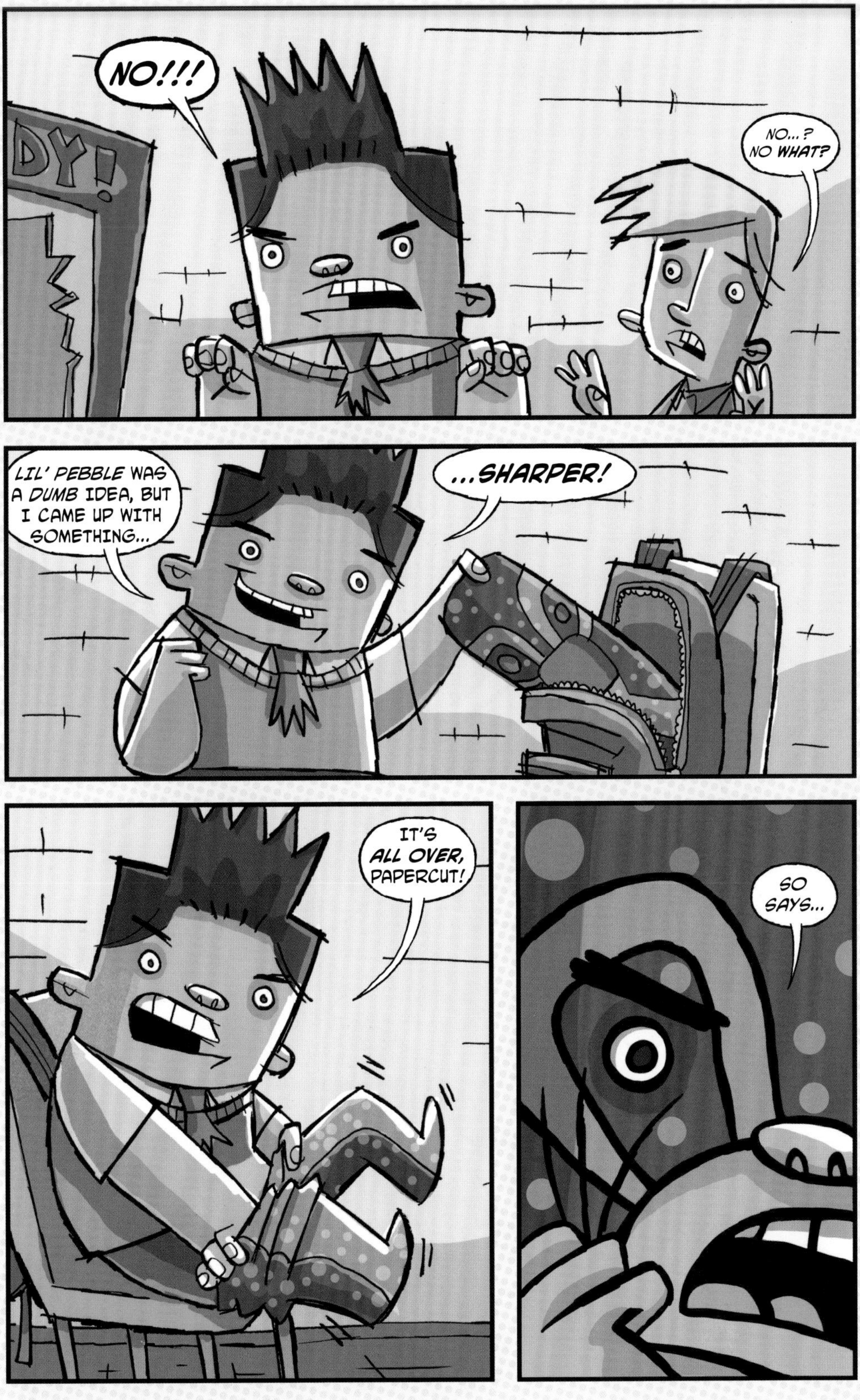
NO!!!
NO...? NO WHAT?
LIL' PEBBLE WAS A DUMB IDEA, BUT I CAME UP WITH SOMETHING...
...SHARPER!
IT'S ALL OVER, PAPERCUT!
SO SAYS...

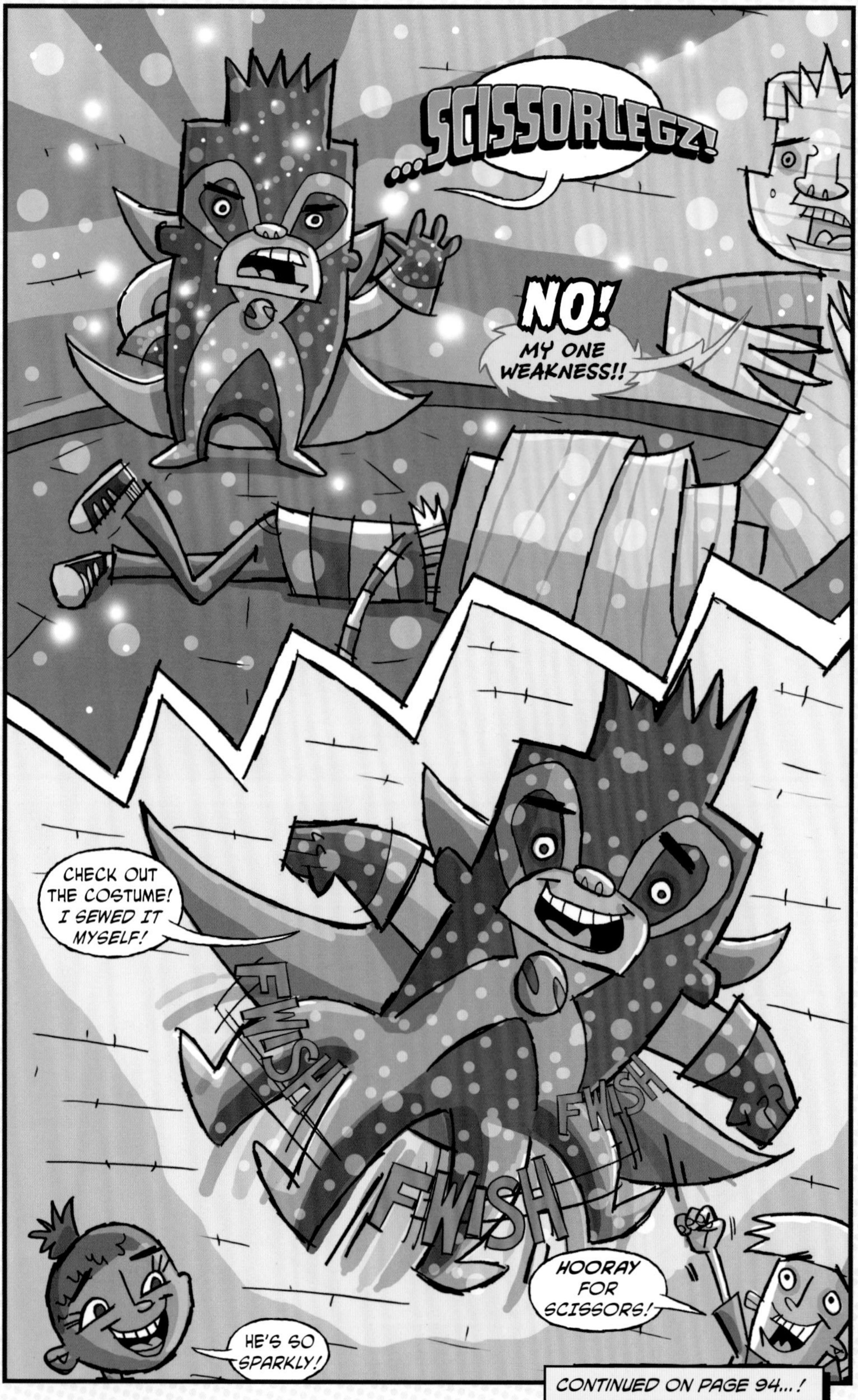
...SCISSORLEGZ!
NO! MY ONE WEAKNESS!!
CHECK OUT THE COSTUME! I SEWED IT MYSELF!
FWISH
FWISH
FWISH
HOORAY FOR SCISSORS!
HE'S SO SPARKLY!

CONTINUED ON PAGE 94...!

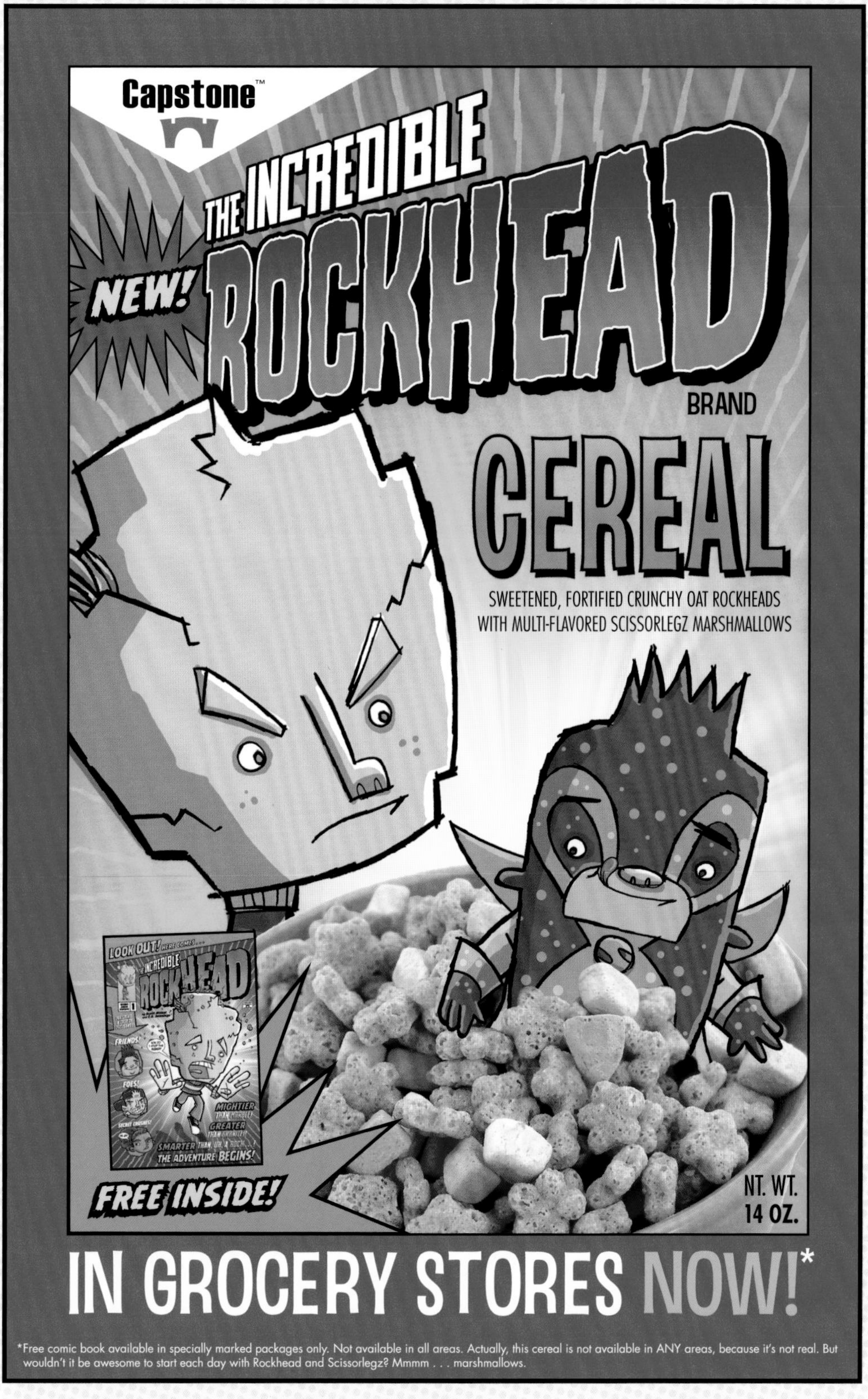
Capstone™
NEW!
THE INCREDIBLE
ROCKHEAD
BRAND
CEREAL
SWEETENED, FORTIFIED CRUNCHY OAT ROCKHEADS
WITH MULTI-FLAVORED SCISSORLEGZ MARSHMALLOWS
LOOK OUT! HERE COMES...
THE INCREDIBLE
ROCKHEAD
FRIENDS!
FOES!
MIGHTIER THAN MARBLE!
GREATER THAN GRANITE!
SMARTER THAN, UH, A ROCK...!
THE ADVENTURE BEGINS!
FREE INSIDE!
NT. WT.
14 OZ.
IN GROCERY STORES NOW!*
*Free comic book available in specially marked packages only. Not available in all areas. Actually, this cereal is not available in ANY areas, because it's not real. But wouldn't it be awesome to start each day with Rockhead and Scissorlegz? Mmmm . . . marshmallows.

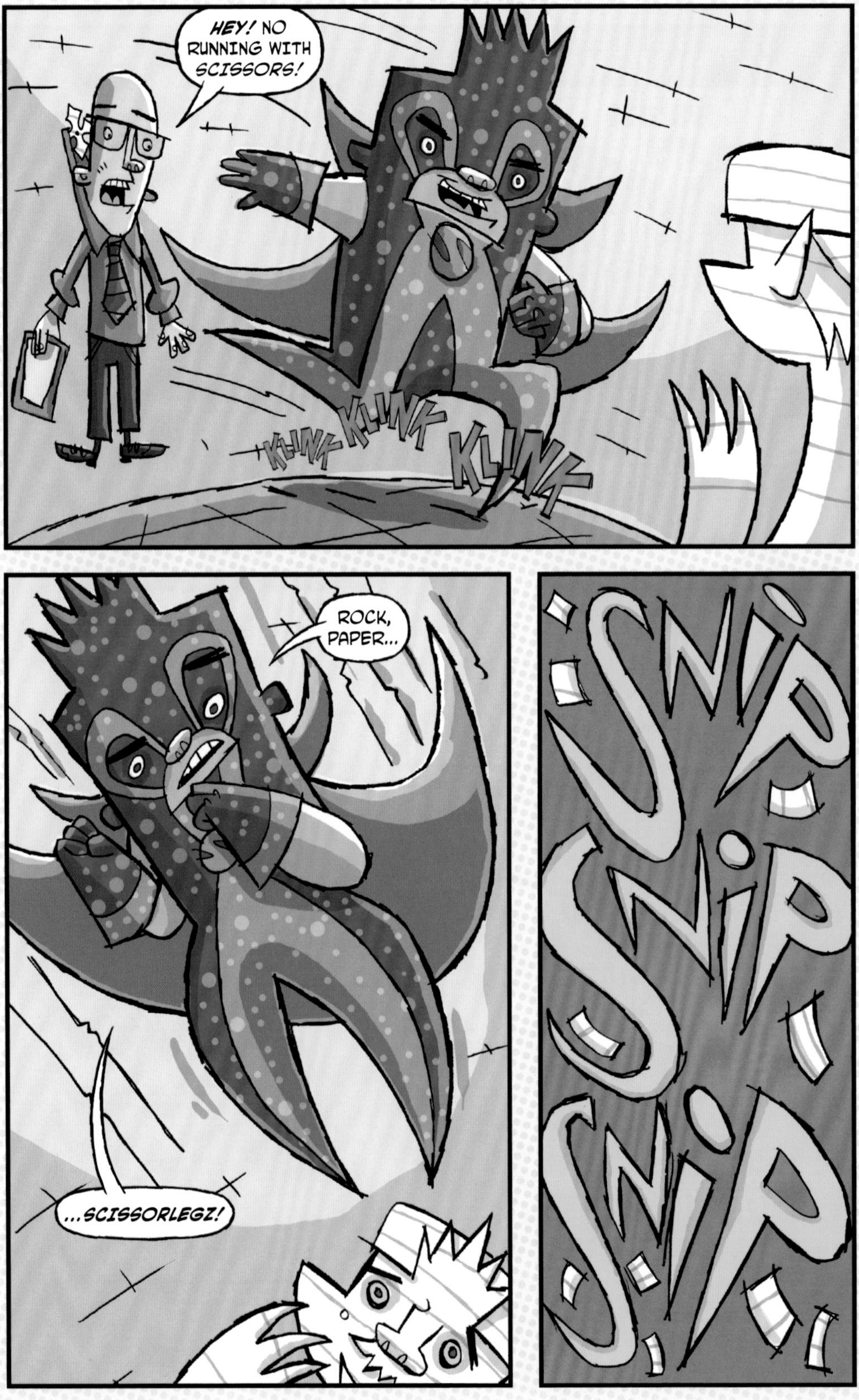

HEY! NO RUNNING WITH SCISSORS!
KLINK KLINK KLINK
ROCK, PAPER...
...SCISSORLEGZ!
SNIP SNIP SNIP

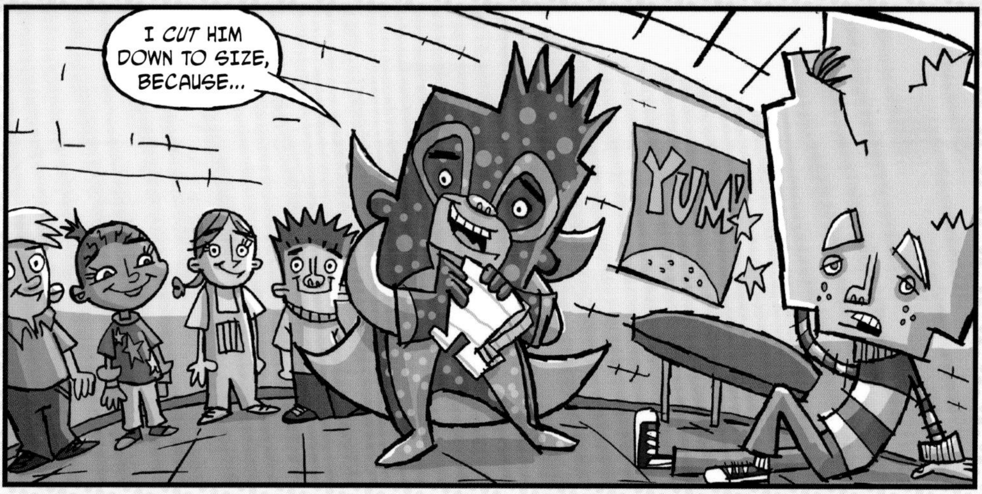
I *CUT* HIM DOWN TO SIZE, BECAUSE...
YUM!

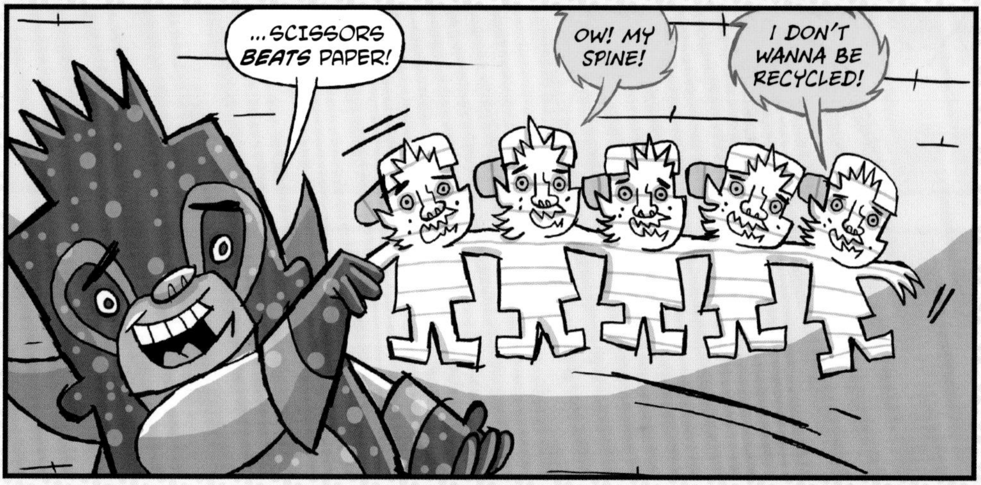
...SCISSORS *BEATS* PAPER!
OW! MY SPINE!
I DON'T WANNA BE RECYCLED!

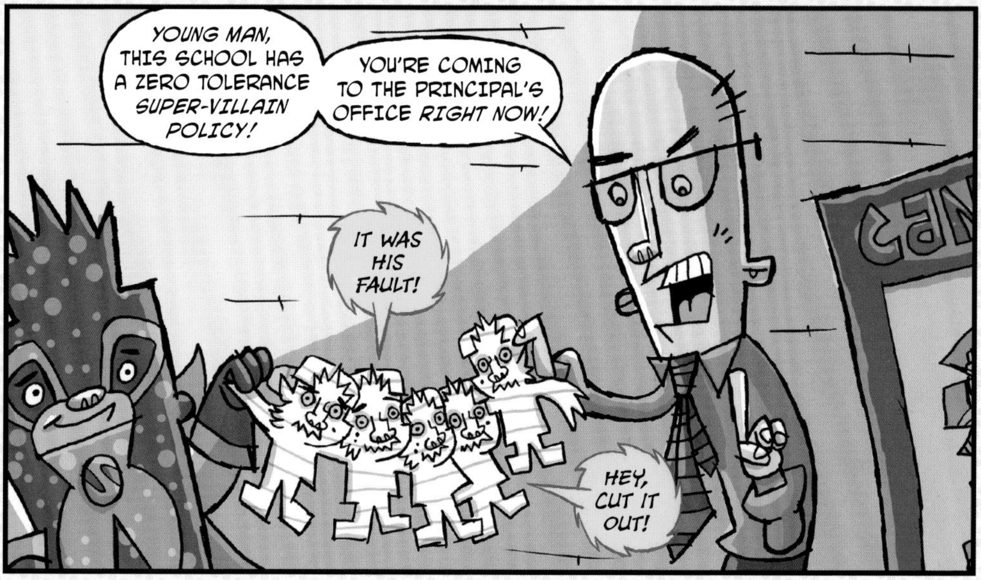
YOUNG MAN, THIS SCHOOL HAS A ZERO TOLERANCE SUPER-VILLAIN POLICY!
YOU'RE COMING TO THE PRINCIPAL'S OFFICE *RIGHT NOW!*
IT WAS HIS FAULT!
HEY, CUT IT OUT!

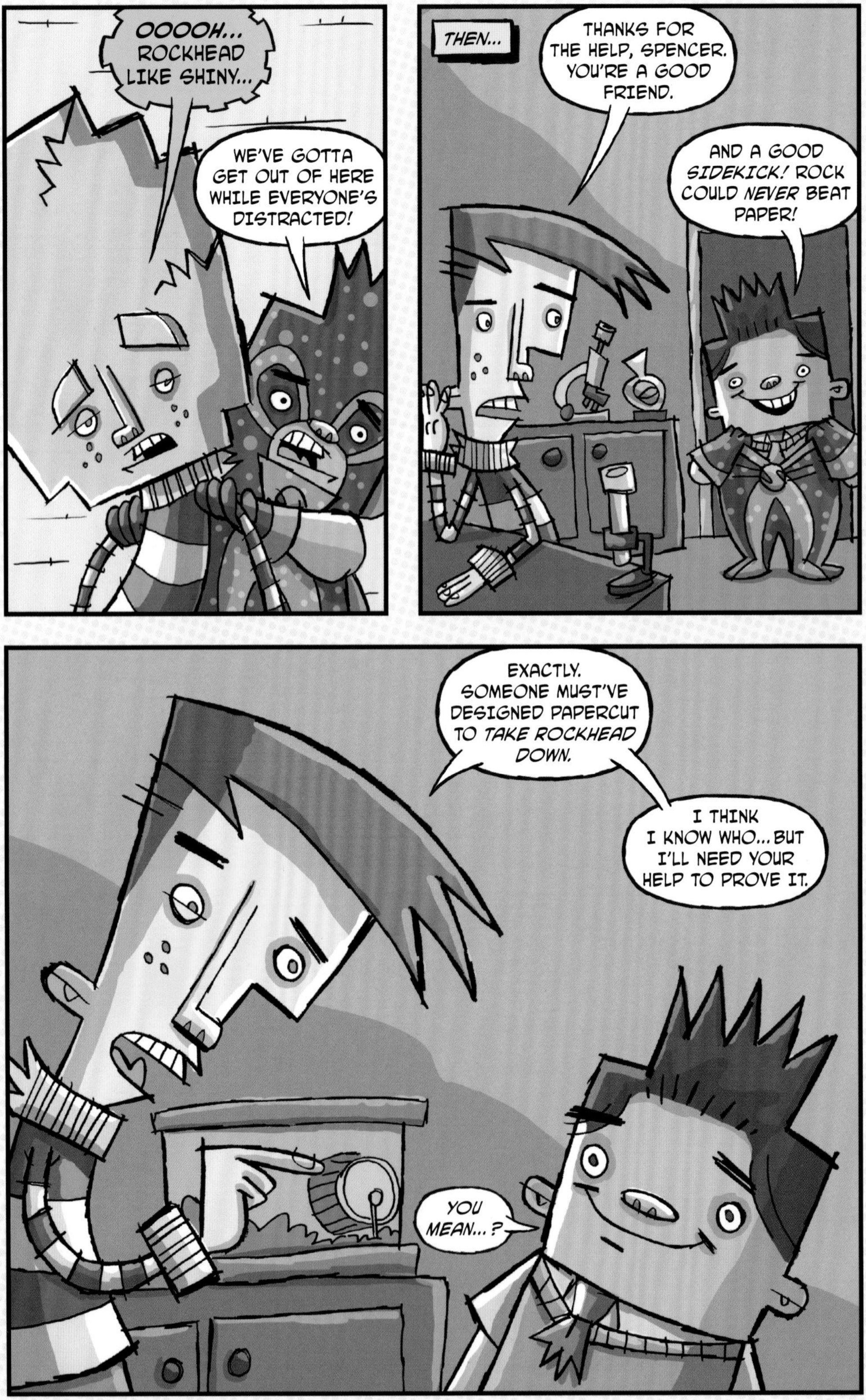
OOOOH... ROCKHEAD LIKE SHINY...
WE'VE GOTTA GET OUT OF HERE WHILE EVERYONE'S DISTRACTED!
THEN...
THANKS FOR THE HELP, SPENCER. YOU'RE A GOOD FRIEND.
AND A GOOD *SIDEKICK!* ROCK COULD *NEVER* BEAT PAPER!
EXACTLY. SOMEONE MUST'VE DESIGNED PAPERCUT TO *TAKE ROCKHEAD DOWN.*
I THINK I KNOW WHO... BUT I'LL NEED YOUR HELP TO PROVE IT.
YOU MEAN...?

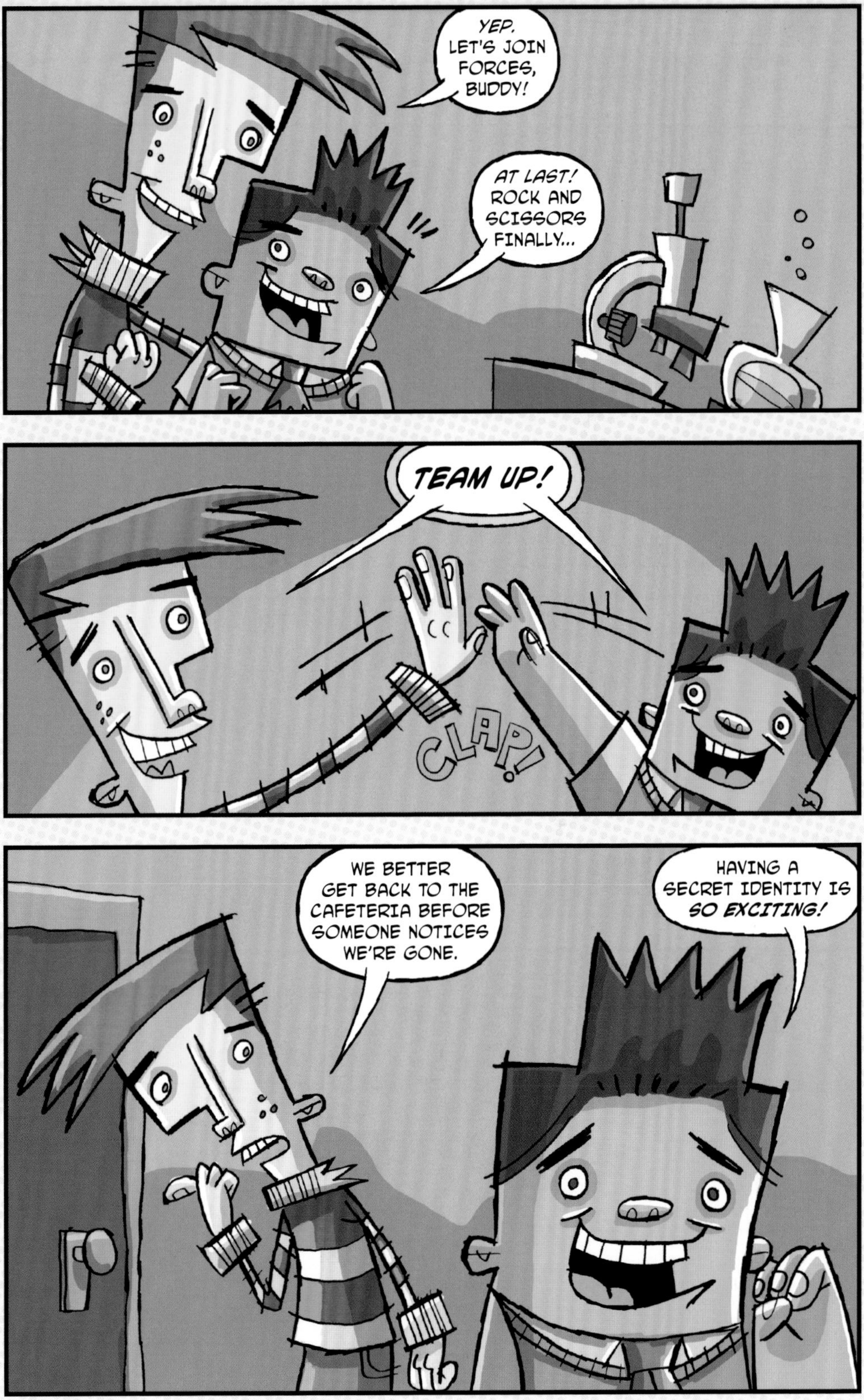
YEP. LET'S JOIN FORCES, BUDDY!
AT LAST! ROCK AND SCISSORS FINALLY...
TEAM UP!
CLAP!
WE BETTER GET BACK TO THE CAFETERIA BEFORE SOMEONE NOTICES WE'RE GONE.
HAVING A SECRET IDENTITY IS SO EXCITING!

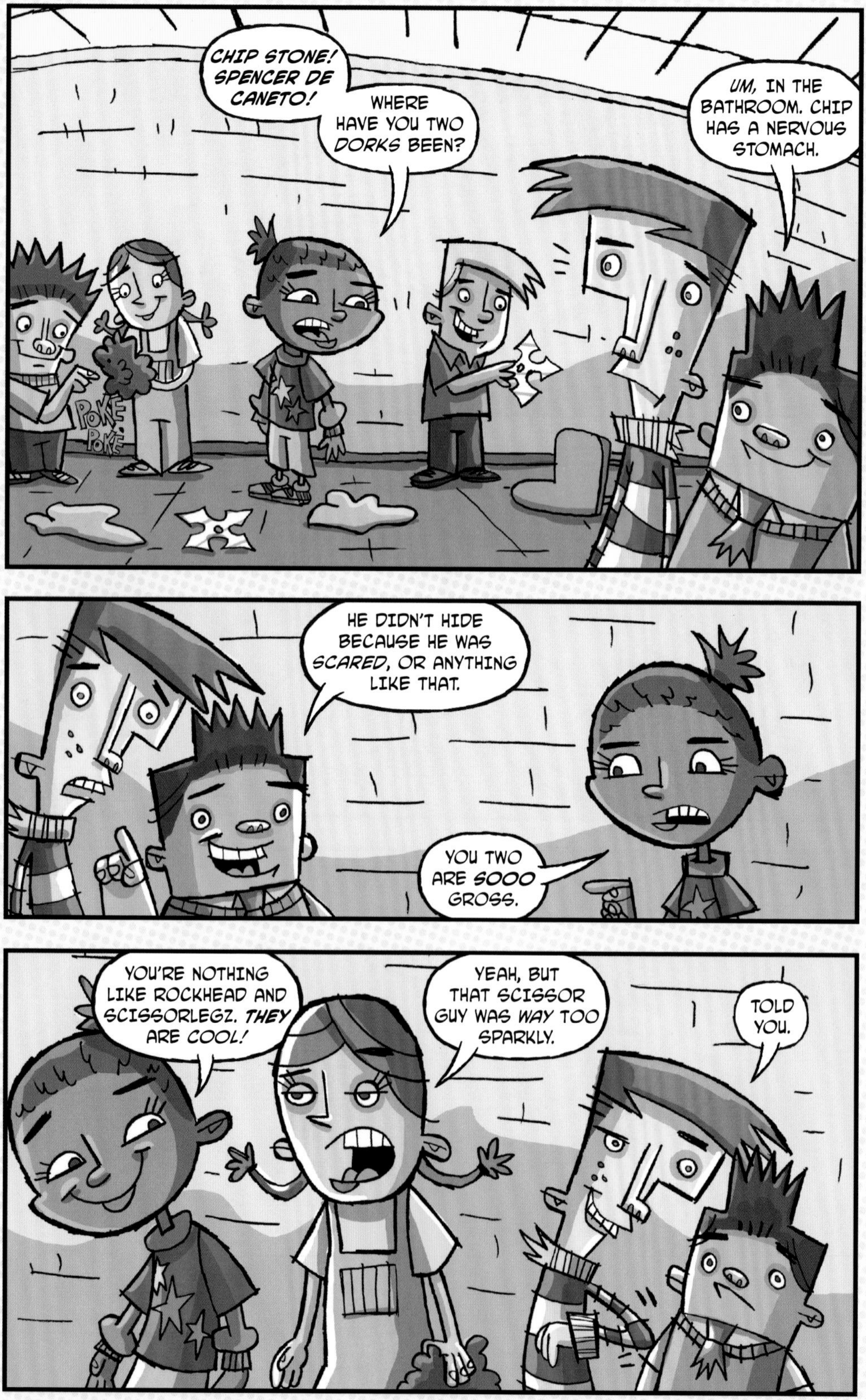
CHIP STONE! SPENCER DE CANETO!
WHERE HAVE YOU TWO DORKS BEEN?
UM, IN THE BATHROOM. CHIP HAS A NERVOUS STOMACH.
POKE POKE
HE DIDN'T HIDE BECAUSE HE WAS SCARED, OR ANYTHING LIKE THAT.
YOU TWO ARE SOOO GROSS.
YOU'RE NOTHING LIKE ROCKHEAD AND SCISSORLEGZ. THEY ARE COOL!
YEAH, BUT THAT SCISSOR GUY WAS WAY TOO SPARKLY.
TOLD YOU.

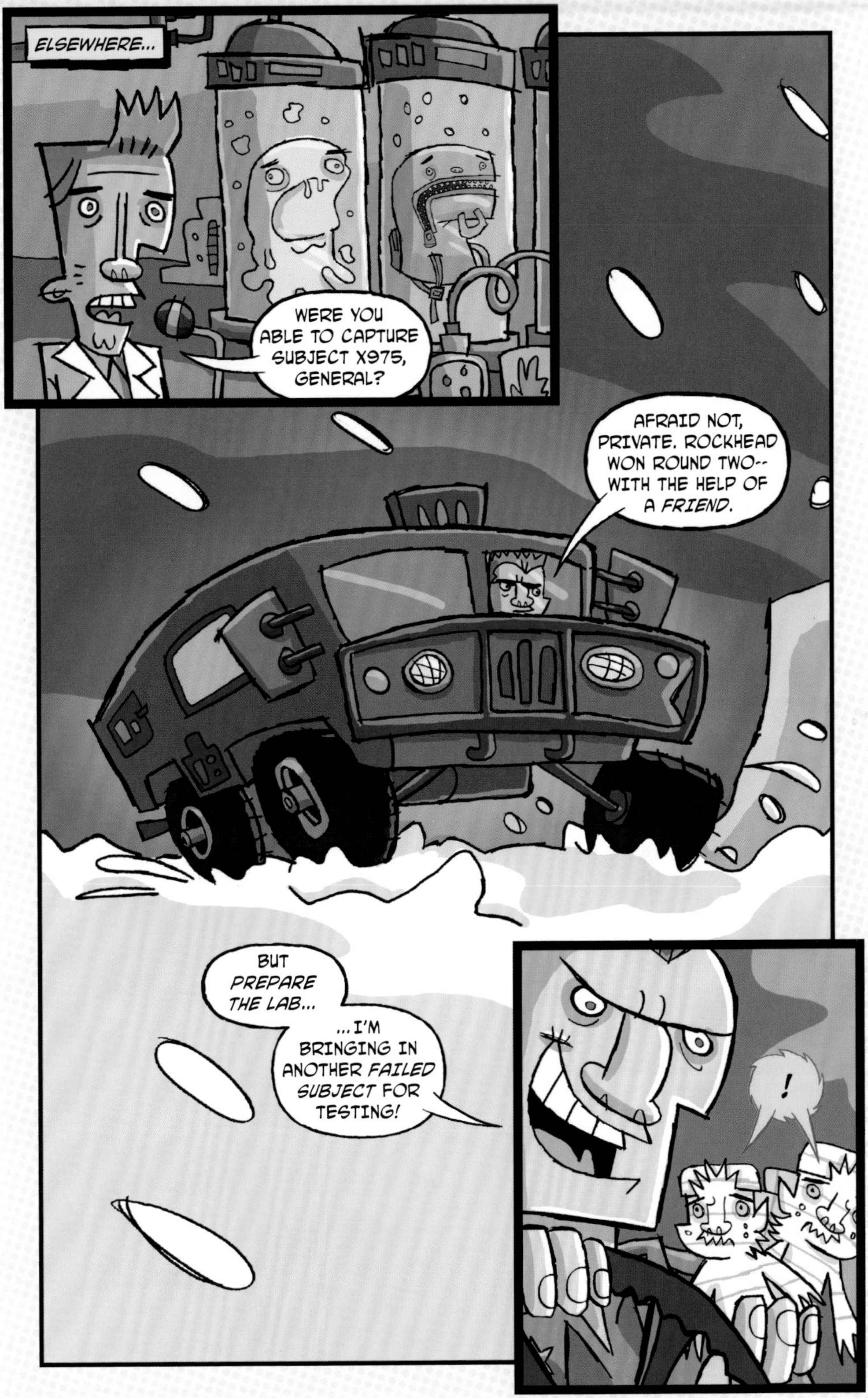
ELSEWHERE...
WERE YOU ABLE TO CAPTURE SUBJECT X975, GENERAL?
AFRAID NOT, PRIVATE. ROCKHEAD WON ROUND TWO-- WITH THE HELP OF A *FRIEND*.
BUT *PREPARE THE LAB*...
...I'M BRINGING IN ANOTHER *FAILED SUBJECT* FOR TESTING!
!

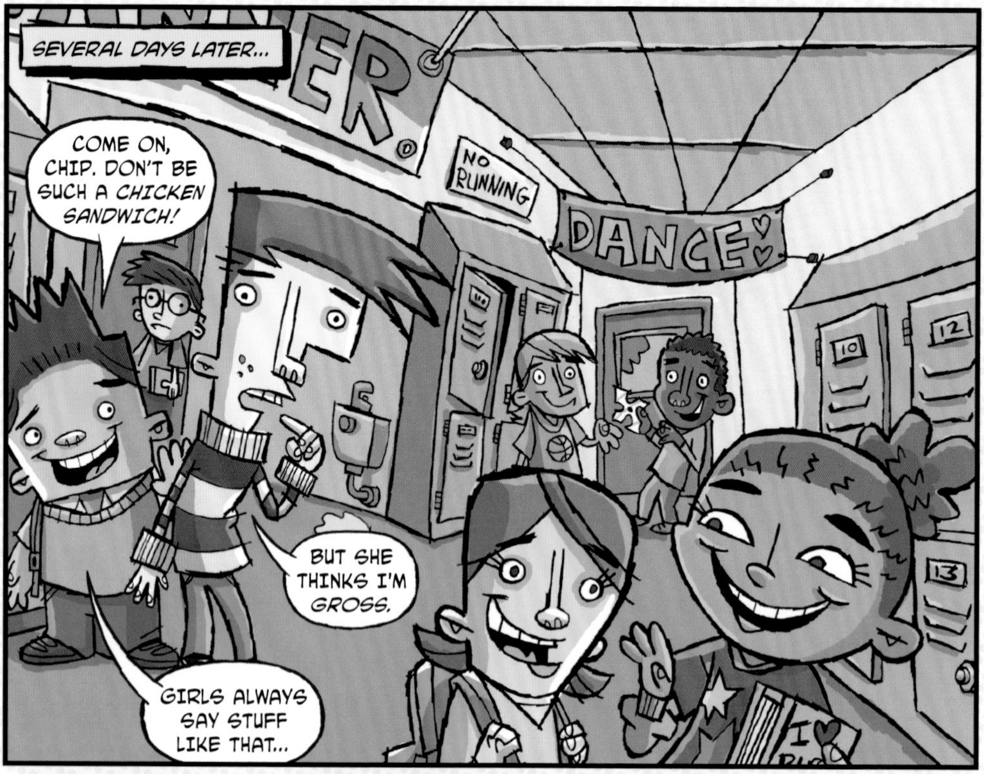
SEVERAL DAYS LATER...
NO RUNNING
DANCE
COME ON, CHIP. DON'T BE SUCH A CHICKEN SANDWICH!
BUT SHE THINKS I'M GROSS.
GIRLS ALWAYS SAY STUFF LIKE THAT...

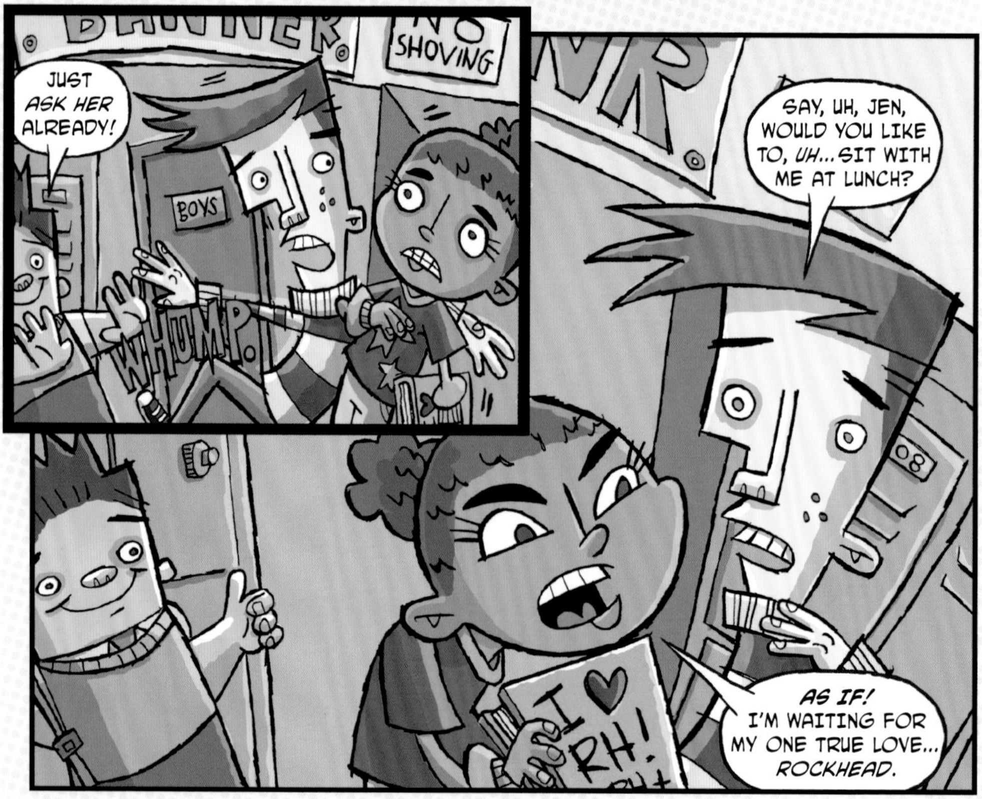
NO SHOVING
BOYS
JUST ASK HER ALREADY!
WHUMP
SAY, UH, JEN, WOULD YOU LIKE TO, UH... SIT WITH ME AT LUNCH?
AS IF! I'M WAITING FOR MY ONE TRUE LOVE... ROCKHEAD.

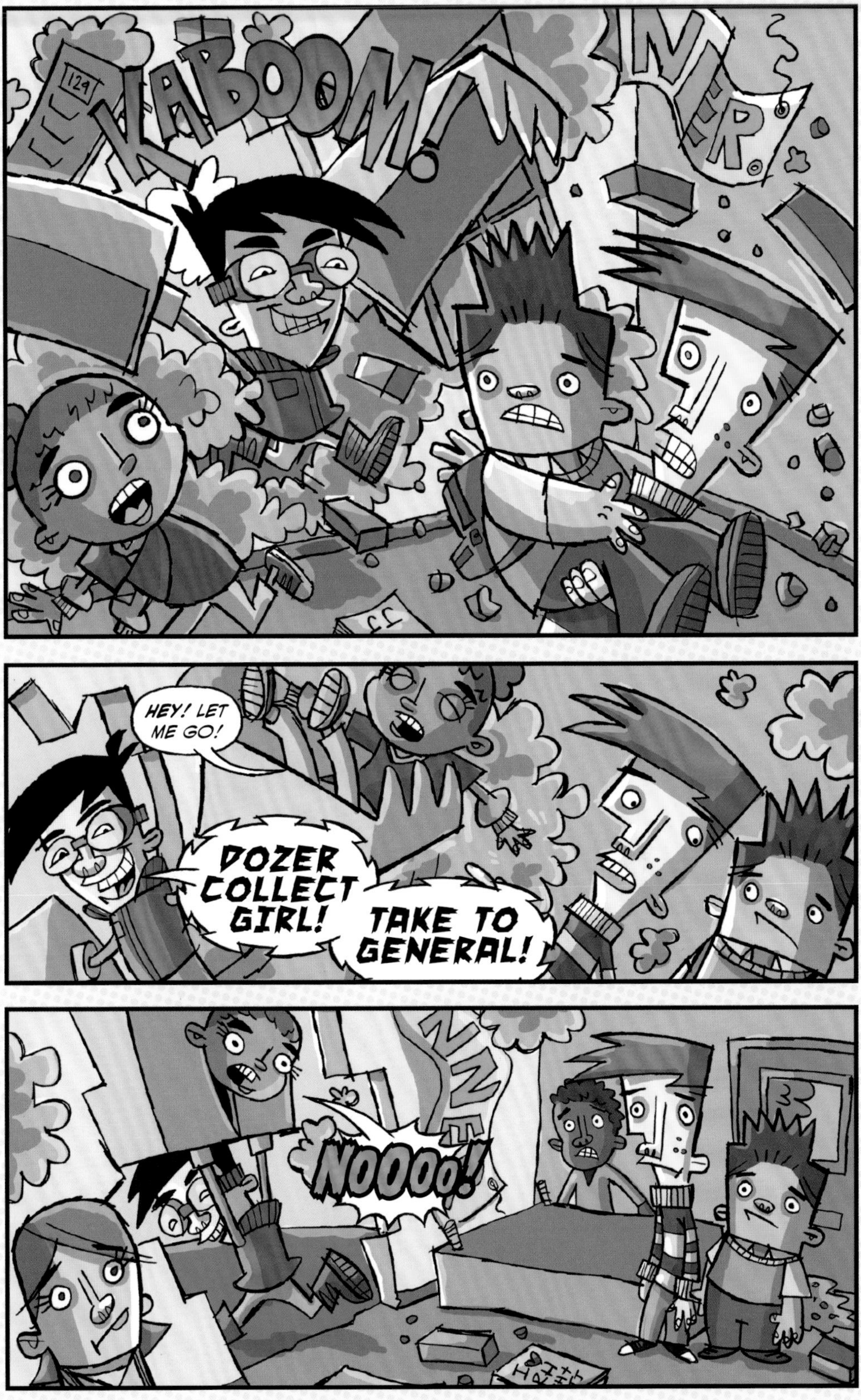
KABOOM!
HEY! LET ME GO!
DOZER COLLECT GIRL!
TAKE TO GENERAL!
NOOOo!

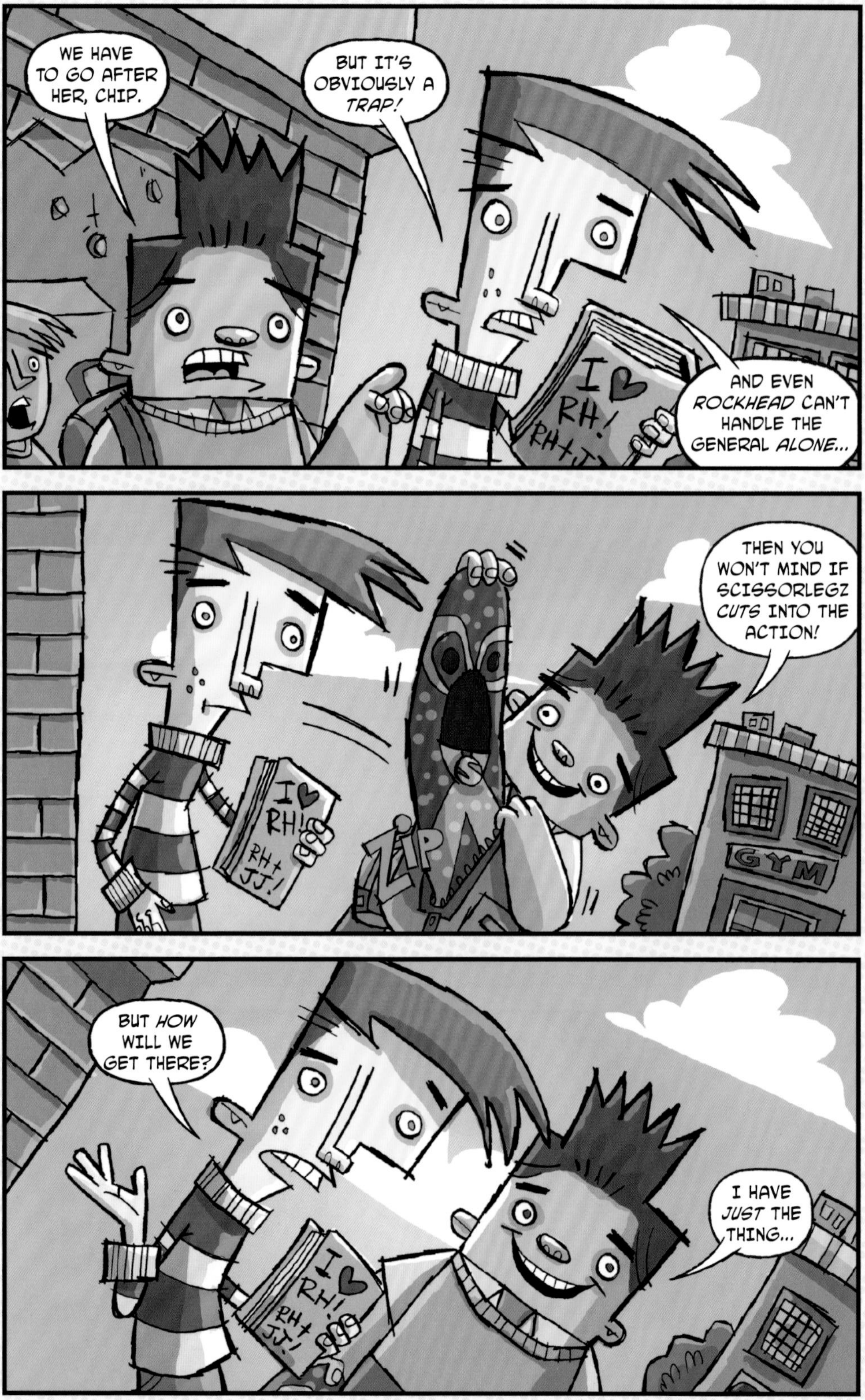
WE HAVE TO GO AFTER HER, CHIP.
BUT IT'S OBVIOUSLY A TRAP!
AND EVEN ROCKHEAD CAN'T HANDLE THE GENERAL ALONE...
I ♥ RH! RH+JJ
THEN YOU WON'T MIND IF SCISSORLEGZ CUTS INTO THE ACTION!
ZIP
GYM
BUT HOW WILL WE GET THERE?
I HAVE JUST THE THING...

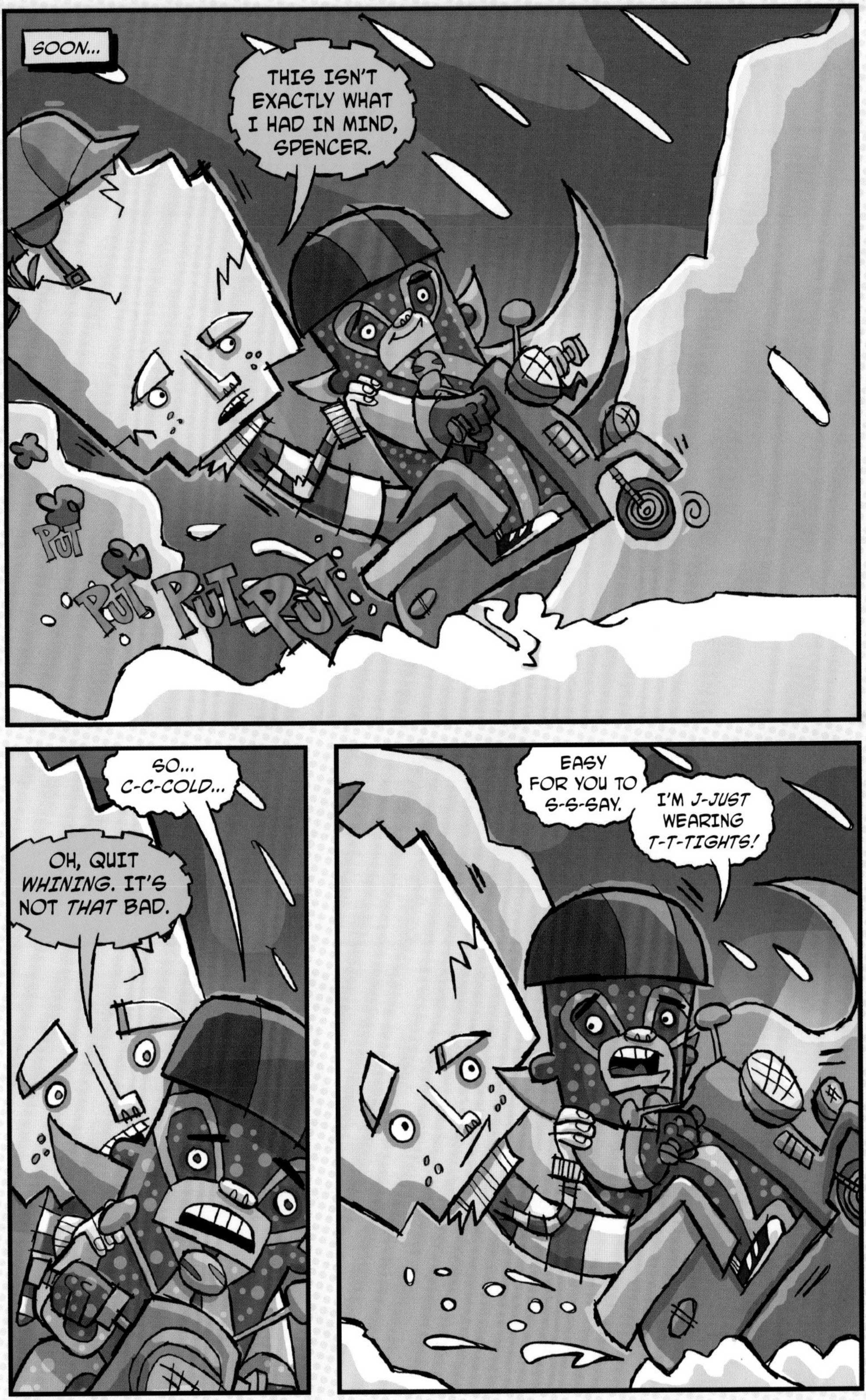
SOON...
THIS ISN'T EXACTLY WHAT I HAD IN MIND, SPENCER.
PUT
PUT PUT PUT
SO... C-C-COLD...
OH, QUIT *WHINING*. IT'S NOT *THAT* BAD.
EASY FOR YOU TO S-S-SAY.
I'M *J-JUST* WEARING *T-T-TIGHTS!*

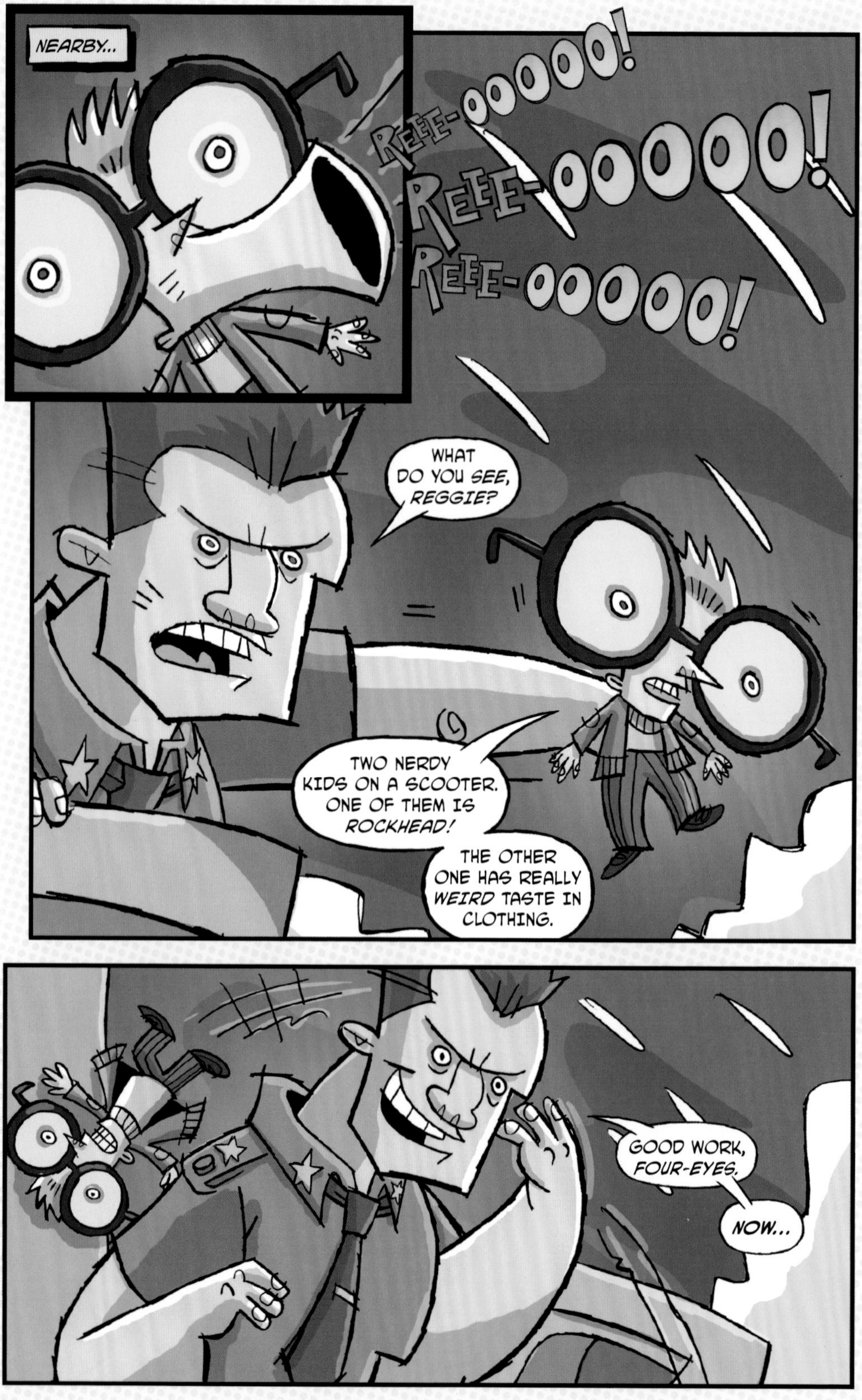
NEARBY...
REEE-OOOOO!
REEE-OOOOO!
REEE-OOOOO!
WHAT DO YOU SEE, REGGIE?
TWO NERDY KIDS ON A SCOOTER. ONE OF THEM IS *ROCKHEAD!*
THE OTHER ONE HAS REALLY *WEIRD* TASTE IN CLOTHING.
GOOD WORK, FOUR-EYES.
NOW...

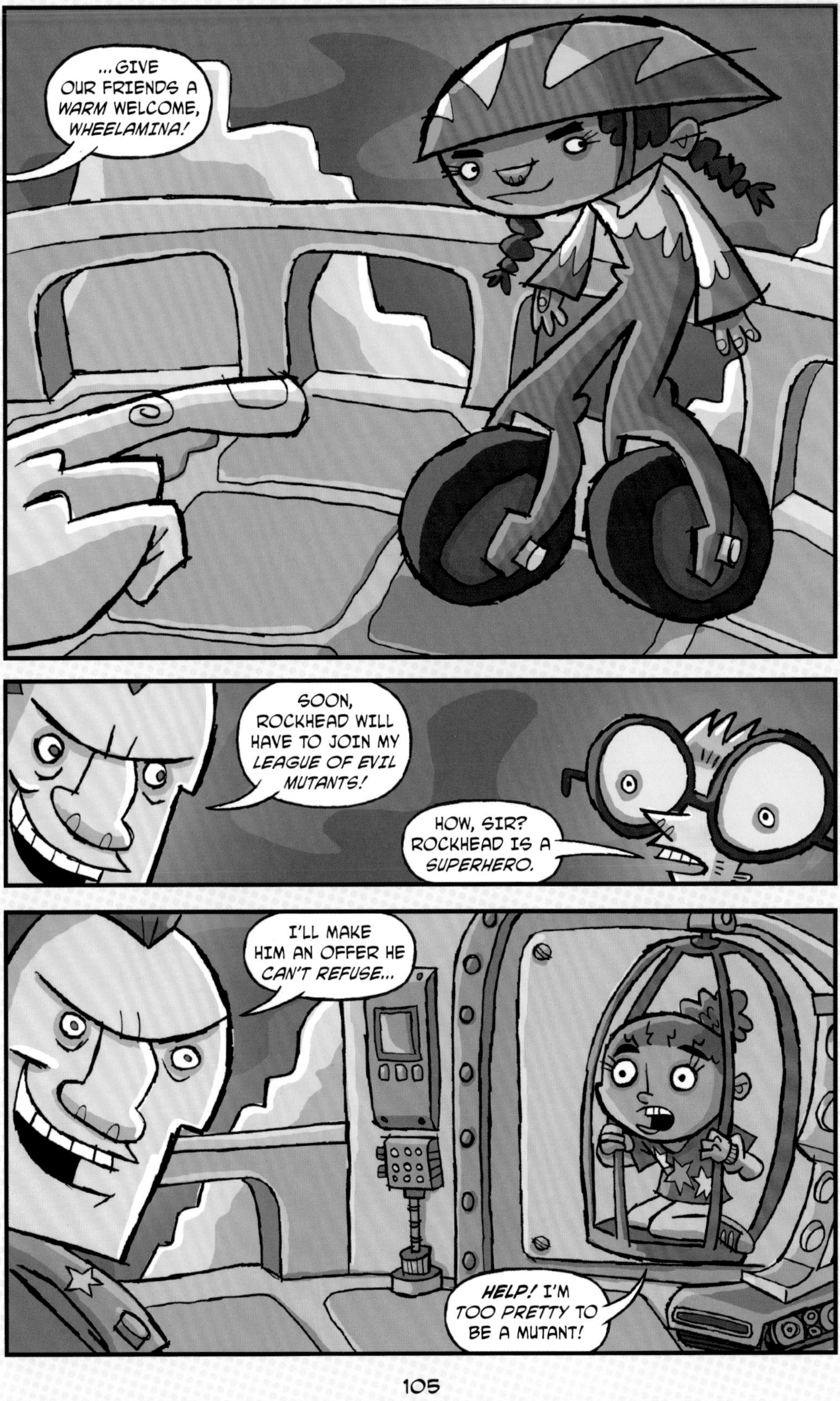
...GIVE OUR FRIENDS A WARM WELCOME, WHEELAMINA!
SOON, ROCKHEAD WILL HAVE TO JOIN MY LEAGUE OF EVIL MUTANTS!
HOW, SIR? ROCKHEAD IS A SUPERHERO.
I'LL MAKE HIM AN OFFER HE CAN'T REFUSE...
HELP! I'M TOO PRETTY TO BE A MUTANT!

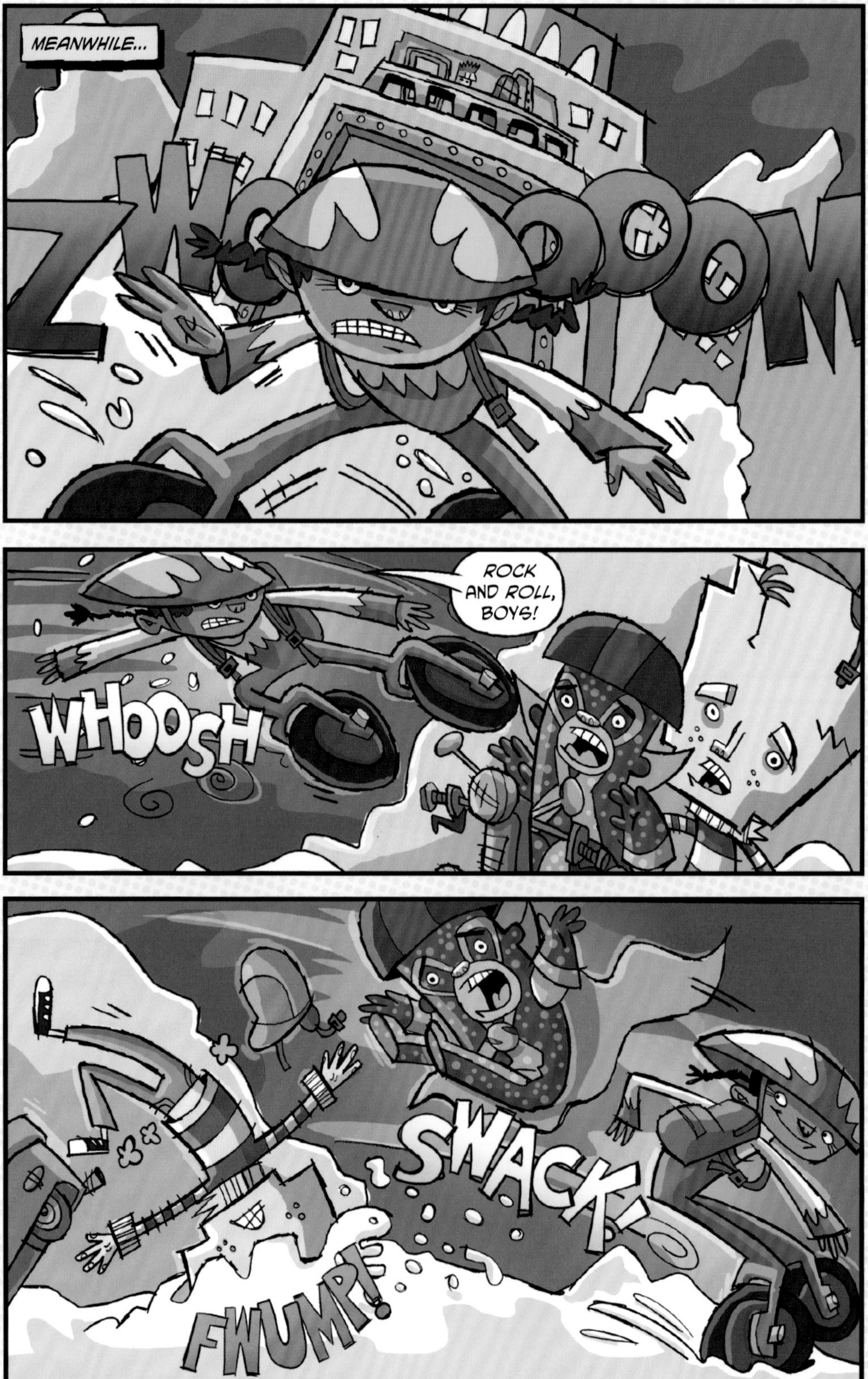
MEANWHILE...
ZWOOOOOM
ROCK AND ROLL, BOYS!
WHOOSH
SWACK!
FWUMP!

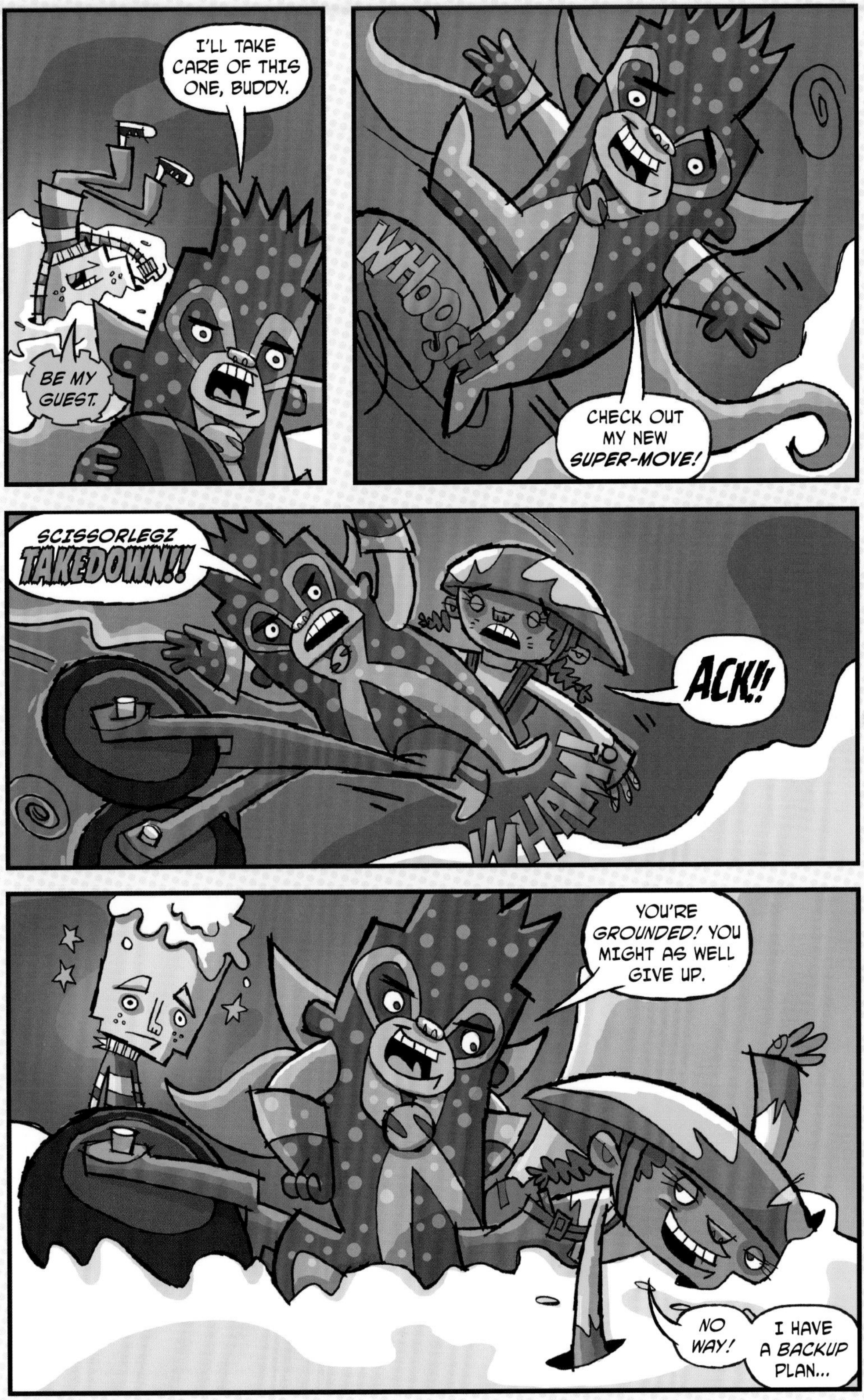
I'LL TAKE CARE OF THIS ONE, BUDDY.
BE MY GUEST.
WHOOSH
CHECK OUT MY NEW SUPER-MOVE!
SCISSORLEGZ TAKEDOWN!!
ACK!!
WHAM!
YOU'RE GROUNDED! YOU MIGHT AS WELL GIVE UP.
NO WAY!
I HAVE A BACKUP PLAN...

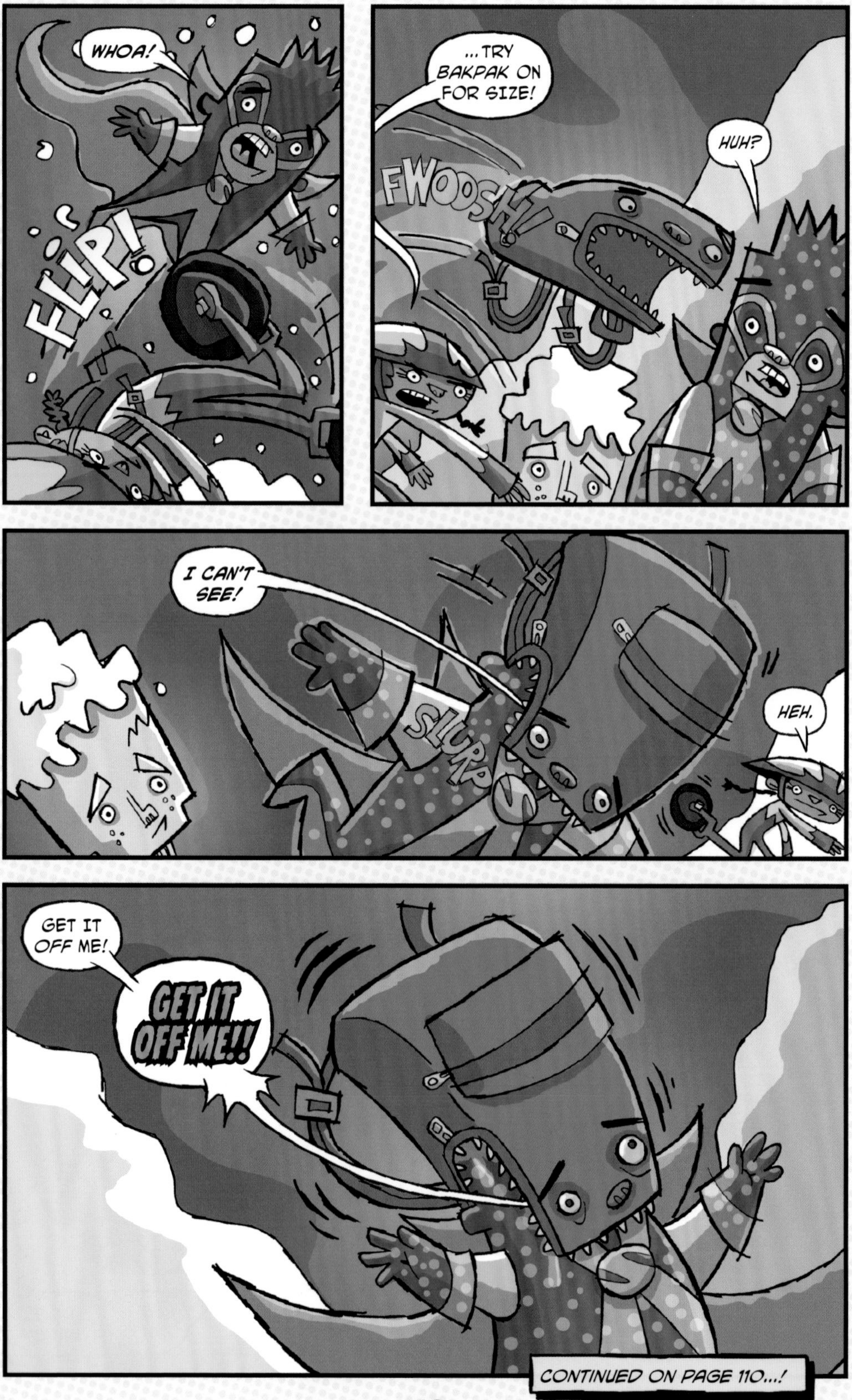
WHOA!
FLIP!
...TRY BAKPAK ON FOR SIZE!
FWOOSH!
HUH?
I CAN'T SEE!
SLURP
HEH.
GET IT OFF ME!
GET IT OFF ME!!

CONTINUED ON PAGE 110...!

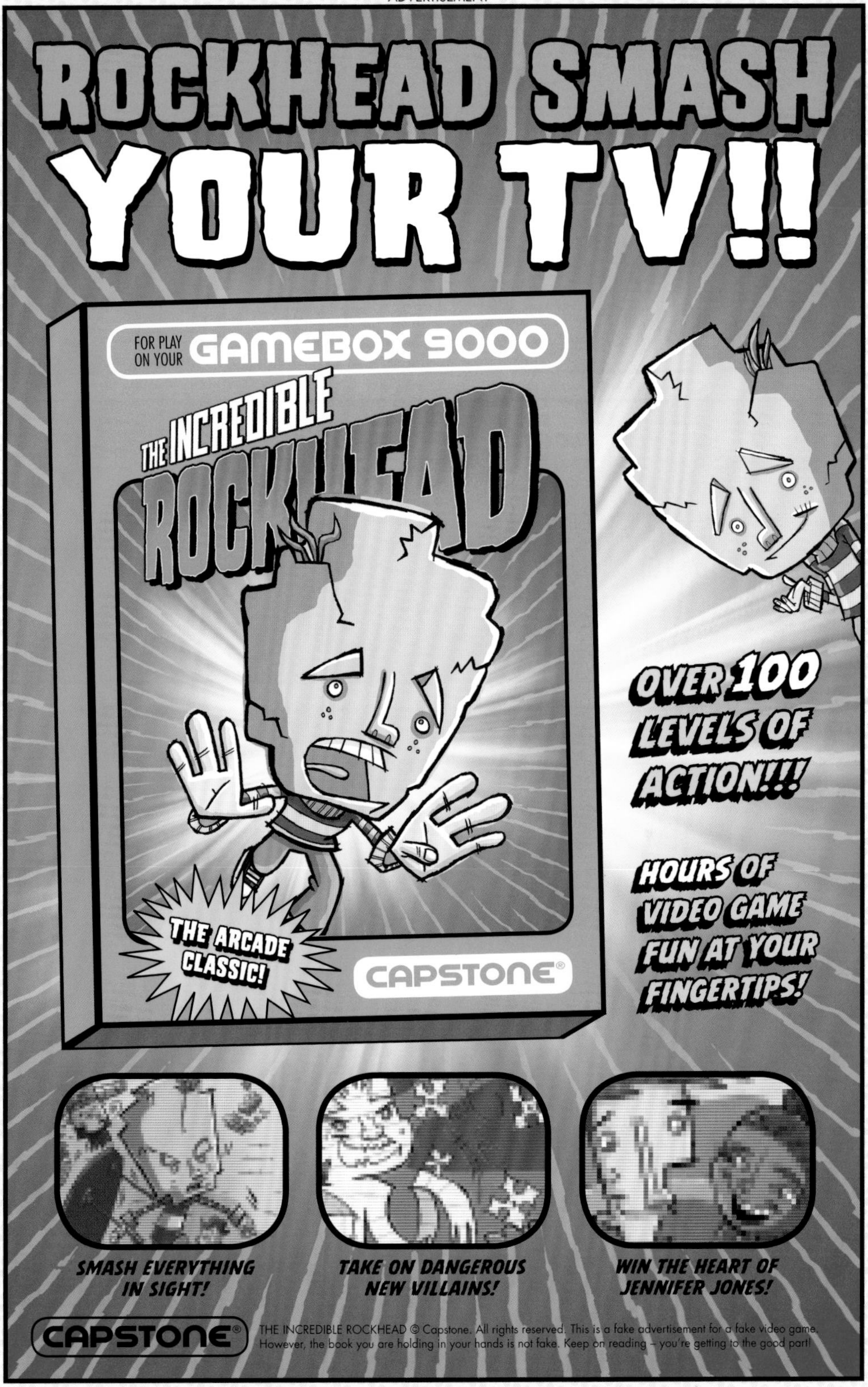
ROCKHEAD SMASH YOUR TV!!
FOR PLAY ON YOUR GAMEBOX 9000
THE INCREDIBLE ROCKHEAD
THE ARCADE CLASSIC!
CAPSTONE®
OVER 100 LEVELS OF ACTION!!!
HOURS OF VIDEO GAME FUN AT YOUR FINGERTIPS!
SMASH EVERYTHING IN SIGHT!
TAKE ON DANGEROUS NEW VILLAINS!
WIN THE HEART OF JENNIFER JONES!
CAPSTONE®
THE INCREDIBLE ROCKHEAD © Capstone. All rights reserved. This is a fake advertisement for a fake video game. However, the book you are holding in your hands is not fake. Keep on reading – you're getting to the good part!

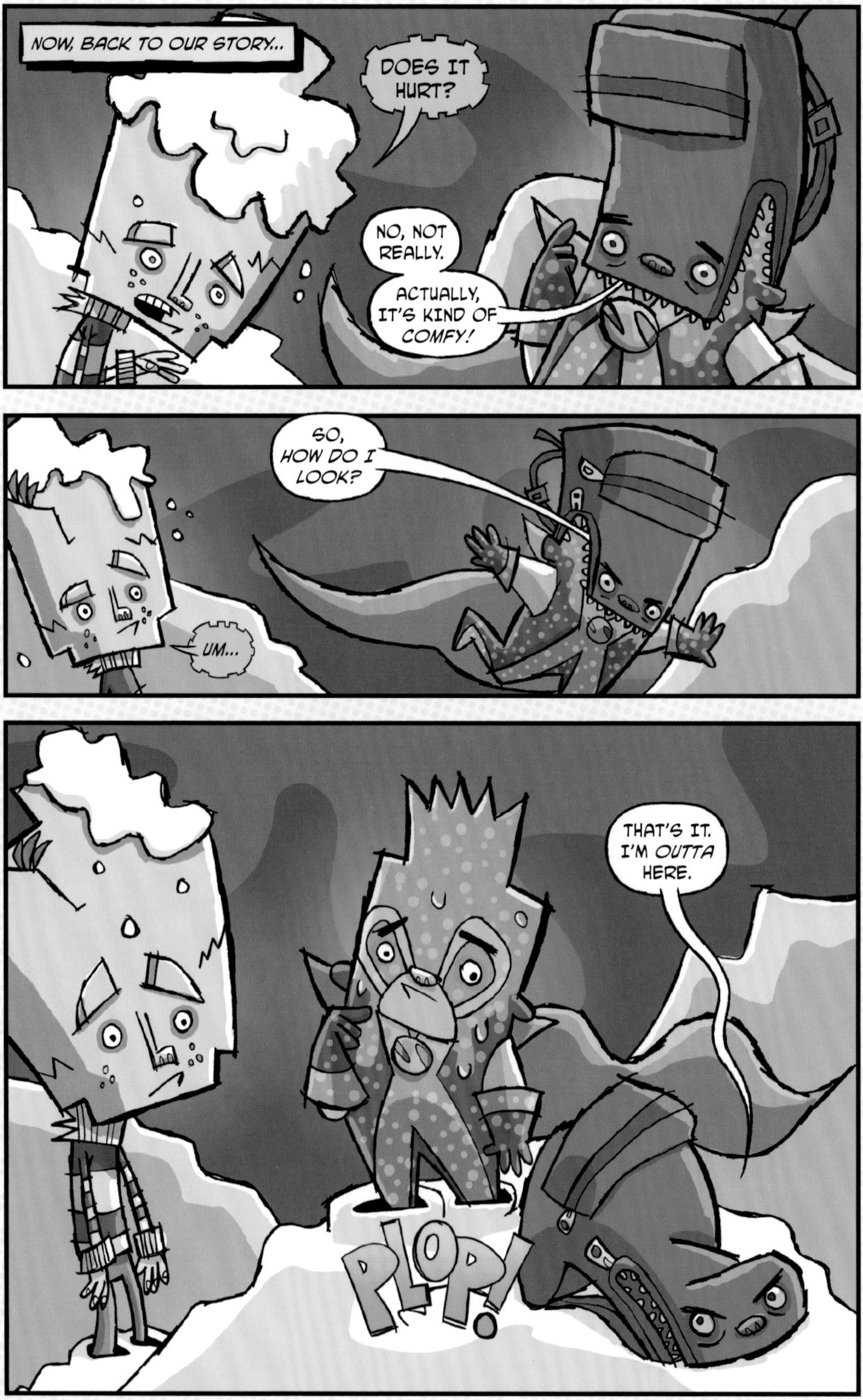
NOW, BACK TO OUR STORY...
DOES IT HURT?
NO, NOT REALLY.
ACTUALLY, IT'S KIND OF COMFY!
SO, HOW DO I LOOK?
UM...
THAT'S IT. I'M OUTTA HERE.
PLOP!

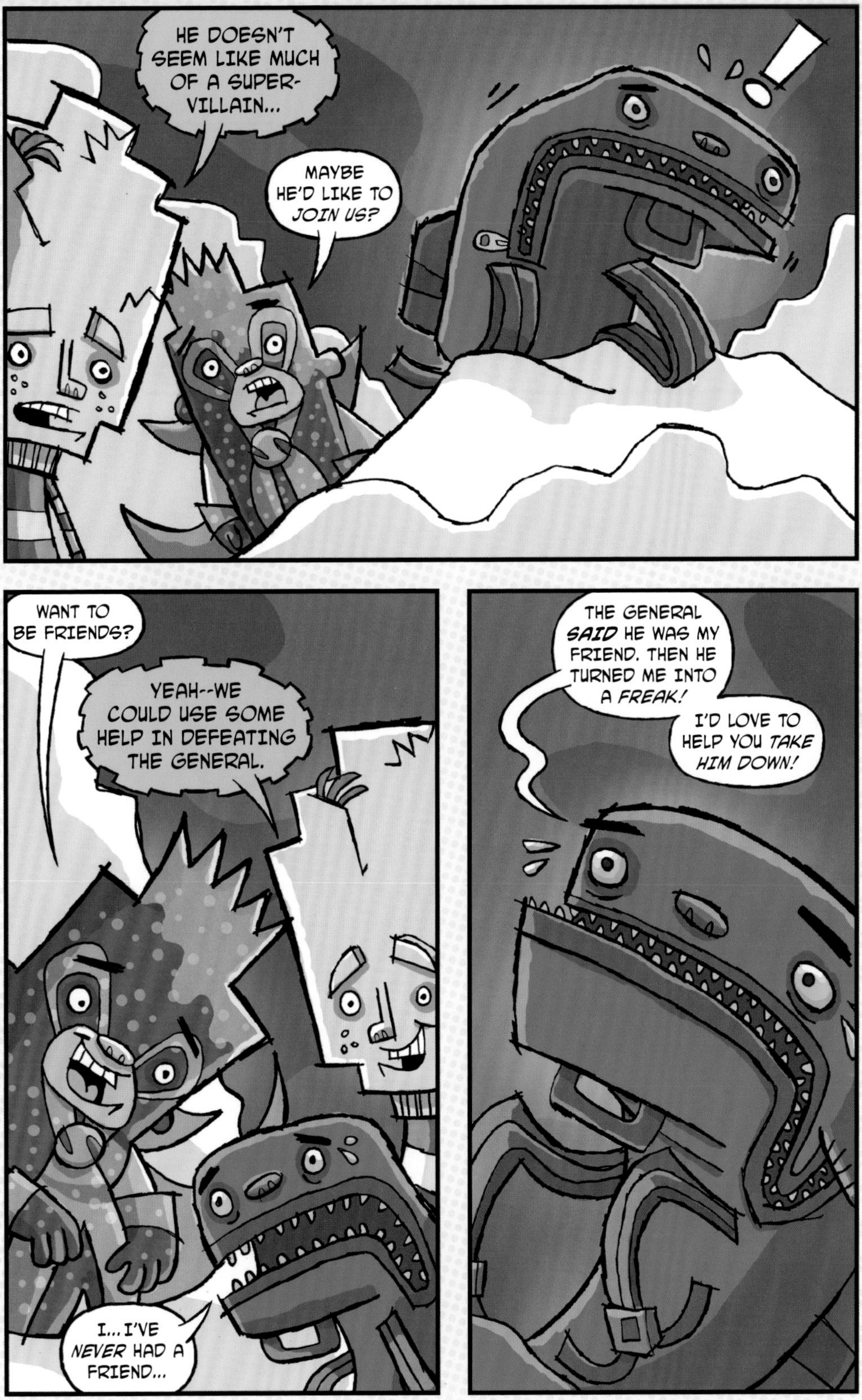
HE DOESN'T SEEM LIKE MUCH OF A SUPER-VILLAIN...
MAYBE HE'D LIKE TO *JOIN US?*
WANT TO BE FRIENDS?
YEAH--WE COULD USE SOME HELP IN DEFEATING THE GENERAL.
I...I'VE *NEVER* HAD A FRIEND...
THE GENERAL ***SAID*** HE WAS MY FRIEND. THEN HE TURNED ME INTO A *FREAK!*
I'D LOVE TO HELP YOU *TAKE HIM DOWN!*

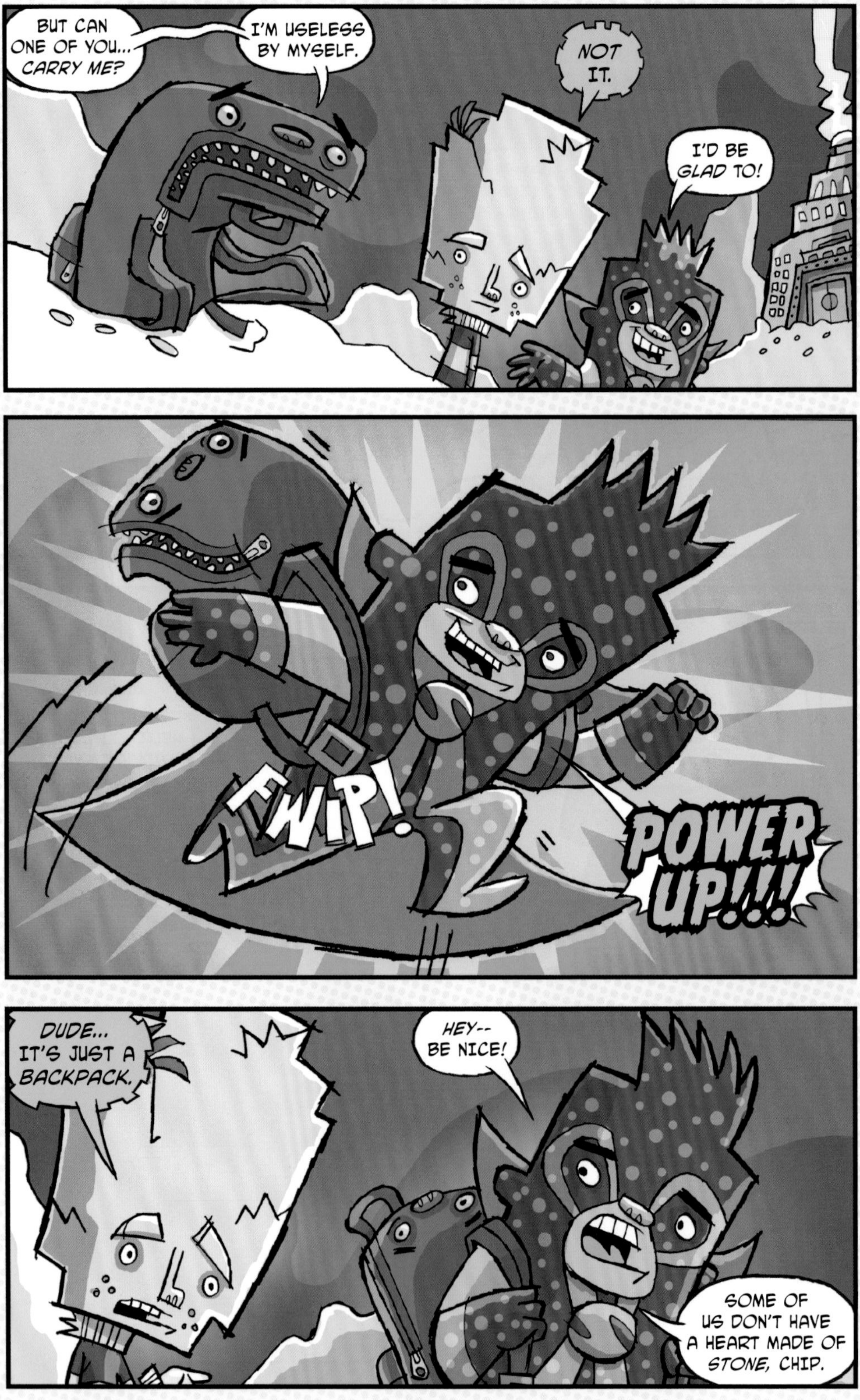
BUT CAN ONE OF YOU... CARRY ME?
I'M USELESS BY MYSELF.
NOT IT.
I'D BE GLAD TO!
FWIP!
POWER UP!!!
DUDE... IT'S JUST A BACKPACK.
HEY-- BE NICE!
SOME OF US DON'T HAVE A HEART MADE OF STONE, CHIP.

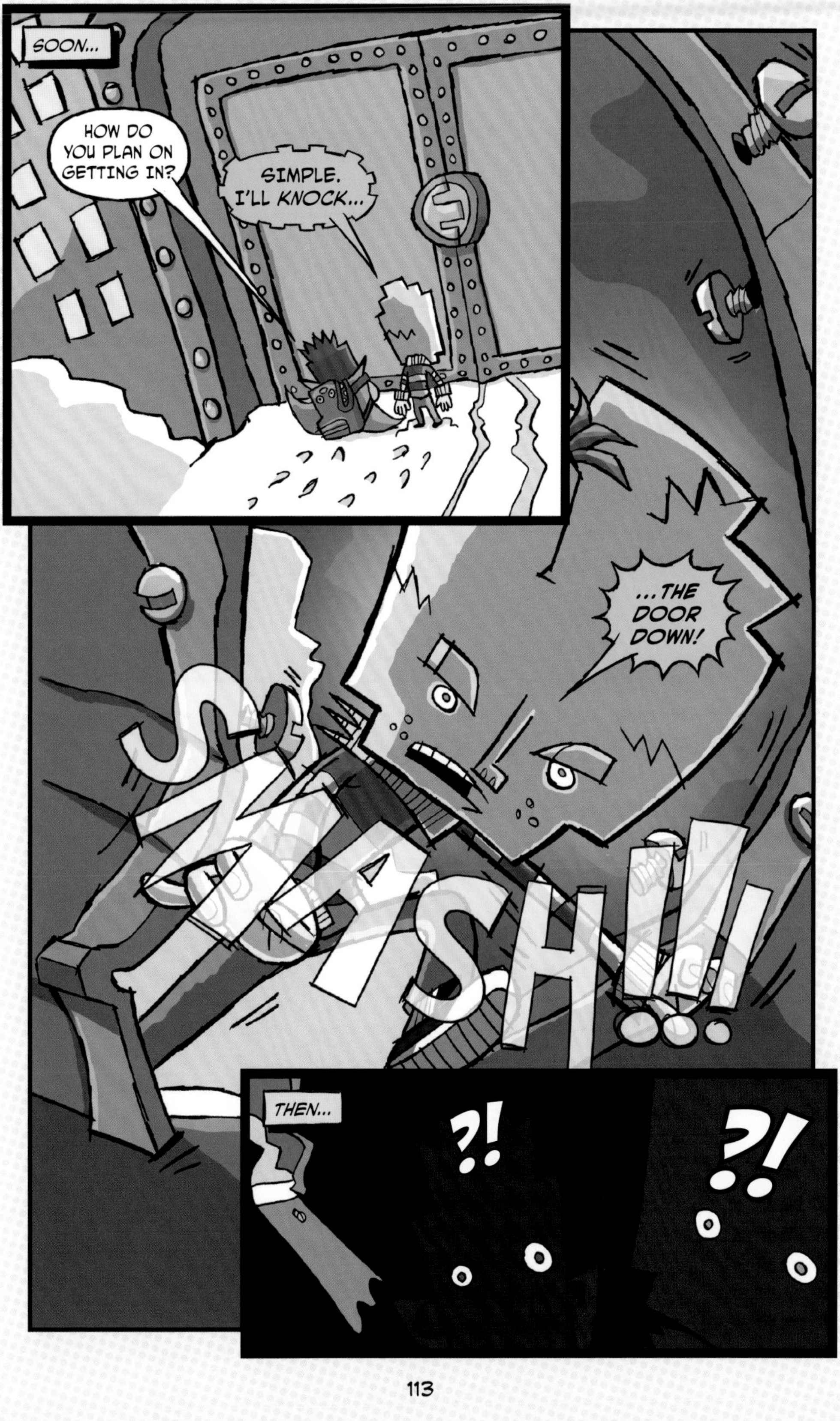
SOON...
HOW DO YOU PLAN ON GETTING IN?
SIMPLE. I'LL KNOCK...
...THE DOOR DOWN!
SMASH!!!
THEN...
?!
?!

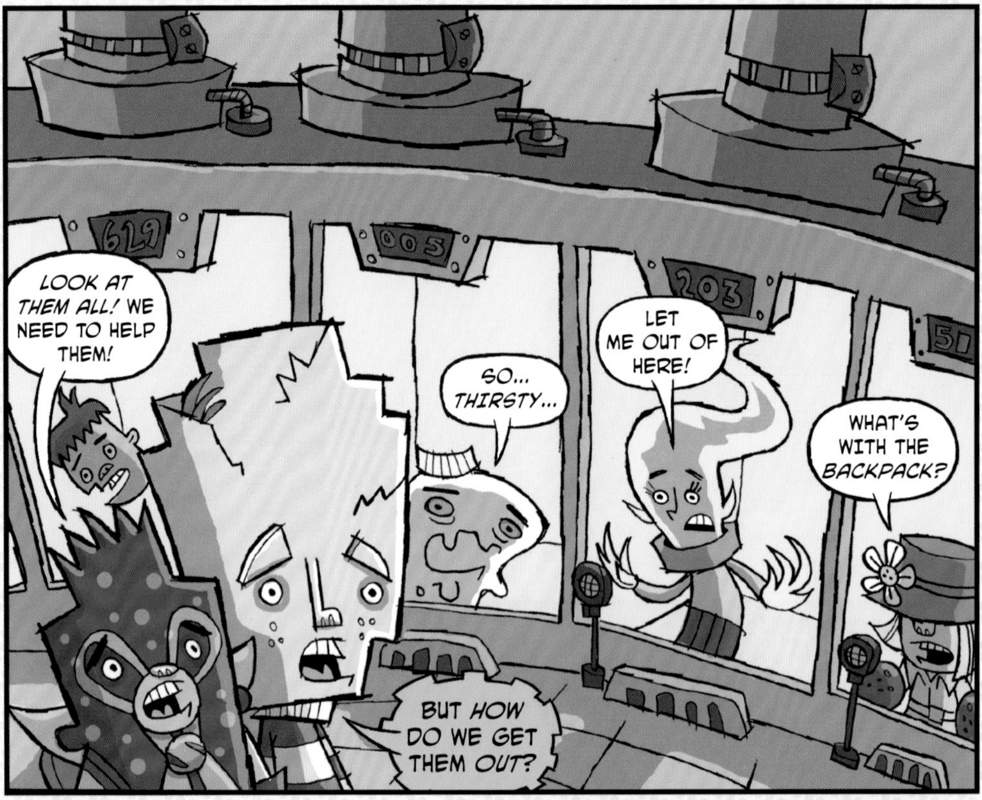
LOOK AT THEM ALL! WE NEED TO HELP THEM!
SO... THIRSTY...
LET ME OUT OF HERE!
WHAT'S WITH THE BACKPACK?
BUT HOW DO WE GET THEM OUT?

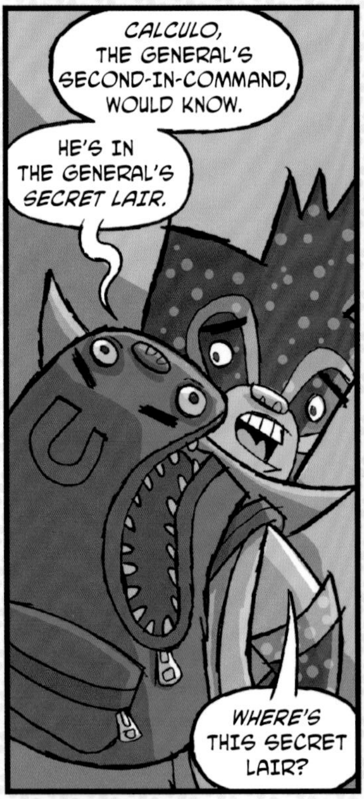
CALCULO, THE GENERAL'S SECOND-IN-COMMAND, WOULD KNOW.
HE'S IN THE GENERAL'S SECRET LAIR.
WHERE'S THIS SECRET LAIR?

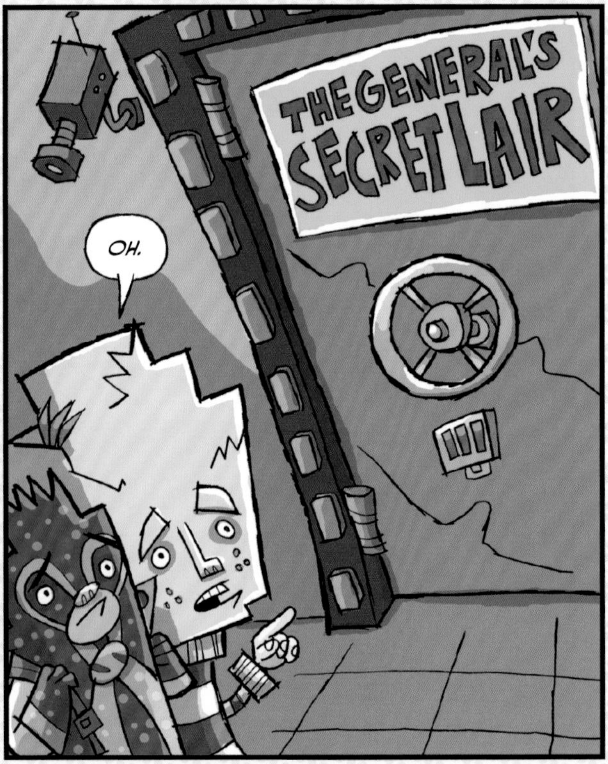
THE GENERAL'S SECRET LAIR
OH.

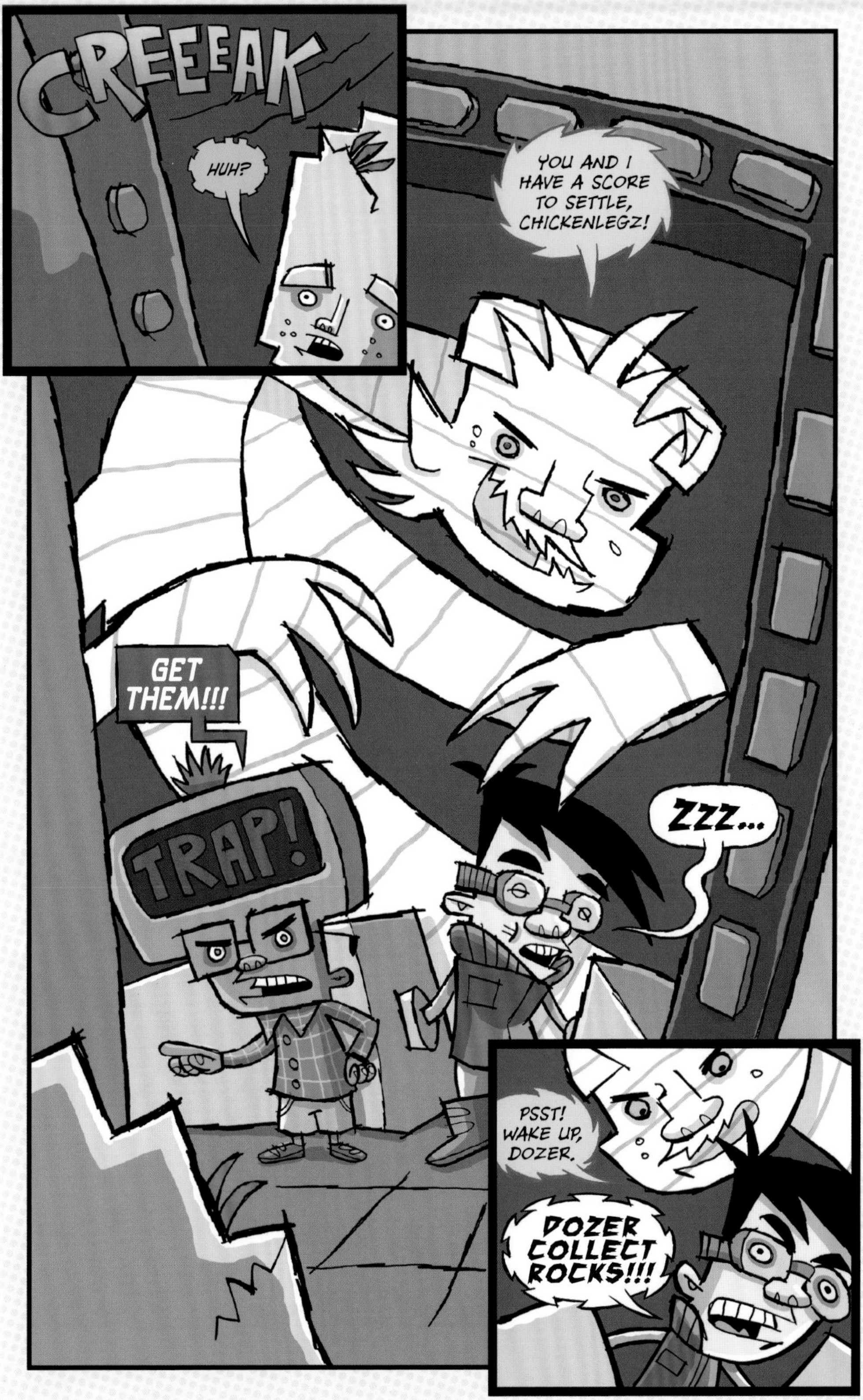
CREEEAK
HUH?
YOU AND I HAVE A SCORE TO SETTLE, CHICKENLEGZ!
GET THEM!!!
TRAP!
ZZZ...
PSST! WAKE UP, DOZER.
DOZER COLLECT ROCKS!!!

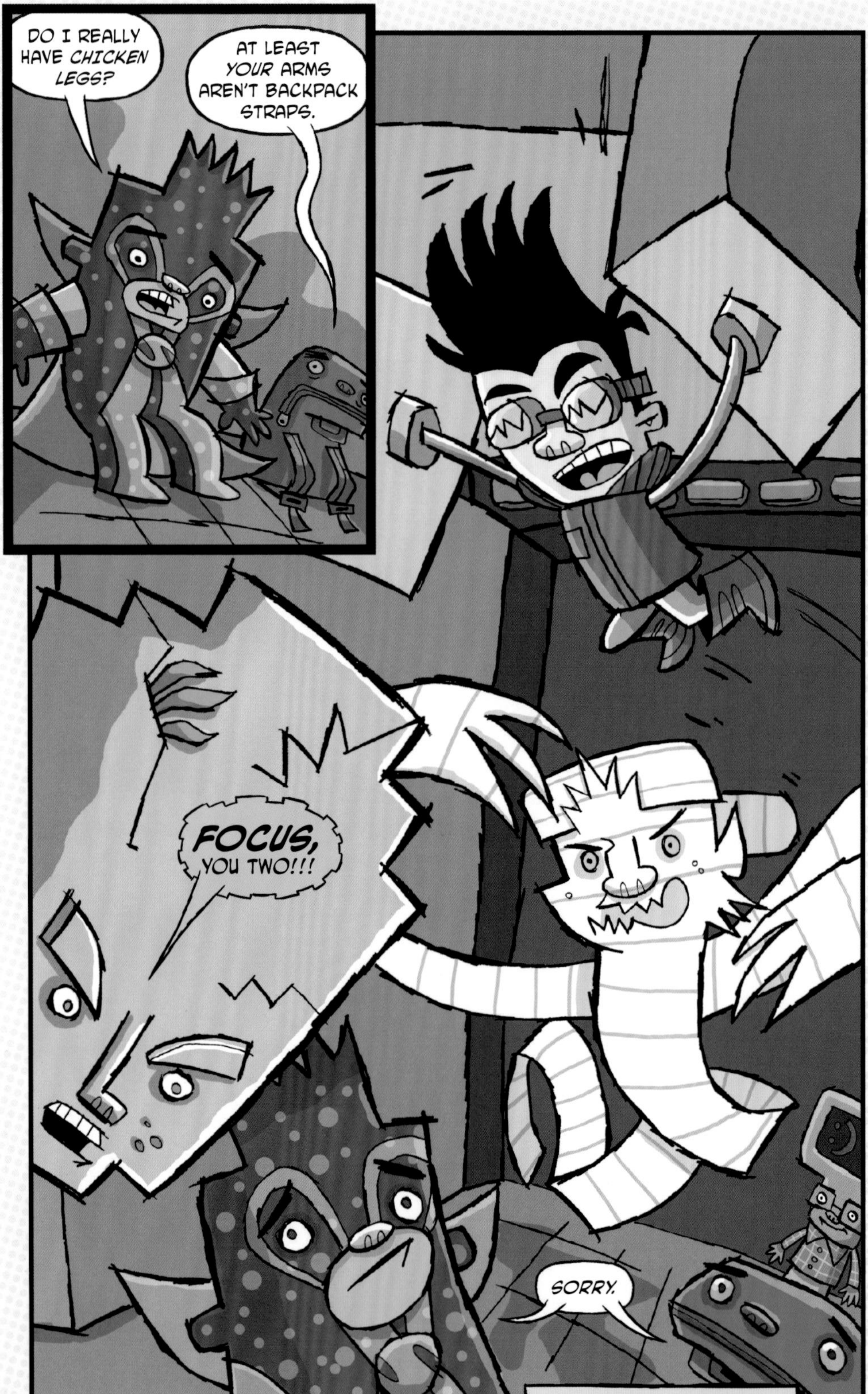
DO I REALLY HAVE *CHICKEN* LEGS?
AT LEAST *YOUR* ARMS AREN'T BACKPACK STRAPS.
FOCUS, YOU TWO!!!
SORRY.

CONTINUED ON PAGE 118...!

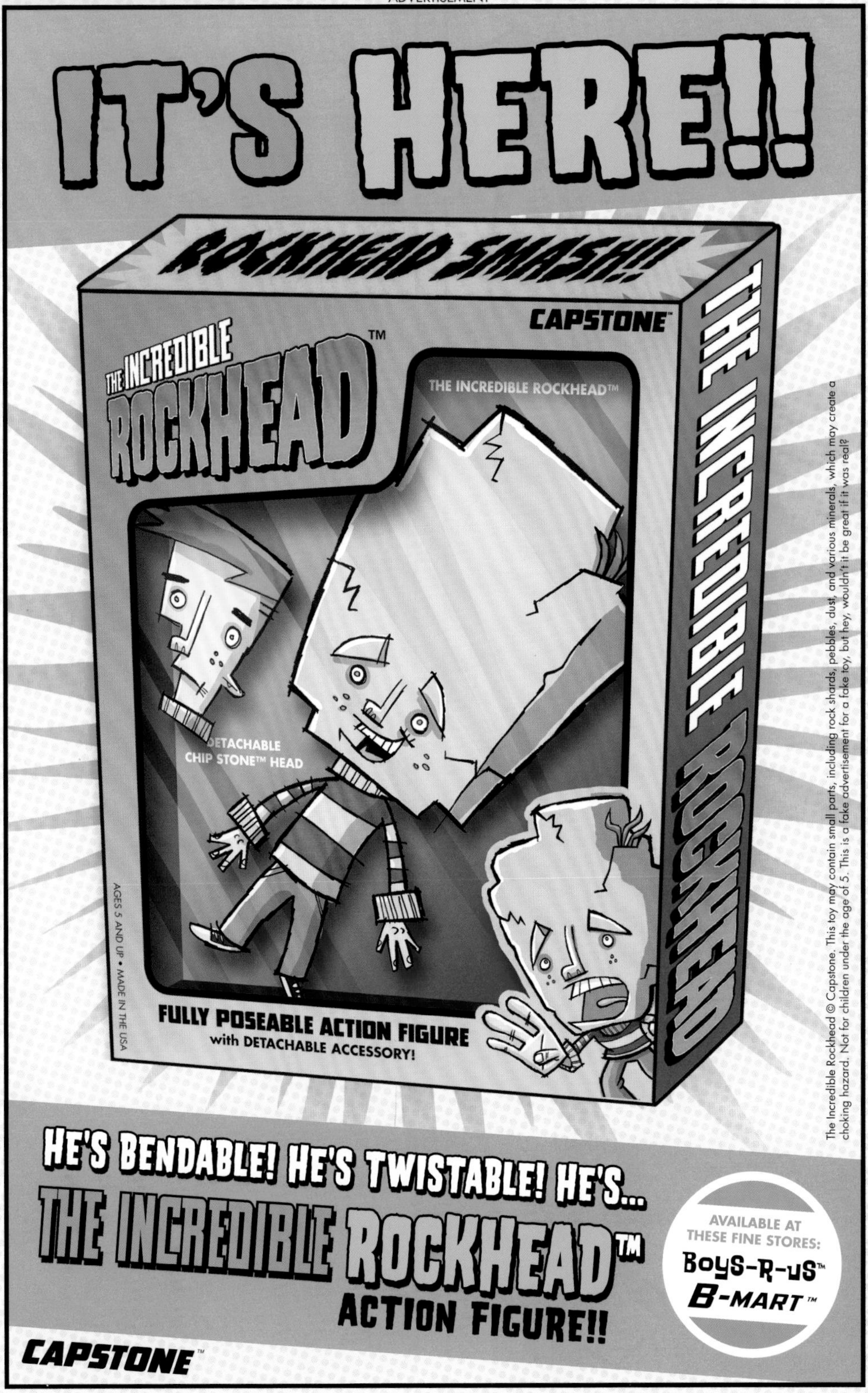
IT'S HERE!!
ROCKHEAD SMASH!!
CAPSTONE™
THE INCREDIBLE ROCKHEAD™
THE INCREDIBLE ROCKHEAD™
DETACHABLE CHIP STONE™ HEAD
AGES 5 AND UP • MADE IN THE USA
FULLY POSEABLE ACTION FIGURE with DETACHABLE ACCESSORY!
THE INCREDIBLE ROCKHEAD
The Incredible Rockhead © Capstone. This toy may contain small parts, including rock shards, pebbles, dust, and various minerals, which may create a choking hazard. Not for children under the age of 5. This is a fake advertisement for a fake toy, but hey, wouldn't it be great if it was real?
HE'S BENDABLE! HE'S TWISTABLE! HE'S...
THE INCREDIBLE ROCKHEAD™ ACTION FIGURE!!
AVAILABLE AT THESE FINE STORES:
Boys-R-uS™
B-MART™
CAPSTONE™

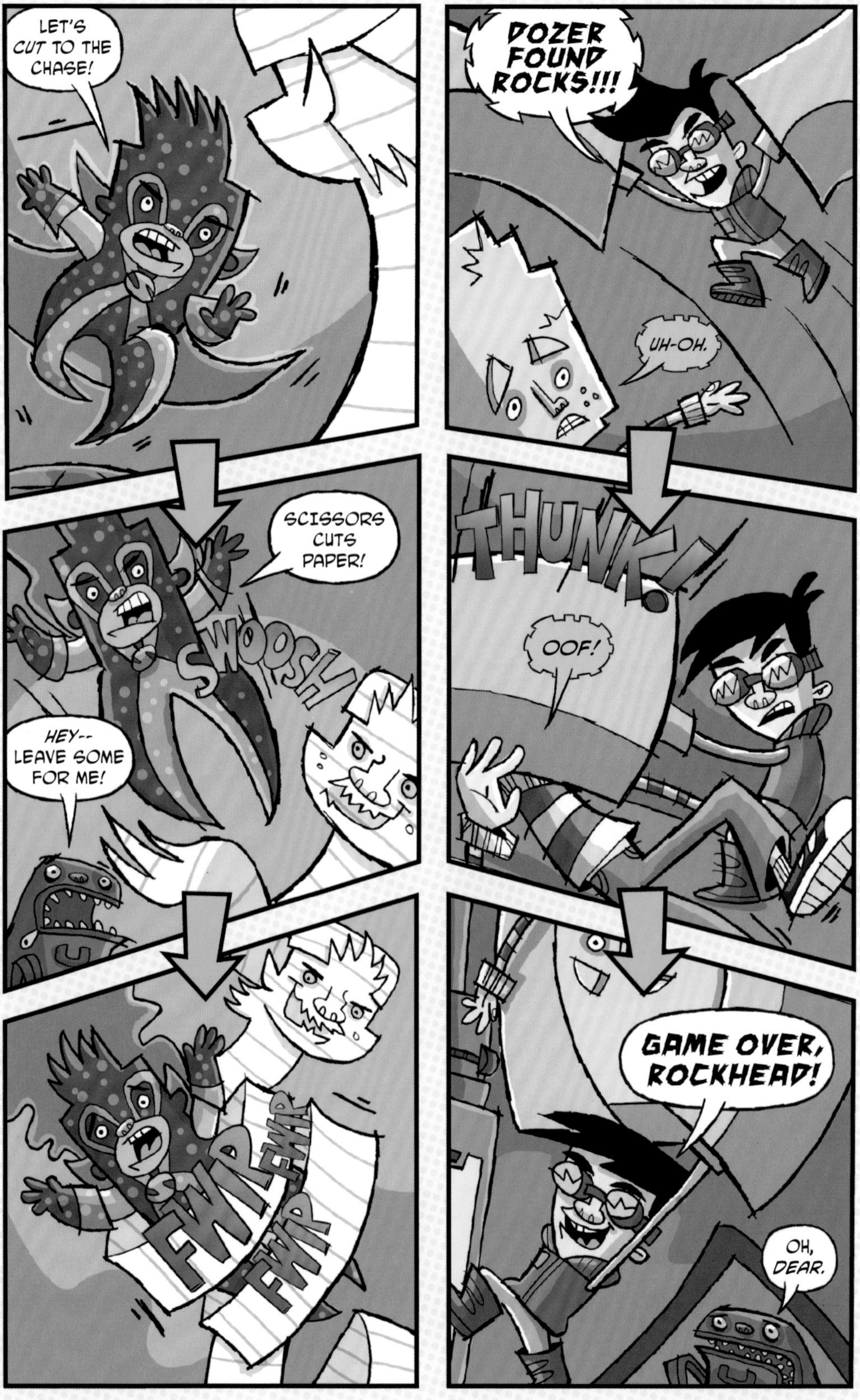
LET'S CUT TO THE CHASE!
SCISSORS CUTS PAPER!
SWOOSH!
HEY-- LEAVE SOME FOR ME!
FWIP
FWIP
FWIP
DOZER FOUND ROCKS!!!
UH-OH.
THUNK!
OOF!
GAME OVER, ROCKHEAD!
OH, DEAR.

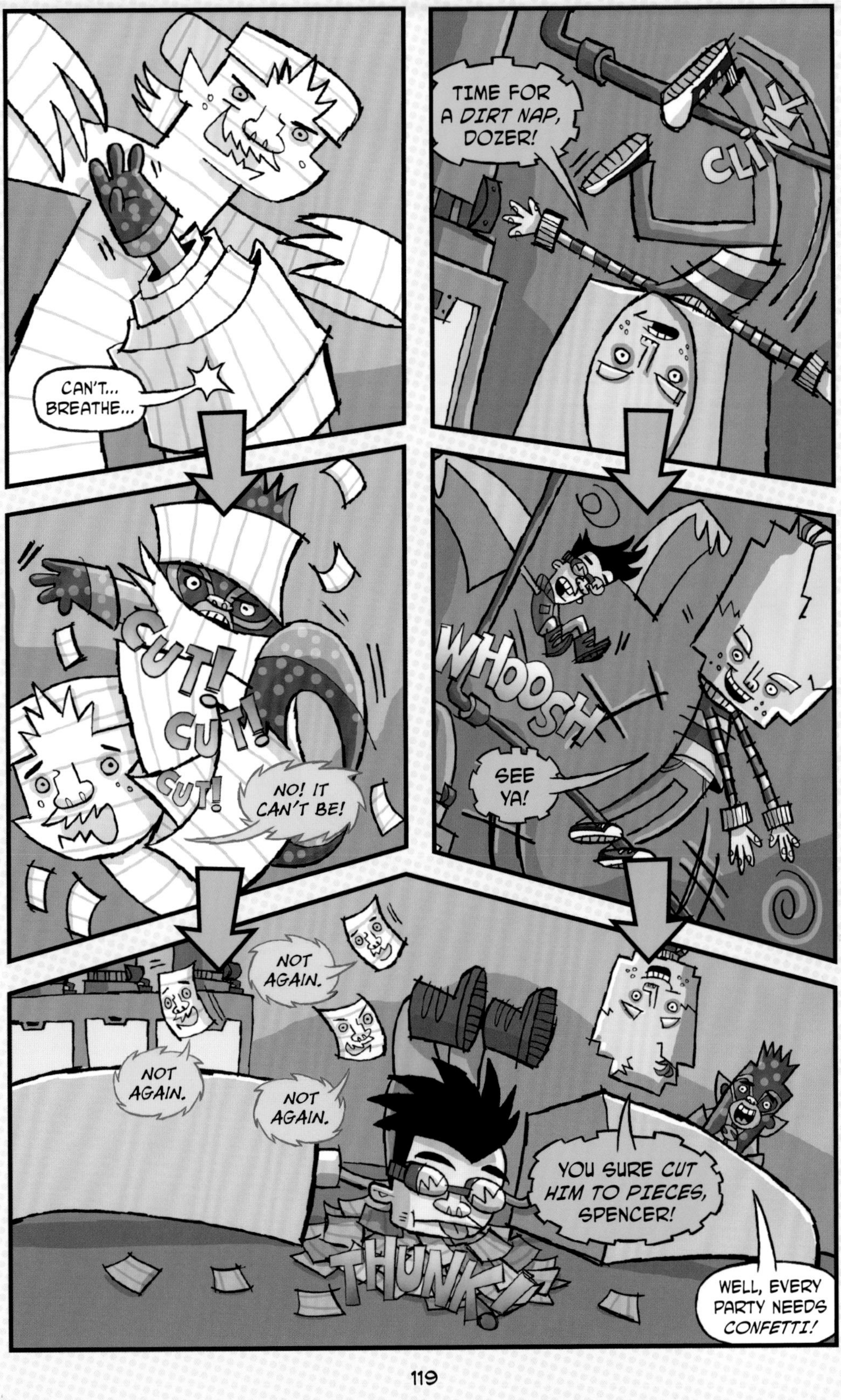
CAN'T... BREATHE...
TIME FOR A DIRT NAP, DOZER!
CLINK
CUT!
CUT!
CUT!
NO! IT CAN'T BE!
WHOOSH
SEE YA!
NOT AGAIN.
NOT AGAIN.
NOT AGAIN.
THUNK!
YOU SURE CUT HIM TO PIECES, SPENCER!
WELL, EVERY PARTY NEEDS CONFETTI!

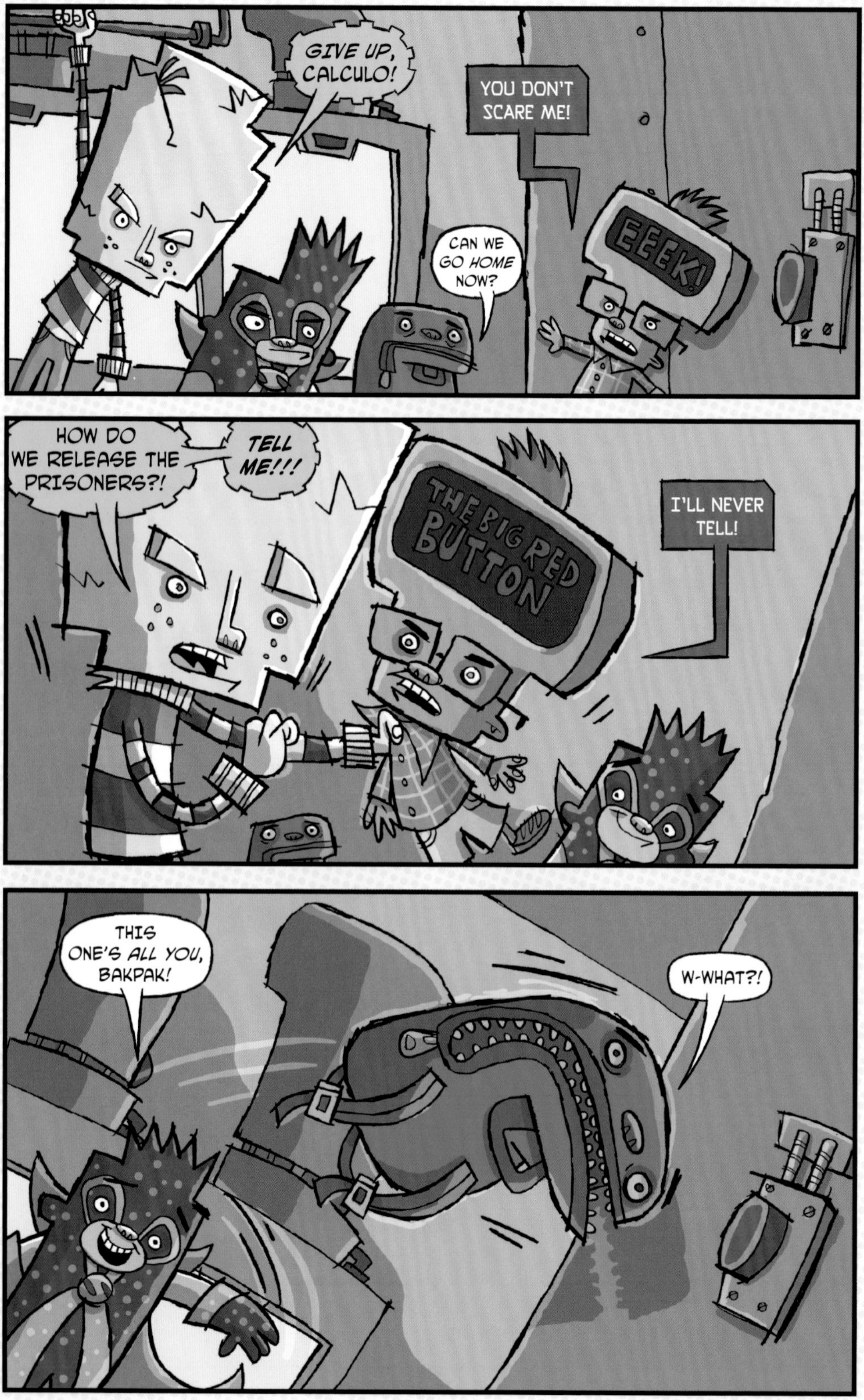
GIVE UP, CALCULO!
YOU DON'T SCARE ME!
CAN WE GO HOME NOW?
EEEK!
HOW DO WE RELEASE THE PRISONERS?!
TELL ME!!!
THE BIG RED BUTTON
I'LL NEVER TELL!
THIS ONE'S ALL YOU, BAKPAK!
W-WHAT?!

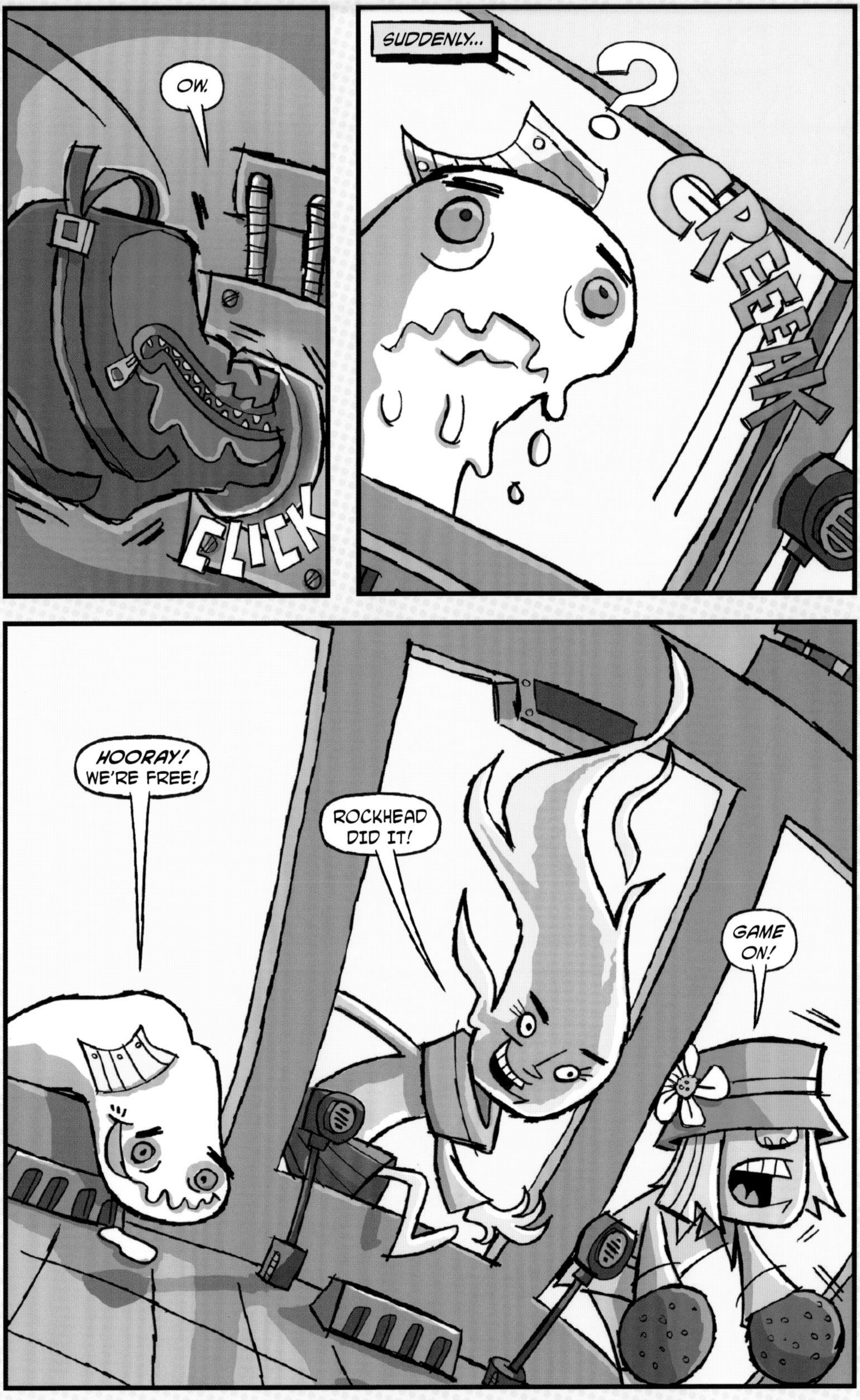
OW.
CLICK
SUDDENLY...
?
CREEEAK
HOORAY! WE'RE FREE!
ROCKHEAD DID IT!
GAME ON!

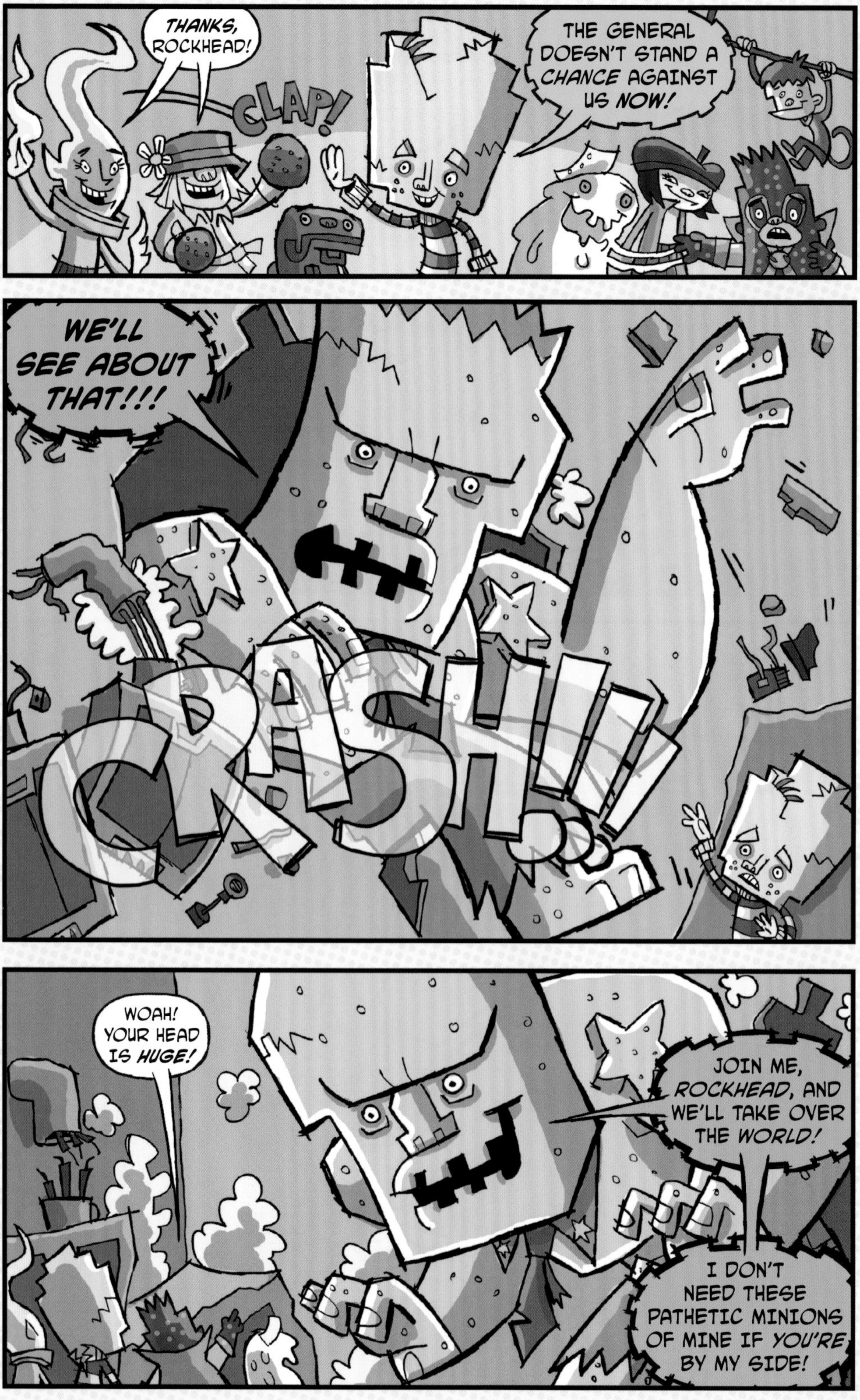
THANKS, ROCKHEAD!
CLAP!
THE GENERAL DOESN'T STAND A *CHANCE* AGAINST US *NOW!*
WE'LL SEE ABOUT THAT!!!
CRASH!!!
WOAH! YOUR HEAD IS *HUGE!*
JOIN ME, *ROCKHEAD*, AND WE'LL TAKE OVER THE *WORLD!*
I DON'T NEED THESE PATHETIC MINIONS OF MINE IF *YOU'RE* BY MY SIDE!

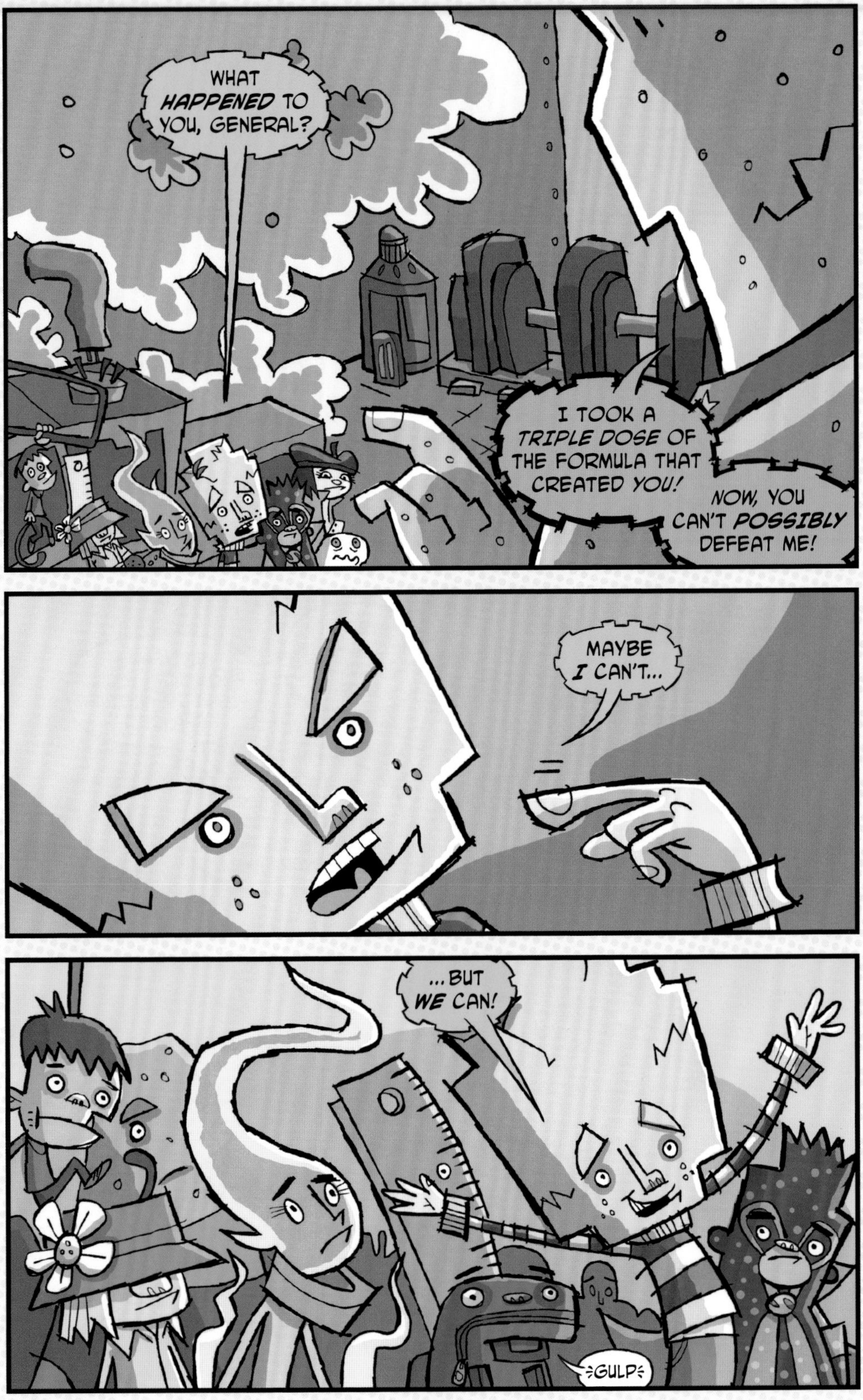
WHAT HAPPENED TO YOU, GENERAL?
I TOOK A TRIPLE DOSE OF THE FORMULA THAT CREATED YOU!
NOW, YOU CAN'T POSSIBLY DEFEAT ME!
MAYBE I CAN'T...
...BUT WE CAN!
GULP

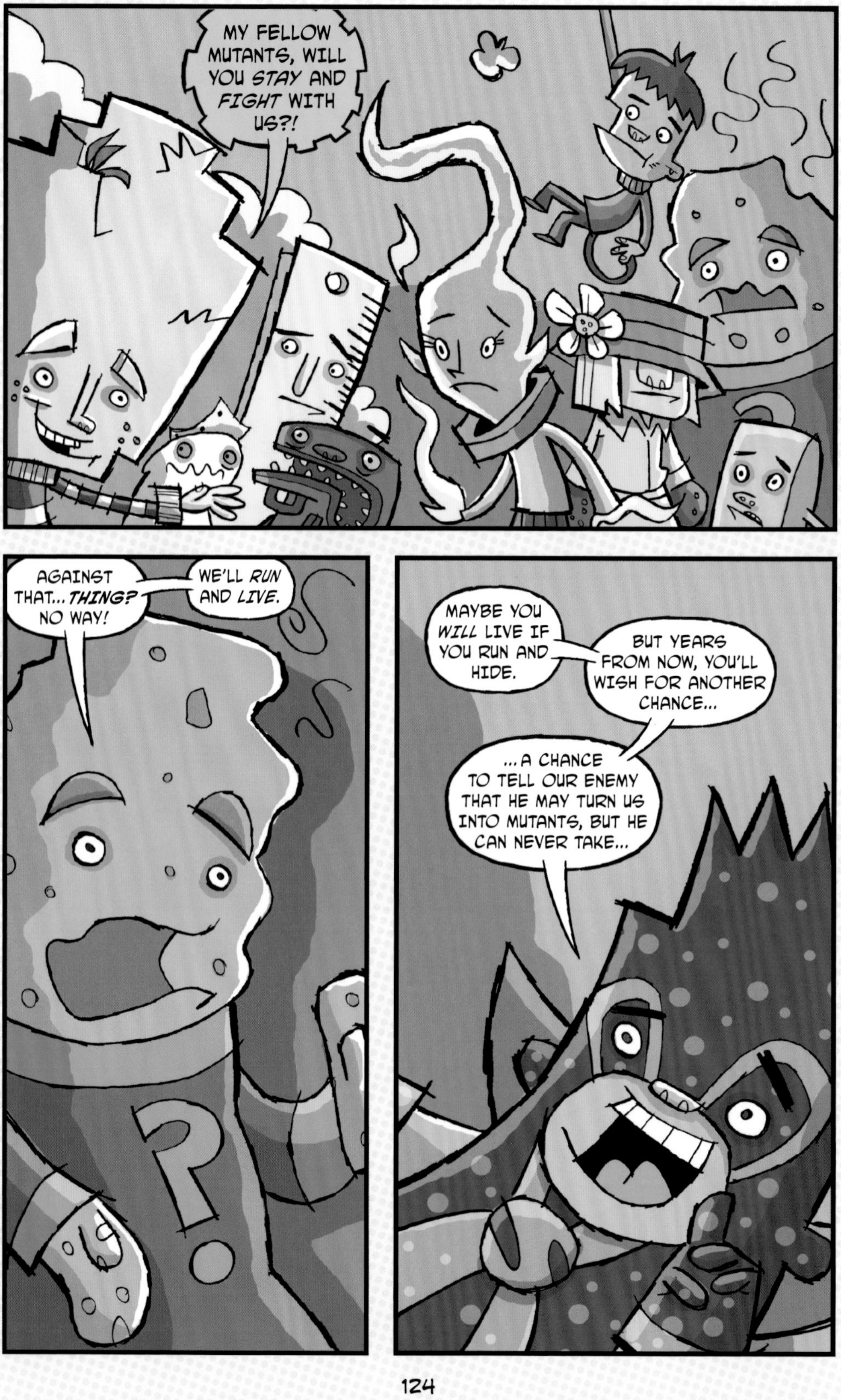
MY FELLOW MUTANTS, WILL YOU *STAY* AND *FIGHT* WITH US?!
AGAINST THAT... *THING?* NO WAY!
WE'LL *RUN* AND *LIVE*.
MAYBE YOU *WILL* LIVE IF YOU RUN AND HIDE.
BUT YEARS FROM NOW, YOU'LL WISH FOR ANOTHER CHANCE...
...A CHANCE TO TELL OUR ENEMY THAT HE MAY TURN US INTO MUTANTS, BUT HE CAN NEVER TAKE...

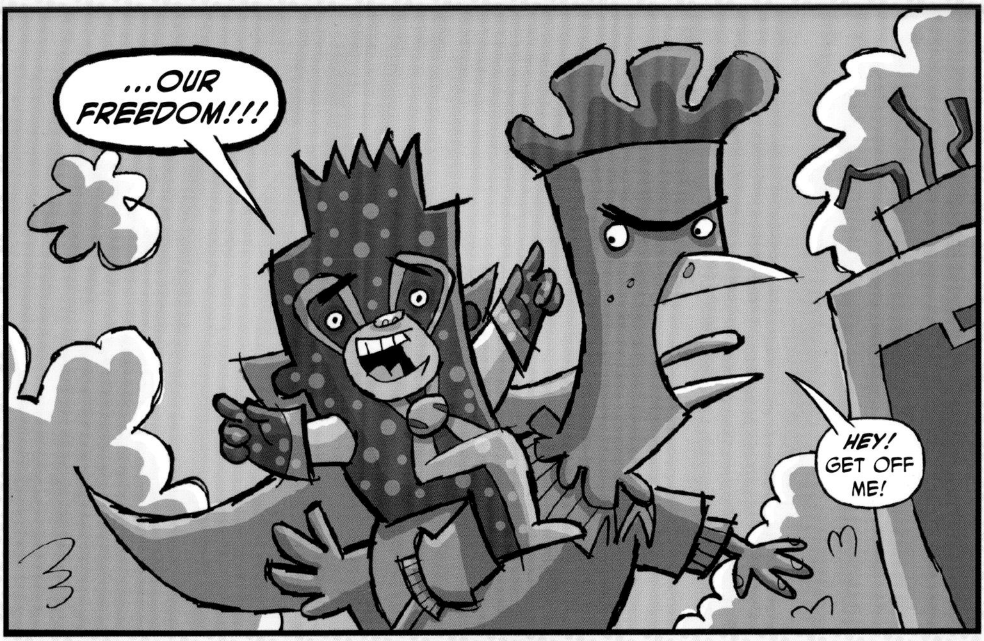
...OUR FREEDOM!!!
HEY! GET OFF ME!

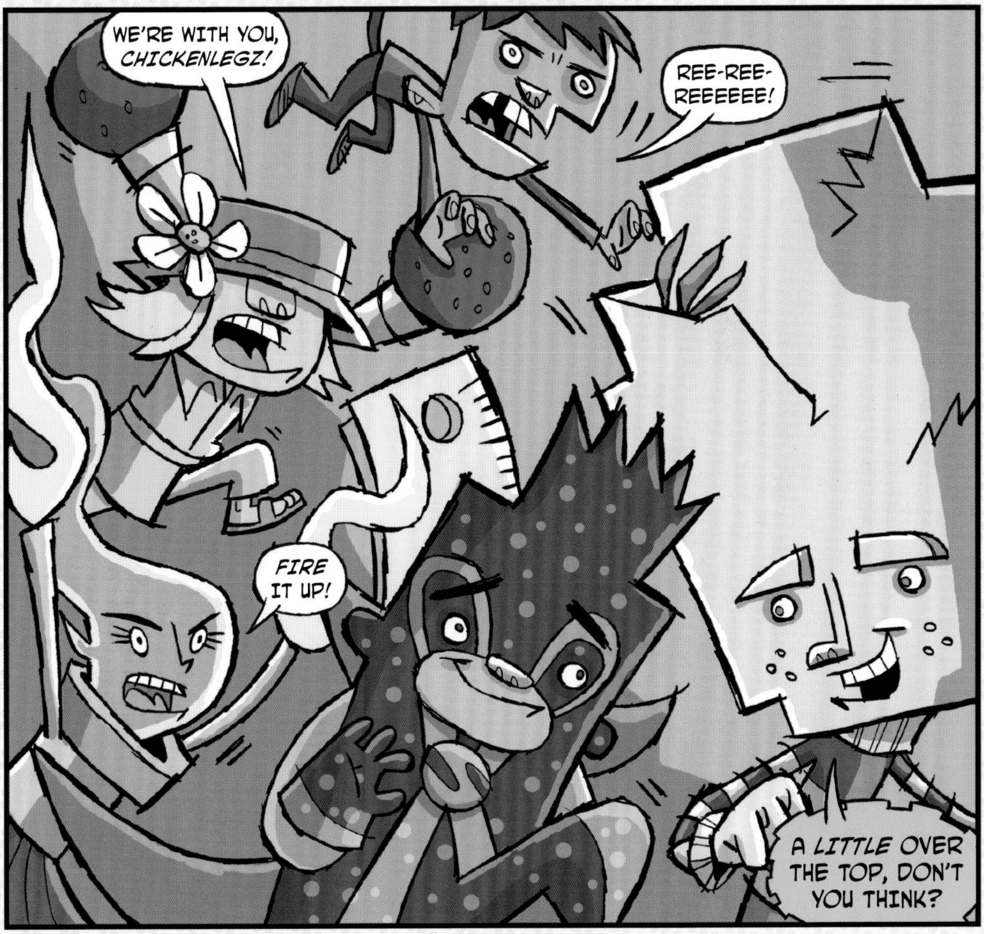
WE'RE WITH YOU, CHICKENLEGZ!
REE-REE-REEEEEEE!
FIRE IT UP!
A LITTLE OVER THE TOP, DON'T YOU THINK?

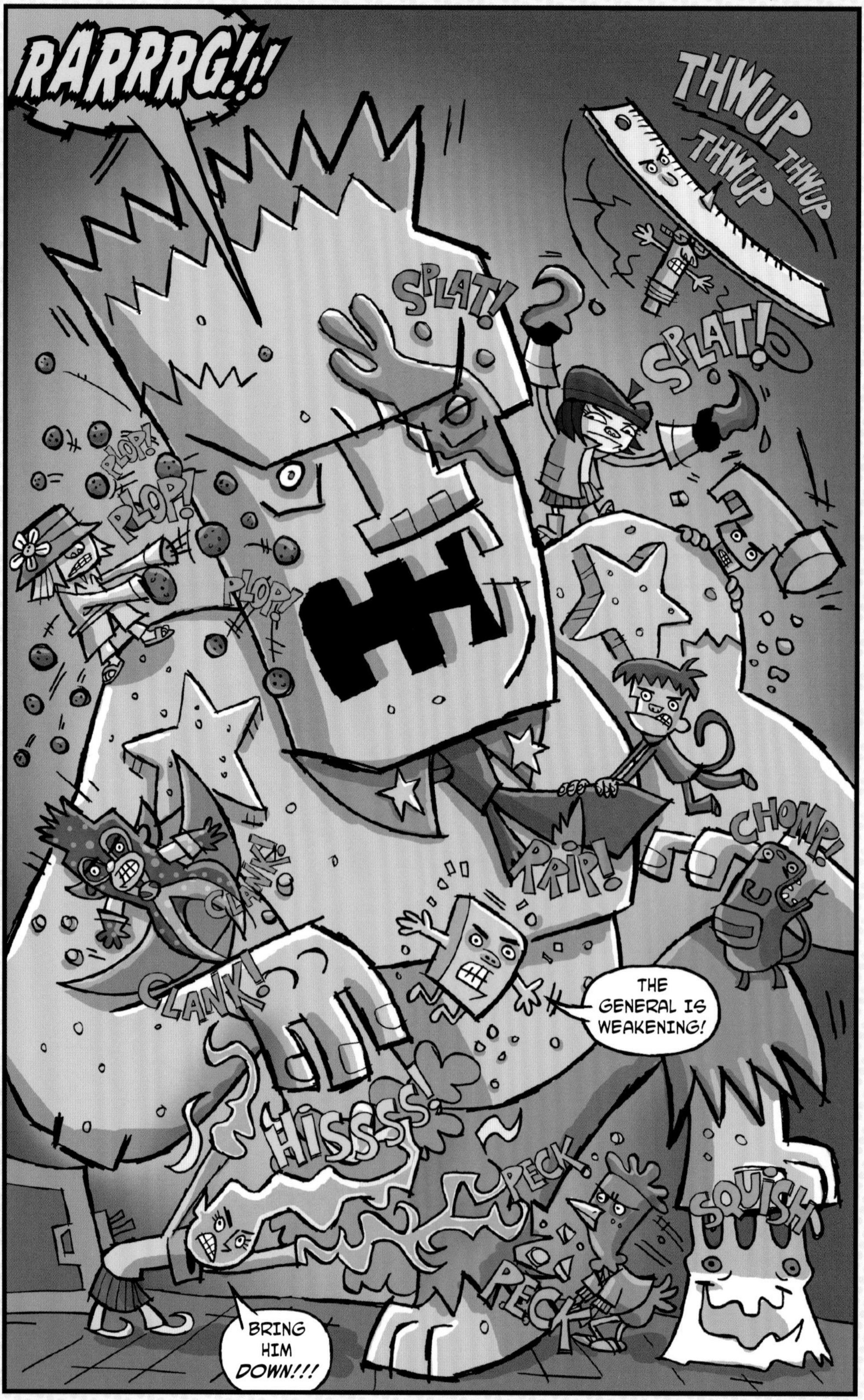
RARRRG!!!
THWUP THWUP THWUP
SPLAT!
SPLAT!
PLOP!
PLOP!
PLOP!
CLANK!
RRIP!
CHOMP!
CLANK!
THE GENERAL IS WEAKENING!
HISSSSS!
PECK
PECK
SQUISH
BRING HIM DOWN!!!

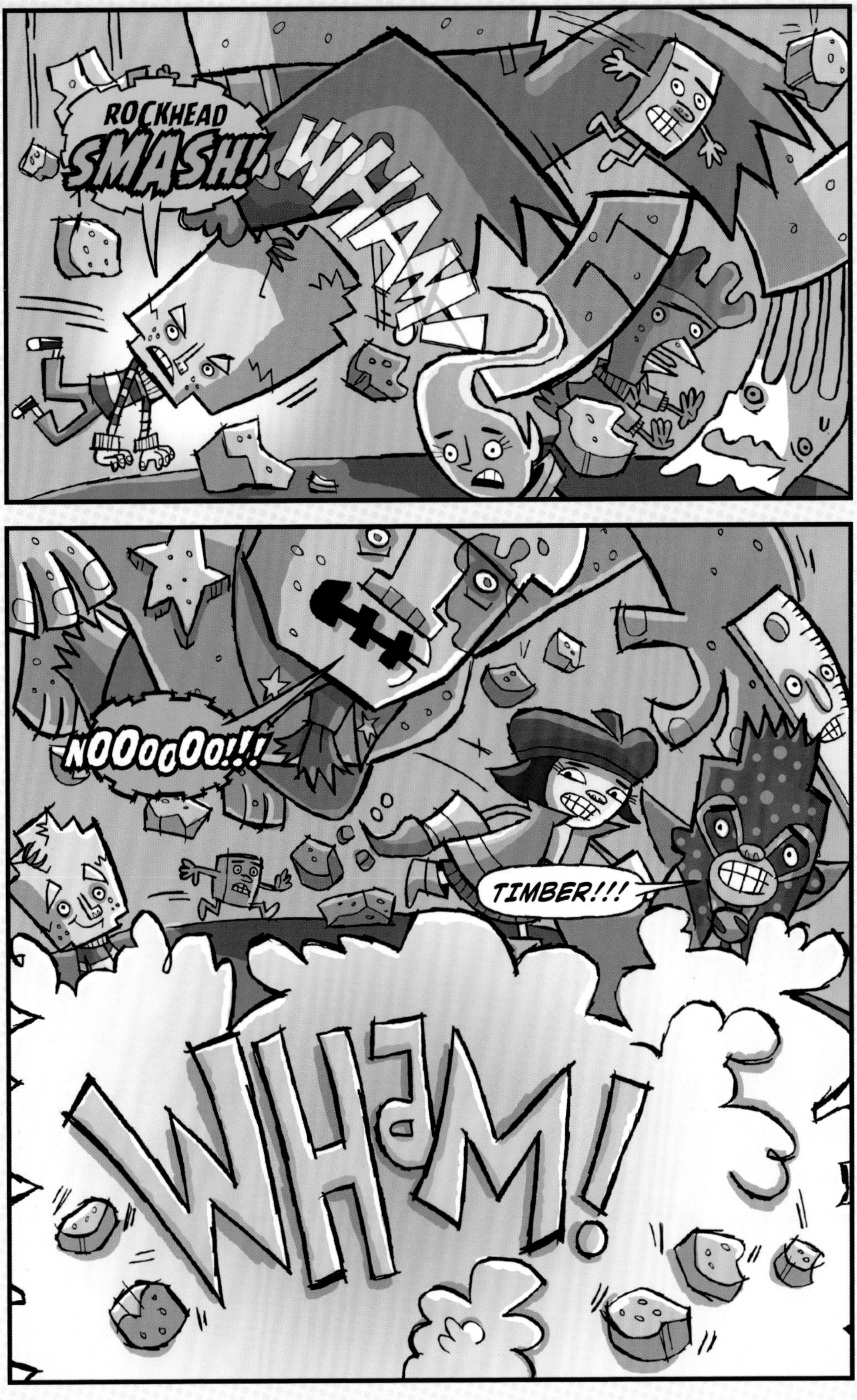
ROCKHEAD SMASH!
WHAM!
NOOOoOO!!!
TIMBER!!!
WHAM!

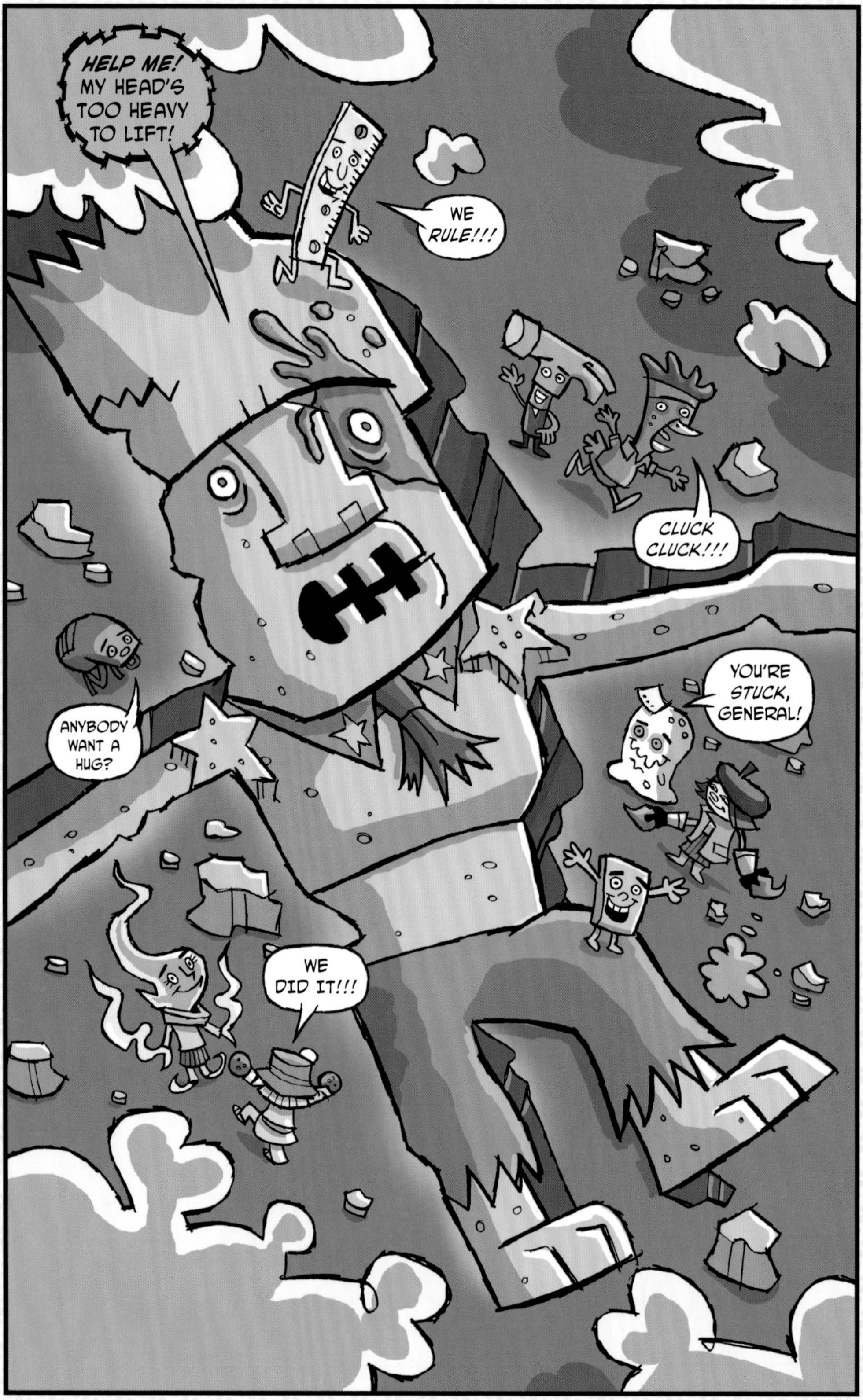
HELP ME! MY HEAD'S TOO HEAVY TO LIFT!
WE RULE!!!
CLUCK CLUCK!!!
ANYBODY WANT A HUG?
YOU'RE STUCK, GENERAL!
WE DID IT!!!

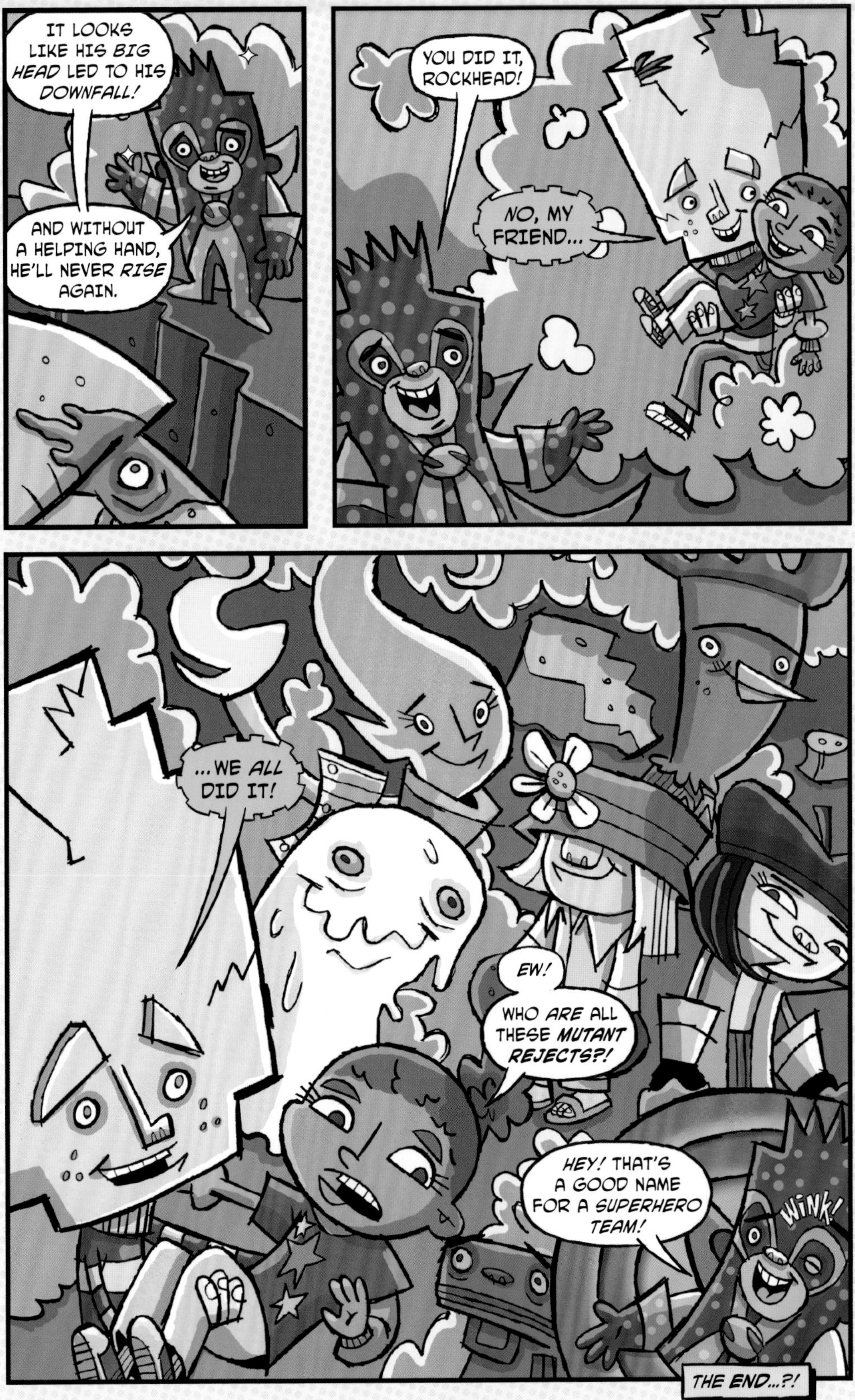
IT LOOKS LIKE HIS BIG HEAD LED TO HIS DOWNFALL!
AND WITHOUT A HELPING HAND, HE'LL NEVER RISE AGAIN.
YOU DID IT, ROCKHEAD!
NO, MY FRIEND...
...WE ALL DID IT!
EW!
WHO ARE ALL THESE MUTANT REJECTS?!
HEY! THAT'S A GOOD NAME FOR A SUPERHERO TEAM!
WINK!
THE END...?!

Banner

BANNER ELEMENTARY - BOULDER, COLORADO · FIRST EDITION

REJECTED!

MUTANTS DEFEAT EVIL GENERAL

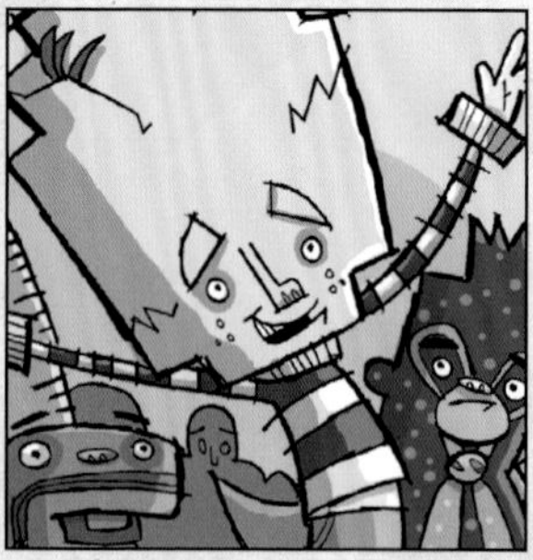
The Rockhead

by Ivana Scoop

More than a dozen missing Boulder children returned home yesterday after defeating their captor, known only as "The General". Although mutated, the children were otherwise unharmed in what appears to be a military experiment gone awry. Still, the experience took an emotional toll on some. "I just want to erase the recent events from my memory," said one victim, who now resembles a rubbery, pink eraser. Others united through the incident. "The Incredible Rockhead gave me newfound strength," stated a boy with the body of a backpack. "I'll always have that kid's back!" Rockhead was humbled by the praise. And, although the stone-faced leader wouldn't confirm rumors of a new superhero team called the Mutant Rejects, he promised to never again be "taken for granite."

THE MUTANT REJECTS

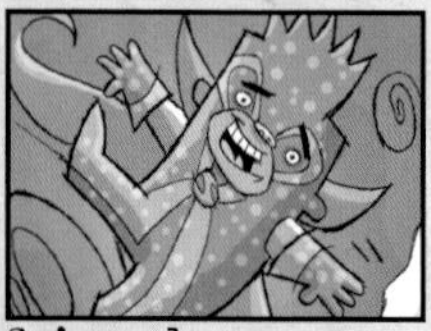
Scissorlegz

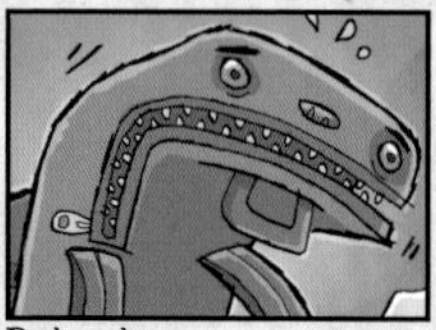
Bakpak

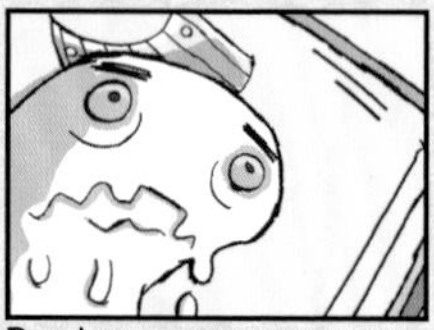
Paste

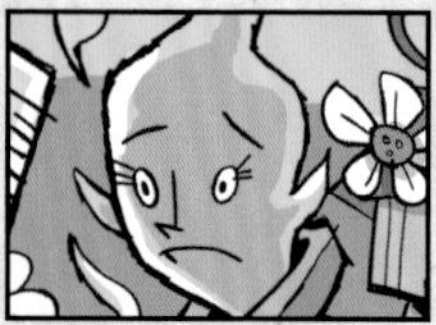
B. Unsen Burner

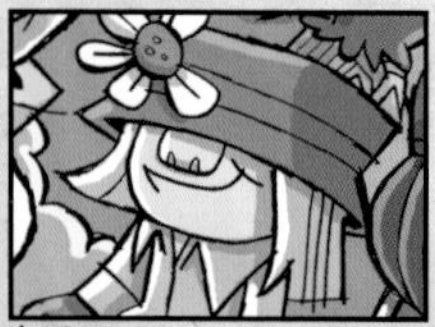
4-Square

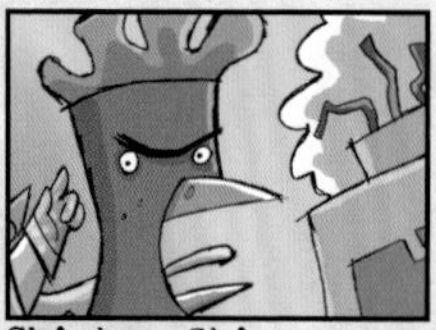
Chicken Skin

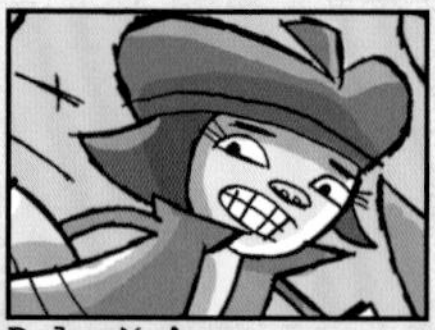
Poly Muir

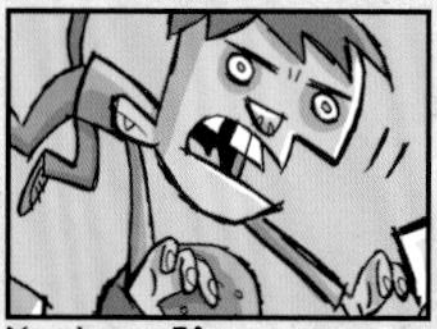
Monkey Jim

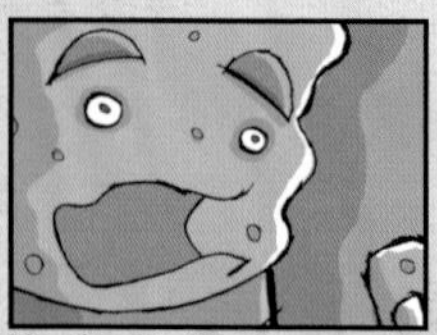
Mystery Meat

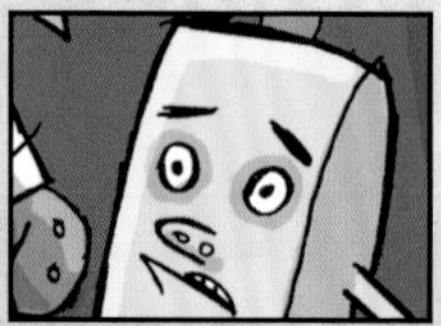
Eraserhead

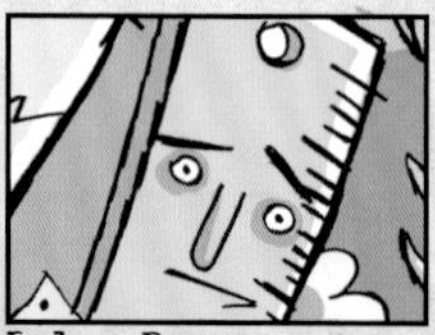
Ruler Boy

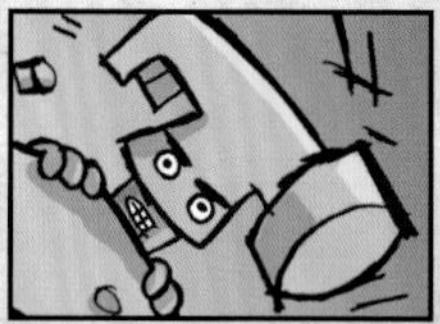
Hammertime

Tribune

THE NATION'S #2 SCHOOL NEWSPAPER

EVIL GENERAL OR MAJOR JERK?

by Cliff Hanger

One day after injecting himself with a self-made mutant toxin, The General, as he refers to himself, is recovering at a local hospital. Although the military refuses to comment, sources close to the story report that this so-called "General" is not, and has never been, a member of the U.S. Armed Forces. In fact, a friend of the criminal testified that The General had been "living in his momma's basement" just a few weeks earlier. "One day he told me to call him a 'General'," said the anonymous source. "If you ask me, he's nothing but a major jerk!"

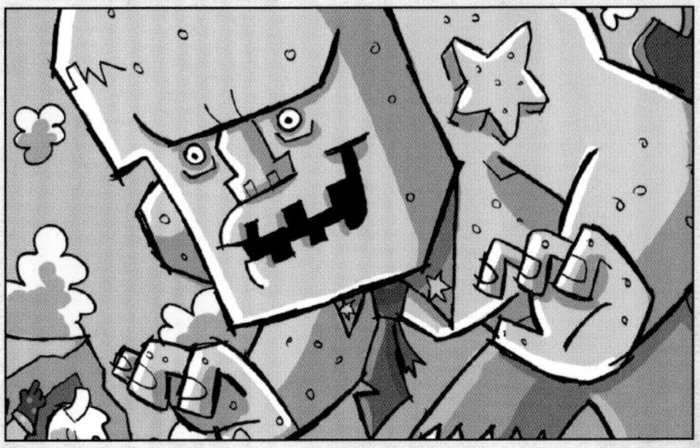

"The General"

Today, the criminal is expected to plead guilty to possession of toxic serums, mutant-making, and impersonating a nurse. The charges could bring a maximum sentence of 10 years house arrest--or in this case, "momma's" house arrest.

EVIL EYESORES

by Penny Pal

In the aftermath of yesterday's events, six local students remain at large. The group, known as the Evil Eyesores, are wanted by their principals for some "serious" detention time. Currently, their whereabouts are unknown. And while some authorities think Papercut is headed for Canada, others believe he's Spiral bound.

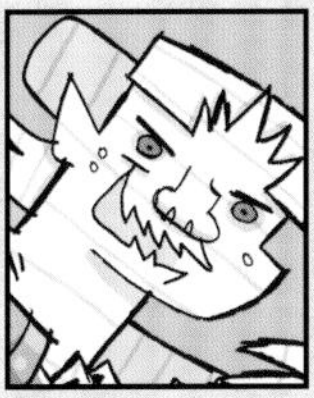

Papercut

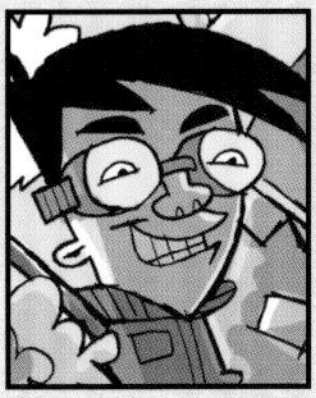

Dozer

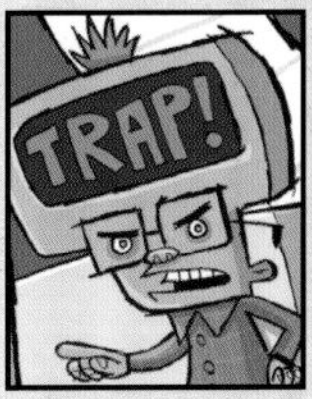
TRAP!

Calculo

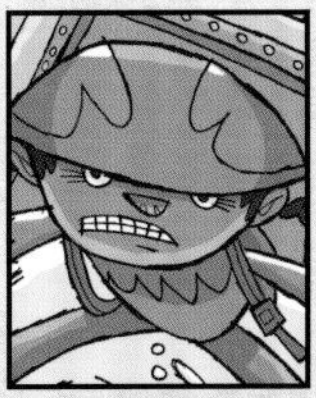

Wheelamina

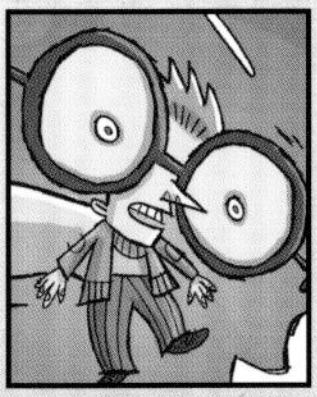

Reggie

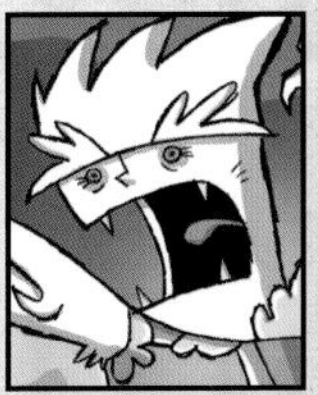

Crystal Frost

INSIDE: EXCLUSIVE INTERVIEW WITH JEN JONES!

WHY HER RELATIONSHIP WITH CHIP STONE GOT OFF TO A ROCKY START...

THE INCREDIBLE ROCKHEAD CREATORS

SCOTT NICKEL
WRITER

SCOTT NICKEL is a humor writer, cartoonist, and a lifelong fan of comics, humor magazines, and monsters. In addition to his day job at Paws, Inc. (Jim Davis' GARFIELD studio), Scott produces the online syndicated comic strip EEK!, creates humorous greeting cards, writes children's books, and draws gag cartoons for national magazines. Scott was nominated for a National Cartoonist Society Divisional Award for Greeting Cards in 2016 and 2018. He lives in Indiana with his wife, son, and cats (Princess Friskamina Von Frisky is his favorite).

C.S. JENNINGS
ARTIST

C.S. JENNINGS has been a freelance illustrator for over a decade. Jennings has created caricatures, editorial cartoons, greeting cards, t-shirt art, logos, children's books, card games—you name it. He also wrote and illustrated the children's picture book *Animal Band*. In 1994, he won an Addy Award for his work in advertising. He currently lives in Austin, Texas.

Q&A WITH SCOTT NICKEL

Capstone: Can you tell us a little about where the idea for Rockhead came from?

Nickel: The inspiration for Rockhead was the Incredible Hulk. We wanted a character with a strong—and somewhat uncontrollable—alter ego.

Capstone: What was your favorite part of this character to tackle?

Nickel: I like coming up with weird and funny villains for Chip/Rockhead to face. I also like the other characters, especially Chip's friend Spencer.

Capstone: What's your favorite part about working in comics?

Nickel: I love the medium. Combining words and pictures is a lot of fun.

Capstone: What was the first comic you remember reading?

Nickel: Coincidentally enough, I think it was an issue of Marvel's Incredible Hulk. I've always been a fan of ol' Jade Jaws.

Capstone: Tell us why everyone should read comic books.

Nickel: Because they're awesome! (And I'm not just saying that because I write comics.)

Glossary

allergy (AL-er-jee)—if you are allergic to something, it causes you to sneeze, get a rash, or it turns your head into a giant rock

diversion (duh-VUR-zhuhn)—something used to distract others, like shiny objects or candy

doomed (DOOMD)—destined to fail, or certain to be eaten by a ribbon-wearing yeti-girl

dozed (DOHZD)—took a nap, or plowed over a nerdy, rock-headed superhero

formula (FOR-myuh-luh)—a scientific recipe often used to turn students into mutants

lair (LAIR)—a place where a wild animal rests and sleeps, or where an evil scientist performs experiments

mutant (MYOO-tuhnt)—something that has been changed or altered physically, or what you become when someone plays mad scientist with your genes

obituary (oh-BICH-oo-air-ee)—a notice of the death of a person. Spencer probably would've had to write Chip's obituary if Scissorlegz hadn't saved the day!

origami (or-uh-GAH-mee)—the Japanese art of folding paper into things like a pretty swan or an angry catfish

secret identity (SEE-krit eye-DEN-ti-tee)—if you have a secret identity, you haven't told anyone that you're also a superhero

sidekick (SIDE-kik)—an assistant, or a close friend, who helps you defeat evil, mutant bullies

status (STAT-uhss)—the condition of a certain situation, or how sickly a test subject has become

subject (SUHB-jikt)—a person or thing who is studied, examined, or turned into a monster of some sort

Share Your Ideas

1. If you could create a superpowered head, what would it be made of? Wood? Pudding? Discuss your choice.
2. Troy Perkins, a.k.a. Papercut, is a bully and a super-villain. Which is worse and why?
3. Who do you think did more to help take down The General—Scissorlegz or Rockhead? Discuss your reasons.

Write Your Own Stories

1. Write your own Incredible Rockhead story. What adventures will Rockhead have next time? You decide.
2. If you became a mutant, what special skills would you want? Write a paragraph describing your abilities. Then draw a picture of your new form.
3. Rockhead and Scissorlegz are heroes. Who is your biggest hero? Write about that person and explain why he or she is your hero.

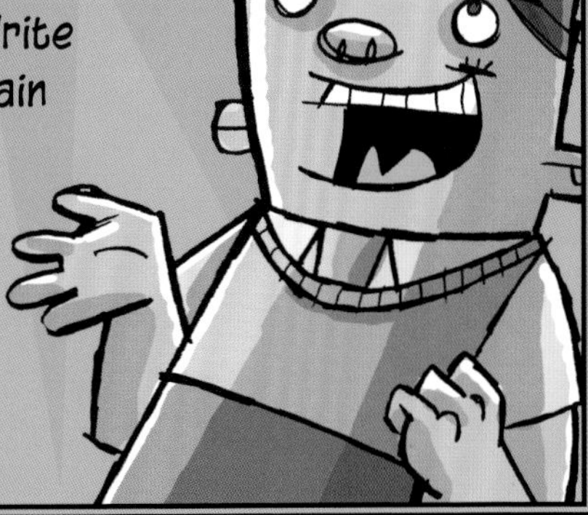

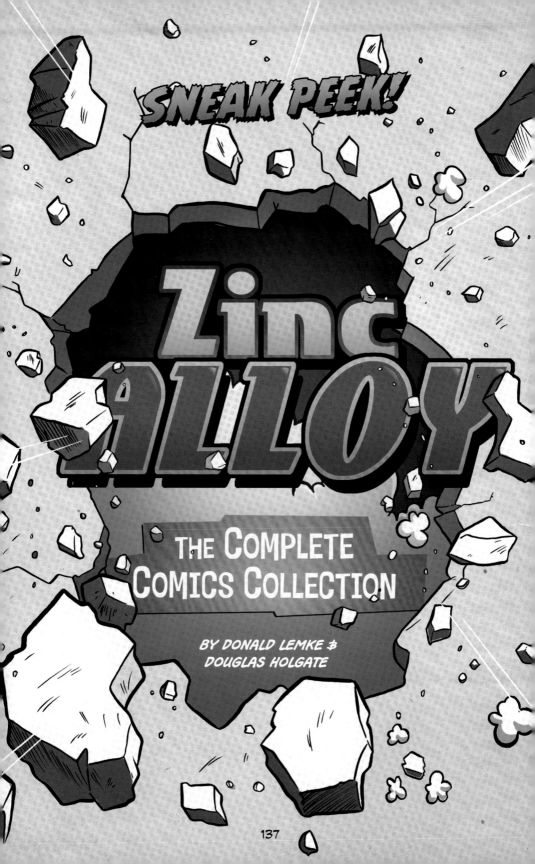

SNEAK PEEK!

Zinc ALLOY

THE COMPLETE COMICS COLLECTION

BY DONALD LEMKE &
DOUGLAS HOLGATE

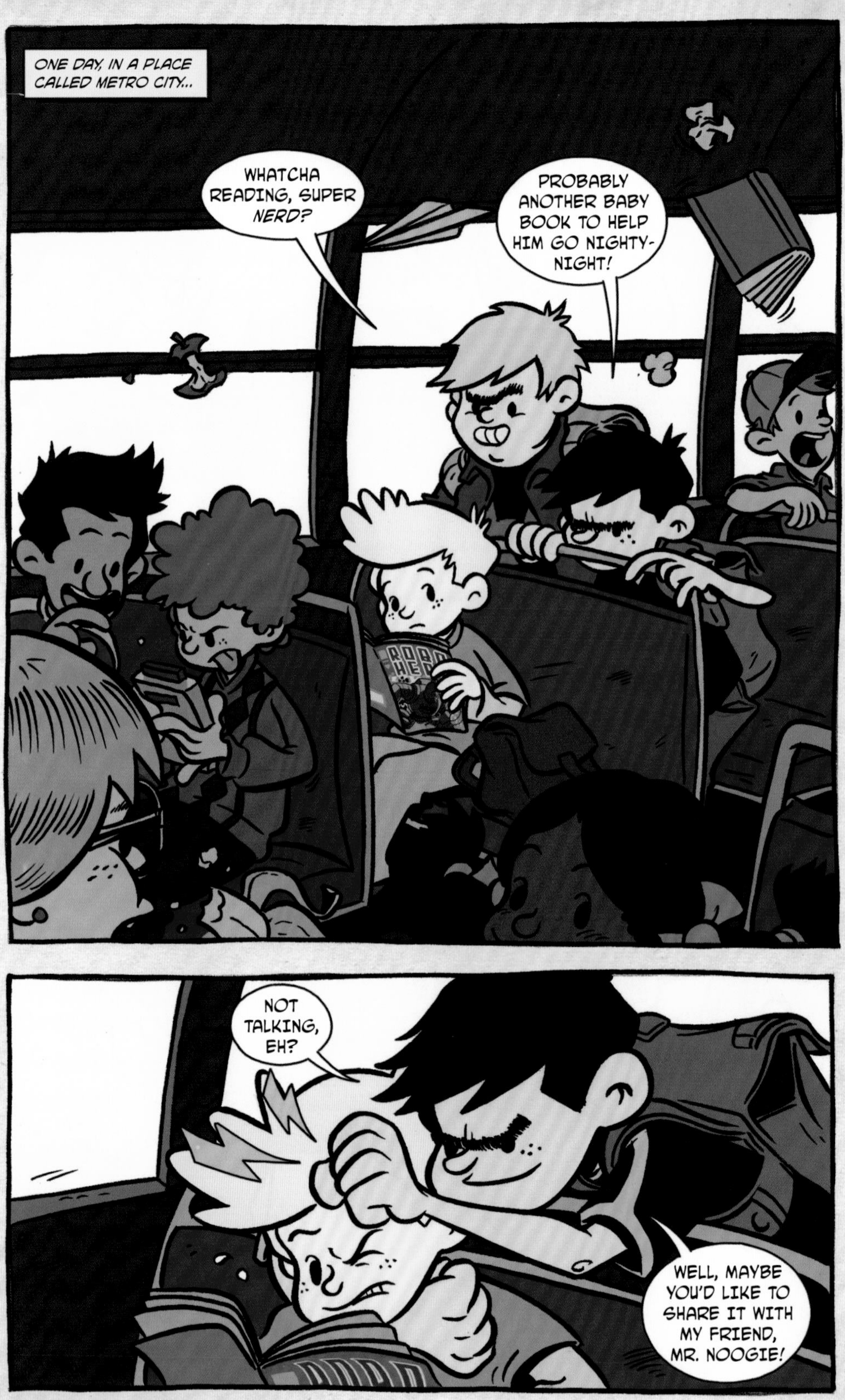
ONE DAY, IN A PLACE CALLED METRO CITY...
WHATCHA READING, SUPER NERD?
PROBABLY ANOTHER BABY BOOK TO HELP HIM GO NIGHTY-NIGHT!
NOT TALKING, EH?
WELL, MAYBE YOU'D LIKE TO SHARE IT WITH MY FRIEND, MR. NOOGIE!

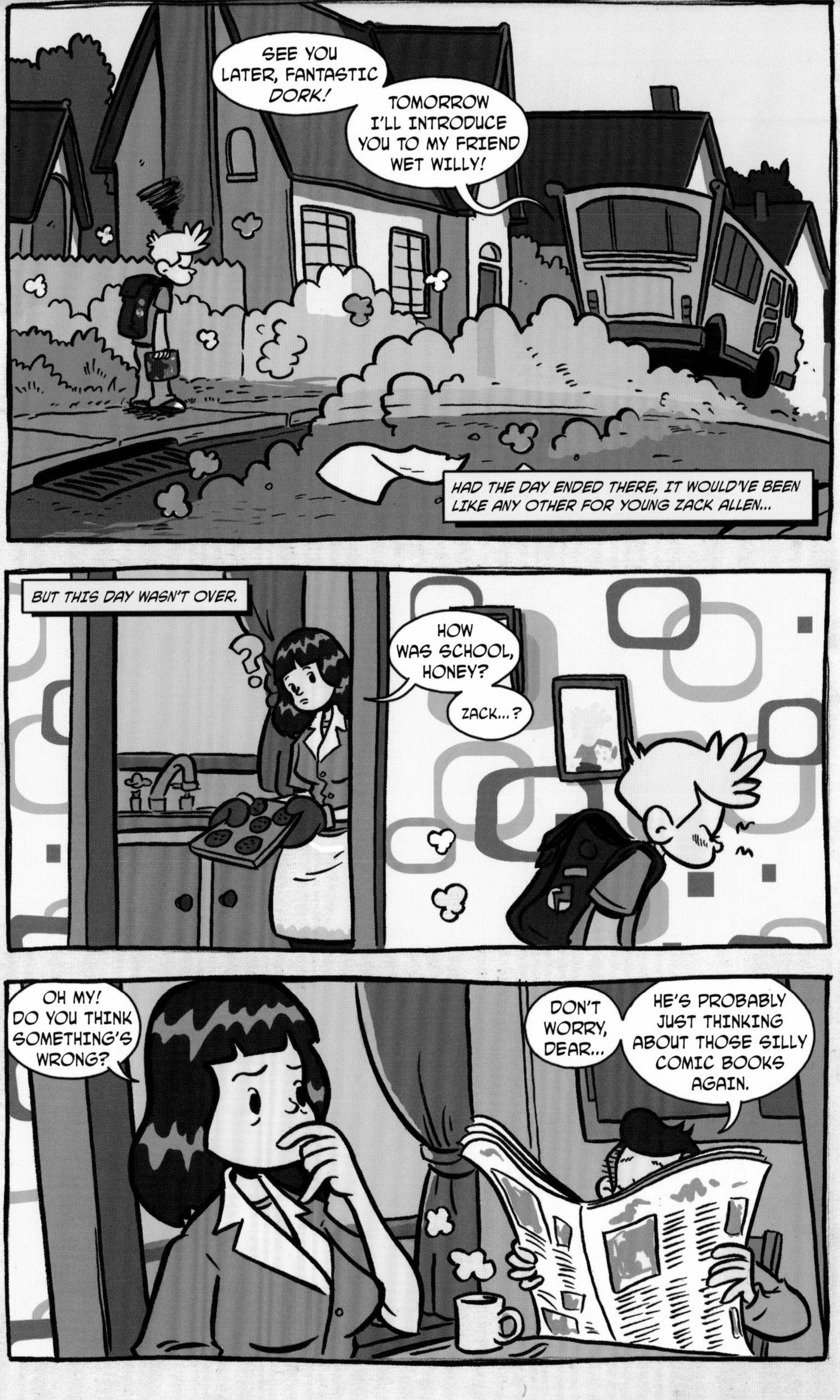
SEE YOU LATER, FANTASTIC DORK!
TOMORROW I'LL INTRODUCE YOU TO MY FRIEND WET WILLY!
HAD THE DAY ENDED THERE, IT WOULD'VE BEEN LIKE ANY OTHER FOR YOUNG ZACK ALLEN...
BUT THIS DAY WASN'T OVER.
HOW WAS SCHOOL, HONEY?
ZACK...?
OH MY! DO YOU THINK SOMETHING'S WRONG?
DON'T WORRY, DEAR...
HE'S PROBABLY JUST THINKING ABOUT THOSE SILLY COMIC BOOKS AGAIN.

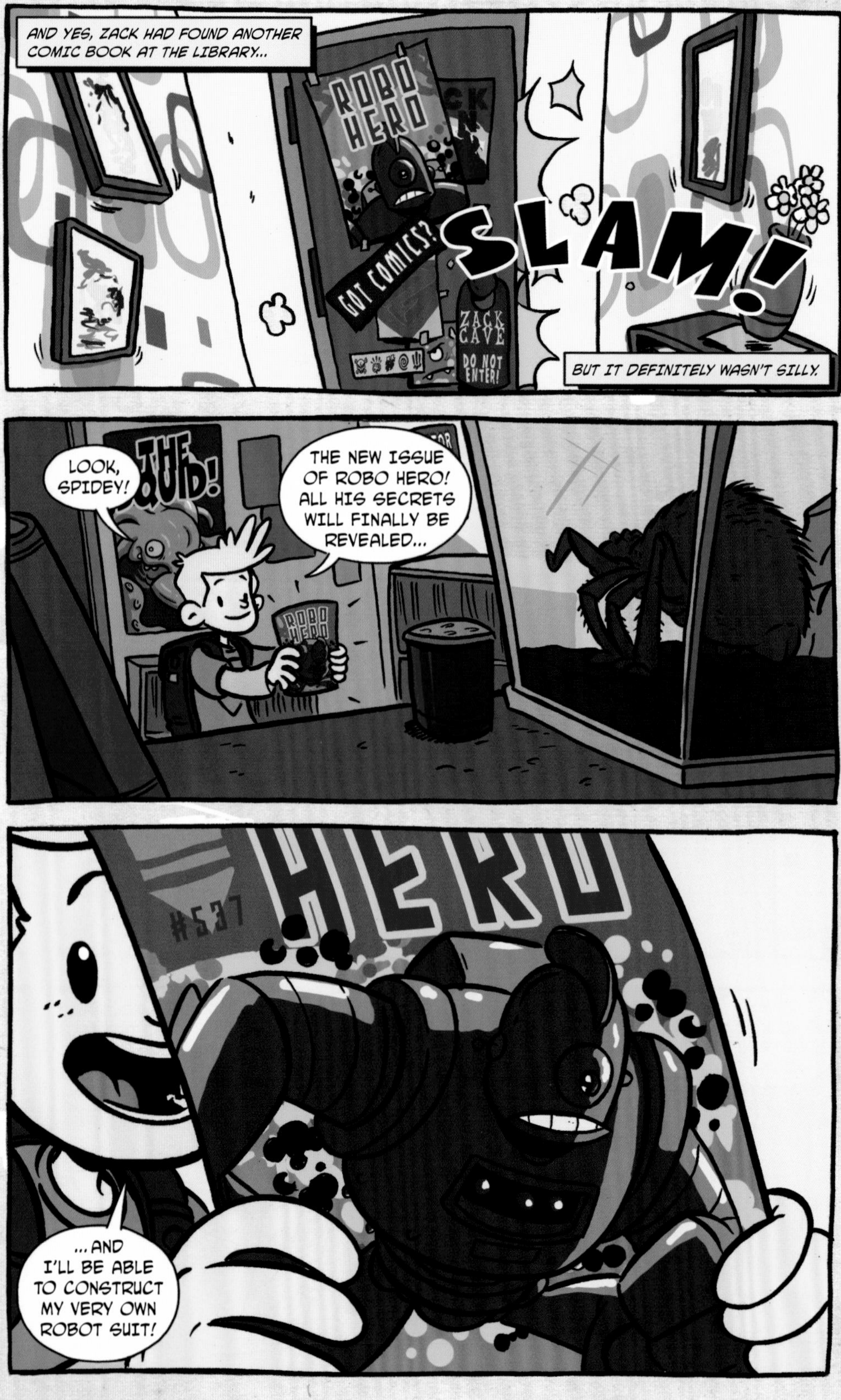
AND YES, ZACK HAD FOUND ANOTHER COMIC BOOK AT THE LIBRARY...
ROBO HERO
GOT COMICS?
SLAM!
ZACK CAVE
DO NOT ENTER!
BUT IT DEFINITELY WASN'T SILLY.
LOOK, SPIDEY!
THE NEW ISSUE OF ROBO HERO! ALL HIS SECRETS WILL FINALLY BE REVEALED...
#537
HERO
...AND I'LL BE ABLE TO CONSTRUCT MY VERY OWN ROBOT SUIT!

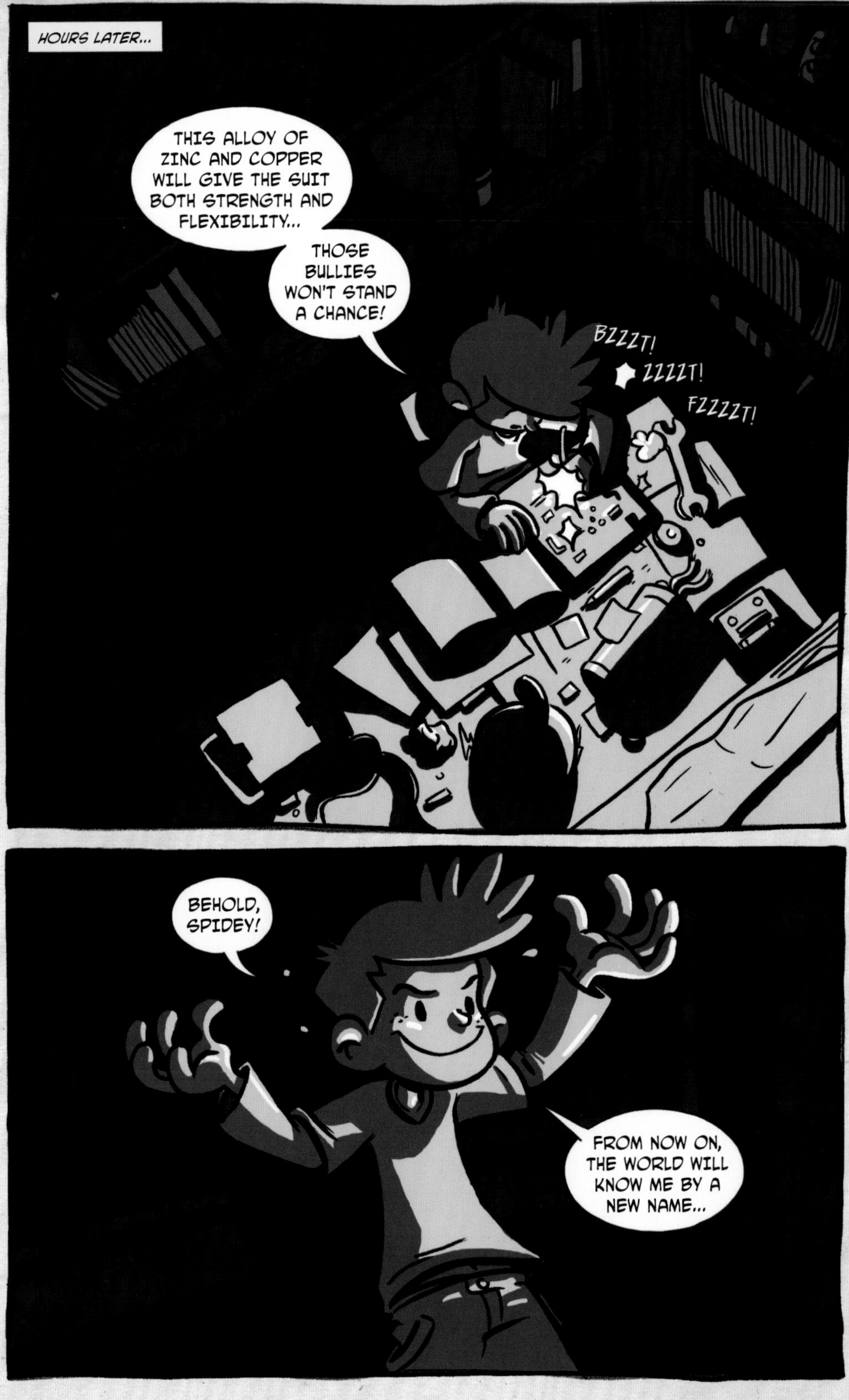
HOURS LATER...
THIS ALLOY OF ZINC AND COPPER WILL GIVE THE SUIT BOTH STRENGTH AND FLEXIBILITY...
THOSE BULLIES WON'T STAND A CHANCE!
BZZZT!
ZZZZT!
FZZZZT!
BEHOLD, SPIDEY!
FROM NOW ON, THE WORLD WILL KNOW ME BY A NEW NAME...

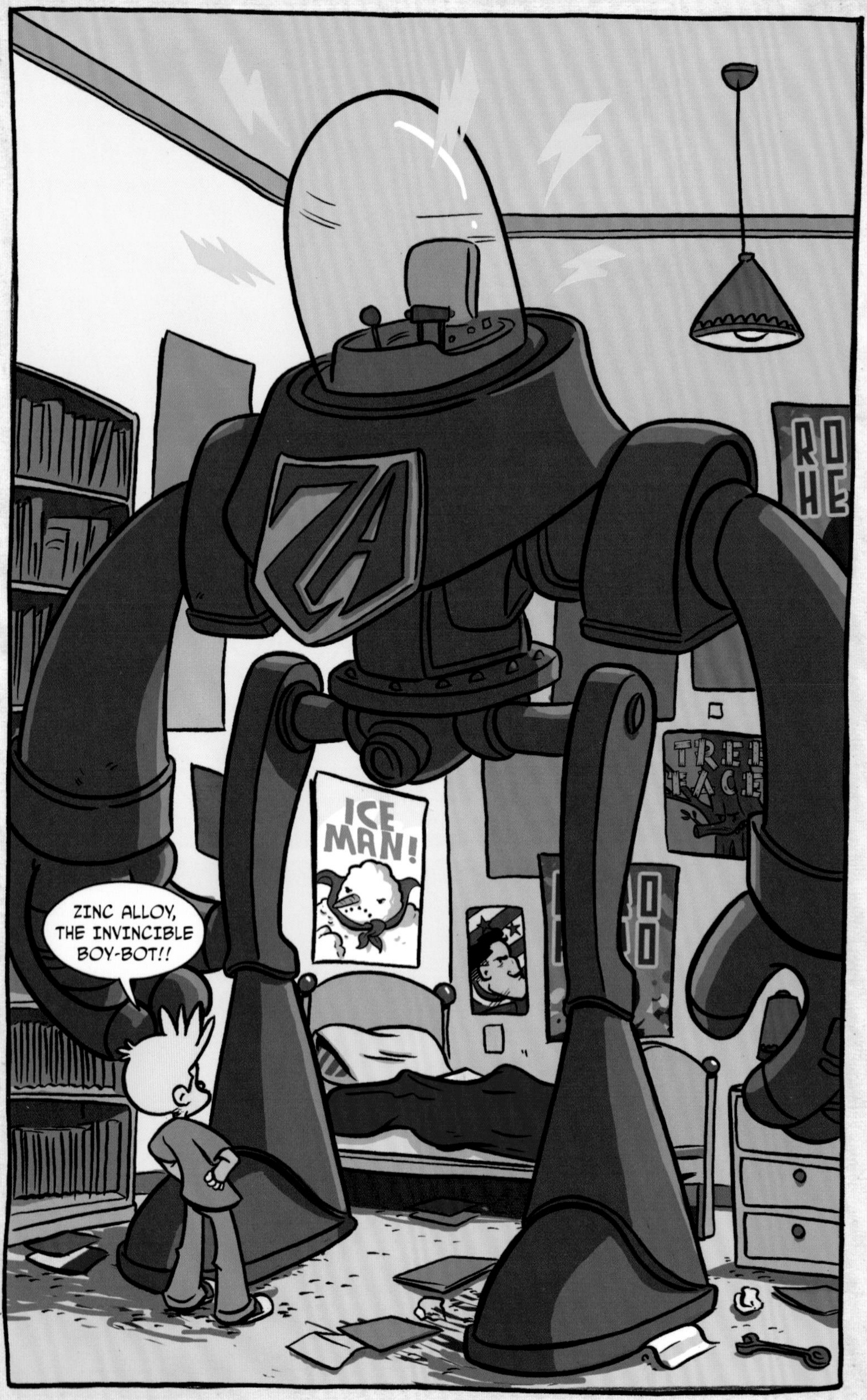
ZINC ALLOY, THE INVINCIBLE BOY-BOT!!
ICE MAN!

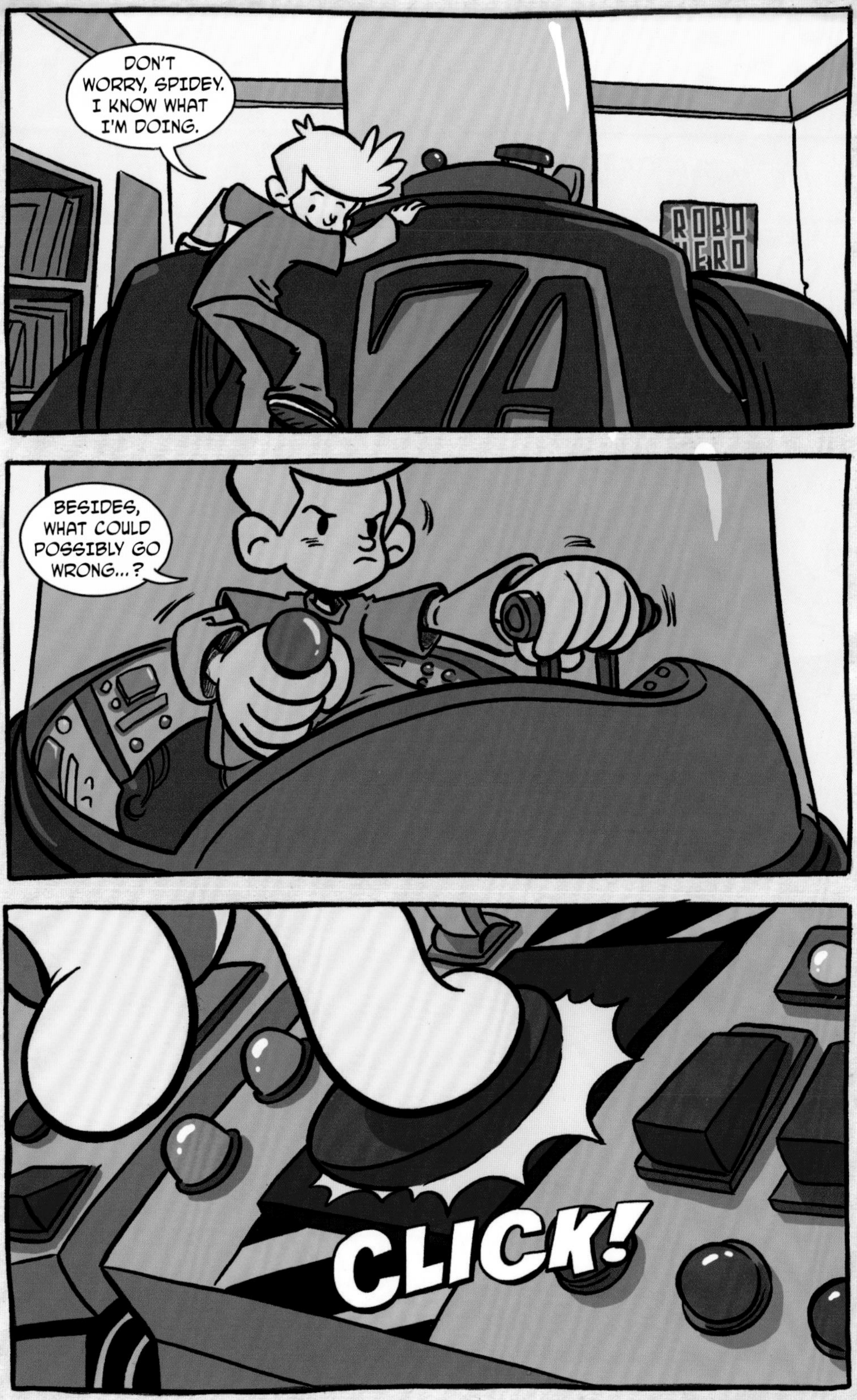
DON'T WORRY, SPIDEY. I KNOW WHAT I'M DOING.
BESIDES, WHAT COULD POSSIBLY GO WRONG...?
CLICK!

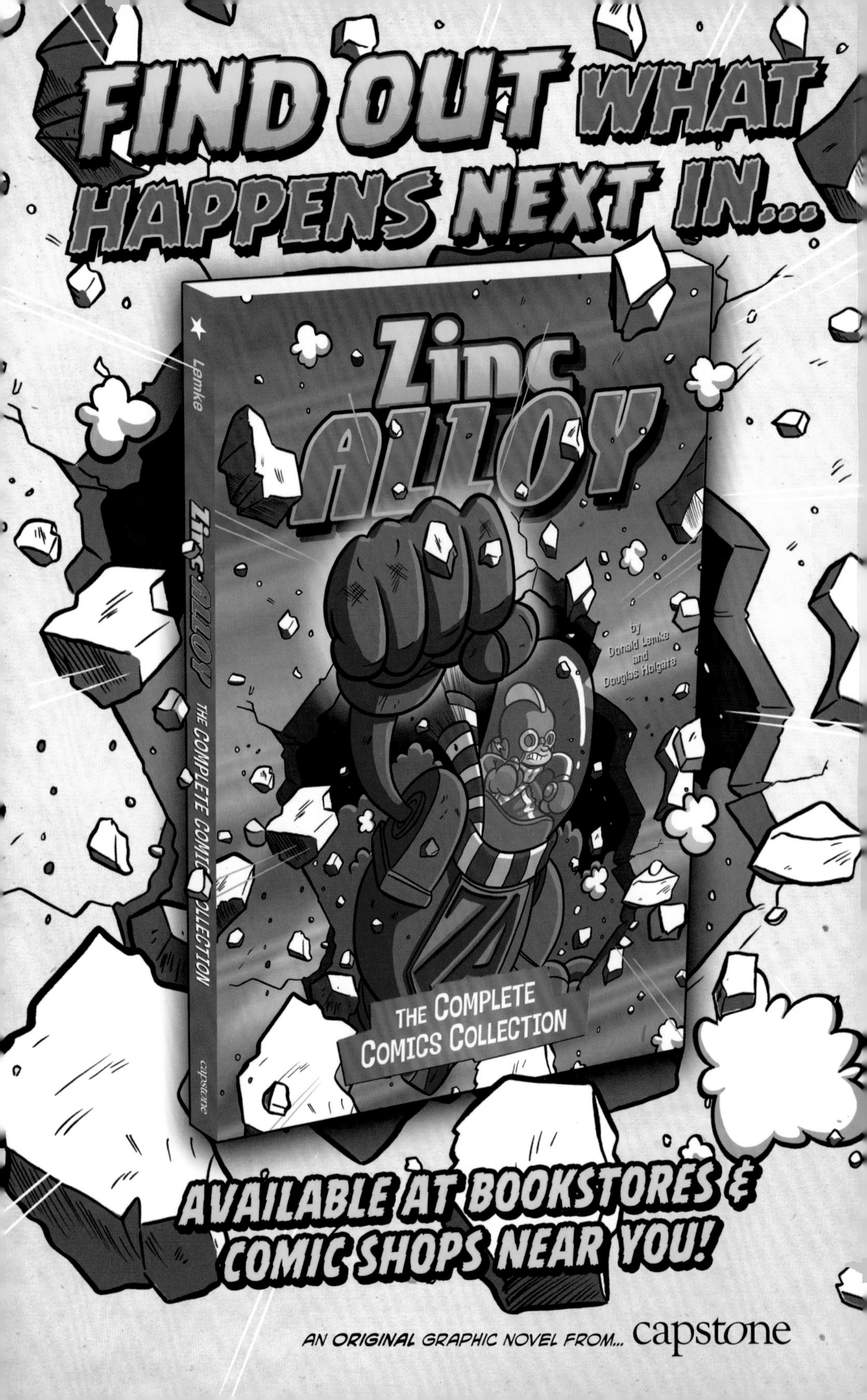
FIND OUT WHAT HAPPENS NEXT IN...
Zinc ALLOY
by Donald Lemke and Douglas Holgate
THE COMPLETE COMICS COLLECTION
Lemke
Zinc ALLOY THE COMPLETE COMICS COLLECTION
capstone
AVAILABLE AT BOOKSTORES & COMIC SHOPS NEAR YOU!
AN ORIGINAL GRAPHIC NOVEL FROM... capstone